MW01504632

THE
FLYING
PHAETON

Edward R Hackemer

THE
FLYING
PHAETON

EDWARD R. HACKEMER

The Flying Phaeton

(Book 5 - Throckmorton Family Novels)

~ a novel ~
Edward R Hackemer

Hardcover ISBN: 9798790389900
ISBN-13: 978-1518707858
ISBN-10: 1518707858

TITLES BY THIS AUTHOR:

THE SIX THROCKMORTON NOVELS

Sangria Sunsets
(Book 6 in the series © 2017)
ISBN-13: 978-542615945

The Flying Phaeton
(Book 5 in the series © 2015)
ISBN-13:978-518707858

Dollar To Doughnut
(Book 4 in the series © 2014)
ISBN-13:978-505245110

A Bridge To Cross
(Book 3 in the series © 2014)
ISBN-13:978-494972820

The Katydid Effect
(Book 2 in the series © 2013)
ISBN-13:978-482669831

In A Cream Packard
(Book 1 in the series © 2011, 13)
ISBN-1 978-1482662801

THE TWO TRUFFAUT TALES

PHRYNÉ ISN'T FRENCH
(Book 1 in the series © 2018)
ISBN-13:978-975926397

PHRYNÉ CROSSING
(Book 2 in the series © 2020)
ISBN-13: 798581963524

AND SOME RELATIVE ANCESTRY

FABLES FOIBLES & FOLLIES
(A quirky anthology © 2019)
ISBN-13: 978-1790613717

COBBLE TALES
(Sussex Stories © 2022)
ISBN-13: 979-8364639899

Titles are available in Hardcover, Paperback or Kindle® format.
Visit the author's Facebook, Goodreads, or Amazon page.

ACKNOWLEDGEMENTS

is given to:

My checker – Edny.

My editor & pen pal – Letitia.

My reader – You.

My inspiration – The song writers, musicians & singers.

DEDICATION

to:
The flyers & their women.

SPECIAL MENTION

Miss Penelope Porque, (Lady Oynke, the Flamboyant Flying Pig)

"With a bit of lipstick and some serious ass-end thrust, this pig flies."

COVER PHOTO & DESIGN:
© 2015 Edward R Hackemer
Photo properties:
Latitude: 34.2291223
Longitude: -84.1226149
Altitude: 1911 feet
Date: 18 August 2014
Location: Forsyth County, Georgia, USA

THE JAZZ:
Phaeton [fey-i-tn, *or* feyt-n]:

(Ancient Greek): Fire God blazing across the sky
(18th century English): Fast, high, horse-drawn carriage
(Modern English): Touring sedan; luxury automobile

THE PLAYERS:

Nicholas & Nora Throckmorton
Gladys Nolan, Leopold & Eloisa Throckmorton
Robert McElvoy, Guendolen Peate, Jovita Vasquello

THE STAGE:

Detroit, Upper Midwest, Texas, California
The Southwest Pacific Theater of WW II.

THE SET & STORY:

The Roaring Twenties, The Great Depression
The New Deal, World War II, The Cold War.

THE QUOTES QUOTED:

"The Flying Phaeton ... Beautiful."
~ USAAF Capt. Nicholas Throckmorton - August 29, 1942 ~

"Ducky! We're going to the cinema ... we're off to see the Wizard, by Jove!"
~ ANS Nurse Sister Guendolen Peate - November 20, 1944 ~

"I want to be at the controls of my Flying Phaeton, holding the stick, flying low, cannon blasting and guns blazing ... and clearing the path for the righteous."
~ USAAF Capt. Nicholas Throckmorton - March 19, 1946 ~

"You will learn to appreciate the taste of Puerto Rican rum."
~ Jovita Vasquello - April 1, 1946 ~

THE FINE PRINT

Sincere effort has been taken to ensure this novel contains the straight stuff for 1927 thru 1946. Please realize that this novel is fiction, except the parts that are not. A reading comprehension test may be given at the end of the book. The needle and names have been changed to protect the record and only the record.

A novel is a work of fiction; therefore, many characters in this book are fictional. Any resemblance in the description or name to any real person, living or dead could be purely coincidental and honestly unintentional. No endorsement is given or implied for any amoral, indecent, dubious, or illegal activity presented in this novel. Any name specific identification, dialogue, comments, or opinions expressed or implied by any character or organization (either actual or fictional) are used solely for descriptive and entertainment purposes. Although totally useless, 3D glasses are optional.

Any lyrics, songs or music annotated in this book are the intellectual property of the individual copyright holders and are referenced only for descriptive purposes. The reader is encouraged to purchase the music, listen, and feel free to enthusiastically tap his, hers, or its foot or feets.

Retail, government, service, or religious institutions mentioned in this book, actual or fictitious, are not included as an endorsement or editorial rejection of their products, services, or doctrine. Descriptions of religious organizations or law enforcement agencies within these pages, either actual or apocryphal, are included with literary license and no negative inference or implication to any past or current agency is intended. Wartime inhumanity is recounted solely for literary reality. The reader is strongly encouraged to research the history. It's not nice.

Verbiage used in this novel is contemporary to the story except what ain't and won't be. A short glossary of common early to mid-20th Century slang is provided at the back of the bus in the Glossary.

Weird things, factoids, tidbits, and footnotes are noted as quirky handnotes, are indicated with a superscript asterisk (*) and recorded at the rear of the bus in either The End Notes and/or The Odd Stuff.

WHAT'S INSIDE:

ENJOY THE READ!

1: DETROIT, 1927-29

Brief history: The fire under the melting pot …

The Austrian-Hungarian Empire and Dmitri Sterescu …

In the rural hillside villages north of Budapest, the townsfolk believed the tall, dark, black-haired, cryptic Dmitri Sterescu possessed a mystical, magical clairvoyance and could see the future simply by gazing upon the fallen oak leaves covering the forest floor. He was a driven man of modest roots who grew his family dynasty from felling trees and cutting firewood to a small, single sawmill before building a financially secure and successful timber firm. He thrived; nothing could block his path. Curiously, it was rumored that his Germanic wife Adelheid was the illegitimate spawn of none other than Emperor Franz Josef. The curious residents of Gödöllö would strain for a glance inside his horse drawn, blood-red phaeton carriage as it traversed the crowded cobblestone streets on market day. If Dmitri should nod or wave a gloved hand, it was taken as an omen of good providence, whereas any greeting from blonde Adelheid was considered ominous. Rain or shine, Sándor the chauffeur sat straight at the reins, stoic and undaunted in his pressed-felt top hat and sealskin cape. Be it daylight or darkness, whale oil lamps emitted an eerie yellow glow at both doors.

It was speculated that Dmitri had foreseen the drastic change that was coming to his homeland. The successful lumberman and his immediate family left the quiet village of Gödöllö and emigrated from the Austro-Hungarian Empire[*] in 1903, a full decade before the onset of World War I, enabling the Sterescu lineage to escape the devastation of war and the resulting ruinous collapse of the Empire. Perhaps the rumors were correct, and Dmitri's emigration was prompted by some sort of sixth sense or gypsy premonition. The population of Gödöllo believed it to be true. All hell broke loose in June 1914. World War I battered and broke Austria-Hungary, split cultures, destroyed dynasties, and spread families far and wide.

By the end of the Great War and the signing of the Versailles treaty in 1919, nearly all the remaining members of the scattered Sterescu family unit followed Dmitri's lead and abandoned Hungary for either England or the United States, escaping through war-ravaged Germany and Belgium. His nephews, Konstantin and Dominik, along with their wives and children made America their destination, and all passed muster at Ellis Island, New York. Konstantin, Dominik, and their wives Lyudmila and Gabi were sponsored immigrants, underwritten by Uncle Dmitri, who held ownership shares with *Fox River Hardwoods* in an out-of-the-way town called Oshkosh; located somewhere in central Wisconsin.

A great adventure lay before them. The imported family unit accepted the challenge of a new life in Middle America with zealous excitement. There was one exception: young Dominik soon became disenchanted with sawmill work and believed the American Dream was to be realized somewhere other than rural, agrarian Wisconsin. He, like many others, was drawn to Detroit by the flashy newspaper ads of the Ford Motor Car Corporation. The promise of five-dollar workdays was too hard to resist and in a matter of three months, Dominik, his wife Gabi, 8-year-old daughter Nora, and four-year-old Marie were on a Milwaukee Railroad passenger coach to Detroit, where Dominik was able to land his dream job with Ford.

The five-dollar workdays turned out to be slick advertising to hook as many laborers as possible for the booming assembly lines of Ford's massive Highland Park and the expanding River Rouge assembly plants. Five dollars a day was indeed possible, but the actual pay was a dollar and a quarter with incentives up to five; provided the line produced at maximum output for the entire shift. From the rubber to the roof, Ford's Highland Park assembly lines manufactured 25 Model T's per hour.

Dominik's dream began to take form. He and his family found themselves at home in Detroit and settled into the growing ethnic Hungarian neighborhood of Delray, situated a fifteen-minute streetcar ride from his job at Ford. Over the course of eight years, Dominik and his family prospered. In 1925, his wife Gabi had purchased a used lunch cart and began a small business of her own, selling Hungarian stews and sandwiches on the streets off Gratiot and Mack Avenue. She was proud of her venture, and her enterprise cleared modest profits from the day she first opened the wood shutters of the lunch wagon. It was decorated in the national colors of Hungary; glossy green, red and white enamel, and proudly displayed the name: *Gabi's Goulash Cannon.* The kerosene stove belched its sooty smoke out of a crooked steel chimney positioned in such an odd manner that it appeared to be the barrel of a formidable piece of field artillery.

Things changed dramatically for the Sterescu family in late summer, 1927. A young man traveling from Buffalo, named Nicholas, had just been hired at the machine shop across the street from where the Goulash Cannon was parked. He had ordered a midday meal of soup and bread and met the young, blossoming Nora. Her raven hair framed her flawless ivory complexion, perfectly pert nose, and rosy lips. Her cocoa eyes warmed him. She captivated him at first sight.

On August 31, 1927, the Goulash Cannon discharged a volley that would echo in Nicholas' heart and mind forever. In the days that followed, he fired back in a way that would profoundly affect the Sterescu family for decades to come.

Poor judgment fueled by immaturity, teenage desires, and the lack of foresight, drove the young man from Buffalo and the innocent fifteen-year-old Nora into unknown territory with unforeseen consequence that would drastically change their lives. During the first weeks of September, Nick and Nora blindly tempted fate and mucked around with the unseasoned carnal expression of their newly discovered sexuality.

1927: 'Deed I Do …

Nick and Nora on their wedding day: Saturday, Oct 15 …

Young lovers Nicholas Throckmorton, eighteen, and his wife Nora were seated on a threadbare, beaten divan in their two-room Gratiot Avenue apartment. It was their wedding night.

Three days earlier, on October 12, Nicholas had turned eighteen. Nora was to mark her sixteenth birthday in seven days, on October 21. They were aware of the heavy, nervous silence sitting alongside them. Nicholas used the fingers of his right hand as a comb and pushed back the coal-black hair off his forehead. He kept it straight back, without a part, and unlike so many other young men, he was clean-shaven. He stood a head taller than his wife, his muscular frame measuring six-foot-two inches.

He scooted his hips closer to her, desperate for any meaningful interaction. "That dress looks very nice on you, Honey." It was a figure-hugging, drop waist cotton print that she would outgrow in the coming weeks. Nora's was the first female form that Nicholas had truly known intimately and had experienced sensually. He was aware that he had explored too much too soon, and learned too little too late, but it was impossible to replace his loving emotion for her with remorse or guilt.

He pulled a cigarette out of his packet of Camel, lit it and offered another to Nora. She declined. A single, hundred-watt bulb hung from the ceiling and cast its harsh light and dingy, incandescent shadows onto the bare floor and papered walls. A fresh cloud of grey cigarette smoke floated through the room. He took another swallow from the bottle of Vernors ginger ale they were sharing, and set it back on the rickety, beaten, and bare coffee table, next to Nora's tattered bridal bouquet of a dozen daisies and sprigs of baby's breath.

Nicholas had been walking on eggshells for the past seven weeks, his toes curling in his shoes. He and his budding wife had not shared intimacy since mid-September, when Nora's mother discovered them during a moment of unbridled passion. Her father Dominik had spewed buckets of broken English verbiage upon him and torrents of harsh Hungarian at his teenage daughter. Since then, all relations with his wife had become increasingly difficult; sparse, tense, and strained at best. Nora's father communicated with him in short, terse sentences and only when it had been necessary. Her mother was brief and superficial on the few occasions when she did speak to him.

He gently put his right arm along the top of the sofa, across her shoulders, and gave her a gentle hug. He tried to force a conversation, "You and your mother put together a delicious pot of chicken paprikash tonight, Nora, my love. Next week I'm planning to buy a double electric cooking plate for us, so we can begin to enjoy dinner at home ... together as husband and wife. And today I saw a sign in the window of Medford's Mercantile that they offer four-week financing on purchases over five dollars with only a fifty-cent down payment. And of course, I'll need to buy a pot to go with our fry pan." His banter and upbeat tone were an attempt to encourage some kind of response; trying desperately to get the simplest dialogue started.

Nora was paging through a two-month-old copy of *Woman's Home Companion* that her mother had given her the day before. She raised her shoulder, rejected his touch, set the magazine down next to her, and deflected his struggle at mild intimacy.

"That's not necessary, Nicholas. And we must stop spending your pay on little things. I appreciate the new shoes that you bought yesterday, but Papa says we will need all your money to provide for us. And besides, you know how much I enjoy our meals with my Mama and Papa. If I discover that I am pregnant, I may not be able to work the family lunch wagon. Our suppers with Mama, Papa and Marie could become the only chance I have to be outside this little apartment of ours."

Lately, their discussions had lasted considerably less than the time needed to soft boil an egg. He fought his nervous trepidation, but still worried that their marriage had already been poisoned beyond repair.

Nicholas had arranged for the day off to be married, but his normal work week was six long days at Garwood Detroit Machine Works. When his day ended at six o'clock, he would walk six blocks to Fort Street, catch a streetcar to the waterfront, walk north to 156 Mackie Street and eat dinner with his wife-to-be and her parents. The meals were standard Hungarian fare: beef goulash, baked potatoes, cheese and sausage casserole, vegetable stew, boiled turnips, or stuffed peppers and dumplings. English was spoken only as a dessert. While the food filled his belly and warmed him to the core, mealtimes were more than discomforting. He sat among the family as a foreigner in his homeland, the outsider, the intruder, and tasted the bitter disdain of Dominik and Gabi's curdled emotions. Even Marie, his wife's younger sister, avoided any interaction with him and was hard pressed to make eye contact. Her mother and father appeared to ignore his presence like he harbored the next catastrophic outbreak of food-borne cholera.

He had deflowered their eldest daughter.

Nicholas' life in Detroit had become a metaphorical bubbling kettleful of Hungarian Goulash: a mixture of ingredients thrown into a simmering pot of emotion and human experience. So far, everything he had tasted could be likened to an overload of fresh garlic, paprika, horseradish, and black pepper. It was foreboding and threatening, yet it teased the taste buds with a curiously tempting bite. He had begun to doubt the reason for his existence. Since he left Buffalo, the singular love and personal affection he knew was given to him by Nora, but since their wedding, her warm touch had grown cold. The only intimate spice they had shared were those few heated, lustful, flash-in-the-pan occasions in the old tool shed behind Garwood's machine shop in early September. Those awkward, teenage sexual rendezvous ended abruptly when Gabi discovered Nick and Nora doing the deed one warm September afternoon. After the dust had settled, Nora's parents not only belittled her and raged on Nicholas, but they immediately took tyrannical control of their daughter's interactions with him. Dominik demanded that Nick marry Nora.

A problem arose when Father Rozsa, in complaisant conjunction with Monsignor Pokemi of Holy Cross Hungarian Roman Catholic Church, flatly refused to join fifteen-year-old Nora into a marriage union with a non-Catholic. A Balkan bastion of the Delray community, the church firmly stood its ground against inter-faith marriages. With dogged pleas, persistence, devotional persuasion, and a generous offertory by Nora's parents, the Detroit Diocese reluctantly agreed that a wedding could take place in the rectory of Saint Hyacinth's, located some miles away in the middle of ethnic Poletown on the east side of Detroit. The young couple had to jump over daunting hurdles, many of them of considerable height and difficulty, before they could be named *man and wife*. The Monsignor Himself needed to sign a waiver of an unavailable Birth Certificate for eighteen-year-old Nicholas and grant parochial consent for underage Nora.

The 15th of October had arrived and after a full week of heart-wrenching stress, tedious paperwork, meetings with clergy, intimate questions and sleepless, restless nights, Nick and Nora were able to recite their wedding vows inside the benefice of Saint Hyacinth Roman Catholic Church. The modest ceremony, necessitated by Nora's embarrassing dalliance with a non-Catholic, had been performed by Father Paul Dabrowa and witnessed only by Nora's parents, Gabi and Dominik.

It had been a month and a half since Nicholas left Buffalo and tragedy behind. Upon his arrival in Detroit, he had hoped to find a new life, a new purpose and a reason to continue living. The August 29th fire that destroyed the only home he ever knew and claimed the lives of his mother and three sisters, had left a bottomless void that Nicholas was struggling to fill. A few days later, upon their first meeting, young Nora had satisfied his hunger for companionship. Once they had been smitten with youthful desire, their hormone-driven emotions had pushed them into the ultimate exploitation of teenage physical curiosity. A seemingly innocent, spontaneous romance had turned to sexual fulfillment. With just enough previous experience, Nick knew the mechanics of the deed, but had an extremely limited grasp on the consequence of culmination. Nora had only the vaguest inkling of what could lie in store. She had given herself to him, and he loved her for it. He loved her with an adoration that steeped the emptiness in his heart with deeply driven emotive longing. He had accepted the outcome with imprudent zeal and promised himself and his Nora that he would provide devotion, love, and sustenance forever.

He was troubled by the guilt and consequence brought to bear by Gabi and Dominik, but kept faith that his love for Nora could only grow stronger with time. He was aware he was fighting stoic Catholic doctrine, and the rule of an ultra-conservative, patriarchal Balkan culture, and could not help but resent the influence and psychological hold her parents had on his wife. He spent a great deal of time scheming and searching for ways he could cut the ties that bound her to Delray. He found himself captured by the circumstance of immaturity.

If only there was a shortcut, a trap door to Eternal Bliss.

Nora's existence was also like a simmering cauldron of ingredients thrown together with no forethought whatsoever. There couldn't be. Spontaneous, heated consequences were boiling over with every stir of the spoon. Daily, she was experiencing unfamiliar, new feelings that evolved with every change her young body underwent. Torn between the romanticism of a handsome, virile husband and the respect, loyalty, and obedience due her father, Nora found herself caught in the middle of a developing, widening chasm separating the only two men on Earth for whom she had feelings. She wanted her husband to discover and unlock that glimmering castle she had dreamed of as a little girl. She wished she could climb the hill with him and live the storybook life happily ever after. Although her father wore flawless armor and brandished the sword of Old-World reason, Nora worried that Nicholas might attempt to fill the moat around their castle with biting crocodiles of isolation.

It was as clear as a starlit night in January that they would never experience any sort of honeymoon, and it certainly would not begin on their wedding night. One week after Nora's pregnancy became known, her parents insisted she begin a study regimen of the seventy-four edicts of the Canisius Catechism at Holy Cross Catholic Church. In private, Nicholas could only mildly protest the arrangement and did his best to convince his young wife that their love was neither a sin nor condemnation. Life in their small Detroit apartment was to be bittersweet for him and at best, a conflicted existence for her. Albeit in different directions, they each wished for their love to persevere. Day to day, they would continue as two young lovers, dreamers, and believers in the fantastic Irish Sweepstakes of life.

Before they went to bed, Nicholas poured some water into the empty Vernors bottle, using it as a vase for six of Nora's wedding daisies. It had come to be, despite their love and marriage, they would spend their wedding night sleeping alone, yet together, upon their small, skinny straw mattress and squeaky, coiled-spring bed frame.

1927: Midnight Special …

Monday October 31, with Littlejohn and Benson …

Supper at the Sterescu household was interrupted by a knock on the front door, made by a banging fist. Around the table, everyone exchanged glances of curious wonder. Dominik pushed his chair back and started down the hall. Dinnertime visitors were as unlikely as a chicken on ice skates. He wiped his mouth on his shirtsleeve. His heavy mustache and two-day growth of whiskers dragged along the flannel like sandpaper. He opened the door.

Four men were standing on the porch: two Detroit police patrolmen stood behind two men wearing wrinkled wool suits, stiff-collared white shirts, and loosened ties. They appeared weary.

One of the strangers held a wallet shield in front of Dominik's face and announced, "Agents Rolf Benson and Dan Littlejohn of the BOI*. We're looking for Nicholas Throckmorton and understand we can find him here."

"He's here." The back of Dominik's neck prickled. Anger churned inside him. Not only had the man from Buffalo spoiled his daughter's purity and laid her virginity to waste; but his presence had brought the police to his door. He hastened his response, "Follow me. He's at the dinner table with my wife and daughters. We have just finished." Four long strides down the hall, Dominik stopped at the side of the doorway, pointed a finger of damnation into the dining room and spoke a fateful condemnation, "There he is. That's him. You are free to take him away." His boiling anger and sticky Balkan accent had become as hot as black tar. The Bureau of Investigation agents stood crowding Dominik and the doorway, the Detroit police halfway down the hall.

Dominik stood with clenched fists and wondered if nosey next-door neighbor Oszkár Vizenjik had noticed the visitors. Petty worries began to torture him; all sorts of scenarios flashed through his mind. If Nicholas were to be arrested, perhaps the Monsignor would annul the marriage. But that would bring further embarrassment with an out-of-wedlock birth. Things were not going well. Perhaps Nicholas would be removed from his home forever. The fellow from Buffalo had brought nothing but trouble. Four policemen must certainly mean trouble, big trouble.

Littlejohn and Benson moved past Dominik and took two steps into the room. "Nicholas Throckmorton?"

"That's me." He had no inkling who these men were or what was going on. He noticed Dominik's foreboding glare and felt a painful knot tighten in his stomach.

Agent Benson's voice was firm, authoritative. "We're from the BOI. We've just arrived from the Buffalo office and need to ask you some questions about the Adams Street fire that claimed the lives of your mother, three sisters and three of the four boarders living in the house at the time. We do not intend to charge you with any crime, and we are not here to place you under arrest, Mister Throckmorton. We need to clear some things up so we can move on with our investigation into the blaze and how it could have started. Are you willing to come with us to Cadillac Square … to the Federal Building, downtown on Fort and Shelby Street? We should be able to clear everything up tonight and can bring you back home after we finish up."

Dominik felt a blanket of disappointment thrown over him.

Nick eyed the agents, "Yeah. Sure. I can do that. But I, I mean my wife and I … we live over on Gratiot. But how did you know where to find me? How did you find me?"

Agent Benson nodded. "We were advised of a marriage license, found your employer, and discovered that you married a tinker's daughter and into the Gypsies, and we found you here in Delray. Where else?"

Dominik growled from the hallway, "We are not Romany! We are not Gypsies! We are Magyar! Austro-Hungarians!" He roared like an enraged lion.

Benson and Littlejohn turned and apologized in unison. "No offense intended, sir. None at all." Everyone took a breath and waited for the dust to settle.

Nicholas voiced a thought, "When we're finished, you can bring me back here, then. Right? You can do that instead? My wife and I can take the streetcar from here to our apartment. After we finish and you bring me back, I mean."

In a split second, Dominik interrupted. He did not want any more police presence, "No. No, Nicholas. The police can stay away tonight and take you alone back to your little rooms on Gratiot all by yourself and alone. It will be dark and late before you return, and I will not permit my daughter to go out that late at night. Nora can stay here in her own bed tonight and longer if it is needed or necessary. I will keep her safe."

The agents shared glances. Rolf Benson always tried to keep away from family discussions. Littlejohn felt empathy for the young Nicholas, and offered a solution, "After we're finished, we can stop here and pick up your wife, Mister Throckmorton, and drive both you and your wife back to your Gratiot Avenue address."

Dominik responded once again with Balkan thunder, "No, no, no! It will be too late, like I said. You take him alone by himself. My daughter stays here tonight."

Over the course of the past two months, Nicholas had become accustomed to the opinions and attitude of Nora's father. He had begrudgingly accepted it would continue to be that way, at least for the foreseeable future. Walking barefoot on thumbtacks was the accepted norm. Oh, how he longed to break free from Dominik's shackles.

He leaned toward Nora and gave her a quick peck on the cheek. "Don't worry and sleep well, Honey. I'll come down here tomorrow morning. And we will go home together in the morning." He shoved his chair back, stood and glanced across the table to Gabi and said, "You made another great meal. Thanks, Mama." He did not look at Dominik, but only nodded in his direction as he walked past him and into the hall, ahead of the Federal agents and two Detroit policemen. His jaw was locked. He felt a slow burn in his gut. He vowed that someday, that man would either accept him or be left behind. He had little hope for acceptance.

Nora, her mother Gabi, and sister Marie sat in silent worry. Dominik followed the officers and Nicholas down the hall, remained inside and watched from the doorway as they walked to the cars parked at the curb. He wondered if he would ever see the young man from Buffalo again. The police presence had upheld his opinion of Nicholas.

Nicholas sat alone on the back seat of a large black Buick for the ride downtown with Benson and Littlejohn. The Detroit police drove off in their Chevrolet patrol car, heading back to their precinct. Next-door neighbor Oszkár Vizenjik and his wife Gröngyi stood watching it all from their porch. On the other side of the street, window curtains on the Jankovick house parted slightly.

Dominik shut the front door and stomped down the hall. Back in his dining room, he sat down at the table, sputtered and grumbled in Hungarian, *"A dolgok meg fognak változni."*

Nora knew exactly what her father meant. He had threatened it many times before. His nostrils flared and veins popped on his forehead as his fist hit the dinner table. The dishes bounced and silverware clattered. His wife and daughters shuddered.

He repeated himself, "Things are going to change! The police at my door are the final insult cast by Mister Nicholas."

Nora drew a breath, reached inside and found the courage to speak. Her voice was thin and fragile, like translucent porcelain, "Papa, Nicholas is not under arrest. The police said so. He's not in trouble. Show mercy. The police are investigating the fire that killed his family." She wasn't sure how she managed to say those words, and an uneasy silence settled. Her mother and sister shifted their eyes from Nora to

Dominik and back, expecting more Hungarian, possible continued rage, tears or another fist to the tabletop.

He looked into the eyes of his wife and daughters, slowly moving his gaze down and along the table. He spoke with conviction, "Things are going to change."

The women knew he meant it. They did not know exactly what was coming, but they realized they had just heard it rounding the home stretch. Dominik was not only a cantankerous man, but unyielding as well.

1927: I Know That You Know…

… the whole truth and nothing but the truth …

The Federal Agents seemed friendly, pleasant and straightforward with him, but Nicholas could not ignore the twisting in his gut or the nervous suspicion constricting his brain. He was not looking forward to this ordeal, had no idea what to expect, and was uncomfortable knowing he would be asked to recall the deadly fire. He could once again smell the putrid stench of wet, burnt timbers and evoke stark, haunting images of the fiery destruction of his boyhood Adams Street home. All sorts of things were flying through his mind; just about everything imaginable from superficial, meaningless, and uncomfortable dialogue to getting locked up in the can. As unlikely as it was, he did his best to force the second possibility from his thoughts. The disturbing memories all came back as if they had occurred yesterday, and he wondered what his life would be like if only the past never happened. If yesterday could only become tomorrow maybe he could change things.

The ten-minute ride downtown passed without conversation or comment. The Federal Building at Fort and Shelby Street was a massive four-story building of white marble, grey granite, and bedrock limestone. An imposing clock tower reached 243 feet skyward into the cloudless, moonlit night casting its long, black shadow two blocks to Campus Martius.

When Agent Benson parked the Buick at the curb, he simply announced, "Here we are." Nicholas' senses had gone numb. His reality seemed to be somewhere locked in a timeless limbo. He didn't remember getting out of the car, climbing the white stone steps or arriving at room 214. He was in a large office with two desks, smaller tables, and several upholstered leather chairs scattered about. Large portraits of Presidents Coolidge, Lincoln, and Jefferson hung on the dark wood panel walls. An expansive bookcase covering one wall was packed with leather and cloth bound volumes colorfully trimmed in gold and red.

Benson and Littlejohn arranged chairs at a four-foot round oak table and motioned for Nicholas to sit down. Both men had full-size notebooks in front of them and pencils scattered everywhere. A black cast iron light fixture resembling a wagon wheel hung from the ceiling with incandescent bulbs burning under green hurricane glass shades.

Benson started, "I want to thank you again for coming down here and helping us with our investigation, Mister Throckmorton. May I call you Nicholas?" He didn't wait for a response. "Some of what you may learn about the night of August 29th may be disturbing to you, but I think with your help we can bring those responsible for the fire and deaths of your family to justice."

Nicholas interjected, "It was the mob, the Black Hand. I already know that. And those Torricelli brothers."

"Right ... right. We just want to clear up the timeline so we can build a solid case. One of the boarders did manage to jump from an upstairs window and lived. He was badly busted up, and bruised a lot, but he's doing fine now. Willy McTell is his name. Are you familiar with him, Nicholas?"

"Yeah, I knew Willy. He stuck pins* at Broadway Bowling. He's a good mug, a decent guy."

Benson spoke, "He told us that four men visited your Adams Street home on the morning of August 28ᵗʰ, Sunday, when you and your family were at church. After he got bandaged up, he fingered one of the men, Lorenzo Torricelli from some mug shots. He said Torricelli and three of his goons had asked the whereabouts of either you or your brother, Leopold. Is that correct?"

Nicholas wanted to be careful with his answer. He did not know for sure, but he believed that his brother Leopold was in Ohio. "Yeah. I think they wanted to see Leopold, but I'm not sure why. I don't know."

It was Littlejohn's turn. His tone was gruff and demeanor direct. He often laced his words with street jargon. "You know why, Nicholas. You know the real megillah. Your brother jazzed with a mick named Dillon Cafferty, and two snake charmers; Ellie Ashworth, and a dame called Frenchy Truffaut. Cafferty was running a bootlegging scheme from Niagara Falls, Canada into the States, and supposedly kept your brother and the muffins in the dark about it. They ran the border late that Saturday night in a Pierce Arrow that we linked to the mob, and then they drove over a United States Customs and Revenue agent, and then headed for the hills. Your brother and his gal Frenchy skipped town and left Cafferty and Ashworth to squirm in the dust. That's what went down."

Agent Benson lit a cigarette. He coughed and continued, "We don't think you were involved in any of this, and we know you were working at the Urban flour mill when everything happened on Sunday night. So, now it would be a good time for you to tell us what you know, Nicholas Throckmorton, so we can put together a solid case to nail Torricelli and his mob for the bootlegging scheme run by Cafferty, then killing Cafferty, and setting the fire that killed your family. Wake up and smell the coffee, kid. We know your brother and Phryné Truffaut are now married. We found his car at the Lackawanna train terminal and followed their trail out of Buffalo from there."

Littlejohn took another turn, "We need your help. There are a few holes in our investigation, and we think you can help us fill them. McTell said he told you about Torricelli's Sunday visit to your home on Adams. So, if you can tell us what you know about your brother's involvement with Cafferty and what you know about the two broads, Ashworth and Frenchy Truffaut, you would be helping us build our case against that scum Torricelli so he can pay for his crimes and the deaths of your family."

Nicholas was aware of his sweaty palms and strong pulse. So far, outwardly, at least, he had held back his emotions and kept his nerves in check, but despite his determination he could feel his ears reddening. He wasn't going to allow these two men to break down the brick wall he built around the torturous, burning memories, he had tried to leave behind in Buffalo.

He answered, "When my mother, sisters and me got back from church that Sunday, Willy told me that four men in a big black Chrysler had stopped by and asked for *Throckmorton*. Willy told them we were at church ... the goons said they'd be back and then they left. I knew it wasn't me that they were after, so I put two and two together and I knew they must have been looking for Leopold. My brother and Cafferty and their ladies often went to Canada, maybe a couple times a month for dancing and a night out and drinking beer. It's legal in Canada, you know. My brother wasn't in cahoots with nobody ... not nobody. He wouldn't do that. And I know that his gal Phryné was nobody's moll or patsy... no way! My brother brought her over to the house a couple times and they were engaged to be married."

"How can you be sure about that? That they weren't involved?" Benson scowled and crushed out his cigarette. Littlejohn was taking notes with a pencil.

Nick gave Benson an indignant glance. "Look, I hopped the streetcar to Leopold's walk-up on Howlett, off Sycamore, and the place was empty. He left a note for me. He addressed it: *Brother*."

This was something the BOI agents did not already know. Benson immediately asked, "A note? That's a new piece of evidence. Something new ... what did it say? What did you do with the note?"

"I found it on the table ... he wrote on a paper sandwich sack and said that he and his gal Phryné were going to catch a train to Cleveland and get married. I found it hard to figure why the hell he would go to Cleveland, but that's what the note said. He said he was leaving his car at the train station and would put the transmission key on top of the right front tire. I took the note home with me and showed it to my mother, so she would know that he left town with Phryné to get married and not be worried."

"Well, Nick, your brother and his girlfriend went beyond Cleveland. In Buffalo, they bought tickets to Chicago on New York Central's *20th Century Limited*. Then in Chicago they got married and on the same day, they bought tickets to Los Angeles, California on the Atchison and Topeka." Rolf Benson lit another smoke from his olive-green packet of Listerine* mint cigarettes, took his first pull and coughed; a deep hacking cough. "Why do you suppose your brother did that, Nick? And those train tickets cost a few bucks. Did your brother have that kind of moolah laying around? Did he?"

"Leopold always had money. And he used it. He used to say that's what they make money for: to spend. The note he left for me said that him and Phryné were going away to get married. They were eloping. That's all it said."

"It was more than that, Nick, and you know it. What else did you find in your brother's apartment?"

Nicholas wanted to defend his brother, and the best way was with the truth. His brother may have skipped town, but he was not a mobster. "His suit and his gal's clothes were soaking in the bathtub. It smelled like Fels Naptha. Some of my brother's things were on the bed, so he must have just packed what he wanted and left. I figure that Phryné must have put on some of his things to wear and ..."

Littlejohn interrupted, "Of course, she did ... she didn't take a train to Chicago naked. She left all of her clothes soaking in the tub; her dress, stockings, dainties, shawl, everything. And without a doubt, they then drove to her home on Lombard Street where she changed out of your brother's pants and shirt. Her family found the clothes and the note that she left behind, just like your brother did, and it said they were headed to Cleveland, just like your brother said. Then she snuck out without waking anybody. So now we know that they each left a note behind and lied about where they were going."

Benson asked, "Why do you think they left their clothes in the bathtub, Nick? What's your best guess about that?"

"I don't know."

Littlejohn lit a cigarette. "I'll tell you. It's because their clothes were soaked with booze and stunk like a distillery, that's why. They carried the stink of Canadian bootleg booze from head to toe. The Pierce Arrow got shot up when they ran the border and drove down that Customs cop, and it leaked the illegal hooch all over them. That fact alone means they knew damn well what Cafferty was up to, don't you think?"

"My brother is no hood. He did not run with the mafia. He knew the rumors about Cafferty, but he wouldn't be part of any scheme of his. No ... not my brother. He may have been stupid blind in love with his gal Phryné, but he didn't have any part of the mob. I'm sure of it. He wasn't that thick-headed. Sometimes he played the cake-eater with his gal Phryné, but he was on the up and up. I'm sure he wasn't working the jazz with Cafferty. And besides, I know the cops found Cafferty dead the next morning in Buffalo Creek by the ship canal. I heard two coppers talking about it over my hotdog breakfast at the Deco restaurant on Eagle Street when I got out of work on that Monday morning. And they talked about a house fire that killed the residents... but I didn't know then that it was my house they were talking about."

Nicholas' speech had slowed, and his rambling words began to trail off. He looked around the large room and took a deep breath. In a few seconds, he began again, "Well, after my breakfast I went home and found my house gone, burnt to the ground and watched them smoke-eaters put my family onto a flatbed Ford. They had seven stretchers. My mother, my three sisters and must have been three more maybe; the boarders. The Fire Brigade Commander told me only one boarder got out. And now I know it was Willy. There were seven stretchers with bodies covered in white sheets, seven of them, surrounded by black smoldering wood and the stench of fire. I puked on my shoes."

"What did you do then? Did you stay at your brother's apartment that night or what?"

Eighteen-year-old Nicholas leaned forward off his chair, took a Camel from his packet, and put a match to it. He fought his trembling hands, rested his elbows on his knees, stared at the floor, and began again, "I walked down Broadway to Main and Washington, sat at a trolley stop, and bawled my eyes out. That's what I did. I cried. Like a kid. A scared kid." He filled his lungs with smoke and sat up. He looked directly into Rolf Benson's eyes, then to Daniel Littlejohn.

Littlejohn put down his pencil and pushed a heavy green glass ashtray across the table.

Nicholas exhaled and continued, "I was lost, alone and had no place to go. Then I walked fifteen, twenty blocks to Leopold's place, my brother's apartment just to see if he was there, I guess. It was still empty. I was alone. All alone. Then I walked back to Niagara Street, then to the Peace Bridge, and then over to Canada. It cost me a nickel to walk across the Niagara River to Canada. I remember the wind in my face and the gulls swooping over the water below. I thumbed a couple rides across Canada and made it to Detroit, and here I am. It took me two weeks to wash the stink of fire off me. Sometimes I can still smell it. There is nothing for me back in Buffalo anymore. Nothing." He took another draw on his cigarette and sat back into the leather armchair. "Torricelli and his dago, wop, mafia mob killed them."

Benson glanced to his partner and gave him the slightest nod. "Well, Nick, first let me and Littlejohn express our sympathies to you, and that said, we want you to know that you have helped us nail down some of the facts. We wanted to see if what you could tell us would fit into our timeline of events. Timelines are important. And we want to let you know where we are; and what we can tell you, so far, about the investigation.

"We got the drop on two of Torricelli's men the day after the Peace Bridge dust-up and caught them in the act: emptying the booze from the Pierce Arrow. They told us that one of the Torricelli brothers, Vincente, was shot through the head in Canada and stuffed into the trunk of Cafferty's car ... and to avenge his brother's death, Lorenzo had Cafferty killed and was looking for your brother, Leopold. So, putting that tidbit together with what we learned from the surviving boarder Willy, we figured Torricelli was good for the arson charge and put the pinch on him.

"We arrested those two mugs in the garage on several charges, and Lorenzo Torricelli for eight counts of murder, arson and conspiracy under the Prohibition Act. The two we nabbed in the garage were knifed in Erie County Jail a couple days later, probably to make sure they didn't spill their guts, and Torricelli got a New York shyster and got out on ten G's bail. But he goes to trial next month, and the DA's indictment and the case we got against him is looking damn good. The prosecutor is asking for the death penalty, the hot squat. It's either that or life in Sing-Sing. The Buffalo arson investigators and Fire Marshalls found traces of kerosene at the front, rear, and basement entrances of your home on Adams. And when we're finished with Torricelli, the canucks can load on some charges of their own.

"We located, arrested, and questioned Miss Ashworth shortly after the Peace Bridge incident. Then we got her account and released her with a witness subpoena for the Torricelli trial, but I don't think her testimony would be worth a damn. We also spoke with her family and that of Miss Truffaut. I can tell you that we are comfortable saying that the Bureau Of Investigation does not believe that your brother Leopold, Phryné Truffaut, or Eloisa Ashworth had any knowledge of the actions of Cafferty or the Torricelli, Black Hand mob. Miss Ashworth said they became aware of the body in the trunk only after Cafferty had run the border. And despite the first reports on the incident, it is believed that nobody in the Pierce Arrow had any weapons or fired upon any Federal Officers. Cafferty simply ran into and drove over that Customs Officer at the Peace Bridge.

"It has been determined that your brother and the two women were accessories to crimes without prior knowledge or willful compliance. The Federal Prosecutor has not filed charges, but the Marshals could issue a witness warrant for your brother and his wife if they are able to locate them in California. They're looking for them now, and all things considered, your brother, his wife, and Ashworth are damn lucky they got out of this alive and as easily as they did. Have you had any contact with your brother?"

Nicholas was taken aback. "And how the hell would that happen? Him and Phryné skipped town as soon as the shit hit the fan! He doesn't know where I am, and I sure as hell don't know where he is, and I don't really give a damn. If he wasn't pals with Cafferty in the first place, my family would still be alive. My father came back from the war and died from rotten lungs caused by Kraut mustard gas and the TB, and my mother and sisters died from lungs full of smoke and fire. Thanks to my brother. Does that sound like the kind of brother you would like to have? I could care less about him. I hope he's haunted. I hope his dreams torture him."

It was past ten o'clock before the agents were finished, and were able to drive Nicholas to his austere apartment on Gratiot. Daniel Littlejohn parked the big Buick at the curb; Agent Benson got out and opened the rear door for Nicholas. Standing on the sidewalk with a cigarette hanging from his lips, Benson gave Nick a hearty handshake. "Take care of yourself, young man. And that wife of yours. I hope you have clear skies."

Nicholas didn't know what to say other than, "Thanks." He nodded toward Littlejohn and started toward his apartment. His stomach felt hollow.

He didn't sleep much that night, haunted by Nora, Buffalo, and his brother. The thought of Torricelli's body convulsing in an electrified chair, however, was somewhat gratifying.

The next morning, he caught the Fort Street trolley to River Road and walked to the Sterescu home on Mackie Street, where Nora met him at the door with open arms, sobs and abundant tears. Gabi made a breakfast of sausage and egg-filled crepes, and Dominik listened intensely as his son-in-law fully detailed his encounter with the BOI Agents. Tempers had cooled since the night before, and although everything was certainly not forgiven, the tension was tolerable. To Nicholas, it was eerily peaceful; strangely amicable. After breakfast and several cups of stark black coffee, he escorted his wife back to their small apartment.

He would never again see Agents Benson or Littlejohn.

1928: Baby Face ...

The birth of Alexander Throckmorton...

The machine shop's home was time-tested, mid-nineteenth century post and beam construction, stretching eighty feet deep, and fifty wide, with brick on two exterior walls.

Massive chestnut timbers supported the heavy, rough-sawn and hand-hewn joists of the roof. The wooden floors were permeated with machine oil and iron filings. Heat was provided by an enormous five-foot wide, potbelly, cast iron, coal-fired stove situated in the exact center of the building. Four oak desks with various standards of neatness and organization stood near the stove: one each for the foreman, two draftsmen and the owner, Garfield Wood*. The one-story structure shared its north wall with Gratiot Fabric Dyers, a textile enterprise protected by a labor 'association' under the thumb of a Detroit crime syndicate called the *Purple Gang**.

Nicholas had a knack for machinery, a feel for the steel, and an affinity for oil and grease. The owner of the machine shop developed a rapport with him and noticed the young man's work ethic and hunger for knowledge. He saw a quality in Nicholas that he claimed was *born of man, envied by gods*. Gar Wood was not only a successful businessman, but an inventor and boat designer, and oftentimes would be seen wearing his seaman's cap and double-breasted, brass-buttoned pea coat under his shop apron. He encouraged Nicholas to seize the opportunity to learn as he earned. Gar loaned Nick the shop's service manuals for Curtiss, Continental, Packard, and Hercules engines that he studied at home. Nick memorized torque and tolerance limits, bore, stroke, and displacement by manufacturer and model. The shop foreman and chief mechanic, Orin Waters, considered the young man from Buffalo to be a diamond in the rough. In short order, Nick had confirmed his worth to the business.

Through the frigid, dark winter months of November 1927 through March 1928, Nicholas persevered at his job, working his ten-hour shifts Monday through Saturday. On Sundays, at about ten in the morning, he would accompany Nora to the trolley stop and wait until she boarded the Delray streetcar to attend morning Mass with the rest of her family. He would then walk to Garwood Mechanical, voluntarily clean out the ashes and clinkers from the stove, load and bank the coal, and start a new fire if it had burned itself out. Keeping a fire burning over the weekend made the biting cold a bit less severe come Monday morning. At the shop, at his own pace, he could dabble on his own for a few hours with whatever caught his interest. This routine also made it possible for Nick to avoid the piercing glances cast upon a non-Catholic by some of the more conservative members of the Holy Cross Hungarian Catholic church congregation. He would join his wife and in-laws just before two o'clock, in time for Gabi's Sunday dinner, which she dished up promptly at three.

The rest of the week, nightly dinners with Nora's family continued to be served Monday through Saturday at six-thirty. Nicholas eventually purchased a double-plate electric cook top, but it was used mainly for toast, coffee, leftovers from family suppers, and the occasional fried egg sandwich. His strained relationship with Gabi and Dominik had eased, just as the tension on a rubber band weakens over time. At best, interactions were amicably cordial, but realistically cautious.

The spring of 1928 broke with the early arrival of a baby boy. On May 14, Nora gave birth to a four-week premature but otherwise healthy, six-pound, and two-ounce boy. The new parents had decided on the name *Alexander*; not only was it saintly, but it sounded respectably similar in English and Hungarian. The infant was baptized two weeks later, on Pentecost Monday, May 27.

Just the Wednesday before, Nora had completed the strenuous study of the Canisius Catechism that her parents had arranged. Nora's circle of personal influence had a small, three-point radius: Nicholas, her patriarchal family, and Holy Cross Hungarian Church. The weakest of those three points of importance was her husband.

Contact with youths and young women outside of Nora's family and the church had virtually ceased when she quit the sixth grade at the age of thirteen. A young man from Buffalo had entered her life just prior to her sixteenth birthday and turned her world upside down and sideways. After she had met Nicholas, things were never to be the same for young Nora. Her structured life and innocence were torn away and replaced with confusing and often conflicting sets of values and mores. She was repeatedly shamed and belittled by her parents, and instructed by the Church that true absolution was a lifetime task. Overwrought and confused, Nora found it difficult to understand or respect her husband.

Nicholas realized that his only way out was to get out, and unexpectedly got his chance in October. Two days shy of their first wedding anniversary, Gar Wood presented the aspiring mechanic an opportunity with a promising new business venture, *Huff-Daland Aero Machine Corporation*, located about 25 miles north of Detroit in Mount Clemens. Enrique Del'aire, a Huff-Daland engineer and veteran French WW I pilot, had contacted Wood looking for an engine mechanic familiar with the Packard 1500, V-12 Marine engines. Del'aire explained that the fledgling firm was working with existing technology, and desired to adapt the higher horsepower for commercial use in aircraft. Nick excitedly jumped at the promising job opportunity, knowing it was his best chance to start a new life. When her husband explained it to her, Nora sat smiling hopefully with five-month-old Alexander on her knee.

He and Nora fully anticipated that their decision would be met with protest from her parents. They were surprised. Dominik listened closely as Nicholas told the news. Nora's father had only one question and he asked it of his daughter, not Nicholas, "You will be going north and away from 8 Mile Road? To the good neighborhoods?"

"About halfway to Port Huron, Papa, about 19 Mile Road … in Mount Clemens. It's only forty minutes on the Inter-Urban train … an hour and a half between trains. We checked the schedule, so we can still have Sunday dinners with you and bring baby Alexander too, of course. And Nicholas' new job pays half as much more."

One year into their marriage, Nick and Nora had renewed hope for their future.

1929: Dead Man's Blues …

Dominik, Gabi and Marie leave Detroit

In February 1929, the anger-fueled promise Dominik had made to his family when the BOI came looking for Nicholas came to fruition. Things were definitely about to change.

The entire front page of the February 15th edition of the Detroit Free Press was devoted to the coverage of brutal mob violence in Chicago that was to become known as the *Saint Valentine's Day Massacre*. Seven members of Bugs Moran's *North Side Gang* had been lined up against the brick wall of a Lincoln Park garage and machine-gunned.

The newspaper account detailed the unsettling connection between Detroit's *Purple Gang* and Al Capone's *Chicago Outfit*. On numerous occasions, Capone had unsuccessfully tried to gain control of Detroit's lucrative location and the availability of illegal Canadian liquor. It was reported that brothers Abe and Ray Bernstein of Detroit's Lower East Side, had joined forces with Hymie Paul, Joe Lebowitz and their *Little Jewish Navy* of speedboats that ran bootleg liquor across the Detroit River from Canada.

Capone was expanding his power to Detroit, echoing his influence with a bang and a splash. Two bullet-riddled bodies were found at the corner of Gratiot Avenue and Russell Street, only a half block from where the Goulash Cannon was located. Two additional corpses washed ashore near the confluence of the Rouge and Detroit Rivers in Dominik's beloved Delray neighborhood.

Violence perpetrated by organized crime forced Dominik to make the rock-hard decision to move his family completely out of Detroit and back to Wisconsin. He had resolved that the best way to protect his wife Gabi and innocent fourteen-year-old Marie was to remove them from the city. It was not only mob violence, but also the bitter memory of Nicholas' trespass upon Nora that prompted his actions. By June 1929, he had quit his dream job at Ford's Highland Park plant and sold their Mackie Street home with its furnishings for $1500. Gabi sold the Goulash Cannon for $170.

While the names *Oshkosh* and *Wisconsin* did not conjure up reveling excitement, *New York Avenue* did sound better than Mackie Street; even with a Hungarian accent.

When Dominik and his family returned to Oshkosh, Dmitri embraced his nephew in a breath-taking, Budapest Forest bear hug. He then prophesized in his deep Hungarian growl, "I knew you would return. Your daughter Nora and grandson Alexander will follow in the coming years. I know. I see it."

Just like they did back in the Old Country, people listened when Dmitri spoke. Dominik was soothed yet mystified and shaken. It was understood that he would keep Dmitri's words to himself.

With his assembly line experience at Ford, Dominik was able to secure employment with Oshkosh Motors[*]: a heavy truck manufacturer. The family moved in and shared the two and a half story Victorian home on New York Avenue with aging Uncle Dmitri and Aunt Adelheid. The Victorian home was snuggled safely between Lake Winnebago and the Fox River. The Purple Gang was five hundred miles away.

1929: No, No, Nora …

A pattern forms …

When Nicholas hired on with Huff-Daland Aero Corporation in October of 1928, he and Nora had rented the back half of a single-story Macomb County bungalow from Gladys Dunn, a widow of the First World War, and a casual acquaintance of Enrique Del'aire, Nick's new boss. She had first met Del'aire ten years earlier at her husband's memorial service at Selfridge Airfield. After a very brief, superficial and thankless romance with Del'aire, Gladys withdrew into the isolation of a war widow in mourning.

Gladys was thirty years of age in November 1928; not quite twice that of Nora. She had a cheerful, yet cautious demeanor, pale blue eyes, and a voice as soft as marshmallows. She was a shapely blonde of subtle beauty who, at five-foot-one, stood almost as tall as Nora. Her deceased husband had been a pilot in the French Air Service, the Lafayette Escadrille* and served with engineer and pilot Del'aire during the Great War, World War I. Gladys, like so many other young women, became a casualty of foreign war without leaving home.

Battle Creek born and raised; Gladys Dodge had married flashy, flamboyant Army Air Service* Lieutenant Nolan Dunn at the age of eighteen only to become a young widow two years later. Nolan Dunn was a flight instructor at Selfridge Air Station when Europe became engulfed in what was to become World War I. He resigned his commission the day after his twenty-fifth birthday, visited the French Consulate on Grand River Boulevard and joined the *Aéronautique Militaire* as a combat pilot. Five months later he lost his life in a dog fight over Douaumont, France*.

Gladys secretly envied young Nora and her role as a mother of a healthy young son and the wife of a handsome husband who held a steady job. In confidence, she bemoaned her situation to Nora, telling of her loneliness and inability to create any meaningful friendships. It had been especially difficult for her to secure any dependable tenants for the rear apartment. When Nora knocked on her door with the second month's rent, Gladys not only thanked her, but gave her a hug. "It has taken nearly eight years for me to have reliable renters, and I am so happy to share my home with you!"

The departure of Nora's immediate family in June left her without the love, righteous guidance, and discipline she had grown so accustomed to. When Dominik moved his family to Oshkosh, he had essentially banished his elder daughter to

Detroit. He told her, "You have married Nicholas, now you must lie in his bed." Her father had the ability to twist the simplest truth into a punitive, authoritarian edict. She knew the chances of her husband moving his bed to Oshkosh were slim to none.

Nora felt as if she were alone and stranded on a desert island. Like Robinson Crusoe, she began searching frantically for companionship. Although she and Nicholas had established lives of their own and set up housekeeping in Mount Clemens, the separation from her parents and younger sister left a nipping hunger that she needed to satisfy. Even though Gladys quickly proved she could be an opportune friend and not just a landlady, Nora desired so much more. She looked to her faith and the Catholic Church to fulfill her appetite for structure and took full advantage of a familiar community and the ritualized organization that her father had provided for her first fifteen years. Four blocks from their apartment on Boehme Street, Saint Peter's church and the Saint Mary School, proudly stood at the corner of Gratiot Avenue and Pine Street. Nora volunteered for everything from cleaning toilets, washing windows, and polishing pews to whatever seemingly menial task was asked of her. She started working a few hours a day at whichever would have her, the church or school, and either brought young Alexander along or left him in the care of Gladys, who had generously agreed to volunteer her services as a babysitter. After the first few weeks, Nicholas persuaded the landlady to accept a dollar a week for watching after Alexander.

Within two months, Nora began *Lectio Divina*, the Divine Readings three days a week with Brother John, a diocesan seminarian. The Church was more than accommodating, and scheduled Nora's readings to coincide with her volunteer duties. Shortly after beginning her studies, it became obvious that Nora needed prescription eyeglasses. Nick, of course, purchased them at once. Nora wore them as a badge of honor, having fully embraced her faith, and believing that she was on the path to redemption. She became a very busy young woman.

By December, Gladys Dunn had found herself in a blossoming and fortuitous new relationship. Nora, Nicholas and Alexander supplied the human contact she longed for and the rental income that she needed to survive. Gladys welcomed every opportunity to share small talk with her new tenants. As circumstances dictated, it was Nora who offered most of the companionship. After the first few months, Saturdays or on Sundays after church, their friendly conversations became family dinners. Gladys and Nora would put together potluck suppers that were followed by games of canasta, rummy, or dominos with Nick until it was time to put Alexander to bed.

Gradually, a strong interaction developed between Nora and Gladys: the sort of familiarity and trust that is found between sisters. Gladys tried to fit the young bride under her wing and began to advise her on everything from laundry soap to fresh eggs. She and Nora knitted small items such as sweaters and coverlets for Alexander and a wool hat and scarf for Nicholas. As the winter drudged on, she taught Nora how to crochet and together they crafted countless doilies, little table runners, and small scarves for themselves, building a stronger friendship with each hank of yarn, crochet hook, and pot of Eight O'Clock coffee. Gladys eventually changed her taste in cigarettes and switched to Nick's brand: Camel. Nora had successfully quit her fledgling habit before it controlled her.

Gladys had a ritual established for the first of the month when it came around on the calendar. On Wednesday, May 1st, it was no different. A fresh pot sat percolating on the green enamel stove, ready for Nora's knock at the door. Gladys expected the rent to be paid on the first, neither a day sooner nor later. The knock came at nine o'clock, and Nora was invited inside along with little Alex. Gladys had an apple cake ready and waiting on the coffee table in the sitting room.

The wood floor was covered by a large, worn Persian rug but still managed to squeak and moan in protest under their footsteps. The room was bright with three large double-hung windows facing the south side. Gladys' yellow canary welcomed the visitors with incessant chirps. The 'first-of-the-month coffee klatsch' was underway and Gladys Dunn was in an unusual, talkative mood.

"I consider myself very lucky to have you living in the rear apartment, Nora. I've been alone more than ten years already and it seems like a lifetime to me. You and Nicholas have rescued me, believe it or not. Counting you, I've had a half dozen renters and now it's been three months since you moved in. You're the best of them all, believe me. It's not easy finding reliable tenants. In fact, I quit renting to single men right after the first disaster who had proved himself to be a drunken sot, and I needed to get the cops to kick him out for good."

She sliced off a piece of cake for Nora and continued, "The last people I had was a young family with two kids and she ended up getting herself pregnant again. And you know that there's barely enough room back there for even two kids, but when she told me that another little one was on the way, I had to ask them to leave."

Nora finished her first bite of the apple confection and added, "You don't have to worry about Nicholas and I having another child."

"I wasn't talking about that, Nora. Heavens, no. What I meant to say was that you and Nicholas are quiet, clean and you pay the rent on time. And you should consider yourself lucky, Nora. You should be thankful that you have an honest husband with a good job who doesn't lurk in dance halls or speakeasies and waste his dollars on painted women or whiskey. It's a mark of a good man when he finds his way home after a day's work." Gladys did not consider that she was a painted lady. In her eyes, nail polish and the proper amounts of lipstick and powder were a modest expression of femininity.

Nora sipped at her coffee. Alexander was on the sofa next to her, wrapped snug and fast asleep. Nora joined the conversation, "My father always said that a good man takes care of his family, and my mother says that if you want to keep a good man, you have to cook for him. Father Andrès says a good man respects his wife and Brother John says a husband must honor his wife. I guess that when you put all that together, I think all of them are right, and so are you ... a good man does find his way home in the evening. But I think Nicholas needs more patience with me. He needs to honor me, leave me alone, and begin following the Holy Word, like I am trying to do. He can put those big engines of his in an automobile or a boat or an airplane, but an engine alone cannot drive, power, or fly anyone into Heaven. The Bible says that a husband should love his wife as Christ loved the Church. It says that in the Epistle to the Ephesians." Nora would remember some parts of the Canisius Catechism for the rest of her life.

Gladys was never surprised by anything Nora said. She was aware that the young wife was barely a woman at seventeen, and all of her home life and education had been highly influenced and controlled by strict Catholicism. She knew that Nora held a very tight bond to her faith. Gladys decided to take a step onto the ice, cautiously tip-toed to the thin part and asked, "What do you mean that Nicholas needs to honor you and leave you alone? Does he have demands that he puts on you?" She tried to keep her tone one of concern and not curiosity.

Nora blinked rapidly, felt a flush and considered that perhaps she had said too much. Slightly embarrassed, she nervously looked down at little Alexander. He was still quite fast asleep and offered no immediate excuse for an escape, so an apology of sorts would have to do, "Oh no, he doesn't have any demands. I just meant to say that I wish he would understand my feelings and fully respect my faith."

Gladys watched Nora's expressions and tried to read her emotions. Gladys ran her finger over the brim of her empty coffee cup and decided to make yet another attempt to pry without appearing obnoxious, "It seems to me like you two are getting along swimmingly. I mean, I never hear any arguments coming through the walls."

"No, it's nothing like that. It's just that I don't want another baby right now, and my Nicholas doesn't understand. That's what I meant to say." With that statement, Nora had said it all.

Gladys tried to tactfully offer a bit of veiled advice and added, "There are birth control* methods ... and things that couples … married couples … can do to avoid pregnancy and still enjoy some … some physical contact."

Nora instinctively recognized the need to make her argument clear, and rapidly defended her position and faith, "The Church positively forbids what you are talking about. Abstinence is the only answer for me now. I must allow time for my body and spirit to heal. Brother John says so."

Gladys caught herself in the middle of an erotic fantasy and set her cup onto the coffee table. She pictured sex-starved Nicholas ravaging her, smothering her with heated kisses and caressing her with strong hands. She smoothed the skirt of her cotton house dress, moving her hands slowly over her thighs, down to her knees, closed her eyes and took a deep breath.

As she had done with her dress, Gladys felt she needed to work the wrinkles out of the conversation, "Well, Nora. It's clear that you, Alex and your Nicholas are a fine young family. I know things will work out for you. You have so much trust and faith, and I admire both you and your husband."

Gladys allowed her mind to wander once again and wondered what young Nicholas thought about abstinence.

She knew that his job had been keeping him busy, working long hours and occasionally taking him away from home for a few days. Perhaps he was too occupied with his work to give much thought to spiritual purity and physical chastity. To Gladys, it seemed to be such a waste of manhood.

As soon as Nora and Alexander left, she locked her bedroom door, surrendered to her erotic fantasy full time, and privately satisfied her growing sexual frustration.

2: MOUNT CLEMENS, 1930

Riding In My Car …

June 1 … starting Gladys Dunn and her engine

At the onset, Nicholas' new job with Huff-Daland was much of the same routine he was accustomed to at Garwood Mechanical. The enterprising aircraft company was working in conjunction with the Army Air Service, developing twin engine aircraft by re-fitting *Cyclops XHB-1* bombers with more powerful Packard V-12 marine engines. As an engine mechanic, he was part of a team of engineers and pilots working to improve the aerial dispersion of agricultural product: crop dusting. He began to travel from Selfridge Army Air Station in Mount Clemens to airfields, farms, and cornfields all over the Upper Midwest, from Ann Arbor, Michigan to Muncie, Indiana. With grease-stained hands and skinned knuckles, he felt that he had the world in his grasp. He was working on engines and the airplanes they powered, getting his hands dirty, his body bumped and bruised while fueling the hope of someday flying above the Earth like Charles Lindbergh.

In a time when the rest of the country found itself wallowing in the initial dire muck of the Great Depression, at seventy-five dollars a week, Nicholas could comfortably provide for his family. Unlike many others, nineteen-year-old Nicholas had a horizon he could set his sights upon. He had dreamed of becoming a pilot since boyhood and when Lucky Lindy crossed the Atlantic, the idea had been fully cemented into his being.

Although he knew he was in the hangar, he wasn't aware that he was about to taxi toward the runway. Takeoff would come soon enough.

Not only did Lieutenant Nolan Dunn leave his beloved wife Gladys behind, but there was also one other item he cherished that remained in Mount Clemens: a 1912 Model T. When he left for France in 1916, Nolan had squirreled it away in the small garage behind their Boehme Street home and covered it with sailcloth. On a whim, Gladys sold it to Nicholas for twenty-five dollars two days after Nora had paid the June rent.

Two weeks later, with a crankcase of fresh oil and a rebuilt carburetor, Nick had the old Ford's four-cylinder, twenty horsepower engine ticking away like a Singer sewing machine. As soon as he had the car running, he knocked on Gladys' door and invited her into the garage. He picked up Alexander into his arms and they all braved the chill of early summer and stepped outside. It was a Saturday evening, at about seven o'clock, and Nora was at Saint Peter's helping to get the church in proper order and squeaky clean for Sunday services.

Nicholas stood at the open door with his son cradled into his left arm and Gladys standing on his right, looking into the garage and admiring the idling Model T. The car was identical to the one Nick's brother had owned back in Buffalo with a few qualifying exceptions: Leopold's breezer did not have doors, windows or a roof. Nicholas fingered an oily denim towel sticking out of his pant pocket. He had a smile as wide as the Detroit River, standing and listening to the Ford's engine happily chattering away. Gladys felt a brief touch of hands between her and Nicholas. The soft brush of his flesh brought the tingle of goose bumps. She moved an inch closer to him, barely touching his arm. Gladys looked up for a reaction and got one.

He was elated, but at that moment, it was the car that had all his attention and not her gentle touch. "Just listen to that! That's music to my ears, Gladys … an engine running as it should … smooth, steady and dependable. Just listen! A mechanical masterpiece! It's beautiful! Thank you, Mister Ford! And thank you, Gladys!"

He put an arm around her shoulder and gave her a fleeting, innocent embrace. Although his gesture of gratitude was over as soon as it began, the recipient felt an unfamiliar, but welcome tickle. He continued, "Thank you so much for selling this car to me. I'll take care of it, believe you, me." He gave her shoulders another soft squeeze, and bumped his hip to hers, ever so harmlessly.

Her senses jolted, she fell deeper into her daydream and pushed further into thoughts of fantasy. She reached for his hand and found it, "You're more than welcome. It wasn't doing anybody any good just sitting in the garage ... I'm glad you can put it to good use, Nicholas." She paused for a split second, waffled her fingers into his and spoke softly, "But you can really thank me by giving me a ride in it someday. I haven't been in that Ford since ... since 1916." She had the hint of a smile; an innocuous, inquisitive smile. She was entering unfamiliar territory, very unfamiliar, and could not explain away what had prompted her suggestion, flirtatious touch, or the flush she was feeling. That evening, and not for the first time in their relationship, Gladys became keenly aware of Nicholas' masculine presence. She had been fantasizing away for some time now. She recalled Nora's vow of chastity and felt sensuous compassion for Nick and hope for herself. For the first time, she wondered if it could matter to him that she was ten years his senior, and immediately discounted her worry as pure foolishness when he turned, faced her and held her hand to his chest.

He returned her smile, "That sounds like a fair trade ... a favor for a favor."

Soundless seconds dragged past, and she searched for something to say.

Then, with impulsive urgency, Nicholas broke the silence, moved away, and asked an excited question, "How about next Saturday, a week from today, June 21st? You and me and

Nora and Alexander … we can all jump in the Ford and go to Belle Isle and watch the boat races. How's that?" Nicholas was captured by the excitement of his spontaneous suggestion. His words came from his mouth at rocket-speed, "We can watch *Miss America* race that morphadike Limey and win the trophy again! Nobody can beat four pounding Packards! Alex will love it! My old boss Garfield will be at the helm and my good old pal from the Detroit machine shop, Orin, will be sitting right next to him at *Miss America's* throttles! I can stop by the shop and see if I can get Orin or even Gar to save us a good spot on the bank … on the grassy bank at the top end ... right by the finish line!"

Given that Garfield Wood was a living legend in Detroit, having racked up eleven international championships, folks eagerly anticipated the annual race.

Nick could not help but get goose bumps just thinking about the roar of four Packard V-12 engines storming around the racecourse on the Detroit River. He knew those thunderous engines inside out and upside down.

Gladys noticed the boyish sparkle in his eye, and confirmed their plan, "Sure. Nora and I can pack a picnic. It will be fun, I know it!" At that moment, she began counting the minutes until the coming Saturday. It warmed her soul to see Nick so elated. He had already warmed her hand and quickened her pulse.

Gimme A Little Kiss, Will Ya Huh? …

The Detroit River, Garfield Wood and Joe Carstairs …

On the Tuesday before the race, Nora had apologized and said she couldn't partake in the picnic or attend the race because of her obligations at the church. After her explanation, it was no surprise to Nick and Gladys that she had made the decision not to go to the speed boat races on Saturday. It was a Holy Week and after the Feast of Corpus Christi was celebrated on Thursday, there would be a good deal of cleanup and preparation that needed to be done for the coming Sunday services. Nora's responsibilities to the Church were foremost in her life and she would not be able to witness the Harmsworth Trophy[*] race on Belle Isle with her husband.

Additionally, there were two dozen Holy Communions scheduled for Sunday, and The Most Reverend diocesan bishop Himself would preside over Sunday Mass, the Benediction, and Communion Ceremony at Saints Peter & Paul Cathedral. It would be a Holy Sunday.

Regardless of commitment, be it boat race or religion, everyone was up with the birds on Harmsworth day. It promised to be a glorious summer day on Lake Saint Clair, with only a few puffs of clouds. After a breakfast of hash and eggs, and a pot of Eight O'Clock coffee in their bellies, the adults were ready for everything the day could bring. Alexander was excited just to be a part of it all.

A half dozen hard boiled eggs, a can of sardines, a jar of dill pickles, a half loaf of Bernstein's pumpernickel, and one bottle each of Vernors and Nehi Grape had been packed into the reed picnic basket and loaded into the Model T. The previous evening, Nora had mixed two nursing bottles of formula[*] for Alexander from a can of Pet evaporated milk and Karo corn syrup, and wrapped them in her linen shopping bag along with a slice of buttered bread, small bits of American cheese, a small tin of Heinz apple sauce and her son's favorite nap blanket.

By seven o'clock the old car was packed and everyone ready for the short ride to Belle Isle. Gladys sat behind the wheel, with her foot on the clutch and hand on the throttle as Nicholas turned the crank. Nora was holding Alexander and watching from the rear stoop. The engine started on the first crank and began to clatter happily. When Nick secured the crank, Alexander was wide-eyed with anticipation and smiling ear to ear.

Gladys slid to the passenger side; Nicholas took Alex from Nora and gave her a kiss on the cheek. Nora told her son, "Alexander, you be a good boy for your father and Auntie Glad."

"We'll see you this evening, Sweetheart. Don't worry about Alexander, he's in safe hands." He didn't wait for an answer, walked to the Model T and handed his son to Gladys. She slid across the seat, holding the boy on her lap, close to her torso and breast. Alexander was ripe with excitement; his eyes moving everywhere and watching everything.

Nicholas nodded, touched two fingers to his forehead, hung his arm out the window, smiled to his wife and teased her, "Be good at church today, all right?"

Nora smiled back. "Of course, I will. I always am. Have fun, and don't let my Alexander in the sun without his hat or coverlet." Nick gave a flick of his hand as a wave, and backed out of the driveway. They were on their way.

Although he had worked at Garfield Wood's machine works and was more than familiar with the big Packards, this was the first time he decided to attend the race. The banks of the Detroit River were beginning to fill with people and automobile traffic was lined up on Grand River Boulevard at the Belle Isle Bridge into the park. The best seats, however, were at the island's Detroit Yacht Club and reserved for the city's elite, select invited guests, politicians and automobile moguls. Nicholas, courtesy of Gar Wood, was one of a few hundred to have a twenty-five-cent reservation ticket for automobile access and parking on the island. It was nine o'clock by the time they were directed to and found their picnic spot about fifty feet from the water's edge and elevated just enough to get a good view. The scene on Belle Isle was like a gigantic county fair. There were roped-off areas, walkways covered in wood shavings, automobiles parked on the lawns, vendors' tents, horse-drawn wagons for transport, children chasing one another and couples on blankets. The

Detroit Mounted Police were an imposing presence, second only to the souvenir mongers.

Nick had a parking spot reserved on the grassy hill: a quarter mile north of the finish line, the judges' stand and the yacht club. Orin had explained that it was the best place because by the time the boats rounded the last turn, the leader was nearly always assured a win and it also served as the staging area, where the drivers would start the engines and cruise to the start line. Nick's main interest was to witness first-hand the four V-12's of Gar Wood's new boat, *Miss America IX* tearing through the water. The first of three races was to begin at noon.

The lively surroundings captured Alexander and as soon as Nicholas parked the car and their feet touched the green grass, the youngster was ready for action. It was with a curious twist of familiarity that Alex informed Gladys that he needed to pee rather than his father, but Nicholas stepped in, "I'll take you over to the toilet, Alex. It's different here; they have one just for us boys. Come on, up we go, and you can ride piggy-back, Buddy, and we can all walk to the toilet." He picked up his son and placed him snugly onto his shoulders, straddling his neck.

Father, son, and landlady Auntie Glad wove their way around parked automobiles, picnickers and pedestrians toward the restrooms. Nicholas had his left arm up to his chest, up and around his son's legs, with Gladys on his right, walking close alongside. She looked up, returned Nick's smile, and deftly searched for his hand. She found it, and he accepted her touch.

It was much more than a touch for Gladys. She scolded herself for allowing a decade to pass without the feel of a man. Although she immediately placed admonition upon her thoughts, she could not release him from her grasp. It felt too good, and she decided not to deny temptation. She moved closer. If only for a slice of time, he was hers.

For the last eighteen months, Nicholas had known Gladys only as his landlady and a convenient child sitter during the times he was working, and his wife was at the church or school. Alex simply loved her and for him, the words *Auntie Glad* literally meant fun. She was always extremely pleasant and provided congenial company during shared suppers or while playing a few hands of canasta. But right then, carrying his son and walking next to Gladys, holding her hand, Nick too, experienced a sense of belonging, a sense of family and togetherness. All of it, while his wife Nora was at Saint Peter's.

Nicholas noticed Gladys differently that day. He discovered her beauty and became keenly aware of her pent-up sexuality. He had gained a sense of familiarity with her that could easily whet his appetite for more. He could not explain it, but he felt the pride of a peacock, having her at his side and his son on his shoulders. Nora was his raven-haired wife of necessity. He reasoned that he could have blonde Gladys as his lover of choice.

Despite the age difference of ten years, he had neither considered her as his senior nor counselor. She was simply Gladys, his landlady, who happened to be an unfortunate widow of the *War To End All Wars**. At that moment, walking across the grass toward the pavilion, refreshment bar, and lavatories, he discovered that Gladys was much more than the person who took his rent money, and babysat his son. For reasons beyond explanation, a door had been opened, an entrance to his soul. Her nearness, soft touches and delicate, intoxicating scent mystified him. Magically and inexplicably, she had suddenly become a desirable woman and her role in his life had instantly changed. Despite these impetuous new feelings, or, perhaps, because of them and the precarious challenges that were sure to come, the walk from the parade field to the pavilion was made without a spoken word.

In the ladies' room, Gladys stood for a moment at the mirror, brushed at her hair and freshened her lipstick. She was wearing a floppy-brimmed royal blue hat over her curled locks, and a mid-calf, pale yellow cotton sun dress with butterfly sleeves. It was a new dress, purchased just that week at J. L. Hudson on Woodward Avenue along with a pair of Kronenberg stockings and a tiny bottle of No.4711 Eau de Cologne.

Looking at her mirrored image, Gladys reflected on how her outlook on life had changed over the last week. During her recent conversations with Nora, she discovered that Nicholas was left wanting for physical attention. For months, she had dismissed her interest in Nick as pure fantasy, simple imprudence and deviously wrong. She recognized that the situation had changed driven by her new knowledge, and it now appeared possible that he could be receptive. And quite literally, hunger can lead to wasting away and ultimate starvation, but given the correct circumstance and partner, she believed physical desire could be fulfilled beautifully. Gladys rationalized further that poets had given written tribute to love and its climax for centuries. She was satisfied with her reflection; it looked good. She was ready.

Back outside, she found a bench, lit a cigarette and waited for Nicholas and Alex to exit the restroom. Judging from the smile on the boy's face, things had apparently gone well. It was also strikingly obvious that a promise had been made and needed to be kept. "Papa said ice cream, Auntie Glad!"

Gladys could only smile, and Nicholas only agree. Their eyes met and thoughts meshed. They were aware that the presence of young Alexander created a boundary, a wall and a fortress of incorruptibility that could not be destroyed. An understanding was reached, and an unwritten accord was silently agreed upon. They needed to show restraint in front of Alex. The boy could talk.

A band could be heard playing Dixieland jazz over the buzz of humanity, voices, machinery and laughter. An unmistakable jambalaya of banjos, clarinets and saxophones drifted from the gazebo bandstand and blended with the smell of hot dogs and popcorn.

One baby-sized, vanilla ice cream cone from the refreshment stand was followed by the purchase of a small, six-inch teddy bear replicating the pair that Gar Wood carried as good-luck mascots for every race. Standing in the shade of a massive, spreading elm, the boy gave all of his attention to the ice cream and held the bear dangling in his free hand. For Alex, it may have well been Christmas.

"Take a look at him, Gladys. If only all of us could enjoy life with the same simplicity, pleasure, and love that a child has."

"We can, Nick. We simply must allow ourselves."

He dared her and moved closer, looking into her eyes and placing his hands upon her hips. "How can we do that without a commitment and without hurting the innocent?"

"Carefully," she said, "Very carefully." She moved her head ever so slightly, looked to Alex and saw him facing the other way, working diligently on the ice cream cone.

Nicholas pulled her to him. There was electricity, a spark and deafness to the world. For Gladys, their first kiss was a passionate welcome into his world. For Nick, it was a kiss that was returned with surrender, willingness and an invitation for more; feelings he hadn't known for years. For Gladys and Nick, it was their first step over a line and down a path that would forever change their lives.

Nick did not relax his hold on her nor did she back away. They looked into one another's eyes for one piercing moment, and then slowly toward Alexander just as he was beginning to finish off his frozen confection. Their lips touched once more; softly, briefly before they broke their embrace. They knew that they had crossed over a line and what it meant. There was no easy retreat.

They walked back to the Model T at Alexander's pace. He was in the middle, holding onto his father's hand and clutching the teddy bear under his arm. "I think your son is heading straight for the noise, Nick. Just like you, he's attracted to the excitement and the power of the engines."

They were aware of their passion and desire, but forced themselves into painful patience, made all the worse by the thrill of anticipation.

As noon neared, the sound of rumbling engines was becoming more persistent. Like Nick and Gladys, the wait was unnerving for the spectators along the banks, but for a different reason. A power plant of engines would start, accelerate quickly and return to a smooth idle and repeat again. Four speedboats sat moored in no particular order at the yacht club's docks. The polished, varnished teak deck of *Miss America IX* gleamed in the sunlight. For Nick, the excitement of the boat race had waned. Gladys was ready and waiting at a different starting line.

All of Belle Isle was warmed in a blanket of sunshine. Families, groups of children, and secluded couples were scattered everywhere. Ladies sported sunhats of every color and style that were adorned with either silk flowers or wide, bright bands of ribbon. Bowlers, fedoras, pork pies, or boaters topped the head of nearly every man, excepting only a few, one of whom was Nicholas. A few dainty, lacy parasols could be seen here and there throughout the crowd. Children ran with pinwheels, catching the wind. The Depression was nowhere to be seen on Belle Isle.

The Harmsworth racecourse at Detroit was laid out on the American side of the Detroit River between Belle Isle and the city of Detroit. It ran clockwise from the Detroit Yacht Club docks, west toward the Belle Isle bridge, around two buoys, turning east toward the back stretch, out into Lake Saint Clair, around a dangerous, well-known, easterly hairpin turn, and finally westward toward the judges' stand. A half-million race fans were crowded on the riverbanks and a few thousand were on the distant Canadian side, straining their eyes with binoculars or telescopes, hoping to catch a glimpse of an Englishman beating the American.

Race preparations of another sort were underway at the old Model T. Nick and Gladys rationalized their choices and decided to have lunch in the car. They reasoned that it afforded them enough personal privacy, yet each wave and wake the speedboats made on the river was still visible. Nicholas used the Ford's right front fender and popped the bottle cap off a Vernors. He then opened every window on the car, worked the blanket into multiple folds and set it behind the front seat on the driver's side floor. Gladys opened the picnic basket and put together lunch for Alex. He nibbled butter bread and barely took any applesauce before he leaned into her and nursed his bottle. Cool breezes rolled off Lake Saint Clair.

Within minutes, Alexander was asleep on the floor by the back seat, leaving the front to Nick and Gladys. They moved to the center, away from the steering wheel. Her left leg went over his, pulling herself closer. His hands slowly, purposely moved over, under and around her. She melted under his heated kisses, hands, and fingers like a pat of butter on a hot plate. Nicholas touched, pressed, and fondled every forsaken inch of her form. He drank in her fragrance and tasted the passion in her kisses. His fingertips covered her warmth; teasing, pressing her patience, as well as his restraint.

Her hand covered his as her breath quickened. Gladys whimpered in quivering ecstasy, shaking to her core. After seconds of euphoria, she quietly wallowed in a shiver of satisfaction that was followed by a trembling climax just as she kissed him, holding him tightly, and murmuring *I love you* in his ear. What ensued was a stark awareness of him. Her immediate reaction was a sexually fueled fervor, moving her hands and fingers over him. She caressed, stimulated, kissed, and stroked him, deliberately giving him the release that she desired to give in return. He moaned in pleasure.

It had ended too soon. Gladys and Nick had satisfied one another with burning touches and sensuous lips.

On the river, *Miss America's* Packards were breathing fire, too.

For Nick and Gladys, the Harmsworth boat races were relegated to second place. The thundering noise of four V-12 Packards was a whimpering whisper compared to the newly discovered roar of passion that was unleashed in the front seat of that old Model T Ford on Belle Isle.

The first heat saw one of the English boats lose control at the east turn and crash onto the Canadian shore. The races were essentially over at the end of the first lap of the third race.

Although she was leading *Miss America IX* at the first turn, England's *Estelle* had spewed oil over her audaciously virile driver, Barbara Carstairs, knocking her out of the race. It was apparent that once again Wood's *Miss America* would take the trophy.

The Harmsworth hoopla was over by half past two and Nick and Gladys were out of the car, onto the grass and blanket with Alex, a dozen wooden blocks, and his new teddy bear. He was paying no attention to the adults. Nicholas finished the last hard cooked eggs and sardines. Gladys was playing her lacquered nails on Nick's thigh, leaning into him. She kissed him.

Nick kept one eye on Alex, leaned to her and whispered, "I don't want to see this end, but it's about time for us to head back."

Gladys was still swimming in a pool of ecstasy and before she got out of the deep end, she wanted to make a statement and a promise. "This will work for us. I'll make it work. I've spent enough time in that desert I was living in. You're my oasis, Nicholas Throckmorton. You have quenched my thirst, wound my life spring, and I shall forever be grateful. Forever. I vow that I will not destroy what you are working for, never. I will cherish and honor and respect you. I will not ruin you. You may set me on fire if I ever threaten you."

He chuckled, "Fine. But how about a cigarette for now?" He reached into his pocket for his packet of Camel. He lit one for her and then another. He did not expect any commitment from her, nor did he foresee her promise of complete discretion. He was caught unaware.

"Thanks for the cig, Nick, but I mean it. I'm serious." She drew in the smoke, and spoke with conviction, "I meant what I said just now. This is between you and me. That's as far as I will allow this to go … just between you and me."

He assured her, "Well, you don't need to worry about me standing on the corner of Telegraph and Eight Mile yelling our secret at the top of my lungs. That's not going to happen. Like you just said, this is between you and me, and that's it."

Nick reached into the basket and brought out Alex's second nursing bottle, trying to shift gears, and hoping to change the serious tone of the conversation. "Do you think Alex's milk is still all right? It's been sitting outside for what, six hours?"

She took the bottle, spotted her wrist with a few drops and licked a taste, "It's fine. It hasn't gone sour. It's not that hot out here." She stood, stepped over to Alex, sat down and handed it to him. The boy didn't make a sound, took the bottle, leaned into Gladys, and began sucking away. She sat facing Nicholas, his son cradled in the arms of his new lover. She was aglow; her cheeks were flushed and her lips in a smoldering pout, wanting more.

She gestured toward little Alexander and encouraged her new partner in passion, "See that, Nick? There's nothing to worry about. Everything is fine with the world. Your son agrees."

She was determined not to let Nicholas walk away from what they had started, only to leave her alone and stranded again in a wasteland starved of intimacy. She did not want to see the well dry up and reaffirmed her promise, "Nora will never know."

She was doing it again, and it gave him a rise. He was conflicted. He wanted her, all of her, but knew the fire that had been kindled must not be allowed to get out of control. "We need to protect Nora. She's easily broken and must never find out … ever."

Gladys reached out and took his hand. "Just take a look at your son, Nick. He's fallen asleep again. Things are just fine. Your son trusts me, and so can you. I will protect you with my vow of silence. I told you that Nora will never know, and I meant it. I have even taken all the precaution necessary. You have nothing to worry about, Nick, nothing. Trust me."

"What do you mean *precaution*?"

She shifted sleeping Alexander off her lap and onto the blanket, leaned forward to Nick, kissed him softly and reassured him yet again, "Don't worry about anything, nothing at all, because just this past week I bought a Dutch diaphragm* for myself at the Rexall on Woodward. So, we can begin to enjoy everything, and I can have all of you, and it's like I said, we're safe. Let's pack all this up, go home and tell Nora all about the race. Tomorrow is another day. It'll be ring-a-ding-ding, I promise. Ring-a-ding-ding!"

She giggled like a teenager. She had surprised him not only with her purchase, but her candor.

"How long have you been planning this, Gladys?"

She had already begun to pack up the basket. "I really haven't been planning it. But I have been wanting, and waiting for it, and I am wishing and hoping that it will happen tomorrow."

Her outspoken honesty amazed him and although he did not see it coming, he understood her motivation. Selfishly, he decided to take advantage of the situation and not deny her or himself.

It was nearing half past four when they got back to the house on Boehme Street. As soon as Nick stopped the Ford in the driveway, Nora came out of the house, snatched up

Alexander, planted a kiss on his cheek, set him on her hip and encouraged everyone inside. "Come on in, I have left-over stew on the warm."

Nora had the table set. She was eager to mention that the Monsignor had visited the church to check on the preparations for Sunday before she could begin to feign some interest in the Harmsworth race. She was much more focused on how Alex behaved, what the ladies were wearing, and if there was any entertainment.

Gladys was ready with answers, "We didn't see them, but we heard a Dixieland band playing somewhere over by the covered shelters; probably at the gazebo there, but that was just about noon, and the races were about to start, so we just stayed at the car. And besides, Alex was tired. All in all, though, it was a good day, a fun day, wasn't it Nick?"

He agreed, "You need to make plans and come with us next year, Sweetheart. You would really have a good time. We sure did."

Nora didn't acknowledge what her husband had said. She obviously wasn't interested in the machinery. "I bet bunches of ladies were getting some sun. Did you get a chance to get a sunburn, Gladys?"

Gladys chuckled, "Goodness, no, Nora. Take a look at me! I'm not like all those other women who can just sit outside barely covered and work on a sunburn. Not me, I'm a blonde with light skin, and I would certainly burn, and not in the fashionable sense. I'd end up as red as those little cinnamon candy hearts. And it would hurt. But I know all of the men, and some of the ladies were there for the excitement, the race, and not the sun anyway. I know I was."

Nicholas had a thought and inserted his opinion, "I don't like cinnamon candy hearts. I don't think many people do."

Nora disagreed, "Oh, Nick! If nobody liked it, they wouldn't make it."

He nodded and grinned. "You're probably right, Sweetheart. They wouldn't make it if nobody wanted it."

I'm Wild About That Thing …

Sunday, June 29, 1930: Twisting and turning …

For the week just passed, simply thinking about Nicholas taunted, tempted, and teased Gladys with a sexual desire and an emotional hunger that grew stronger with each day.

Mere minutes after Nora had left for church, Nicholas knocked on the landlady's door. It was a day that she had held in lustful anticipation. She had coffee and cake on the table and a bottle on the warm for Alex. She knew Nora was always at Saint Peter's until at least one-thirty, and as a rule, Alexander took a late morning nap. Gladys' planned promiscuity was coming to fruition.

After his bottle, she had no sooner covered Alexander than he was asleep on the sofa. Nick was standing close behind her, smelling her bath salts, and looking over her shoulder as she tended to his son. His arms were around her, and he gently pulled and pressed her to him. She felt his enlivening, and pushed her buttocks into him, twisting suggestively, subtly, side to side. He kissed her neck, and she turned to him.

Her fingers fumbled with his shirt buttons, feverishly undid his trousers and lifted his undershirt over his head. She kicked off her pumps, stepped out of her dress and moved backwards to her bed, grappling and pulling at his undershorts. They eased their bodies onto the mattress.

That morning Nicholas and Gladys shuffled, weaved, double-stepped, and dipped through the first of three horizontal waltzes. They marked the beginning of countless dalliances that would span several years. What they had started a week earlier on Belle Isle was a passion-fueled afternoon appetizer for that Sunday's lustful brunch. The full gourmet menu was served while innocent Alexander napped and his teen-aged mother helped prepare for, and attended weekly worship. The new lovers enjoyed two heated entrées and a warm dessert while wrapped in one another's arms.

A soft breeze pushed the muslin curtains aside, creating a silent, gentle ballet in the bedroom while the morning sun spread its liquid light upon the sheets. At Sunday's first blush, Gladys ended her love-starved role as a chaste, withering widow twelve years after the Great War had claimed her husband. After their tête-à-tête, her feelings gushed. She was physically spent, but still held plenty of emotion in the bank. She thought of young Nora and felt a flash of dread before simply pushing it aside. Shame on Nora for neglecting Nicholas. Gladys rationalized that she could lustfully accept what Nora chose to ignore. She was satisfied and guilt-free.

She was resting on her side, one leg over his and drawing invisible heart outlines on his chest with her fingertips. "I so loved Nolan that I would not imagine being with another man. I felt that once married, it meant always married. I was devastated when the Germans stole him from me and I felt that I was violated by the Kaiser himself, and a hatred fermented within me that soured my soul for years. Then for a time, the hatred turned into misguided anger at my Nolan for joining the French and leaving me behind. Finally, maybe wisdom comes with age, I don't know, but finally … I realized it was my fault. During my talks with Nora, I discovered that faith in yourself is the first rung on the ladder that leads up and out of the darkness. It was I who poisoned the well inside me. One morning your wife was telling me about Daniel and the lions … it's so unbelievable that Nora helped me discover my way out. I needed to get over myself, and you helped me with that, Nick. You pointed the way for me and offered me your hand when I offered mine … when I sold you the car, remember? Remember that day? And that beat-up, forgotten old car wasting away in my garage ... like me … wasting away. Your eyes sparkled when I offered to sell you that car. Yes, and there was something in your eyes, too, I think. Dark mysterious eyes, you have. Your eyes drew me inside your heart. You gave that old car what it needed: care and attention. All I ask is that you let me stay near you. I need attention and care, just like that neglected car. Maintenance, that's all … I need affection … tenderness … someone to hold me. I know what love is … I had it once and it was taken from me. I don't need love, I need affection. We can nurture one another, Nicholas."

Her rambling touched him. Her spoken words flowed like warm oils off an artist's pallet. He saw vibrant color in every word, every thought, and every feeling that she had brushed onto the canvas. Her honesty had drawn a portrait of sincerity with soft strokes of sexual desire and subtle shadows of insecurity. Twenty months into an arid marriage, Nicholas rediscovered intimacy very close to home. Gladys devoured him. And he let her.

"You're one fabulous woman, Gladys. You have loved me like I've never been loved before. I'm not an expert at this nookie jazz, not by a long shot, but I can promise you this: I'll always be here when you need me. I'll give you all the affection you can handle, Lover. I think we will be good for each other. We're just what each of us needs. You need more than one noodle to make a plate of spaghetti, and it seems to me that we wind around each other pretty good."

He sat up, reached to the bedside table, grabbed his pack of Camel, stuck two between his lips and put a match to them. He set the ashtray onto the sheet and handed a cigarette to Gladys.

They sat smoking, their backs to the headboard and looking out into the front room through the half-open door. They could barely see Alexander covered, and fast asleep on the sofa, safely behind a kitchen chair.

The lover's brunch was over, and their appetite satisfied. They had swallowed their pride and stepped over the cheating line. Nicholas and Gladys had shared comparatively harmless samples the day before, but that morning they tasted what they lusted after, and experienced the spicy satisfaction of coition.   The main course had gone down smoothly and warmly, tingling their palates.

The hard part was yet to come: digestion.

It is an unwritten mandate that lovers on the sly must follow certain rules.   These carnal rules can be found in the fine print on the bottom of the cheaters' dessert menu.

1. The number one rule about stealing cookies is not to get caught with your hands in the jar.   Gladys and Nick were clearly successful with Step One.   Nora was not at home when the deed was done, and two-year old Alexander was asleep.

2. Secondly, you must put the lid back on the jar and be careful not to leave any tell-tale crumbs on the counter, yourself, your clothes, or between the sheets.   Gladys had showered with Nick following the consumption of the sweet goodies.   Step Two was covered.

3. Third, both parties need to be extremely careful not to let the cat out of the bag by either looking guilty or being overly nervous.   Step Three had yet to be tested.

4. Lastly, you must not spill the beans and keep the secret, no matter what.   Like number three, Step Four was still up in the air.

Nick and Gladys believed that they had memorized the rules.   In the front and the back of the Boehme Street bungalow, they awaited their first test.

Gladys had Sunday's chuck roast dinner in the oven by eleven o'clock and the table was set.   Her bed was made, and fresh towels were in the bath.   The coffee cups and plates from her morning toast with Nick and snacks with Alex were washed and put away.   She tuned the radio to WJR, fidgeted with some crochet work, and paged through an old bi-monthly copy of The Saturday Evening Post.   However, she smoked more than usual, and drank her fifth cup of coffee.

Gladys was the first to see Nora walking up the drive after church, and gave the usual wave out the kitchen window.   She imagined her heartbeats becoming faster, stronger.   In that instant, she felt pity on young Nora. Gladys felt dirty, sooty, like she was covered in the black creosote and ash of the coal furnace in the basement, starkly aware that she had just philandered with the teen-aged mother's husband. She walked to the kitchen sink and busily lathered her hands with a bar of Ivory.

In the back apartment, Nick went about the place, filling the role of husband and father. Twice he picked up Saturday's Detroit News only to become instantly disinterested. His son was his only distraction, and together they repeatedly worked on creating the largest building-block tower possible, only to knock it down, and begin building another.

Having walked down the driveway, Nora simply opened the kitchen door, walked in, and set her handbag on the counter. From the living room floor, Nicholas acknowledged her arrival, "Was it a good mass this morning, Sweetheart?"

3: TAKING OFF, 1931-36

Blue Skies ...

Nick and Jenny fly from Lima, Ohio to Lima, Peru ...

Within six months, Nicholas' job description and duties had changed yet again. He began sitting behind the pilot in the mechanic's seat of a converted Curtiss Jenny biplane that dispensed fertilizer and insecticide over farm fields for Huff-Daland Crop Dusters. He had begun doing double duty for the company as an in-flight mechanic and co-pilot.

After ten months on the job and with training, in April of 1931, he was flight certified at Selfridge Airfield by the Army Air Corps and awarded Pilot License[*] #4376. He immediately began his career as a pilot and enjoyed a weekly wage of $125. It was more money than he ever dreamed possible and one hundred dollars more per week than he had brought home when he started working at Garwood Mechanical. At a time when a room at the Waldorf Astoria in New York went for three dollars a night, young Nicholas prospered.

At the age of twenty-one, Nick had fulfilled his dream of becoming a flyer. To him, becoming a pilot wasn't simply a boyhood dream fulfilled. It was a feeling of boundless freedom that came with the ability to provide comfortably for his family. After his first payday as a pilot, his very first purchases were a white silk scarf and a brown, calf-leather, fleece-lined flight jacket. The scarf became a permanent part of his working wardrobe.

As a pilot[*], Nicholas earned his generous wages and travel allowances flying low and slow, his wheels perilously close to fence posts and standpipes, the wings of his Jenny barely missing power and telephone lines either above or below. It was an unwritten job qualification that if a pilot never nipped a telephone line or clipped a tree limb, he wasn't flying low enough to spread the product. The *Huffer-Puffers*, as they came to be called, garnered a favorable reputation with farmers over the Midwest and South, but they were also the spark of some controversy. Some zealous environmentalists took to their soapboxes and declared that aerial crop dusting contributed to the heat and drought of the Dust Bowl*, arguing that the planes were stirring up the cloud cover and pushing all the beneficial rain to the east and north. The pilots and planes were lumped into the fermenting pickle barrel of blame along with the blossoming air travel industry, the supposed drift of World War I mustard gas, the turmoil of the Russian Bolshevik revolution, hot air balloons, and even the Kaiser's lighter-than-air dirigibles and Zeppelins. Some farming groups pointed the finger of condemnation to the ongoing construction of Hoover Dam on the Colorado River, the creation of Lake Mead and finally, the oil and gas drilling boom in Oklahoma and Texas. The environmentalists proclaimed that the world would never be the same.

Huff-Daland had grown its agricultural business rapidly, and by 1932 was able to expand internationally. Nick's job began to keep him away from home for longer periods of time, up to a month or more. Nicholas, one other pilot, two mechanics and a half dozen trained ground crew were transferred from McCook airfield in Dayton, Ohio to Monroe, Louisiana as a new branch of Huff-Daland to be named *Delta Dusters**. The company sought out and discovered new markets and began dusting farms in Mexico, Nicaragua, and Peru, where the seasons were much longer or even reversed, thus creating a year-round business plan. His weekly pay packet arrived either courtesy the Post Office Department or in his pant pocket whenever he was able to get back home to Mount Clemens.

Meanwhile, in late 1932, Nora began working five hours a day at Saint Mary School assisting the sixteen dedicated Immaculate Heart Of Mary nuns who taught the four hundred plus students of the first through twelfth grades. Nora's dedication to her job and its mission continually became stronger. Young Alexander was left in the care of Aunt Gladys from Monday through Friday.

When Nicholas did get time off from work, it was sporadic and unpredictable. Although her husband's on-again-off-again-come-and-go schedule didn't seem to bother Nora, it forced Gladys to adjust her expectations. She didn't complain, but in fact began to long for him much more with each of his departures.

Breezin' Along With The Breeze ...

Everyone goes to the race this time ... 1933

On Labor Day, September 4, 1933, Nick, Nora, Gladys and Alex were able to witness together Garfield Wood winning his last Harmsworth Trophy on the Detroit River. Nearly five months earlier, Alexander had his fifth birthday and for the first time he was old enough to fully enjoy the noise and excitement that enveloped Belle Isle on race day. He would remember that race for the rest of his life, and it was destined to become one of his best childhood memories. All day, Nick and Gladys secretly drew from their memories of their first Harmsworth race three years earlier, in 1930. Nora spent the day looking after Alex and doting over the picnic basket lunch. She did, however, watch the race with detached indifference. Not much else on Belle Isle piqued her interest.

The day after the race, Alex began kindergarten at Mount Clemens Grade School. Nora had tried to enroll him at Saint Mary's but had been turned away because both parents were not members of a local Catholic parish. For Nora, it was a huge disappointment. For Nick, it was what he had come to expect as part and parcel of his banishment from the faith.

On school days, young Alexander and his mother would leave and return to the Boehme Street apartment together.

Gladys was effectively relieved of her job as part-time nanny. The only time Gladys was needed to babysit was on frequent Sundays when Nora attended mass at Saint Peter's and Nicholas was out of town.

In confidence, Gladys bemoaned her situation to Nicholas, "What good is life if I have to live it alone? I feel like I have become the forgotten, feeble-minded family member, pushed aside for convenience. Your Alexander had become the main outlet for my love and just to remind you: the heart you leave behind is the one beating in my chest, Nicholas, not your wife's. I realize that it's not my position to force change of your job, your life, or your mind. But please remember that when you do come home, I am the friend and lover who you left behind."

Nick argued his case, "One thing I've learned is that this world is too damn big to be stuck in one place all your life, Gladys. The horizon never ends; it has no limit. You need to grow some wings and get out of Detroit. Fly, spread those wings and go. So many people don't have any idea how big this world is. People are meant to live life. You are still young enough to make something of yourself." His intention was to encourage her and not to offend, but for Gladys, it didn't come across that way. She felt emotionally bruised and gruffly ridiculed by a lover ten years her junior. It was the first time that some petals wilted and fell from the bouquet of roses.

With the passing of time, Gladys and Nicholas struggled through the rough patch almost as if it never happened. Despite his shortcomings in tact and timing, she found him easy to forgive. Adult atonement was usually on Sundays, when Alex was napping, and Nora was at Saint Peter's.

Prohibition ended on December 5th of 1933, creating a rare atmosphere of celebration for the nation. Roosevelt's New Deal was still trying to stimulate a struggling economy with social work-for-pay and make-work projects. New Year's Eve, which rang in 1934, was the first time Nora had consumed alcohol, and it did not end well. With three glasses of wine in her belly, she was in bed by ten o'clock, oblivious to the party that continued on at the other side of the house. Nick and Gladys were never sure, and nothing was ever mentioned, but they always believed that his wife had discovered their secret that night. On New Year's Day, Nora vowed that she would never again partake of an alcoholic beverage.

Nick's pilot pay enabled him to live without financial worry. He continued to provide everything his family could need and consistently give his darling Gladys tokens of his appreciation. He did not like the connotation of cash, but Nicholas did manage to keep his lover in silk, nylon and fragrance, not in disregard of Nora, but for his wife's choice in apparel and scent. Nora was religiously practical with wool, cotton, linen and Fels Naptha soap.

When Nicholas wasn't in the cockpit of a Jenny or Stearman, he dressed well. He kept his off-duty clothing separate from the broadcloth and khaki and didn't mix the stain and sweat from work with the crease, starch and cut of his dress slacks or jacket.

Nick spent much of his time in the air, often regulating his time on the ground only for sustenance and sleep. A duster's base of operation could be anywhere the work was. From time to time, the fields he served were his runway and the nearest barn became the hangar or repair shop. Raw product was delivered by truck, rail, or even donkey ahead of the dusting crew's arrival. It was hard work, and glamorous by no measure. In 1934 Nick christened his new Curtiss-powered Stearman C-3 and painted her name on the nose cowl: *Home*.

By its nature, Nicholas' job dictated that his time with his wife, son and lover was irregular, limited, and unpredictable. His love affair with Gladys was strained and its future was up in the air. His job paid comfortably well, had an inherent air of adventure, and enabled him to expand his horizons over the

American heartland, Central and South America. Lovers, one-night stands, and bed-warmers were scattered like the four winds, but precisely marked in blue pen on flight charts. He became acquainted with bar rooms, back alleys, and if the situation demanded, the opportune house of ill repute.

In the spring of 1935, while the country was still struggling to pull itself out of the stubborn economic quicksand of the Depression, Nicholas purchased a two-bedroom cape cod with a detached garage on Second Street, Mount Clemens, for $1000 down and a $1500 five-year mortgage with the Bank Of Detroit. Owning a house and providing for his wife and son had been second only to his goal of becoming a pilot. The new Throckmorton home was within walking distance of Saint Peter's as well as Gladys' one-story bungalow on Boehme Street.

It was on Sunday, April 14, 1935, when Nicholas told Gladys the news. Sitting on the davenport, still basking in the glow of their morning lovemaking, she seemed worried. Nick had a sense that his lover thought he was leaving her in the dusty vacuum of his back draft. He assured Gladys that his feelings for her were genuine, but stressed that he was still concerned as well for her long-term welfare and fortune. He tried to explain, "The time comes when a man needs to read his own compass and go where the little needle leads him. That's why I bought the house; stability for my family … something I really never had as a kid. I am not leaving you, Lover. The fact is, Gladys, that these little differences we have, just go to show how exactly the same we are. Me and my family are only moving five blocks away, for Pete's sake. It's not like I'm pulling up roots and moving to Kalamazoo or Wichita. You're my hangar, Darling. This is where I feather my propeller, dope my wings, and grease my joystick."

Their lips met, she welcomed him, and they shared a soul-deep kiss. She always listened to Nicholas, and his optimism helped soothe her. "Well, don't forget where I live. And stop by when you come home and need some good loving, a sweetheart to hold, or a friend to listen."

"Of course, I will. That's what I've been doing all along."

After another passionate kiss, intimate whispers, and Gladys' gentle, persistent persuasion, they were in the bedroom again.

From the time they had begun their affair in June of 1930 up until he bought the house on Second Street, Nick and Gladys took advantage of one another's company at every opportunity. Still, Gladys saw the purchase of the home as a threat to the status quo and believed that her standing as the recipient of Nicholas' ardent desires was in jeopardy. She feared the masquerade could come to an end and save for Nick's infrequent gifts of cash; the rent was her sole source of income. Gladys had come to depend on Nicholas' support, financially and emotionally. She needed to quickly find a new tenant for the apartment. Nick promised to help, and spread the word at the old machine shop, the boat works and at Selfridge Airfield. It was important to him, very important, that Gladys should have respectable tenants. Through the years, she had been his port in the storm.

As it turned out, within a week Gladys was able to find what appeared to be a reliable renter: Ellis Coulman, an electrical engineer employed with Detroit Edison, his wife Isabella, and four-year-old daughter Cora. Ellis touted himself as dependable and stable and was able to provide a list of references as long as his forearm.

I'm In The Mood For Love …

Three years later … a new five-window coupe arrives on Valentine's Day … Friday, February 14th … 1936

The view through the windshield of a new car casts a gleaming shine over the world, no matter what the season. It seems that everything is sparkling bright and dewy fresh. If it isn't, it ought to be. It should be a law.

Nicholas had purchased his new car only an hour earlier at River Rouge Ford Sales. He felt full of life, reborn, and rejuvenated behind the wheel of his factory-fresh, steel grey Ford V-8* coupe. When he parked it at the curb in front of the cozy white bungalow with blue trim on Boehme Street, he felt life was better than grand: it was glorious. The afternoon sun sparkled on the fresh snow. Things were going his way. He had telephoned Gladys on Wednesday morning from Shreveport, Louisiana, and spoke only long enough to tell her that he would be home on the 14th, Valentine's Day. He still called the Boehme Street bungalow 'home'. He never gave it much thought; he just called it that, just as he had named his plane.

After being away for three months, he was excited about this reunion. He had spent half of November and all of December in Peru, and the last six weeks flying sunup to sundown, seeding rice in the bayous from Jena to Morgan City, Louisiana. It was gratifying to be back in Mount Clemens again, if only for two weeks. His loins ached with the thought of Gladys' legs wrapped around him. He couldn't wait to see her again. He longed for her essence.

She met him at the side door and led him into her kitchen. It smelled of apple cake, coffee and home. His wife Nora did not bake, and never had the interest.

He set a bottle of champagne on the countertop, along with a small, neatly wrapped gift, and a superfluous Valentine card he had toiled over at Goodson's Rexall. His hands then covered her behind, pulling her to him. Between heated kisses and wandering embraces, Nicholas' hands, thumbs and fingers had her dress unbuttoned and on the floor in less than a minute. Once he had the match lit and touched to the tinder, it wasn't long before the real fire started.

It was the most raucous session of love making that Gladys could remember. For some unknown reason, with a fervent drive she had never before experienced, Nicholas went absolutely Elliot Ness* gangbusters in her bed that afternoon.

She pulled his powerful arms and chest to her, daring him to smother her. For the first time, she nearly lost her breath. His shoulders quivered in climax. At that point she felt she was set afire by white-hot lava, having been torched by a tremulous, fiery volcanic eruption.

They lay on top of the sheets, satisfied and satiated, her head cradled on his arm. She was studying him. He was in need of a shave, his face toughened by propeller-forced air and browned by the Southern sun. He looked to her, smiled and crushed out the cigarette he had just lit, "I've missed you so much, I could stay in your bed for a week." He kissed her.

"That was a Valentine to remember, Nick."

"And that was just part of it. I swear, if I didn't have to come up for air, I'd live within your arms and between your legs forever. I'd be flying high, wide, and deep."

His brassy comment flattered her pride and caused her cheeks to pinken. She sat up, shook out her curls and gently fingered her bangs. She straddled him, pushed her breasts to the wind, poked a finger into his belly and teased, "You mean there's more?"

He had a boyish smile. "Yes, ma'am. There's that little something I set on the kitchen counter ... and I'm taking you out to dinner tonight ... to a nice little supper club called Club Canadian, over in Windsor, right on the other side of the Ambassador Bridge to Canada. They got music so we can dance. Tonight, I'm all yours, Darling. I'm all yours."

She tightened her knees against him and shifted her hips upward: just enough to sense the burgeoning renewal of his lust. With only the slightest encouragement, she had convinced him to accept her tacit offer of an encore.

An hour and thirty minutes later, they had showered together and were on their way across the Ambassador Bridge to dine, dance, drink, and celebrate Valentine Day, the lovers' holiday.

The next morning while Nicholas was still asleep, Gladys was in her kitchen, waiting for the coffee to trickle down.

She was wearing her favorite bath robe; the one that he had given her last year, on her 34th birthday. After coffee and breakfast, she was certain that he would leave her. He would leave his lover, his Valentine, to shrink into the presence of his wife and wallow in the company of his son.

She was sitting crossed-legged, a Camel in the corner of her mouth as she picked up her Valentine card. It was adorned with roses as red as could be and inside was a simple, straight-forward message, embossed in flowing Elizabethan script: *I will always love you.*

Wrapped inside the neat little package on the counter she found a delicate silver bracelet. She put it on her wrist and shoved the little package and card aside. After one last, deep drag on the cigarette, she crushed it out.

Gladys didn't know or care that her bracelet was hand-crafted Incan silver inlaid with Andean opals. It mattered only that he had thought of her.

From the bedroom, she could hear the sounds of her lover stirring. The bed springs squeaked. Nick was awake.

She knew what would happen next: he would have coffee, a piece of cake, give her a kiss and leave. As it turned out, she was correct. What she wanted to talk about would simply have to wait.

Footprints In The Snow ...

... and a helping hand from Hazel Stockdill ...

Remembering the night before and still savoring the memory of Gladys' silky touch, Nicholas drove through the slushy snow toward his home on Second Street. Winter was hanging stubbornly on. Knee-deep snowbanks lined the streets, stained black and grey from the cinder and sand mix the Mount Clemens Streets Department had thrown down as winter road treatment.

He couldn't wait to see Nora's surprise and Alexander's excitement when they saw his new car.

The alley access behind his home was impassable with months of snow, forcing him to park on the street. He stuck two small parcels under his arm, grabbed the paper sack off the front seat, and started up the sidewalk to the front door, shuffling through a few inches of snow along the way. He expected that his wife would have at least swept the white stuff off the steps. When he left Louisiana the day before, he was in canvas shoes and shirtsleeves. Winter in Michigan can be a startling wake-up call.

He had telephoned Nora the previous weekend and said he would be arriving on or about February 15th, his first chance to visit his wife and son since November. He tried the door, and it was locked. He had expected they would meet him at the door with open arms. One minute later, after several bare-knuckle knocks and a half dozen pulls on the mechanical doorbell, he set the bag on the porch and fumbled for his keys.

Once inside, he immediately noticed the eerie stillness and sensed the chill, but managed to call out, "Nora! Alexander! Nora! Are you home?" His deep breaths formed frosty clouds. Something was awry; the whole scene was twisted. He walked to the kitchen, set the packages and sack on the table, looking around for some sort of note, some sign of life. He bounded upstairs and discovered Alexander's bed empty, but made. The bed he shared with Nora was stripped of its blanket and quilt. His eyes touched everything, feeding his senses and looking for answers. It was as if his wife and son had vanished … without a trace … sucked up and away within a Dust Bowl tornado only to vaporize into a cloudless, grey, winter sky. He discounted that his wife would leave for Oshkosh and her parents without telling him, or at least leaving a note. The home was cold, without heat, so they had obviously been gone at least one entire day. Perhaps the boiler was on the fritz, and the cold forced them out. Regardless, things weren't right. It just wasn't normal, and one thing that Nicholas did not like was things not being as they should.

He considered a kidnapping, such as the Lindbergh baby incident, but there certainly was no ransom motive. A twisting pain developed within the deepest darkness of his bowels. He feared the worst, the very worst; nearly on the disastrous level he had experienced in August of 1927. The shellacked hallway floor had dried puddle spots where snow had melted off shoes or galoshes. Nora's hat and coat hung in place on the clothes pegs, but Alexander's were missing. He headed for the front door once again and thought to look for footprints in the snow. He discovered only his own on the steps and walkway. There was nothing but virgin snow around the side, the shortcut through the alley to Third Street, and at the back of the house. Frantic, he rushed back inside. Bothered and bewildered, heart pounding, he stopped at the kitchen doorway and caught his breath. He looked around him, and he was still alone. Before he realized it, he found himself on the neighbor's porch, calling out "hello" and pounding on her door.

Mabel Fleckenstein appeared in her own good time, unhurried and unshaken. Nicholas didn't allow the white-haired, eccentric spinster any time for platitudes and spoke as soon as the door opened, "Where are my wife and son?"

"Mister Throckmor …" She didn't finish before Nick interrupted and repeated his question.

"Please! Where are my wife and son, Mabel?"

Mabel's eyes moved excitedly from side to side, "Little Alexander came over on Wednesday afternoon all excited and nervous and said his mother was terribly ill, so I put on my hat and coat and went next door to see what the matter was. Alexander was a brave little boy, and he was so serious." Nicholas could never stand her heavy, Colonial Boston accent or snobbish and aloof tone.

"Get to the point, Mabel. Where in the hell are my wife and son?"

"Nora had bad stomach pain, really bad, so bad she could hardly move. I called her doctor for her, Krakhauer, I think his name is, and when he got here, he said she had an appendix rupture and had to go to the hospital ..."

"Where is my wife, dammit?! Where's Alexander?" He had lost what little patience remained.

"Alexander is staying with Hazel and Robert Stockdill. You know them, next block over, behind yours, the blue house. Nora is at Harper Hospital in Detroit, I think ... Mister Stockdill had her all wrapped up in blankets and drove her there himself."

Nick managed to say two words, "Thanks Mabel," speaking as he turned and started down the steps toward the curb. He gestured a quick wave as he got into the Ford. The Stockdill family lived on Third Street, diagonally behind the Throckmorton home. When Nicholas had looked for footprints in the fresh snow around the house, he noticed there weren't any on the path through his back yard. It was often used for visits between Nora, Hazel, and the children. He was immersed in a mixed bath of freezing cold anxiety and tepid, lukewarm relief.

The Ford slid to a stop in front of 13 Third Street. Nick curbed the wheels to the snowbank and let the engine idle. He took long, bounding steps toward the home. Hazel opened the door as he reached the top step and allowed seven-year-old Alexander to push past her and onto the porch. He hopped up and into his father's arms, throwing his arms around Nicholas' neck.

Little Alexander piped up, "Mama is sick and, in the hospital, and I was staying here with Georgie, but now you can take me home, right, Papa?"

Nick stepped into the hall, carrying his son. "Our house is really cold, Alex, so maybe just one more night with Missus Hazel, Mister Robert, and your friend George, OK? I'm going into the city now to see Mama and then when I get home I can start the furnace, and we can stay there tomorrow night, OK?" He gave his son a hearty hug and set him to the floor. "Play with George for now and let me and Missus Hazel talk for a minute, OK?" Alexander remembered the Tinkertoy* bridge he and George were working on and was gone in a flash to the construction site on the parlor's braided oval rug.

Hazel Stockdill was the mother of two children, eight-year-old George and twelve-year old Grace. Hazel was a thin woman in her mid-thirties, like his lover Gladys, and barely five feet tall with short, tightly curled brown locks. She spoke nervously, trying to quickly give Nicholas all the information she could, "Your neighbor Mabel called your doctor on Wednesday, and we've had Alexander since. The doctor said Nora had a ruptured appendix, and Bob drove her to Harper Hospital. I telephoned that Doctor Krakhauer fellow on Thursday morning to find out more, and he only said that she was at the hospital. And the hospital was no help at all. They told me that she had the operation on Wednesday night, and they would only say that she was recovering from major surgery. That's what I know, so she's downtown at Harper, Nicholas. And don't worry about Alexander ... he can stay with us as long as it takes. He's a good boy."

Nicholas gathered his emotions just enough to take advantage of the offer. "Thanks, Hazel. Can you watch Alexander one more night? The fire went out on the furnace, so I've got to start that up, but first I've got to see my wife. I'm going to Harper."

Hazel agreed, "Absolutely. Alex can stay as long as you need. Give Nora our best wishes and drive carefully and good luck." She didn't want to discourage him. Harper Hospital was struggling with a poor public image for efficiency and visitation standards that had started during the tuberculosis crisis of the previous decade.

It was a slow, tediously aggravating, forty-five-minute, twenty-five-mile drive through snow-packed, rutted and slushy streets from Mount Clemens south to central Detroit. He turned the defogger fan on high, fighting the fingers of frost trying to cover the Ford's windshield. He cursed winter, and once again made an empty promise to himself that someday he would be living someplace where the snow doesn't blow, and the flakes don't fly. The cold nibbled at his fingers and toes.

It was one-thirty in the afternoon when he arrived at the hospital. A cold, dark sky blanketed the city.

Harper Hospital was on John R Street[*]: a four-story building with brick exterior walls, towering spires and parapets, resembling an 18th Century French castle. Once inside, Nick witnessed first-hand an institution that ran with the grandiose efficiency of a bloated feudal kingdom. The entry foyer had a vaulted ceiling, reaching upward through the second and third floors to skylights on the roof. The metallic click and strain of a mop wringer echoed throughout the long halls on either side of the reception area. An elderly custodian wearing a uniform of grey denim was deftly going through the motions of swabbing a marble chip terrazzo floor.

The weekend administrative staff had left for the day, leaving a single shift supervisor to oversee the operation of a four-hundred bed hospital. It was quiet, nearly devoid of humanity, save for Nicholas, the mop jockey, and two women behind a large desk in the lobby. It was nearly half an hour before he could confirm that his wife was a patient and, in fact, alive. Nicholas loudly protested the abhorrent inefficiency that confronted him at the Information and Admission counter. When he was informed that patient visitation[*] was strictly limited to immediate relatives and only permitted between four and five o'clock, he growled at the receptionist and her boss, "I've been standing here for the better part of an hour and all I've heard is gobbledygook."

Dorothy Featherton was a woman of perhaps fifty years with beady, hazel eyes closely set on either side of a long, narrow nose. She had a lean, thin neck that held her elfin head disproportionately above her squat frame. She peered over the top of her wire-frame spectacles at Nicholas. "First and foremost, you will need to control yourself, Mister Throckmorton. You should be advised that Harper is a premier hospital, and our singular obligation is to our patients. I sympathize with you and have compassion for your situation, so I feel obligated to, at the least, call the Charge Nurse in the Recovery Ward and see if she can make an exception for you just this once, mind you, considering that you have been out of town with your job." Dorothy over-emphasized the pronunciation of every hard consonant with a click of her tongue. It mimicked the cluck of a spring pullet running in panic from the biggest rooster in the henhouse.

Nick picked up on her intonation and made an impulsive, rude comparison, "Fine, I understand. But getting any help from you people has been like pulling teeth on a chicken ... awful hard to find if you know what I mean. But please don't you take any offense ... because I'm really not trying to be indignant. I'm expressing my frustration and anxiety to see my wife." His tone was not as apologetic as his words were, and he intended it to be. His eyes had been locked on to those of the administrator, who suddenly seemed to be drawn into a submissive trance and was wearing a passive smile.

The receptionist was shocked and taken aback by Nick's harsh tone and candid remarks. She looked wide-eyed at Nick and then to her boss, expecting a strong verbal retort, warning, or an unconditional denial of his visitation request.

Instead, Dorothy was genuinely conciliatory. An involuntary twitch moved her head sideways and back again. The tall, black-haired visitor with the strong profile and deep voice had her mesmerized like a chicken in a trance. Her eyelashes fluttered and her words floated from her lips with the softness of a feather, "I am sorry for your trouble, Mister Throckmorton. Rather than just calling the Charge Nurse, I will personally escort you to the second-floor ward and talk to her personally. Come with me and you should be able to see your wife in just a few moments."

The receptionist sat, bewildered and astonished, at the surprisingly timid response of her boss. She had never before witnessed her supervisor's surrender.

Dorothy moved her frame out from behind the admissions desk and walked to the elevator with Nicholas. Her white stockings accentuated her thin legs, reminding Nick of Humpty Dumpty's. The heels of her brown pumps tip-tapped along the composite floor and her sharp shoulders swayed with each step. At the elevator, she pulled the folding wood lattice doors closed, gave the up-rope a tug, engaged the electric motor and the machine groaned upwards. "Again, please remember that this is a hospital Mister Throckmorton, and we make every effort to keep things quiet for our patients. When we exit on the second floor, we will go to the Recovery Ward, where I will hopefully be able to arrange for your out-of-hours visit, so try to be pleasant. Abigail Windward is the Charge Nurse and her title says it all … she's in charge, so let me do the talking."

Just One More Chance …

… please and thank you …

When the elevator clunked to a stop at the second floor, Nicholas opened the squeaky accordion door and exited ahead of Dorothy, only to wait for her to lead the way down the empty, lifeless hall. Together, they walked toward a dimly lit enclave with a ten-foot-long counter in front of a half dozen cluttered desks, only one of which had an occupant. A hacking cough echoed through the walls. A barely audible moan answered back. The woman behind the desk noticed them and looked up from her paperwork.

Nick stood at Dorothy's side in front of the counter. "Hello, Abigail. This is Mister Throckmorton, and he's been out of State, away from home since his wife became ill, and I was wondering if we could make an exception just this once and let him see his wife? The roster at Admissions says she had an emergency appendectomy on Wednesday, and her status is now listed as stable. And she's in 207 … the name is Throckmorton."

The Charge Nurse stood and walked from her desk and around the counter. She was standing directly in front of Nicholas, speaking in a meek, high-pitched voice, and pointing her skinny index finger at him, "Just this once, then. Mind you: just this once. And only thirty minutes, that's all: thirty minutes." Abigail was a thin, middle-aged woman of small frame with mousy brown hair and a small round nose perfectly placed in the middle of a small, round, pink face. She resembled an immaculate, prim and proper public librarian: single, demanding, and a stickler for perfection. Nicholas imagined her at home, sitting in a Victorian parlor with a pampered calico cat on her lap.

Dorothy thanked Abigail, smiled and wished Nicholas a good visit with his wife and started off toward the elevator.

Nicholas turned and accompanied Abigail down the hall, past some rooms that were pitch dark, others with doors wide open and a few with small, lighted bedside lamps. Perhaps the sound of Abigail's heels set off some sort of alarm, but as they passed the first half dozen doorways, other nurses appeared and disappeared in and out of rooms. The inhospitable smell of bleach and soap was a stark reminder of what Harper Hospital was all about. The farther down the hall they walked, the moans and coughs got louder and more frequent. They stopped outside room 207.

"Just let me poke my head in here first and see if your wife is awake."

Nick crooked his neck, straining to see inside the light-starved room. He could only see the footboards of two beds along one wall.

Abigail reappeared and whispered, "Be quiet; there are patients sleeping. Your wife is awake, but sleepy from the medication. Remember, a half-hour and no longer. And be quiet or I'll put the kibosh on any more visits." She pushed past him and waved her finger in warning as she left.

Nora's form looked frail and insignificant under the bed sheets. A meek smile crossed her lips as she noticed her husband approaching her bedside. A tiny wall lamp with a frosted globe cast its weak light upwards along the white wall to the towering ceiling. The poor lighting accentuated her tallow color. His eyes scanned the room and found one wooden straight-back chair against the outside wall. His wife was one of four patients in the room. One of the patients moaned. It sounded like a woman's moan. He could only assume that all of Nora's roommates were women.

He moved the chair as close as he could and sat holding her hand. "Oh, Nicholas ... where is my Alexander?" Her hand was cool and limp, like a wet dishcloth.

"With Hazel. He's having fun with his pal Georgie. Hazel and her husband Robert are taking good care of him. And I'm back now for two weeks, and I can stay longer if I need to. So, you just get better, all right?"

She was struggling to keep her eyes open. They seemed to be lifeless and iced over, no doubt from the morphine.

"Are you feeling better, Sweetheart?"

Nora could barely garner a smile before her eyelids fell shut. As a rule, Nicholas had full control of his emotions. That afternoon and evening, as he sat at his wife's bedside, he forced his eyes closed and pressed out a single tear.

Before he left the ward, he checked in with Abigail, the Charge Nurse, and ended up having a cordial and informative conversation. She told him that Nora was progressing as expected and the greatest concern now was that she stays clear of any post-operative infection. The nurse once again explained that Nora was sedated, specifically with morphine* and her lethargic state was to be expected.

After he left the hospital, Nicholas drove to Gladys' home on Boehme Street, and stayed the night. His overnighter was an unheralded landmark in their six-year intimate relationship. One of the few times that they could have shared the entire night together in the same bed, it did not happen. Nick was restless, couldn't get to sleep, and out of concern for his lover, he ended up on her sofa. Gladys did not get much sleep either. She spent hours on her back, staring at nothing but the ceiling and walls. When things go wrong, they can go really wrong.

Sunday was hectic. After a fried egg sandwich and two cups of coffee, he drove to Saint Peter's and spoke to the Parish Curate, Father David. The Priest expressed thanks and said the parish was aware that Nora had been absent since mid-week and assumed that she had taken ill. He mentioned that he and the Sisters would pray for Nora's recovery.

Nick started the furnace at his Second Street home and banked enough coal for an eight to ten hour burn before he visited his son at the Stockdill house. Nick would pick up Alexander that evening when he finished at the hospital.

In the afternoon, he was lucky enough to catch Doctor Reinhold Krakhauer on his wife's floor. The doctor assured Nicholas that his wife was progressing as expected and that she would be in the hospital until, at the minimum, the coming Friday or Saturday. Doctor Krakhauer also praised young Alex, saying that Nora was a lucky woman to have a seven-year-old with enough mettle to get help when it was needed.

Easy Come, Easy Go …

Brother John, Sister Anna Maria, Betty Grable, the King of Mount Clemens and Clancy the Clown …

The next few days were a chaotic string of small successes and memorable milestones. Father and son spent more time together than at any other point in their lives. Nick made breakfasts and packed lunches. After school, Alexander walked from Public School #2 to the Stockdills and stayed until his father returned from the hospital.

For Nora, the marquee event of the week was Monday's double-header visit of Saint Peter's Brother John and Sister Anna Maria of Saint Mary's School. Nicholas watched in curious envy as his wife's spirit soared when the clergy entered the room and walked to her bedside. She glowed. He could not recall ever getting a reaction like that in eight and a half years of marriage.

Nora politely asked him, "Nick, can you allow me and my new visitors a few minutes?"

Nicholas was taken aback and thought it was a strange request. What response could his wife expect … a denial of spiritual comfort … a maniacal tirade or a roaring, negative 'No'? He nodded to the seminarian and nun, smiled meekly and answered, "Of course, Sweetheart. I'll be down the hall."

Nora's visitors reflected her purpose on Earth. She did not so much as bat an eyelash before she had asked her husband to afford her time alone with the ambassadors of her church. Nora acknowledged her role as mother and primary source of influence for her son Alexander but could not define her marriage as one sanctioned by the church. She accepted the support Nicholas provided for her Earthly well-being, but her spiritual and physical selves were reserved for the work of her church. Hers was a no-frills existence, steeped in faith.

In as few words as possible, Nicholas introduced and excused himself from his wife and her visitors. He exited the room graciously and considered his departure as an opportunity to walk to the waiting room opposite the Nurse's Station to have a cigarette or two. Once there, he found himself alone with a few pieces of tattered furniture, old magazines, dim lights, full ashtrays and his thoughts.

Nick felt more beleaguered than bewildered by his wife's request. What bothered him was that when Nora's religious entourage arrived, she reflected a demeanor that he had not been able to invoke with his visit, a smile he had not seen on her lips for years and a cheerfulness that had all but completely eluded their marriage. Over the years, Nora's indifference toward him grew, and it seemed she was able to completely ignore him at times. It had become a way of life. For Nicholas, it had become the accepted norm. He regretfully understood it to be his due reward; a natural retribution for deflowering a young woman of fifteen years.

Their relationship had become a deep-seated guilt, a burden saddled upon his conscience that became tethered by Nora's pregnancy and spurred into a religious gallop. Nicholas' self-reproach and regret fed upon itself with the reprimands and derision of Nora's parents and their departure from Detroit. Nicholas found himself in a quandary of remorse and insecurity. Sixteen-year-old Nora had turned away from her husband to seek consolation and redemption and found it in her faith.

Years earlier, when his wife first became heavily involved in her religion, he had left her to it. Nora sought answers to her problems and Nicholas admitted that he obviously had no spiritual solutions to offer. At the onset of their forced marriage, he had tried to fit in, and began to attend mass with his wife and her family, but after the first few weeks he could find neither the serenity he anticipated and hoped for nor the acceptance he desired and expected. He had refused her parents' suggestion that he undergo the Rite of Initiation and be baptized into Catholicism. He had further infuriated Nora's father when he stated that such sectarian conversion was an exercise in absurdity that he could only reject. Growing up in Buffalo, he regularly attended church services with his mother and sisters at First Reformation Lutheran, but after the tragedy that claimed his family, he had become so disenchanted with spirituality that it was beyond difficult for him to accept the concept of divine mercy or justice. The idea of heavenly intervention seemed convoluted and contradictive to him. Soon he found excuses to avoid worship altogether. He began going to Garwood's machine shop on Sundays, just to keep the coal fires lit and committed to hours of voluntary, unpaid overtime while studying and tinkering with the engines.

Nicholas had grown up hard and fast in Buffalo, becoming the head of household at the age of sixteen. His father had died from TB after a long struggle with lungs weakened by poison gas in the Great War, and only a year later his elder brother had moved out of the home. He had been the sole male influence in a struggling environment that he'd shared with three sisters and his mother.

Providing for his wife and son was an objective that became his paramount duty. As a husband and father, he faced the onslaught of the Great Depression. At a time when barefoot children scoured railroad tracks for a few spilt chunks of coal or back alleys for a bat of firewood, Nora and Alexander had a roof over their heads and a warm bed to sleep in. Every day, hundreds of hungry souls stood in soup lines that stretched for blocks, but Nicholas' job enabled him to bring home the bacon and then some.

Until he and Gladys had discovered each other a year and a half into his arid marriage, he had a life devoid of intimacy. Their ongoing dalliance had been satiating their lust for over six years.

He found a pound of solace in the fact that, had he returned directly home to his wife on Valentine's Day rather than into the warm, welcoming arms of his lover, the current state of affairs would have been the same: Nora would still be in the hospital, Gladys would still be sitting alone on Boehme Street, Alexander would be forced into the temporary care of a caring and convenient neighbor, and his marriage would still be chaste.

His time alone in the waiting room allowed his thoughts to send him into a self-induced hypnotic sleep. He dozed off, his chin in his chest, having lost track of time. He was awakened by one of the nursing staff, "Visiting hour is ending sir. It's ending in five minutes."

Before he left, he stuck his head into Nora's room to find her with closed eyes. She was asleep, having been covered and her pillows arranged. Nicholas assumed that Brother John and Sister Anna had lent their helping hands.

During visiting hour on Tuesday evening, Nora told Nick that her friends from church would be visiting her daily and that it really wasn't necessary for him to take the time and drive all the way downtown to spend only an hour with her. Brother John had circumvented the hospital's visitation rules by hinting that he and Sister Anna Maria were administering spiritual reinforcement and enrichment. After eight and a half years of marriage, Nicholas was well aware how important the church was in Nora's life, but this was the first time his wife had informed him that he was in fact, a second-tier priority. Initially, he felt hollowness in his heart, but could not help but admire her honesty.

Nicholas drove Alexander to school on Wednesday morning but did not pack a lunch for his son. It was the first time Alex had the chance to ride in his father's new car. It was like Christmas for the boy. The little bits of chrome on the dashboard, the radio, the chocolate brown steering wheel and the big round knob atop the two-foot gear shift lever were things that Santa just couldn't fit in his sleigh. Alex listened to his father ramble on about marvelous mechanical things he had never heard of and describe precious parts that would certainly be fantastic fun if he understood them. He sat on the front seat with his hands folded on his lap, looking at his father, at the dashboard lights and little dials, listening to the wonderful mixture of static and music coming from the radio, and marveling at how new everything was. When his father mentioned Betty Grable* and something about the car's headlights, Alex had already lost interest and worried about what time it was.

Nick parked the Ford at the curb, right at the main doors. There was not one stranded soul, not a single hapless student outside; classes had already begun. Alexander was understandably nervous, "I think we're late, Papa."

"No, we're not, Alex. We're right on time. Just you wait and see … we're right on time."

They walked to the office and Nick requested that his son be allowed to play hooky through Friday. After he fully explained the current family predicament, excused absence was reluctantly arranged for Alexander, but not before an extended dissertation on the merits of education by Principal Clancy Yarborough.

Young Alexander had witnessed a miracle performed by none other than his father. Time off from school meant citywide bragging rights. He walked next to his father, his hero, back through the hall, out the door, down the steps and onto Dickinson street feeling like he was the sole heir to the throne. Alexander had crowned his father as the King of Mount Clemens.

"That was magic, Papa! No school for the rest of the week!"

Nicholas turned the key on the Ford and let it idle. "There's a lesson to be learned here, Alex. Don't let some twit in a suit scare you. If you have something to say, say it. If you want a favor, don't be afraid … just ask for it. The worst that can happen is that he tells you: *NO*."

Of course, Alexander didn't fully understand. "You weren't afraid of Principal Yarborough were you Papa?"

"Hell no, son. Principal Clancy looked like a circus clown to me with that yellow tie, his red nose and that chrome dome."

Alex let loose a belly-laugh that any self-respecting eight-year-old would envy. Nicholas immediately corrected himself, "Don't disrespect adults, Alex. Respect the grownups around you and don't talk bad about people. You and me can joke and have fun when we're together, and you can fool around with your best pals, but don't misbehave in front of people you don't know or other grownups ... especially your mother ... respect your mother."

For the following week, father and son were bound together by necessity. They attended several matinee films at the Orion Movie House, guffawing at the antics of the Marx brothers, laughing along with Laurel and Hardy and admiring a curly-top Shirley Temple.

For three midweek afternoons, Nick plotted and convinced neighbor Hazel Stockdill that he could arrange out-of-hours visits with Nora if she watched Alexander. Hazel readily agreed, and Nick was able to sneak into Gladys' bed.

Drop In Next Time You're Passing ...

1936: It will have to wait until next time ...

Nine days after her hospitalization, on Friday, February 21st, Nora was discharged from Harper Hospital to finish her convalescence at home. Nicholas' time off was quickly coming to an end. He held a rail ticket back to Monroe, Louisiana on the 29th. From there, he was part of two flight crews scheduled to fly off to the bean fields of Matamoros and Reynosa, Mexico for a month or more and then back to the Deep South until late spring or early summer.

On Saturday and Sunday, Gladys stopped by and made meatloaf and roast chicken dinners. Despite Nora's mild protests, neighbor and friend Hazel did some light housework and laundry. When Brother John came for a visit on late Sunday afternoon, Nora's mobility had improved, and it was much easier for her to get up and around. It was apparent that Nora had a bevy of helpful hands around her.

Doctor Krakhauer made a house call* to the Throckmorton home on Monday, and removed the forty-five continuous sutures* he had used to close the ten-inch incision on Nora's abdomen. In the afternoon, Gladys stopped by and brought a copy of Saturday's Detroit Free Press, remembering how much Alexander enjoyed following the comic antics of the

Katzenjammer Kids, Tailspin Tommy, and *Little Orphan Annie.* Nicholas rarely bought a newspaper and insisted that everything that was printed was either bad news or advertising. The headlines affirmed his opinion; all of France was on strike and the Nazis continued to spread political turmoil throughout central Europe.

As Nora, Gladys, and Alex sat on the sofa reading the funnies, Nick picked up the paper with indifference, glancing at a picture and the coverage of Sonja Henie's[*] figure skating performance at the Winter Olympics in Garmisch, Germany.

His last full week in Mount Clemens was spent largely doing minor maintenance on the home, running errands, and stocking the pantry. On Washington's Birthday, he shared the entire day with Alexander. In the morning, it was a visit to his old employer, Garwood Machine Works, and because it was winter, *Miss America IX* was in the indoor boat well. The first half of the day was full of hands-on adventure for the youngster. The afternoon was a guided tour of Selfridge Air Field and all the aircraft inside the maintenance hangar.

For Alexander, his mother's medical emergency became a rare opportunity for him to spend time with his father. Nicholas' stature grew in his son's view during that February in 1936. In between movie matinees, his father shared boyhood tales and tidbits of paternal advice disguised as anecdotes. During their evenings at home, they sat together on the floor in front of the Philco parlor radio, propped up with sofa cushions listening to the broadcast adventures of *The Green Hornet, Gang Busters,* and *Ann Of The Air Lanes.* Not only did his father arrange an absence from school and give him a taste of all things mechanical, but Alexander also began to appreciate what his father did for a living. Although his father held a job that kept him away from home for lengthy stretches that could range from a week to months, it was a job with stature: an airplane pilot. Nobody else in the entire third grade could say that.

Nicholas' two-week vacation turned out much differently from what he had anticipated. While flying under the clear blue skies of the high Andean plains, he had daydreamed of rolling in his lover's embrace. His next opportunity for time off would occur nearly five months later in June, between the spring seeding, fertilizer application, and the summer pesticide dustings.

For Gladys, Nora's unfortunate appendicitis attack was an inconvenience that robbed her of the devoted intimacy she longed for and left her with only a few hours on singular afternoons. She could only look forward until the next time Nick had time off, in the warmth of June and his embrace.

Nora had a positive outlook during her entire medical ordeal, and her faith helped her through the infrequent, few, fleeting moments of despair. Her greatest disappointment was the unavoidable disruption of her work with the school, the nuns, and the students. Nevertheless, her hospitalization not only gave her the chance to appreciate the friendship of her neighbor Hazel, and former landlady Gladys, but it also allowed her to fully understand her devotion to the school. The good news came when Doctor Krakhauer said she could resume her duties at Saint Mary's by mid-March, with the restriction of no lifting for an additional month.

Nicholas suggested that Nora and Alexander take some weeks during the summer and make a long overdue visit to her parents in Oshkosh. Her Great Uncle Dmitri and his wife Adelheid had passed earlier in the year, and a trip to Oshkosh was certainly in order. Nora initially balked at the idea, but after some consideration, reassuring support from Sister Anna Maria, a telephone call to her mother, and some subtle encouragement from Gladys, she agreed. The plan was to stay in Wisconsin with Dominik and Gabi for four weeks.

Nicholas' two-week respite from work seemed to have ended as soon as it had begun. As they so often do, daily events in the Throckmorton home ran together like watercolors on tissue paper. The lines of time became blurred beyond comprehension, confusing everyone to the point where all the players on that stage of life's drama stood in the spotlight, looked at one another and asked, "What the hell just happened?"

It was Leap Day, February 29th, and once again, it was time for Nicholas to leave. He parked the new Ford inside his Second Street garage at noon. Moments earlier, he gave Alexander a goodbye bear hug and advice to listen to his mother. He gingerly, carefully embraced his wife, so as not to cause her any post-surgical discomfort, and kissed her on the cheek. "I'll be back in June, and I'll telephone you when I get the chance." Goodbyes were a common occurrence for all the roles of the Throckmorton players: son, father, husband, mother, wife, and last but not least: the lover.

He walked to the corners of Cass and Gratiot and rode the Interurban streetcar to Michigan Central Station for his train ride south to Louisiana. Accustomed to slipping around, Gladys boarded the trolley two blocks down the line and joined her lover at Robertson Street. Inside the train station, they sat at a corner table inside the Ambassador Lounge, where they captured the last of their stolen moments before the beginning of another extended absence. Gladys sipped at her Blue Aviator* while Nick finished his second bourbon.

Two years shy of forty, Gladys sensed that the only permanence she held in the relationship she shared with Nicholas was his absence. Within his embrace, she felt part of his life. The painful reality was that, even if she could claim him exclusively as her own, when he was gone, she would still be alone. And he was gone most of the time. She had tasted love and its passion and had become addicted to his sweet touch. She longed for more and pled her case, "You know that you fly away with my heart every time you leave, Nick. For the last seven years you've flown my heart over every acre of Earth that your airplane's wings have cast their shadow upon."

She made a point. He looked into her eyes. For the first time, he could fully appreciate their color: sky blue.

"We'll be together for weeks on my next trip home, Darling, sometime in June. I promise. When I get back, we'll get back to me and you. We'll do it up big; real big."

Over the previous year, his departures seemed to evoke more and more poignant farewells from Gladys. She had been clinging closer and tighter. He dreaded the possibility of flying into an unpredictable emotional storm of tears.

4: MEXICO AND LITTLE ITALY, 1936

Cielito Lindo (A Beautiful Sky) …

Matamoros, Mexico and Bonita Del Querida …

After spending nearly every minute of daylight for two months airborne, the flight crews of *Delta Dusters Wing One* were ready for a night of drink and high times. Thursday, May 1st was that night, and it happened to be not only a pay day, but *Día del Trabajo* (Labor Day), a national holiday in Mexico. They bought fresh cigarettes, split a pack of condoms, hailed a taxi and crossed the Rio Grande.

In 1936, Matamoros was a booming agricultural city that had grown rapidly across the border from Brownsville, Texas. Tamaulipas Avenue was lined with white and brown adobe shops, barrooms, bordellos, and hotels interspersed between narrow alleyways and crooked side streets that disappeared through a mixed maze of mud, brick, and wooden structures. Without the requirement for a diploma, license, or credentials; dentists, bankers, blacksmiths, pawn brokers, surgeons or lawyers could call Matamoros home. Dust, dogs, donkeys, pigeons, pigs, and people were everywhere. Faded curtains wafted from inside dingy, small mud cap homes, drunkards propped themselves against brightly painted doorways, and the sounds of mariachi music was thick enough to fill a thousand tamales. The setting sun cast a filtered glow of red pepper over the city. It smelled of dirt, drink, and debauchery.

At nearly twenty-seven years, Nick was the oldest member of the two Stearman Duster flight crews. Will Gules, Nick's flight mechanic, pilot Isaac Skrood, and general mechanic Gene Gillette each marked their twenty-first year.

The pilots and mechanics had been dodging twelve-foot telephone poles, low-hanging power lines, fence posts, barbed wire, donkeys, sheep, goats, and cattle over Mexican soybean, corn, and bean fields for weeks. On the recommendation of a local rancher, they made their way to Cantina La Rosita, a cabaret that catered to güeros and their greenbacks. Breathing clouds of dust, fertilizer, and insecticide created a thirst that begged for the temporary relief that tequila and beer could provide.

The floor show was fronted by a well-endowed señorita songstress, Antonia Verdeja. Guitars, trumpets, drums, and Antonia's castanets were the backbone of a unique brand of Mexican Banda jazz. She had a voice that flowed through the cantina like heated chocolate and coffee syrup. Bodies were packed two-deep at the bar, couples on the dance floor writhed, and the entire cantina throbbed with a pulse of its own. Nick and his crew had arrived early enough to claim a table for themselves, but not long after sunset, four young local lovelies had managed to work their magic and cozy their way to seats at the Yankee flyers' table.

One bronze and beautiful young woman concentrated all her charms on Nicholas. Everyone else inside the cantina disappeared into another dimension and left the world to only the Mexican vixen and the Yanqui flyer. She was mesmerized by the tall American. His white shirt stood alone in contrast with every other dusty and dirty thing in the room. Her eyes drank down his entire form, his black hair, and brown eyes. He did not flinch an inch when she slid her hand under the table and squeezed his taught thigh. She studied his face, his two-day stubble and became fascinated with his pilot tan. She traced the tan-lines of his goggles with a lacquered red nail, giggled and tipped her head in curiosity. Her ploy worked.

"I'm a pilot, Baby Doll, an airplane pilot."

She answered in excitement, "Piloto … piloto de avión! Si!"

She managed enough English to say her name was Bonita Del Querida, was nineteen-years-old, and that she lived in

Reynosa, the next town upriver. When they danced, she pressed to him like a second skin. Her hair was shoulder-length, softly curled, the color of burgundy wine, and brushed with the sweet smell of jasmine. She moved on the dance floor like olive oil spreading on a warm plate and breathed the words of Spanish love ballads in his ear. The soft cotton bodice of her red and blue dress clung to her form, accentuating her firm breasts and taut nipples. The white lace trim on her hemline wandered up and down her burnished legs with her every sensuous step on the floor. With all the fire of a matador, Nicholas stopped abruptly and gave her a kiss that would halt any high-stepping Cha-Cha-Cha. His hands covered her behind, kneaded her softness, and pressed her to him. Before long, he and Bonita had plotted to escape the confines of the cantina and search for a softer, horizontal dance floor.

On his way out the door, he gave his crew a wink and a nod. It was a familiar gesture, and true to his nature, he was leaving with yet another beautiful but unfamiliar share crop under his wing.

Nicholas by no measure was a novice at dalliance, but Bonita had challenged him. This spicy, hot jalapeño from across the Rio Grande had enough heat to set the world aflame. The spice burned long into the night before slowly cooling to a warm, deep satisfaction. She fell asleep satiated. He fell asleep exhausted.

The morning sunlight came charging through the open window and rudely pulled back their blanket of sleep. Still groggy, he remembered that he and Bonita had checked in at the Hotel Reál and continued their dance between the sheets. With mild relief, he looked down and affirmed that it was Bonita in bed with him and the sheets were whole, white and clean. She was as beautiful as she was the night before.

From the noisy street below, he could hear the shouts of pedestrians, vendors, the occasional bray of a donkey, and the harsh protest of a goat. A large ceiling fan wobbled and moaned precariously over the bed. Bonita was asleep next to him, her lips still as red as he remembered them, her scent still as sweet. Her smooth skin looked like delicately browned brass against the white sheets.

On the bedside table was a nearly full bottle of Luna Azul mescal tequila, complete with the dead gusano worm floating on the bottom, his watch, wallet, a pack of Camel, and an empty bottle of Victoria beer. He pushed his pillow to the metal rails of the headboard and lit a cigarette. On impulse, he checked his wallet. Everything seemed intact. It was past noon. He had an ache at his temples.

Bonita stirred, opened her green eyes, and whispered with a smile, "Buenos días, amante … my lover."

"Good morning, Baby Doll, my very own, darling Mexican Spitfire[*]."

She reached for his cigarette, took a puff and cuddled on his arm. She struggled with her words, but managed to say, "You must know Spanish, Nicholas. Spanish is the love language." She smiled, licked at his ear and purred like an Aztec leopard.

With one fluid motion, she slid on top of him, reached to the nightstand and crushed out the cigarette. At first, he assumed that he was about to get his first language lesson, but not a word was spoken. He lost himself in her heat, and once again Bonita Del Querida slowly burned her memory onto his soul.

He visited Bonita twice more, the last in early 1937. He later learned that she had married an American truck driver and moved to Amarillo. Her suggestion that he should learn Spanish was one that he would heed a decade into the future.

Pistol Packin' Papa …

Nick, Will, Gene and the finicky Izzy Skrood …

The experience that Nick had that night in Matamoros differed from that of his crew mates. The tequila worm wiggled in another direction for Nick's mechanic Will Gules, pilot Izzy Skrood, and his mechanic, Gene Gillette. Their evening did not wrap them in the scent of jasmine or the warmth of a woman. At around midnight, a minor ruckus transformed the dance floor of Cantina La Rosita into a Mexican wrestling* match. Shots were fired, bones and chairs broken, and machismo badly bruised, but no deaths were reported.

The beaten and bleeding Americans were arrested along with about a dozen Mexicans and spent the night packed into two jail cells. They were able to leave Matamoros on late Sunday afternoon after paying about fifty dollars apiece in unexplained fines.

They met up with Nicholas on Monday morning in Texas at Padre Island Airfield and shared their respective war stories over coffee, corned beef hash, and eggs. They had been intimidated, humiliated, and their egos trounced. A night in a Mexican jail wallowing in the stench of sweaty clothes, beer, rotten breath, putrid body odor, and human waste was enough to prompt three of the four to purchase and carry revolvers from that day forward. At about thirty dollars each, they considered the pistols an investment in safety. On their future Mexican escapades however, cool heads and prudence prevailed. Despite their precaution and purchases, the flight crews never found it necessary to fire a shot in Mexico. Izzy was the lone flyer to option out of buying a revolver*. His decision was dictated by his orthodox religion and the fact that he was a third-generation pacifist. It also saved him thirty dollars.

Downhearted Blues ...

There's no need to worry ... Ellis Coulman ...

Banking his time off by working overtime, and saving his free days, Nick had accumulated a full month of vacation. The entire month of July was at his disposal. It was his to squander whichever way he wanted. He flew his Stearman C3 from its home base in Monroe, Louisiana to Walker Airfield, Kansas. The plane was due for its standard four-hundred-hour engine maintenance and a complete linkage cable replacement.

He sent Gladys a telegram as soon as he got settled in the crew quarters on Sunday night. Once he had his ticket securely in his hands, he telephoned her from the train station Monday morning. At a whistle and water stop in Topeka, he fulfilled his obligation to make a telephone call to Nora, said that he was on his way home and expressed his love for her and Alexander.

He then set his devious plan in motion and told his wife that he only had two weeks off. He plotted that he would spend one night with Gladys before going home to his wife and Alexander on Wednesday. Thursday, he would drive the family to Oshkosh and stay for perhaps a week before returning to Detroit and Gladys for the remainder of July. His wife and son would spend at least three weeks with her parents in Wisconsin before taking the train back to Mount Clemens. His plan worked out in his mind's eye so well that he was convinced it would even look good on paper.

True to form, as soon as Gladys opened the door, he landed a kiss on her lips, set his suitcase and duffle on the floor, and handed her an unwrapped gift; a stylish little half ounce bottle of Chanel #5.

She had been expecting him. Her makeup was impeccable, her hair was in tight curls, and she wore a scalloped chenille dress that clung to her form. The kitchen table was set for two, and the neat, compact home smelled of fresh-baked bread and hot coffee. Dinner was in the oven and most importantly, she seemed pleased to see him. It warmed his heart to know that someone had anticipated his arrival. He could rely on Gladys to please him and dependably so, he was in her bed in a matter of minutes.

After dinner, they rode the interurban trolley downtown, watched *The Great Ziegfeld* at the Odeon Movie House, imbibed a few drinks at the Inside Out Blues Room on Woodward Avenue, caught the streetcar and were back home on Boehme Street just past midnight. The lovemaking wasn't as intense as their earlier afternoon delight, but they fell asleep in each other's arms satisfied and content.

Gladys was up early on Wednesday morning and had a hotcake breakfast ready when he walked into the kitchen. First to touch his lips was a Camel, then a sip of black coffee and lastly, a peck on his lover's cheek. The green wooden chair creaked in mild protest under his weight and squeaked along the linoleum floor as he moved up to the table.

Nicholas wrenched his shoulders backwards, wriggled his neck and took a gulp of coffee. "Good morning, Darling."

Gladys set his short stack in front of him; a thick pat of butter already melting its way down and over the pancakes. "Good morning, Nick. Did you sleep well?"

He was pouring Log Cabin syrup over his hotcakes. "Of course. I always do here. You know that." He wiped the sleep and smoke out of his eyes, and crushed his cigarette into the ashtray.

Gladys sat across from him, and a bland smile came over her lips. Her words seemed rehearsed, possibly memorized, and flowed steadily without pause or hesitation, "I've got some news, Nicholas. Some important news. I'm selling the house to my tenant and it's cash on the barrelhead, to my tenant Ellis Coulman, you know, he's married with a five-year-old daughter and works for Detroit Edison. And for a couple of reasons, I'm moving back to Battle Creek where my family is. Reason number one being that my parents are getting on in age, so I'll be helping them just by being there, you see. Reason number two is that my brother said that he can get me a job at Kellogg and he said the prospects for promotion are good for women."

Nicholas set his fork down and pushed his plate away. He sat wide-eyed, incredulous and stymied, "I'm about to get hit by a frigging freight train, ain't I?"

His bewilderment effected his reaction, temperament, and vocabulary, "No shit. When did you decide all this? This morning … last night … yesterday … when? I can say this: you got goddamned outstanding good timing, Gladys, I'll give you that. You got me by the short hairs, for sure. Talk about a kick in the head … wow. You just kicked me right smack-dab square in the family jewels."

She sat still, hands folded, taking rhythmic, calculated breaths. She squeezed out a tear, "It's nothing new, Nick. It's been slowly coming ... slow, but sure. You said yourself one time that maybe I should get out of Detroit and spread my wings. You told me that once and, well … it made me think. I have remembered everything you ever told me. I loved you and wanted you, but you won't leave Nora, you can't. You feel too obligated, and too guilty to hurt poor, fragile Nora, and I'm not getting any younger sitting here like a frog on a lily pad just waiting for some prince to plant a warm wet kiss on my lips and take me away from this little polliwog pond. I know we each had our reasons for what we did, and we promised each other up front not to make waves, but I'm tired of swimming against the current, Nick. I mean, I'm almost forty years old for goodness' sake. I'll never have you for my own, and I cannot keep going blindfolded down this one-way street that I'm on. What we had was great. But it wasn't permanent, not by a long shot. You know that."

He wondered if he had just seen a flash and heard the crack of lightning and was nervously waiting for the thunderclap that would certainly follow. He knew that the sooner the thunder is heard, the closer the storm is. It was wishful thinking, but he wanted to avoid the noise altogether. He was angry and his gut ached from a sucker punch he never saw coming. She had stunned him and landed a painful blow below the belt. He had always thought that he could count on trustworthy Gladys.

"I'm sorry it's ending this way Gladys, but to be honest, you're right and I suppose we are obligated to follow our own star through life. Maybe yours is hanging directly over a bowl of toasted corn flakes in Battle Creek. I think mine might be somewhere just west of the sunset and it's surely not in Detroit … and maybe calling it quits is a good thing after all. My father once told me that *everything happens for the best*. Well, I can tell you one thing … I won't be looking for any goddamned search lights in the night skies over Detroit to guide me back to my home airfield. I am already familiar with more than one landing strip between here and Tampico, and most of them are newer and smoother. And them Mexican dames are even warm to the touch. Everyplace."

His words burned slowly into her mind. She managed to fight back a tear and released her steam, "Holy mackerel! Have you ever listened to yourself, Nick? You keep acting the modoc! Did I actually hear your words correctly? You are one self-centered, fly-by-night, mean-spirited, no-account flyboy! You bastard, you!"

It was the first time in her life that Gladys had spoken with hostility. And it was the first time she was angry with Nicholas.

Nick snarled his reply, "Well, now that we've been properly introduced, and you've finished hurling your thoughtless insults, I can say: pleased to meet you, lady. Abyssinia, honey. A*dios, auf wiedersehen* and *fare thee goddamn well*."

Not another word was uttered. He moved about the place, ignoring her, and picked up what odd, little items were his, stuffed them into his case and was out the door.

He didn't look back. He left her sitting at the kitchen table and watching him, her chin resting on her clenched fist and holding a hankie.

Nick walked five blocks to his Second Street home. Alex met him at the door.

"Papa, Papa, we knew you were coming! Auntie Glad telephoned and told Mama that you were on your way!"

After he heard his son's words, the three steps up to his front porch were like walking to the gallows. He could only anticipate his fate once he reached the doorway and his wife.

Traveling The WPA Road …

… from air to asphalt …

The first hours of the ride across Michigan were torment. In front of Gladys, he had masked his feelings with a veil of anger-laden regret. He spitefully believed that he needed to refuse her the satisfaction of watching him squirm. He couldn't wish her ill will, but he could deny her the sight of his anguish. For nearly seven years he had never anticipated the end of his illicit love affair, and never could he have dreamed that he would suffer heartbreak. Gladys had been his home field; his hangar.

South of Benton Harbor, US Route 12 turned westward, ironically through a small town named New Buffalo. He was driving on smooth new pavement laid down by the Works Progress Administration[*] along the expansive shoreline of Lake Michigan. The town's name prompted his thoughts to wander in all directions and with the navigational mind of a pilot, Nicholas looked westward to the horizon and witnessed the twinkling blue grey waters melt into an endless faded blue sky, and completely blur his destination. He decided to rely on his compass; rather, his willpower, his determination. Gladys had ended their affair in much the same manner he left her so many times in the past: flying off without a care or commitment. Perhaps it was his due desserts, a looming hazard in the flight plan that he should have seen coming. The whole affair could have sent him into a fateful tailspin, like he had been caught by low-hanging power lines. Now that Gladys had called his bluff and placed her cards face-up on the table, all he could do was to pick up his chips and navigate away from any emotional thunderstorm. The day before, she reminded him that the relationship they had shared was non-committal from takeoff.

He felt uneasy about the telephone call that Gladys had made to his wife and had difficultly reasoning why she would have done such a thing. When they were leaving Mount Clemens, he nonchalantly asked Nora, "So what did you think when Gladys called and ruined my surprise arrival, Sweetheart?"

Nora had shrugged her shoulders and seemed to minimize the conversation with Gladys altogether, "Nothing. She gets emotional and doesn't make sense to me sometimes."

He took a deep breath, filled his lungs with the humid air of late afternoon and convinced himself that it was time to stand tall and walk like an aviator: chin up, frame tight and trim, eyes, toes, and nose facing forward.

Nick looked to the passengers in the front seat beside him and affirmed his responsibility to keep his hands on the wheel and try to ensure a safe ride. Nora was nodding off with her head cradled on a pillow against the passenger window and front seat. Alexander was in the middle, half asleep with a nickel comic book on his lap; one of the five his father had bought for him.

Nicholas felt alone and bored. He couldn't have a meaningful conversation with himself without talking aloud. To take matters from bad to worse, his conscience was stubbornly mute, and unwilling to keep him company. The silence was ominous. He had a headache as big as Texas.

I Know Why (And So Do You) …

It's a long way back …

Nick broke their Wisconsin road trip into two parts: day one to Michigan City, Indiana and the second to Oshkosh.

When they arrived on Saturday, it was the bittersweet reunion that Nicholas had expected. Nora was reunited with her parents after seven years of separation. Together, they disproved the adage that says, *'you can't go back'* because that's exactly what happened; it was as if they had never parted. Everybody and everybody's behavior had not changed a jot.

Despite his successful career and clear ability to provide more than a bare-boned existence for his family, Nicholas was still on the receiving end of Dominik's piercing stares and Gabi's conditioned disdain. It went without saying that no matter what Nick's position in life was, it wasn't good enough to forgive the transgression he committed in 1927. Nora boasted about her ability to donate freely to Saint Peter's coffers only to be admonished by her father, "You cannot buy your way into Heaven, Nora Jolan." It was always Dominik's habit to use full Christian names for emphasis, particularly when he was proving a point.

It was impossible for Nicholas to get beyond the embarrassment of his guilt. He had hoped that one day he could forget how uncomfortable he felt around Dominik. He hungered for the forgiveness that he knew was never to come. Old memories had been dredged up, and Nicholas perceived a renewal of the emptiness that he had hoped was buried and forgotten.

Young Marie had taken a path that was similar to her sister's role at Saint Mary's in Mount Clemens. She had just finished her two-year studies at Oshkosh State Teachers College and was to begin teaching elementary school the following year twenty miles away in Fond Du Lac. Like her sister, Marie was also married, specifically to David Withersby, who worked in the family's Fox River sawmill. The defining differences between Marie's marriage and Nora's were that so far Marie's marriage was childless, and David had been welcomed into the family fold.

Nora and Marie shared more than parallel vocations. They shared family; something that Nick had been tragically denied in 1927. As soon as they arrived in Oshkosh, he tried to envelop his son Alexander and claim him as his sole companion, but it was impossible with two grandparents and a doting aunt vying for his son's attention.

Nick stubbornly denied it and refused to admit to the ache that Gladys had given him. His heartbreak was crammed together with the grieving memories of his family that had painfully landed once again like a nagging hunger, deep in his belly. His brother Leopold had vanished, and his mother and sisters perished in one fell swoop of circumstance. He had no sense of resolution, and no definitive conclusion to the violent upheaval he had experienced as a young man in Buffalo. He felt the need to go over the last chapter of his family history and put that giant volume of personal devastation away on the shelf for good.

Monday evening over his second helping of Gabi's pörkölt ragout*, Nicholas announced that he was leaving Oshkosh the next morning and driving to Buffalo. He explained his decision with a tone of certainty, "I've got to find my mother's grave." It was a pronouncement of his desperate attempt to finally close the book on his past.

His remark surprised Nora and shocked her parents.

Dominik pointed out the obvious, "You know that you will be driving a car and not flying an airplane. Buffalo is not exactly around the corner, you know."

"It's about five hundred miles as the crow flies, but as you just reminded me Dominik, I'm not a crow. But I can cut about a hundred miles off the trip if I drive through Canada. Anyway, my mind is made up. I'm going to Buffalo. I've got to do this."

Nora did not understand her husband's quest for closure. She could easily brush away any emotional upheaval that could come her way with the help of her faith, and she knew if more help was needed, Brother John, Sister Anna Maria, and the Church would provide it.

Nicholas had always been a mystery to Dominik and Gabi. He came from a world beyond their borders of domination and this sudden pilgrimage of his to Buffalo was just one more manifestation of their son-in-law's bagful of confusing behavior.

Eight-year-old Alexander was accustomed to the comings and goings of his airplane pilot father. It was what he did.

Nick announced that he planned to leave for Buffalo on Tuesday afternoon. In the morning, he took Alexander to Albertson's in downtown Oshkosh and bought his son a fire-engine-red Road King tricycle. Back on New York Avenue, the good-byes were short and on-point. Surprisingly, Dominik offered a handshake, and Gabi gave him a passing kiss on the cheek. He and Alex shared the usual bear hug.

He believed Nora was still holding back and would never reveal the entire conversation she had with Gladys over the telephone. Despite the tension, he was congenial, though superficial with his goodbye. He left her with two-hundred-fifty dollars to cover her stay and the train fare back to Detroit and Mount Clemens.

She left him puzzled by her farewell, "The shortest, safest way to the solution is to drive with Faith, Nicholas. May the Lord Jesus Christ guide you and God's Angels guard and keep you."

After a light kiss on Nora's lips, he was gone again.

Hold Tight …

Cleveland: Fats and Llewellyn D'Arcy …

Rather than shifting north to Detroit and across Canada, he decided to stay on US Route 20 all the way to Buffalo. Nick spent fifteen hours behind the wheel of his five-window Ford and arrived in Lorain, Ohio at nine o'clock Wednesday morning. He filled up at a Sinclair station, had his oil level and tire pressure checked, and got recommendations for a local restaurant and a Cleveland hotel from the gas jockey. The fellow worked hard and earned every penny of his two-bit tip scrubbing the motor freckles off the windshield and headlights. Driving along the Great Lakes has it hazards, no matter the season. In June, it's the sand flies, mosquitoes, and moths.

He wasn't much company or very talkative during the drive. The questions he asked aloud went unanswered. Nick was aware that nobody was listening, and that forced him to spend all of his time alone with his thoughts. While traveling through the darkness of night, WSM radio out of Nashville twanged above the monotonous grind to keep him awake, aware and alert. Jimmy Rodgers and The Carter Family weren't Benny Goodman, Vera Lynn, or Tommy Dorsey, but they got the job done. He was able to stay awake.

He checked into the Hotel Bruce, located on Route 20, Euclid Avenue and 63rd Street, at 10 AM. He was able to ignore the buzz in his ears, and fire in his eyes, and finally passed out with a pillow over his head. He awoke at 7 PM, limped to the dining room for a pork chop dinner, found a seat at the bar and in a mere two hours (thanks to Canadian Club and Carling Black Label), drank himself into a haze.

Thursday evolved into a marathon fistfight with his memory and an oratorical debate with his conscience. Both matches turned out to be nothing more than a waste of time. There was nothing on this schedule, so he decided once again to get drunk. When he learned that Fats Waller[*] and his Six Piece Rhythm were playing the Bruce's Club and Lounge on Friday, he had no choice but to stay yet another night.

Friday afternoon he was in high spirits for the first time in a week, and anxiously anticipated the show. He walked to the Montgomery Ward store at 65th Street and bought a dark blue, pin-striped suit for fifteen dollars, a two-dollar silk shirt, and a fifty-cent tie. He decided against a pair of shoes, reasoning that his pants would conceal most of his Acme western boots.

He spent much of the afternoon in the hotel lobby, paging through tattered magazines, smoking cigarettes, and watching women. His thoughts drifted ... up and away from the cornfields and rice paddies, far from the power lines and train stations. Of all the women he had bedded, he could not think of one who would appreciate the musical performance he was hoping to witness. Nicholas could attribute his love of music to his brother Leopold. From the family's first crank-and-gear gramophone and black wax record, he recalled his brother's love of song and the stories that the singers told in rhythmic rhyme.

Had nothing else happened the following night in Cleveland, seeing Thomas 'Fats' Waller perform live at a jazz club was something that Nicholas Throckmorton would never forget. Unexpectedly, memorable events can sometimes come packed together like sardines.

As a hotel guest, he was able to order dinner and claim a small table near the left side of the small, raised stage. He had decided to leave the drink alone until show time, and proudly ordered a bottle of Saratoga Spring water with his meal. It was a show night, and the selection and quality of food was diminished by volume and demand. He nervously worked on his over-cooked ham steak, limp string beans, and cold sweet potato while watching Fats' Rhythm and stage crew set up for the show. Fats had an entourage that changed with the wind, shifting from Louis Armstrong to Adelaide Hall and Lena Horne, so the audience could never bank on who would show up.

As ten o'clock neared, the Bruce became noisier as more patrons pushed through the doorway, claiming their seats and ordering libations until magically, at quarter-to, a blanket of expectation covered the room. Minutes later, the conversation dimmed, laughter abated, and voices vanished. Eyes strained through the dim light and smoke, anticipating the show. A pair of cigar and cigarette girls in skimpy red flare skirts swayed and sauntered among the tables, advertising and declaring the obvious, "Cigars ... cigarettes ... matches." They displayed their wares in compartment trays hanging just below their pushed-up, barely covered bosoms. Uniformed waiters in flowing black tuxedos moved around the club with the grace of ballet danseurs, holding trays of bottles and drink high over their shoulders.

The Rhythm entered stage right and took their positions in the trenches near the first row of tables; packed with anxious club crawlers, jazz club opportunists, and fly-by-nights such as crop-duster Nicholas Throckmorton. Fats Waller was a big round man and boldly appeared in full form, walking across the stage from the left curtain fall, taking four giant strides to his piano. He was nursing a glass of whiskey from his left hand and had a large hand-rolled, Cuban cigar between his lips.

There wasn't an arm without goose bumps or a neck without prickles anywhere in the club. Fats acknowledged the applause with a broad smile full of white teeth, raised his right hand and sang his trademark line half an octave lower than a growl: *"Latch on, baby, latch on!"* The crowd howled. Nick was electrified.

Fats stepped to his gleaming, black upright piano and settled his large frame onto the bench. He leaned into the circular microphone, thanked the room, and introduced his vocalist as *Lovely Lulu, the Carolina Chickadee.*

Nicholas noticed her the second she appeared from behind the curtain. Long and lanky, with legs to the sky, the olive-skinned songstress captivated the room, flowing over the stage like warm sorghum syrup. Fats, Lulu, and the Rhythm wasted no time, and began the night's entertainment with *Hold Tight.*

The alluring vocalist caught his glances from the start and played to him along with all the other men in the audience. She teased, taunted, and touted some of the ribald lyrics that were uniquely scattered through Fats' scat jazz and Harlem stride; all while she focused her gaze on Nick.

He had seen New Orleans jazz, Memphis blues, and Kansas City bebop, but nothing like what was going on in Cleveland that night. Vocalists came and went like the blat of a gobble pipe, but Lu was electric, puzzling and hypnotic. Her voice was like vanilla tapioca: soft, blended with sweet little bumps and sprinkled with brown spice. Nick sat mesmerized. Memories of Mount Clemens, Memphis, Monroe, Tampico, and Matamoros were pushed aside.

Around midnight, when Fats declared that he needed to *wet his whistle*, Lulu took ten soft steps away from the bandstand to Nick's table. She wasted no time before she boldly declared, "I need a glass of champagne." A waiter had followed her like tail feathers on a peahen, wearing a broad smile and carrying a tray full of various drinks, ready to take Nick's money.

"Thank you, sir." Without doubt she was genuine, but her Yat, twang and drawl betrayed her origin, and it surely wasn't Carolina, North *or* South. Nick pinned her to Louisiana. She grabbed two full flutes of champagne, immediately downed one, pulled a single, misshapen cigarette from the inside of her revealing neckline and waited for Nick's match. She puffed, exhaled from pursed red lips, eyed him from head to toe, smiled and asked, "You must be here just for the show, because you sure as hell ain't dancing in them cowboy stompers, are you?"

"I suppose not. But it's not because of my boots, it's because I don't have a partner, you see."

It was tit-for-tat: he amused her, and she mystified him. She gave her name as Llewellyn D'Arcy and proudly claimed her Louisiana Creole* heritage, "I'm not a Negro, but an old-time hybrid going all the way back to the French colonialists, Bayogoula Indians, and African slaves. So, you can think of me as a blended whiskey: smooth, tasty, and easy on the pocketbook. Take me as I am: slow and smooth. Remember though, you treat Lulu bad, and she will give you a hangover you won't ever forget."

After that introduction, the next twelve minutes were filled with coy small talk, earthy teases, forthright flirts, and the confirmation of an after-show rendezvous in room 315.

Two hours later, Fats, the Rhythm, and Lulu ended the show as it started, with an extended, rowdy encore of *Hold Tight*.

After the show and a few more glasses of champagne, Nick and the songstress took the elevator to his room on the third floor of the Hotel Bruce. Once inside room 315, they *latched on*, as Fats himself freely expounded and encouraged in song. Lulu's long legs certainly latched on, and Nicholas held tight.

He left the Hotel Bruce, Lulu, and Cleveland late Saturday morning on his way to the next big city on the shores of Lake Erie: Buffalo. The taste of Lulu's kiss and lips lingered until noon, and her voice for days.

Shave 'em Dry ...

Home not-so-sweet home ...

There was no denying that he had reached his destination and was back in Buffalo. The heavy, putrid smell of sulfur spewing from the coke and iron ore ovens of Bethlehem Steel blanketed the waterfront. When he crossed the Buffalo River and drove over the Ohio Street Bridge and away from Lackawanna's odor, past the Russell Miller flour mill, and onto lower Main Street, it was like he had never left.

The city seemed grimmer, greyer, and grimier than he remembered. Time wears the gleam and glamour away. The Depression had quieted the roar of Buffalo's Roaring Twenties.

He drove deftly, almost in a trance, up Broadway and left onto Adams Street. The Ford moved at a snail's pace and came to a silent stop at the vacant lot where his boyhood home once stood: the home where his mother and sisters were burned to death. They lost their innocent lives in vile, wrong, mistaken blame and retribution for transgressions against the mob, and the Torricelli crime family of the Black Hand Mafia.

Weeds, grass, wild raspberries, and sumac had taken over. The oak tree that once shaded the backyard now stood as an eerie, macabre scarecrow. It had broken down and rotted to a pitiful charcoal skeleton of trunk and black, twisted limbs. A few young maples had claimed their own little piece of earth where the front porch used to be. Old memories flooded back; good and bad. The pain in his head and gut returned but it wasn't as debilitating as it was nine years earlier.

Nicholas sat there, thinking and reminiscing until dusk before he turned around in the tall grass and drove back downtown. He got a room that night at the Genesee Hotel for seventy-five cents and a thirty-cent hamburger platter at the Deco restaurant. Mulling things over and over, he decided to visit his mother's brother, his uncle Wilbur Abenstern, early the next morning and find out where his family was buried. He hoped to nail down the lid on the troubled past and box in some sense of finality. He hoped that tomorrow would bring him all the answers he needed.

Nick fell asleep that night thinking about Fats Waller's *Hold Tight*, Llewellyn D'Arcy's sweet vocals, and latching on.

He had not seen his fire-eater uncle Wilbur in over a decade, long before he left Buffalo in 1927, and needed to check the voluminous Bell Telephone *City Directory* to verify his address. When he arrived at the Strauss Street home and took a seat in the front room, long-forgotten memories of his grandparents appeared through the cobwebs in his mind. The old furniture, faded upholstery, heavily worn rugs, and dated drapery took him on a journey back through time. The room had the dank odor of an airless attic, stagnant and stale with the hint of naphthalene mothballs.

Aunt Minnie brought in a pitcher of lemonade and a plate of apple tarts and set them on the heavily varnished coffee table. As the first order of business, he asked about the resting place of his mother and sisters and discovered that it was at Parkview Cemetery on Elmwood Avenue. Meaningless but mandatory prater followed about his life in Detroit, wife and son, and his job as a crop duster.

When the trivial updates were over, his uncle gave him a bit of unexpected, curious information.

Uncle Wilbur told Nicholas that he had heard from a reporter at the Courier Express a year or so earlier that his brother Leopold was a city police officer in San Francisco. Nick tasted the lemonade and finished one of his aunt's little pastries. Memories exploded like fireworks and flashed through Nick's mind. He couldn't imagine Leopold as a cop and wondered if his brother ever gave him or their childhood any thought. He wanted to believe that he did.

Then, Wilbur Abenstern unwittingly opened a can of worms. The next bit of news Nicholas got from his uncle was unsettling at the least, troubling, and quite virtually disgusting. What the FBI had told Nick nine years earlier led him to believe that justice would have been rendered for the deaths of his mother and sisters. It did not turn out that way.

In 1927, Lorenzo Torricelli was charged with murder for the beating death of Dillon Cafferty, arson for the Adams Street fire, and second-degree murder for the resulting deaths of Nick's family and three boarders. Jailhouse justice was served when two FBI informants in the case were knifed in the Erie County Penitentiary following Torricelli's arrest. Soon afterward, all the arson evidence collected by Abenstern himself and the Buffalo Fire Inspector disappeared from the evidence locker of Precinct #2, Buffalo Police Department. Lorenzo Torricelli was quickly represented by a high-priced New York City lawyer associated with the Callamarise mob, immediately posted a five-thousand-dollar bond, and walked away a free man when the District Attorney dropped all charges with prejudice. The gangster got off scot-free and couldn't be charged again.

When Nicholas asked if Torricelli was still in Buffalo, his uncle said that the mobster had been pushed out of the mob hierarchy years earlier by Salvatore Magladino and banished from Buffalo's *Little Italy* neighborhood. However, he believed that the aging crook was still living somewhere in the city. Torricelli's two sons, Joseph and Salvatore, were running small-time protection and Numbers' rackets in the Lovejoy neighborhood on Buffalo's Lower East Side.

Nicholas immediately became agitated, impatient, and detached. He withdrew into his thoughts. He abruptly stood, thanked his uncle for all his information and his aunt for her hospitality. His visit with his newly retired uncle and matronly aunt had lasted as long as a glass of lemonade and a few apple tarts. The seasoned fire-eater and Brigade Commander unsuccessfully tried to convince his nephew to stay for lunch or return for dinner. Nicholas graciously declined, mentioned that he needed to spend time at the gravesite, and boldly lied that he had to be back in Detroit by Tuesday. He'd had about all he could stand of his uncle's disconcerting revelations, and the old house, with all of its memories and odors.

"Be careful, Nicholas, and don't make any rash decisions. That dirty, slippery, wop family down in Lovejoy isn't worth your spit. Remember that ... and you drive carefully on your way back to Detroit ... and take care of that young family of yours."

Her husband's brash ethnic remark evoked a "Wilbur, hush that ethnic prejudice talk!" from Aunt Minnie in the middle of his commentary.

Nick was a bit perplexed by his uncle's comment and didn't understand what could have prompted it. Ready to leave, he walked to the hallway and gave his aunt a perfunctory hug.

He shared a hearty handshake with his uncle and tried to allay any unfounded concern, "You don't have anything to worry about, Uncle Will. I try to give most things I do a lot of thought, and I wouldn't go about shaving anybody dry, anyhow. Torricelli can go straight to Hell as far as I'm concerned, and it couldn't be soon enough for me."

The scaled-down family reunion was over. What Nicholas had learned was unexpected and disturbing. The revelations turned his stomach. The biting, harsh aftertaste of bile and stomach acid lingered. He was fully disgusted with a dysfunctional justice system that had been stymied by organized crime.

Back at the hotel, he bought a bottle of rot-gut blended whiskey from the desk clerk, hoping to dilute Uncle Wilbur's distressing news and all the musty, painful memories that came along with it. He paid for another night and disappeared into all the seclusion his dingy, seventy-five cent room could afford him.

The cheap rye whiskey purchased in a flea-bag hotel on a Sunday night in Buffalo had no mercy on its victim whatsoever. Monday morning landed on Nick's head like a cinder block, allowing his brain to function no better than a ball of cotton.

The Deco restaurant on Niagara Street didn't have enough coffee or Bromo Seltzer to quiet the steam roller crushing his skull and it wasn't until well past noon before he could open his eyes wide enough to recognize daylight. When he did, he managed to drive to the cemetery on Elmwood and found his mother and sisters' graves on Serenity Knoll, just as his uncle had said. He discovered an oak and iron bench and sat there, staring at the manicured lawns, marble angels, and granite headstones until dusk. His head still ached and pinged like a blacksmith's hammer. That night he bought another bottle and fed the insatiable thirst of his alcoholic and emotional hangover.

It was midday Tuesday when he checked out of the Genesee Hotel and drove two blocks north to Niagara Square and got a room at the Hotel Statler*. He had over two hundred dollars stuck inside his Acme boot and some everyday cash in his wallet. Although he couldn't put his anguish to bed, Nick convinced himself that he should be able to get some sleep in a better hotel, a better room and a better bed. It was obvious: he needed not only a good night's rest and to clean up, but a change of scenery. It was depressing at that cheap hotel on lower Main. There was a big difference in the clientele and amenities, but there also was a small premium to be paid. The room cost a dollar and fifty cents; twice what he had paid at the Genesee, but it was a hundred times more comfortable. The Statler proudly stood in the middle of downtown and close to the clubs and dancehalls. The newer, upscale hotel had a tub and shower in every room, highlighted a nightclub and lounge with entertainment, and a full-service restaurant. It also had a lighted parking lot on Court Street.

Nick had earned this time off and had planned this supposed vacation for more than a month. Unfortunately, his plan to spend a few passionate weeks with Gladys had gone sour as soon as he returned to Mount Clemens, but for Nicholas, it did not mean that the good times were over for good. He had resolved not to flush the entire month of July down the crapper, and was determined to make this impromptu Buffalo visit worth his while. Just like Cleveland and every other big city north of the Rio Grande, Buffalo had jazz dens, dance clubs, gin mills, night culture, and available companionship. There were plenty of ways to open the valve, release steam, and simply enjoy the free time he had worked for.

He needed to clean up after two rough nights at the Genesee and took immediate advantage of the Statler's hot water before venturing out onto the city's streets. After a shower and shave, he felt that some new clothes would refresh him further. He needed an invigorating change.

Nicholas never was a man to wear a hat, save for his leather aviator's headgear, but he was beguiled into a purchase that afternoon at Kleinhanns Men's Wear. A coy, cute, and clever salesclerk named Iris had caught and kept his attention. With a flitter of eyelashes and a come-on smile, she had convinced him to try on a particularly handsome hat. It was a black, beaver-belly fedora with a grey, wide silk band. After perusal of his reflection in the small mirror at the sales counter, he amused himself as well as the flirtatious young saleswoman. Once he decided to buy the hat, the rest was easy. He augmented his purchase with a pair of two-tone, black and white wingtips, black slacks, and a white silk shirt.

"Please, allow me one comment before I ask you something ... I must say that you have the most stunning eyelashes and most striking blue eyes I have ever seen ... blue as the skies over the Gulf of Mexico. How about dinner tonight, Doll? And your name ... Iris ... it's gorgeous. I'm a stranger in paradise here in Buffalo, a flyer without a landing strip, and I'm staying at the Statler ... you could show me the way as my special tour guide and maybe allow me a chance to soften up my new shoes on the dance floor...what do you say? Come on Doll, flutter those blinkers, flash me a smile, show me your pearly whites, and say *yes*!"

Like other women in his past, he had charmed her into submission. Twenty-year-old Iris Black agreed to his invitation. For the next four evenings and nights, she played the escort to an out-of-town flyer, accompanying him to dinner and clubs, clinging on his arm and becoming part and parcel of Nick's Buffalo *vacation*.

On Thursday, he was able to use his Army Air Corps federal pilot license and Selfridge Air Field identification card to gain admission to the Curtiss-Wright Aircraft manufacturing plant on Genesee Street, adjacent to the WPA-built, federally funded, Buffalo Municipal Airport. He spent the day touring the massive facility that employed 30,000 men and women. Nick was particularly fortunate and took full advantage of the opportunity to fly in the gunner's seat behind seasoned test pilot Chester Goodson *(nicknamed Test* *'er Good)* for a demonstration flight of a Curtiss A-12 Shrike[*] fighter plane.   Although it was only twenty minutes in duration, Nick was amazed at the maneuverability and speed of the new design of single-wing Air Corps attack aircraft. He quickly befriended the case-hardened test pilot and on Friday, he did it all over again.   Nick was able to fill the afternoon, the week, and entire weekend with what he loved: flying new, fast and exciting aircraft during the day and landing alongside his new, convivial, and willing Iris at night. He had discovered a landing strip in Buffalo.

Two days earlier, he had made himself a promise that Buffalo was going to be a holiday to remember.   In ways unknown to him at the time, it proved to be a prophetic promise.   On Sunday, July 12th, Nick awoke in room 338 of the Hotel Statler with blue-eyed Iris in his bed and a new mission on his mind.   Over a breakfast of bagels, cream cheese, smoked salmon, orange juice, and coffee at the Statler Café, he said good-bye to young Iris.   He told her the boldface lie that he was leaving for Detroit that afternoon. Nick no longer had the time for his tender, flowering Iris.

Looking Around Corners For You …

One week later: outside the Pour House …

For 360 days of the year, *hot, humid, and uncomfortable* are words not used when describing the weather in Buffalo, New York.   But for one particular night in July of 1936, the phrase was a fitting summation.

It was two o'clock on Saturday morning, July 18th, on the two corners of Great Arrow and Elmwood Avenue when a screeching feral feline could be heard announcing the intimate, ultimate arrival of her current tom.

A full Buck Moon[*] illuminated the night sky and allowed the limbs, leaves, and branches of proud American Elms and Norway Maples to cast eerie, shifting shadows down onto the sidewalk and street.   Black crickets rubbed their barbed hind legs, resonating their mating song. From the alley behind Elmwood, a barking dog vainly protested his pent-up frustration.

The shadowy figure of a tall man appeared from a parked five-window, sloped-back, coupe three doors down the block on Grote Street. The tall dark shadow stood under a broken, burned-out streetlamp and lit a cigarette. Two days earlier, the stranger had paid a local sling-shot artist a two-dollar windfall to extinguish the light. The brief flash of the match revealed that the figure wore a hat, but the light was not enough to identify the unknown soul. His form cloaked in the dark of night, he went unnoticed, and the dog continued to bark. The cats persisted in their noisy tussle. The lurking silhouette vanished into the thick, dense foliage, and darkness provided by a privet hedge along the sidewalk.

At the corner of Great Arrow, the lights inside the *Pour House* bar and grill went out. In the dim glow of a twenty-five-watt bulb, the form of a large man could be seen exiting and locking the door behind him. The thick smoke and heavy smell of a half-burnt *Dutch Masters President* drifted up and around his pockmarked face. Heel cleats and leather soles echoed his footsteps on the sidewalk and pavement. He had closed the bar and was headed home to his wife Agnes. Home was 37 Grote Street, an immaculate two-story Victorian just two doors down from Elmwood Avenue. The rhythm of his steps and a tell-tale shuffle betrayed his age as he wobbled his way to the other side of the street and onto Grote. An automobile sped down Elmwood Avenue behind him.

Thirty steps and thirty seconds later, the tall stranger appeared from the shadows and stood on the sidewalk directly in the big man's path.

The sharp report of a gunshot pierced the night.

The force of the bullet* pushed the big man backwards. He staggered, caught his balance and fell to his knees, clutching his hands to a gushing stomach wound. He looked up, slack-jawed; his gaze locked on the dark figure before him and mumbled, "What?"

The grey shadow answered, "I'm Nicholas Throckmorton. Remember me, you bastard ... remember my name ... remember me as you burn in Hell."

A second, fatal bullet entered the large man's forehead and exited from a hole big enough for a Mack truck. The slug pushed the old gangster's beefy body backwards onto the sidewalk, with arms and legs sideways, askew, and out of kilter. The deed was done. It was simpler and much quicker than Nick had anticipated.

Nicholas stood over Torricelli's body and pointed the barrel of his snub-nose Smith & Wesson at the dead Mafioso's chest. His words went unanswered as he methodically squeezed off the remaining four rounds, "That's for my mother, Wilhelmina ... and my sister Johanna ... and Ottilie ... and Hilde ... you son of a bitch."

The barking dog went silent. The lovesick cats had scattered and forsaken their frolic. The cicadas continued their piercing cry from the elms and maples and the crickets defiantly sang on. For the bugs it was high summer, and the gunshots meant nothing. A faint light appeared in an upstairs window of the house across the street.

Nicholas dragged the mobster's bloody corpse onto the street, awkwardly lifted and set it onto the tarpaulin he had spread out in the trunk. Nick smelled something amiss and nearly vomited when he discovered what stunk. The old mobster's dying act was messing his pants. Nick cursed the dead gangster one last time, closed the lid, took a quick look around, slid into the driver's seat, started the engine and was gone.

Ten minutes later, Lorenzo Torricelli's corpse was cast aside like nothing more than vile carrion and dumped onto a lifeless railway siding at the Hertel Avenue waterfront.

Nick tossed the canvas over the body, closed the trunk lid and paused for a moment. He looked skyward and took a deep breath to give his heart a chance to catch up and his pulse to calm. He suddenly knew how much he missed the sky, sun, white clouds and wind in his face.

It was hot, muggy and weirdly quiet. The only sound was his breath and the soft ripple of the Niagara River lapping at the breakwater. Moonlight sparkled off the river like liquid stars.

He removed his hat and flipped it onto the back seat atop his suitcase and duffle. Nick retrieved the empty revolver from under the front seat and threw it far into the powerful river. The distant sound of a splash signaled that the Smith & Wesson had hit his mark one final time.

Nick put a match to a Camel and leaned against the driver's door. He flicked the butt away after one long draw and took a final look down at the dead gangster's covered remains heaped behind the car. He wiped sweat from his brow onto his sleeve, noticed the blood splatter on his shirt, muttered a profanity, and stripped down to his undershirt. As the last scene in a one-act play, he threw his blood stained, two-dollar Chinese silk shirt from Kleinhanns to the ground and cursed Torricelli yet again.

Nick checked his watch as he got behind the wheel and set the Ford in gear. It was ten past three; he had a full tank of gas and estimated that by ten o'clock he would be able to sit down for breakfast in Cleveland. He dismissed the thought of driving across Canada, reasoning that he was at the least, somewhat familiar with the route through Ohio. The V8 rumbled in anticipation as he drove slowly through the rail yard and onto Hertel Avenue.

His thoughts drifted as he turned onto the smooth pavement of Niagara Street and began his trip back to Mount Clemens. There was so much to absorb, so much to classify, categorize, remember, and justify. He needed to collect his thoughts. He cricked his neck, rolled his shoulders, and shifted into third. He was going home. He stuck his head out the window just to feel the air on his face. It felt good.

After all the preparation, forethought and soul-searching, the conclusion seemed anticlimactic. Nick found it curious that he did not feel an iota of regret. He wondered if guilt could take a while to settle into his brain, like the insecticide dust he dropped on soybeans or the fertilizer on corn.

He would never forget the fire, nor could he forgive the massacre of his family. For the previous week, Nick had studied each of his options from timid passivity, to accepting a pathetic, humanitarian, hands-off, laissez faire approach to the injustice, or to personally deliver Torricelli the fate he deserved.

He had decided that Torricelli needed to die, and that he needed to make it happen.

What had finally tipped the scales and cast the die for Nick to commit to his ultimate vengeance was the purchase he and his crew mates had made months earlier. It came as a bolt of lightning on Tuesday afternoon in the Statler Lounge while he was nursing his second boilermaker*. He was smooth talking some nameless sweet patootie while waiting for Iris Black to get off work when it struck him.

When he was a kid, his brother Leopold would often tease him about being a *good boy* and not getting into mischief, *"Remember, Nick: it's not what you do that gets you in hot water ... it's what you get caught doing."*

He recalled what happened in Matamoros, Mexico one evening in March and the subsequent purchase of revolvers the following day in Brownsville, Texas. His Smith & Wesson and a box of a dozen S&W shells had been packed in the trunk of his '36 Ford and were just taking up space. It was a kiss of fate from Lady Luck, a confirmation that he was destined to use that weapon from the day he bought it. Nick had found a wobbly excuse and blamed it on a spin of the wheel of fortune. After all, he had always been told that everything in life happens for one reason or another, and it's all part of some big plan that has been written in the stars since the beginning of time. Assassination was the ultimate solution to resolve his absolute disgust of Torricelli, lack of faith in the law, and the legal system that held it in reverence. He perceived that it was his duty to give the aged crook the ultimate eye-for-an-eye biblical comeuppance.

Nick had ended his party nights and high times in Buffalo to give his new plan plenty of pre-flight preparation. While Nick was learning to fly in 1930, his boss, mentor, and friend Enrique Del'aire impressed upon him that no matter the field, no matter the target, it's always best to know the lay of the land before you fly over it. A pilot who knows the ground underneath holds a distinct advantage. Whether it's by studying maps, a fly-over from a safe altitude, driving past or walking through the field on foot, the more knowledge the pilot has, the safer the mission will be.

For the previous week, Nicholas had frequented the beer joints, billiard halls and bowling alleys in Little Italy like a gumshoe from a Dick Tracy comic. Just as his uncle Wilbur had told him, he confirmed that Torricelli had handed off what remained of his graft and protection racket to his two sons. Kicked to the curb years earlier by a power-play between the New York City and Canadian mob families, the elder Torricelli was running the Pour House and lived less than a half block away from the gin mill. Nick shadowed the broken-down mobster's routine for days and felt confident with his planned course of vengeance.

Nicholas broke off his heated relationship with Iris and instead filled his days and nights with plotting, conniving, research, and reconnaissance. His thoughts had traveled full circle from idea, to development, to anxious anticipation, and finally, fulfillment. It was over. The one-man firing squad had emptied its weapon. He could relax and drive back to Mount Clemens.

Nick was sharply alert and almost alone on the road. Oncoming vehicles were few and far between. His side-view mirror reflected the blackness he had left behind in Buffalo. What he saw in the mirror differed greatly from what he could see through the windshield. His headlamps lit the way forward. He couldn't go back. It was darker back there.

Iris did not enter his thoughts. Nick had nothing else on his mind but the justification he was granting himself. His memory of staring into the evil pit of Torricelli's soul as he pulled the trigger gratified his conscience. He likened killing Torricelli to a hapless pigeon getting sucked into the cold-forged propeller of his Stearman: it would be instantaneous and noisy, the blood would splatter, and the feathers would fly, but the final result could be considered nothing more than assisted suicide; an unfortunate happenstance at the worse, and the only thing to do was to keep flying. And as expected, the ground crew would clean up the bloody, feathery mess when the flight was over.

He lit another cigarette, cranked down the driver's side window and settled in for the ride. The warmth of summer rushed through the hood cowl and open window. It felt good swirling around inside the coupe. The breeze invigorated him. It was during that trip back to Michigan that Nick first acknowledged how much he truly loved the air.

5: LIFE ON THE FLY, 1936-38

1936: Inka Dinka Do …

… *or somebody else will …*

After eleven and a half hours behind the wheel, Nick arrived back in Mount Clemens. He stowed away his Ford inside the alley garage behind his house on Second Street and brought his bags inside his silent, lifeless home. Nick opened nearly every window in the house, letting fresh air in for the first time in nearly three weeks. He then opened a tin of Campbell's pork and beans for dinner and washed it down with a can of warm Pabst Blue Ribbon beer*. The house was too quiet, too empty. His thoughts were too loud. The events that he had generated in Buffalo on Saturday night, put together with the long, lonely hours in the driver's seat of his Ford coupe, made it difficult to think. He needed a place to lay his head and rest.

He hungered for human company, decided to leave his Second Street address, and walk the five blocks to the Boehme Street bungalow. For eight years, Gladys had comforted him emotionally and satisfied him physically. He hoped that she could again, if only for one last time. She did not answer his knock, but rather it was lanky, freckle-faced Ellis Coulman who told Nick that Gladys had left Mount Clemens for Battle Creek the previous week. Disappointed and dejected, Nick's mood was sputtering and quickly losing altitude.

He then walked to Lawrence's Tavern on Cass Avenue and with the help of bourbon and beer, began to thread his way through the tangled fabric of deceit he needed to weave for his wife. Nick was learning first-hand that once a lie is told, many others are required to continue the ruse and cover up the original deception.

By seven o'clock and after a half dozen boiler-makers, Nick considered that he was ready. He got a pocketful of silver from the bartender and telephoned his wife in Oshkosh from the telephone booth at the corner of Gratiot. After sliding twenty-two quarters down the slot, the Michigan Bell operator connected him for a three-minute person-to-person conversation.

"Sweetheart! My trip to Buffalo went as smooth as Ivory Snow*. I visited my mother's brother, and the gravesites ..." He stammered throughout and didn't know what to say next. There was nothing more that he could tell her.

Seconds passed before Nora spoke, "You've been drinking, Nicholas. I know. I can tell. Where are you?"

He steadied himself inside the booth and straightened up as if his wife could actually see him through miles of telephone wire. The cigarette at the corner of his mouth dropped an inch of ash onto his shirt. He juggled and nearly dropped the handset trying to brush it off. It clunked against the glass before he had the chance to answer. He tried his best, but stammered nonetheless, "I'm in Kansas ... Topeka. We fly out tomorrow and back to Louisiana then back to Texas and Mexico." He knew he had stepped in it, but it wasn't the bourbon or beer, nor was it his brain, but rather his tongue that wobbled his words and poisoned his prologue.

For the first time in nearly nine years of marriage, Nora spoke to her husband with unbending honesty. She told him exactly what crossed her mind; "My glasses may be as thick as the bottom of a milk bottle, but my ears work just fine, Nicholas. You're on the drink, and I know you're not in Kansas. The operator told me that this was a person-to-person telephone call from Detroit, so I know you just told me a big lie. There is an old Hungarian saying that says *trust a thief before a liar*."

He was cornered, with no way out and nothing else to do but continue to weave the lie. "Yes, of course ... I'm home in

Mount Clemens ... I meant to say that I'm leaving for Kansas in the morning, Sweetheart."

"Like I just said, my eyesight may be bad Nicholas, but my ears and instincts are fine, so there's no need to tell me what's coming down the track. I can hear it loud and clear, and I won't let your train of lies run me over or hurt me or our son. Gladys told you goodbye, I know that ... she told me so. And she sold her house, and she is leaving Mount Clemens to live with her family in Battle Creek. She told me that, too. And don't you think that I didn't see her blonde hairs on your shirts over the years. And don't you dare ever expect me to bow to your wayward ways or warm your bed. You will continue doing what you do ... and I understand why. I can forgive you for not honoring me, but we are married, and you must still respect me ... and I will keep doing my best for our Alexander, the children at Saint Mary's, the unfortunate, and the needy. Brother John says penance is the righteous path. You should heed those words, Nicholas."

Nick gave his wife's religion some due respect, but always a wide berth. "You and that Brother John and Sister What's-Her-Name could wear out your knees praying for me, Nora. Why anyone would want to waste time doing that beats the Devil out of me."

Nicholas' only line of defense was humility. He dropped his cigarette to the floor and crushed it out with his shoe and continued, "When are you and Alex coming home? Is he awake? Can I talk to him?"

"I have tickets for the end of the week ... for Friday, so I can be back and help get ready for Wednesday's Solemnity of Saints. And Mama is getting Alexander ready for bed now, so I think it's best to wait until next time to talk to him ... when you are not under the spell of drink. I will tell Alexander that you said hello and leave it at that. Remember, don't forget; I will need some money for groceries and the milk man."

Although his senses were dulled by several beers and whiskey chasers, Nick was painfully swallowing the most devastating, verbal drubbing his wife had ever served. "I have always provided for you, Nora. You know that, and just as always, there'll be cash in the cigar box in the dresser, and the savings in the bank. And my pay packet will still come in the mail ... I'll be back as soon as the job permits, Sweetheart ... please give Alex a hug from his father." He struggled with those last words.

"Goodbye, Nicholas. May Christ Our Lord bless you and Mary, Queen of the sky and Earth, guide you until your safe return. Good-bye." For the second time in a month, Nora had asked for blessings to be granted her husband.

A far-away click sounded through the handset, followed by an annoying, incessant buzz. He stared at the handset indignantly and hung it up. His head was spinning like a demagnetized compass, leaving him off-course, disoriented, and confused. Nick did not know whether to feel humbled, angry, insulted or shamed. He did not expect that Nora could understand his current situation, regardless of whether he was drunk or stone-cold sober. He found himself missing Gladys and tried his best to put her out of his mind. He reasoned that since Gladys had willingly departed and no longer wanted to be a part of his life, she could no longer hold any part of his heart. She was gone. That aileron had broken off. It was a bumpy ride.

Nicholas Throckmorton had touched down on an unfamiliar runway that night. It had been a rough landing. He needed to reassess his bearings in life. He was essentially a stranger in his own home and in his own bed. He was accustomed to being in bed alone, but the silence at home was maddening. Even while sleeping in a bunk house on the high plains of Peru, the snores, sneezes, and flatulence of the flight crews could be company.

He left a letter to Nora on the kitchen table; telling her that he always loved her and always would. He also wrote a note to Alexander and promised that he would take him to a Tigers baseball game at Navin Field the next time he was home. While Nicholas wrote those words to his wife and son, his thoughts were somewhere else: in the clouds.

Nick needed to rethink his current situation and reconnoiter his course. He knew he could detour and navigate around this inconvenient, rogue thunderstorm and the easiest way was to catch a train to Kansas the next morning.

Two days later, he was in the air and flying back to Louisiana. His job was not only his lifeline but his way of life.

For seven long years, the country had been struggling and was slowly breaking the bonds of The Depression. Nicholas, however, had been able to maintain a safe altitude above it all. Delta Dusters was one of many entrepreneurial, private enterprises that had thrived in an era overwhelmed with federal work relief schemes and public works projects.

The reliability and viable success of a product, dependability of a service, honesty of management and the dedication of the employees are the best advertising and publicity any company could hope to achieve. By August of 1936, the company spanned the United States from the Deep South, west to California, north to Michigan, and south to Mexico, Central and South America. The Dusters continued to expand their agricultural branch with twenty aircraft based out of Monroe, Louisiana and Nicholas began doing double duty as a pilot trainer with new Duster hires. The rookies flew in the back seat of his modified Stearman for a week before solo testing and certification.

After his guest experience in a monoplane at Curtiss-Wright in Buffalo, Nick fantasized about flying something other than biplane dusters.

Although elusive, the right place, the right time and the right connection can sound like the proverbial knock of opportunity at the door. Nick's flight supervisor took him aside and suggested that he should consider a course in commercial flight safety and technique training, and grasp at the chance to pilot the new Stinson tri-motor for the reborn passenger service of Delta Air.

At first, Nick was enthusiastic and gave the idea serious thought but reluctantly decided against it. He knew the bumpy history of *Delta Air Service* dating back to 1929, and that profitable passenger service was totally dependent on fickle mail contracts and plagued with political shenanigans and bribes. Even though Delta Air had routes from Texas to the Carolinas and had established a firm foothold and headquarters in Atlanta, Georgia, Nick looked away and declined the opportunity to change his job description.

For the next two years, Nicholas was content flying low and slow. He was kept busy dusting and seeding farmland, fields, hillsides, and bayous. He managed to get back to Mount Clemens every few months for a week or two and visit his wife and spend time with Alexander. He was transparently happy with his job, making an outrageously good dollar, constantly meeting new people, flying somewhere between the clouds and ground above the plains, hills, and mountains of the Americas.

Delta Duster flight crews came and went like a warm wind off the Gulf of Mexico. Fliers arrived by bus or train and before a year had passed; most of them usually left exactly the way they came. Unfortunately, there were a hapless few who departed in a casket, either by accident or mechanical failure. In general, it was death due to human error. At age twenty-six, Nick was a seasoned veteran who knew the difference between an aileron and an axle, air and dirt, life and death.

For Nicholas Throckmorton, it was his personal life that needed attention. He had no trouble either gaining their confidence or becoming familiar with women. The intimate companionship of a woman was not an issue, but separation certainly was.

What familial love he had shared with his mother and sisters in Buffalo was violently stolen from him.

What physical connection he had experienced with fifteen-year-old Nora in 1927 was denied after their marriage.

What he had enjoyed with Gladys for eight sexually charged years was forsaken for a corn flake factory in Battle Creek.

The comfort his bed warmers provided him with was a shallow, tepid bath, that always drained away with the morning sun.

What conscience he possessed had disappeared in Buffalo. Nick categorized the murder of Torricelli as a victory of righteousness over evil. He allowed most of his moral sense to dissolve and vanish as a matter of self-preservation. As if a magician had waved his wand, it was gone.

Instead of accepting his lot, lamenting the obvious, or attempting to salvage what he had lost over the years, he stubbornly ignored his scruples, his marriage and his son. It was simpler to ignore rather than acknowledge.

1937: Goodbye to Summer ...

A line drive to left field ... going, going, gone ...

When October arrives in Michigan, the air cools faster, the sun sets earlier, and the dark of evening settles quicker. It also signals that the baseball season is virtually over. On October 3rd, the Detroit Tigers' last game was at home against their league rival, the Cleveland Indians.

Young Alexander Throckmorton loved baseball. In the middle of the street or some back-alley sandlot, he, his buddies, and like every rag-tag kid in greater Detroit took any opportunity to play the game. It was hands-on fun that could not be substituted. It was common knowledge that radio heroes such as *Jack Armstrong (The All-American Boy)*, *The Green Hornet, The Shadow* or *Flash Gordon* could not hold a candle to the Detroit Tigers baseball team. Fans, young and old would chant, *"The Detroit baseball players are the best baseball players!"* and would yell *"hurrah!"* in unison.

It was Saturday evening. Nick had been home for a week and a half, and the family had just finished supper when he pulled two dugout tickets for the Indians – Tigers game out of his boot and presented them to his son across the dinner table.

"What do you think we can do with these, kiddo?"

Nora smiled. Now and then, her husband's actions could please her and she knew what her son's reaction would be.

Alex was excited beyond Christmas. When his father was home with time off, it usually meant that he could skip Sunday Mass. That Sunday, October 3, was more than a day on the calendar. His father had just made it very special: a Tigers game ... his first real, big-league stadium game ... the season finale at Navin Field with his father ... the airplane pilot. His father's old promise of Tiger tickets came to fruition.

Sunday morning, Nick and Alex left Mount Clemens behind for a day of baseball. Forty-five minutes later, Navin Field appeared before the boy as a concrete and steel shrine to the National Pastime. His eyes gleamed and his rosy cheeks sat at each end of his almost illegal, ear-to-ear smile. Pipe organ music throbbed *Take Me Out To The Ballgame* through the public address system. Nick handed the tickets to the gate attendant, and they awkwardly pushed their way through the turnstile. On the other side of the gangway and railings was the first line of concession and souvenir stands. It was a windfall for the boy: a team pennant with a snarling Bengal Tiger, a navy-blue baseball hat emblazoned with a huge white Edwardian letter 'D,' a box of Cracker Jacks[*], a bag of shell-on peanuts, and a paper cup full of bubbling Vernors ginger ale.

It was a game that Alexander would forever remember. In the bottom of the first inning, Alex and his father witnessed *Hammering Hank* Greenberg smack one to left field to score Pete Fox for the first and only run of the game. At the crack of the slugger's bat, Nick reached over, grasped his son's shoulder and asked with unanswerable excitement, "Did you see that, kid?! Son of a bitch!! Hank hit the hell out of that ball, didn't he, Alex?! Damn-it-all! He hit that goddamn thing! I guarantee they heard that shot all the way to Cleveland!" Father and son had smiles ear to ear and goosebumps head to toe.

Nick recognized of course that he had once again used bad language and apologized yet one more time for his choice of vocabulary. Alex knew very well that his father freely salted his words, and would not have paid the coarse language any mind had his father simply ignored it. Nevertheless, this was not Nick's first apology, nor would it be his last.

"Alex … don't say what I say. Don't talk like I do and don't use those words that I do. You know what I mean. It's a sort of man-talk, you see. You know them words and I know them, but don't say them in front of your mother. It's a show of respect for your mother if you don't use those words so she can hear you. All right? She has to go to church and everything, so don't use them. All right?"

"I know, Papa. I know."

Alexander, his father and about twenty-two thousand other fans watched the Detroit Tigers end their American League second-place season with a 1 – 0 victory over the Indians. Tiger pitcher Jake Wade threw a near-perfect one-hit game. For young Alex, it was an afternoon in Paradise filled with loud, boisterous vendors hawking peanuts, snacks, hotdogs, and a big-league stadium packed with hollering fans. Nine-year old Alex sat proudly alongside his father for the most exciting nine innings of his life.

On their way out of the ballpark and into the parking lot, Alex stopped in his tracks, and looked up to his father. His new baseball hat sat crooked, pushing his ears outward and his black bangs onto his forehead. "Papa that was the best baseball game ever in the whole world. The Tigers might be in second place but they're still the champs!"

With that, Nick knew he had forged a memory his son would never forget.

During the drive back to Mount Clemens, father and son shared a genuine conversation, talking about everything from the horsehide covering on baseballs to the aluminum skin on a Stearman Model 75. Alex loved riding in the front seat of the Ford coupe, watching his father magically use the clutch, shift lever, and gas pedal. The words and music coming from the dashboard radio were spellbinding. Alex rolled up and unfurled the souvenir pennant time and again. He turned his head and listened as his father raved about the design of the car: how the softly curved, sloping rear end, and the fender-mounted teardrop headlamps evoked a vision of Betty Grable in an evening gown. Alex shrugged his shoulders and didn't understand the comparison that his father had made. The boy took off his baseball hat and studied the embroidered big white 'D' one more time as they crossed Eleven Mile Road. The Ford's dashboard with all its instruments, dials, needles, and numbers fascinated him. He imagined the cockpit of his father's airplane to be much more enriched with instruments of all sorts. Alex needed to ask a question he had wondered about lately.

"Hey, Papa ... how come Mama says it's all right to call Grandpapa *Papa*, too? It seems dumb. It just don't make no sense."

Nicholas was quick to reply, "That's because Grandpapa is Mama's Papa. That's all."

Alex wondered, "How will you and Mama or anybody know who I'm talking about if I call two people the same name?"

Nick pulled a Camel from his pack, struck a match on the dash and lit it. He took a long drag, pushed out his lower lip and exhaled the grey smoke from the corner of his mouth. "I'll make a deal with you, my boy. You can call me anything you want. Papa, Father, Daddy, Pops, anything. Anything but *late for dinner*. How's that?"

"Freddie Frick calls his father the *Old Man*."

"You can call me that. I don't mind. Call me whatever you like, Alex. Like I said: anything but *late for dinner*." A few other terms crossed his mind, but he restrained a wanton urge to say them.

Nick moved his eyes to his son and back to the road as he added, "Tell you what, Alex ... how about you call me the *Old Man* and call your grandfather the *Older Man*?"

Alexander thought for a moment, smiled and laughed at his father's frolic with logic. He decided that he liked the way his father talked and the words that he used. He didn't understand what some of them meant, or what Betty Grable had to do with the Ford, but everything his father said sure sounded good. Bumping gums with the Old Man was fun.

Alex went to bed that night with tangled emotions. He had experienced perhaps the best day of his life so far, yet he knew his father was leaving for Louisiana the next morning, and there was no way of knowing when he would see the Old Man again.

1938: The Masquerade Is Over ...

... the handwriting is on the wall ...

In less than two years, the international events of 1938 had given testimony to the ineffectuality of the League of Nations, the disastrous result of appeasement diplomacy, and the unfortunate consequence of ignoring the handwriting on the wall. The world was a simmering pot about to boil over.

A rejuvenated, recycled, reinvented World War I corporal named Adolph Hitler had become chancellor of the new German Reich, had annexed Austria, and was about to lay claim to Czechoslovakia.

President Roosevelt[*] declared that the United States would not join a British-French *stop-Hitler bloc* and declared that America would remain neutral in the event of German aggression against Czechoslovakia.

Italy's Benito Mussolini proclaimed the country was under totalitarian rule with his Doctrine of Fascism.

With the help of German Nazis and Italian Fascists, Spain's Francisco Franco was fighting and winning a civil war against Spanish Royalists.

In the new Soviet Union, Joseph Stalin was eliminating his political enemies in violent purges by banishment to Siberia, imprisonment, or execution.

On the other side of the world, Japan ruthlessly occupied wide swaths of China as the two nations fought the Second Sino-Japanese War.

The world was either simmering, smoking, or about to catch fire. Nicholas sensed it.

In Mount Clemens, Michigan, Nicholas had arrived home on Wednesday, May 11th, for five days off. He had spent the last six months bombinating over Mexican farm fields, sweet-talking señoritas, filling up on tamales, drinking tequila and Victoria beer. As his first order of business, he drove to the Bank of Detroit on Griswold Street, opened another savings account in his name, and paid off the $1500, three-year mortgage he had secured in 1935. The Throckmorton home on Second Street was theirs, free and clear. He also opened a safe deposit box for his pilot license, marriage certificate, and the deed to the home. For lack of reason, he also stuck in the opened box of Smith & Wesson shells from the trunk of the Ford.

There were three more things he wanted to accomplish during the five days he would be home. He had allotted three days to get the first two done; expecting that the third bit of business could possibly use up the last two.

Nick's next task was to create birthday memories that Alex would not soon forget. He used Thursday and Friday to accomplish the second goal he had set for himself.

Saturday, May 14th was Alexander's tenth birthday. At first light, Nick had awakened his son and made a bunk-house breakfast of a *Popeye egg* for him and Nora: an egg snuggled and fried within a cut-out circle in a slice of bread and served with bacon.

After breakfast, Nick suggested to Alex, "It might be a good idea to go down the basement steps and see if there is anything new and shiny down there, but be sure to turn on the stairway light first. I think there could be a birthday present hidden away on the other side of the coal bin. You should be able to scrap that Montgomery Ward relic and ride in style for a change."

His father's words tipped Alex off. The mystery of the birthday gift was over. It was certainly a bicycle. Alex guessed right. Just as his father had told him, there was something hidden in the dusty darkness: a new, blazing red Schwinn with smooth-riding balloon tires. Once he and his father muscled it upstairs and outside, there wasn't one full minute before he was sitting upon the saddle and peddling up and down Second Street.

At noon, Nora needed some of her strongest language to coerce him inside for lunch. The tomato soup and cheese sandwich were only the appetizers. Afterwards, Alex sat wide-eyed behind ten tiny flickering candles freely dripping wax onto the white confectioner frosting of his chocolate birthday cake. Nick and Nora sat close, watching the candles burn quickly down to the icing while they finished singing two hurried verses of *Happy Birthday* right before Nora pleaded, "Blow them out Alex! Make a wish and blow them out!"

With a lungful of air, the flames were extinguished; lines of grey smoke circled upward to the ceiling, and the smell of paraffin and burnt sugar frosting drifted over the kitchen table. Alexander was triumphant. Nora pulled the candle stubs and dried wax from the cake and sliced off three pieces. Nick stepped to the Kelvinator and brought out the paper half-quart tub of Stroh's* vanilla ice cream and spooned out three servings, emptying the container.

Afterwards, they went outdoors to take a few photographs that Nora could share with her family in Oshkosh. As soon as the camera was put away, Alex was back aboard his Schwinn.

Part two of Nicholas' plan had gone very well. Later in the evening, he would tell Alex that he could expect another present the next day; it would be a Sunday surprise.

Nick was ready for the third part of his grand plan. Over the last months, he had decided it was time to have a long, meaningful conversation with Nora. Things were about to change, and he felt it was necessary to set the record straight and air out the linens. They sat in the living room with two cups of freshly brewed Eight O'Clock coffee.

When Nick started talking, he spoke steadily and nearly in rhythm. Nora knew that her husband had something on his mind; something important to him, at the very least.

"It's been ten years, Nora. Ten years since Alexander was born. He's a wonderful boy, a wonderful son. He loves you to bits, you know. I'm especially proud of him, and even more proud of you. You're one helluva good mother ... and ..."

Nora made a face and groaned at those words, but Nick continued, "... and don't you say anything about my words. I get tired of explaining myself, damn it all ... please, just accept that it's just the way I say things and leave it at that, all right? You're a good mother and that means a lot. A lot to me, and I imagine it means a lot to that Man Upstairs that you worship and pray to."

"What exactly are you trying to say, Nicholas? Go ahead and spit it out. There's no need to mince your words. I'm a big girl."

"Give me a minute, please ... be patient and listen. We have to talk about this and quit ignoring everything that's happened over the years and pay attention to what's going on now ... once I wondered if we could ever love again like we loved way back then, back in '27 ... eleven years ago when I first laid eyes on you at your mother's lunch wagon. We knew love, Nora. We really did, and you cannot deny that. There's no way you can deny that."

She did not know what to expect. Her eyes were fixed on him. She had an expression that defied both emotion and definition.

"I was wrong and should've known better and it's a mistake that I've been burdened with ever since. But don't misunderstand what I'm saying, Nora. Oh, I don't regret the birth of our son, far from it. From the day he was born, he has given me reason to carry on. And I love you for giving him to me ... to us. When you were in the hospital, sick with that appendicitis, it made me think how much you've given me. You saved me in '27, Nora. You saved me in ways you may never understand. It's unfortunate ... maybe that's a bad word ... I think it's a sin that the Church had to drive a wedge between us. I know that you and your priest and nuns don't think so, but I sure as hell do."

"I will not let you talk to me like that, Nicholas. It's blasphemy."

"Listen, Nora ... you can believe what you want, and let the Church tell you what to think, but know this: people have made babies, and more babies, and more babies since the beginning of time. It's too late to change anything now, but think about this: where was the forgiveness for you and me that the Church talks about all the time? I got the big old finger of damnation pointed right at me. The Detroit diocese handed me a one-way ticket to the Devil."

He lit a cigarette and took a gulp of coffee. Although his voice was steady, and matter-of-fact, his pent-up frustration and disappointment was evident. "But all that's just water under the bridge, and it ain't going to change. You are my wife and as your husband I must provide you and our son with a roof over your heads and clothes on your back. I paid off the house on Wednesday and the deed is free and clear, so you never need to worry about paying a mortgage. Ever. The place is paid for."

He took a long draw on the cigarette, looked into his wife's dark chocolate eyes and began again, "Maybe I should've swallowed my pride and dove into the Church with you in 1927 ... but I didn't. They never did nothing for me and they sure as hell didn't offer me a hand up. I am what I am, and that's what I am. And like I said, things ain't going to change now."

A single tear rolled downed Nora's cheek.

"But then I started dancing with the Devil, didn't I? I found solace and a warm bed with Gladys. And I'm sorry about that ... I am ... but she tempted me, and I needed her loving. I can sometimes end up cold and alone at night, and I hate that feeling. My desires were real, and my actions were awfully well-intended ... but they all turned out bad, didn't they? And sometimes I wish I would've had the guts to quit and cut my losses and just leave. But I have a debt to you, Nora. I promised to provide for you. And after Gladys, I finally was forced to get my mind straight. I went to Buffalo and did what needed to be done, and I dealt with the death of my mother and sisters, and I have accepted their passing. It has taken me some time, but finally I have come to peace with it all."

Although none of this was news, and she couldn't accept his point of view, Nora was surprised that her husband was trying to explain his logic, actions, and the consequences that accompanied them.

"Maybe it sounds like I'm talking in circles, but what I'm dancing around is this, Nora: I'm going to enlist in the Army Air Corps as a pilot if they'll have me. It'll be the same thing I'm doing now ... just flying around, except that I'll have a uniform and better equipment. And besides, the Air Corps will need pilots ... I really think so ... I know so. And as a matter of fact, one of my ground crew, a kid from Carolina, mechanic Bob McElvoy, is going to sign up with me on Monday."

Nora opened up, "What brought all this on, then? Sometimes I wonder if you have a conscience, Nicholas, and if you know why you do what you do. Nothing bothers you; nothing. You just fly away, like you're free as a bird. You've been gone so much I don't notice you anymore. Are you in trouble or something?"

"No, no, no ... no trouble. Nothing like that. And make no mistake, I've got a conscience. Gangsters, bank robbers, cold-blooded killers, murderers, and arsonists are the ones that don't have a conscience. I've got a conscience, all right ... don't you think twice about that. And like it says in the Bible, *an eye for an eye*. The reaper of vengeance can look the guilty in the eye and watch him die, because the death sentence is justified. If only I could make tomorrow hurry to yesterday and today tomorrow, life would be a helluva lot easier."

"You're not making sense now, Nicholas. You're talking nonsense like a parrot in a pet shop."

"I'm just being honest here, Sweetheart. I'm tired of it all. Tired of flying around spreading lime and killing bugs. I want a meaningful job ... a goal, a mission ... something with duty and purpose. Maybe in some religious sense I'm looking for redemption. You, of all people, should be able to understand that."

"Why are you telling me all this now? About what you want? Why now? It's Alexander's birthday!"

"Put it this way: I had to tell somebody, and I picked you. I owe it to you and after all, you're my wife. And believe me, I've tried talking to myself ... just to have somebody to talk to ... but it turns out that I'm not a very good listener.

"And the sky around here just isn't big enough for me. I'm only comfortable with twenty miles of elbow room."

Nick wondered if his words had merely muddied the water. He knew fully well that secrets are only secrets if they are kept. He really wanted his wife to understand what brought him home this time. He knew she couldn't, and he wouldn't tell her.

1938: Something To Remember You By ...

Goodbye, good luck and God bless you ...

No matter where it landed, the 15th of the month was always Visitor's Day at Selfridge Army Air Field. The day after his son's birthday, Nick drove there without mentioning one clue of their destination to Alex. Upon their arrival, the boy was walking on the moon; intense and silent with his eyes flying from plane to runway to plane to hangar and back to plane.

Nick parked the Ford at Hanger 2C, reached under the front seat, pulled out a paper sack and gave his son the last of his birthday gifts: a white silk scarf purchased in Brownsville, Texas and a silver pocket watch from a pawn shop in Lincoln, Nebraska. He explained the practicality of each gift to his son, "That scarf will keep the cold wind from pushing into your jacket and shirt while you're peddling that new Schwinn, and that pocket watch will let you know how fast you can get from one place to another. So, when you think about it, you got all the tools that a pilot needs to get somewhere fast and warm, just like your old man."

Alex was examining the gifts, fingering the scarf and pocket watch. "Is this where your airplane is parked, Papa?"

"Not now, but maybe someday. Tomorrow I'm signing up for the Air Corps, Alex and because I'll be an Army pilot, I could be away from home longer than usual. But I'll be back, you can count on it. But in the meantime, I want you to be good for your mother, listen to what she says and always be back home before the streetlights come on. All right?"

Alexander was studying the pocket watch in the palm of his hand. "Do you think about me when you're flying in your airplane, Papa?"

"Sometimes ... when I'm not busy doing my job."

"I think about you a lot ... almost all of the time." Alex wrapped the scarf threefold around his neck and hooked the watch chain to his belt loop.

"This has been my best birthday ever, Papa. Thanks for all this stuff." He looked to his father and smiled like the Cheshire Cat. His grin forced dimples into each cheek.

"What I really want to say is: thanks for all the darb, Old Man!" Alex's chuckle quickly progressed to laughter.

It was the first belly laugh Alex had ever shared with Nicholas. His ten-year-old son had aped him with all the swagger and confidence of a border town bartender. It meant something to Nicholas, but he struggled to understand exactly what it meant.

It was clear that Alex had a quick wit and could use it. His son also had shown that he could be sentimental without getting emotional. At that moment, Nick gave credence to Nora's parenting skills and appreciated her more than ever. He knew his son was worldly enough to get along with only a *part-time, here-today, and gone-tomorrow* father.

It was, perhaps, their best day together. They walked for the better part of three hours in and out of the hangars and mechanics' sheds. Alex sat in the cockpits of a Jenny, which was the first plane his father flew, and a factory-fresh P-36[*] Mohawk from the Curtiss-Wright factory in Buffalo. It was indeed a birthday that neither Nick nor Alex would forget.

Nicholas had spent five days doing what he wanted to get done. It was Monday, May 16th when Nick was ready to complete the fourth and final task that he wanted to accomplish in Mount Clemens. He said his goodbyes to Nora and Alex that morning, and drove off to meet young Duster mechanic, Robert (Mac) McElvoy at the enlistment office of the Army Air Corps at Selfridge[*]. Neither Nick nor his buddy Bob had any inkling of what they could expect, but it did not surprise them that after their initial bend-over-and-touch-your-toes physical, they ended up spending the entire day taking hearing, eyesight, equilibrium, and aptitude tests.

Mac was eighteen years old and hailed from Asheville, North Carolina. At sixteen he was a capable engine mechanic at his uncle's garage and looking for the chance to expand his horizons and get out of the Appalachian mountains. A world of opportunity opened when young McElvoy happened upon a Delta Dusters 'help wanted' ad in the Candler Gazette. After a twenty-hour bus ride from Asheville to Montgomery, Alabama, a handshake and a scribbled job application, he was hired. During the spring of 1937, he met Duster pilot Nicholas Throckmorton at Walker Army Airfield in Victoria, Kansas. They embarked on a friendship that would last for more than a decade.

Nicholas Throckmorton and Robert McElvoy qualified for the Aviation Cadet program and enlisted as corpsmen with the rank of Private. Although he would not be granted any special privileges, Nick could finish his initial training cycle as a Lieutenant Cadet. He had the advantage of experience and an Army Air Corps pilot certification from 1931. Bob McElvoy could qualify as a Staff Sergeant, *'flying sergeant'*, pilot upon his satisfactory completion of training.

The men were to report back the following morning at ten o'clock to be sworn into service, and for orientation before leaving for eight months of Primary and Basic Training, and an additional four months of flight and tactical training. In total, Nick and Mac could expect a minimum of one year of training* as Air Corps Flight Cadets. The enlistment officer made an empty promise that if they performed well during training, and finished the course with merit, they could be assigned to the same unit after graduation.

That particular Monday night, May 16th, was the proverbial 'last hurrah' of men going into the service of their Country. Nick and Mac drove to the Ambassador Bridge end of Grand River Boulevard, parked the Ford on Fort Street and got two rooms at the Windsor Gate Hotel. Taking the suggestion of the desk clerk, they walked a block to 24th Street to a Canadian-owned, British-themed barroom named The Cock and Hen. The anticipation of the next day put a thin blanket of caution over their celebratory mood. Their lives were about to drastically change from the daredevil attitude of crop dusting to the disciplined rigor of military life. Without saying so, neither Nick nor Mac wanted to start flight school on the wrong foot. They claimed a small table, ordered shepherd's pie and a cold, frothy pitcher of Stroh's Bohemian. They settled in for an evening of beer drinking, cigarettes, stories, anecdotes as well as lies, about women, and speculation about their future in the Air Corps.

"Do you really think war will break out in Europe, Nick?"

"Don't know for sure, but I expect it will. You don't always need a weathervane to see which way the wind is blowing."

Nick had known scores of mechanics and flight crew over the years, but Mac had a special quality: an eye for perfection, a sixth sense of sorts, an ability to detect flaws. Just two weeks after he had been hired, the young fellow from the Blue Ridge Mountains spotted stripped threads on a tension bolt on the control column of Nick's Stearman. After all the pilot's close calls and numerous near-misses with wires and nipped tree limbs, McElvoy's keen regard for niggling detail had caught Nick's attention. The kid from Carolina always began any assigned task by jumping in feet-first, ready to work, willing to learn, and able to see it through. He shrugged off bumps and bruises, never belly-ached about any job, and wasn't in the least bit squeamish. Mac had witnessed an inattentive, careless Mexican field spotter get decapitated by the center landing strut of a 1923 Jenny Standard and helped gather up all the bits afterwards without a whisper of distress. Nick liked having Mac around and could see a bit of himself in the young man from Asheville. Blood didn't seem to bother Mac the way a loose bolt or frayed cable did.

The two men were working on their second Cock-and-Hen pitcher when they were approached by a tall, thin fellow in a badly wrinkled ten-dollar suit. He had a cigarette in one hand

and a half-glass of beer in the other. He appeared lost, as if looking for directions.

"Do you fellows know a good automobile mechanic nearby? I'm afraid my '26 Essex blew a bearing and is probably all frozen up and whockerjawed." The stranger was in his mid-to-late thirties with thinning light brown hair and appeared to be extremely exasperated. He was certainly tired and feeling his beer.

Mac started laughing. "Sorry, Bud. Just that I never heard that *whockerjawed* word before. Where you from?"

"The name's Walter ... Walter Hendricks from East Wisconsin ... Appleton, just south of Green Bay."

Nick broke in, "Essex is just another name for a Hudson, and everybody knows that a Hudson has crappy bearings ... so ... I think your buggy is ready for the junk heap, my friend. It's ready for scrap, I'm afraid ... but you're quite a ways from home ... aren't you? What do you do for a living? You need the car? It seems to me like you need a car."

"I'm a salesman ... a salesman for Fuller Brush* ... you know brushes, brooms, cleaners ... household items ... and I travel quite a bit and yes, I need the car. Well, let me say I need ... *a* car. Me and my job depend on it. Maybe I should ask where I can find a good automobile dealer ... come to think of it, this is Detroit. Of all the cities in America, I should be able to get a car here, right?" He forced a chuckle from a beer burp.

Quick as a cat on a mouse, Nick asked, "Do you have a hundred and fifty dollars to spend, Bud?"

After a moment of feigned caution, Walter answered, "I have maybe a hundred and a bit more, but I could write a check for the rest. Why?"

"It's your lucky day buddy. Me and my pal ... Mac, here ... well, we're going in the Air Corps tomorrow, and I got a '36 Ford, five-window V8, maybe 5000 miles on her and she's spent most of her time just sitting in my garage. She's parked half a block down the street, she's dark grey and got a

140

nice smooth, rounded ass-end and headlights just like Betty Grable's tits. Interested?"

"How much? You said one-fifty."

Nick stood, pushed his chair back and took the traveling salesman's hand, "Tell you what, Walter … a hundred dollars cash money, and I'll sign over the title right now, and you can ditch that shit Essex, and peddle your mops and brushes from a good car."

Nick swallowed a mouthful of beer, struggled a bit with his balance and continued, "My wife doesn't drive, and the coupe would just sit in my garage gathering dust anyhow. And at least the car will do somebody some good. I know I'll miss her, but where I'm going, I sure as hell can't take Betty's boobies or backside with me."

6: FINDING FENNARIO, 1939-43

November 1939: What's New? ...

Happy Franksgiving ...

Had Lieutenant Nicholas Throckmorton enlisted in the Air Corps, or did he muster the Air Corps into his life?

Quite simply, it was a two-way street, a mutual tit-for-tat coterie, and a calculated means to an end. His conscription was a self-imposed exile from his life in Mount Clemens, an extended tour of duty away from his family. A full year and a half after his enlistment, he had not returned home. The letters that he and Nora exchanged were merely lightly salted tidbits of trivial news and platitudes. He missed his son and wrote to Alexander regularly, relaying whatever anecdotes, stories or humor he could. Nick would enclose comic strips from *Stars and Stripes** and an occasional five-dollar bill. His son wrote short letters and sent some Detroit Tigers box scores and clippings about the football Lions and hockey Redwings in season. Following Torricelli's execution, Nick sought isolation and had devised a way to get it. He felt vindicated.

With his Duster experience, attitude, attention and devotion to the job, Nick excelled at Army Flight School. After a year in and around San Antonio, Texas, he received his commission as Second Lieutenant in the United States Air Corps on June 5, 1939.

Nick's world immediately started to evolve in ways not even a gypsy fortune teller could have foreseen. It began with gradual changes that came in subtle, nondescript, innocuous increments that went unnoticed. He and Sergeant McElvoy were assigned to the 20th Pursuit Group at Barksdale Airfield, near Shreveport, Louisiana for bombing and gunnery training. It was at Barksdale that he was first noticed by an up-and-coming staff officer: Major Dennis Blackburn. Nick didn't know it then, nor would he recognize the name, but half a world away and years later, they would cross paths in a way that would alter Nick's life forever.

On November 15, Nick's outfit (the 20th) was mobilized to Moffett Field, California, about forty miles south of San Francisco. His squadron was empowered with the Curtiss P-36 Mohawk, the new closed-cockpit fighter fresh off the Buffalo assembly lines.

Upon his arrival on the West Coast, opportunity and proximity prompted him to make an improbable, spontaneous decision. Following more than a decade of separation, he would at least try to connect with his brother. Three years earlier, his uncle had told him that Leopold was a San Francisco cop, but knowing how the passage of time can change things, and the uncertainty of where to begin looking for him, Nick searched for the name *Throckmorton* in the city telephone directory* first. His hunch was rewarded. What he discovered on page 114 quickened his heart and teased his expectation:

Throckmorton Leopold   SF city police
96 Cayuga Av   Balboa Pk 689

Nick secured a twenty-four-hour pass for Thanksgiving* and bought a coach ticket for the midday Union Pacific express train from Palo Alto to San Francisco. After a short Yellow Cab ride from Union Station, he stood rapping his knuckles upon the front door of 96 Cayuga Avenue in the city's growing Balboa Park neighborhood. It was one o'clock in the afternoon, November 23rd.

Nicholas had expected the fearless, gorgeous, flirty Phryné whom he remembered from twelve years earlier to answer his knock. She didn't, but he appreciated what he saw, regardless of his confusion. A smiling, proportioned blonde in a clinging cotton house dress had appeared at the door. A curly-haired, wide-eyed, curious toddler was snuggled close at her side. The woman's shapely form, hair color, and blue eyes summoned his memories of Gladys and the fleeting emotional pang that came with them. He wondered momentarily whatever could have become of Phryné. As a young man of sixteen and seventeen, he could not help but fantasize after his older brother's frisky dame. She was, in fact, deliciously delectable.

Time stalled, lost altitude, and crashed to a halt. The next two seconds passed as an eternity. The pilot's eyes instinctively went skyward, and Nick assessed the weather. The morning fog was stubbornly holding on. The wintry air was thick, damp and dingy, with visibility limited to a quarter mile or less and an uncomfortably low ceiling. Conditions were far from ideal, but navigable with due diligence. His anticipated reunion had been dampened by a wet blanket of questions and doubts.

Although Nick knew full well that he was not on a military installation, he found himself standing at parade rest. He swallowed his pride and accepted the humbling that resulted from his situation. He blamed it on the training ... and every Corpsman knew that Army Air Corps training was the best damned training.

He removed his aviators* and stuck them in his breast pocket. In one flowing motion, he then removed his service cap, stuck it under his left armpit, nodded and introduced himself, "Good afternoon, Ma'am. I think maybe I made a mistake and have the wrong address ... but ... my name is Throckmorton ... Nicholas Throckmorton. I'm looking for my older brother, Leopold ... Leopold's my brother."

He felt defenseless, pitiful, lost and looking for direction; like a newly weaned whelp pulled from its mother. He could feel his wool slacks prickle on his buttocks, thighs and calves. His tie uncomfortably pushed at his Adam's apple with each beat of his heart. Nick's olive brown dress jacket itched through his khaki shirt and once again, he silently cursed the laundry service for starching the stiff collar that was biting into his neck. The starch further validated his decision to stop wearing jockey shorts.

"Golly! It's you! Nicholas! Yes! I see the resemblance! Come in, come in!"

Her welcoming voice ended his torturous wait. He followed her and the little girl inside, along the shellacked hallway floor to the living room. His eyes surveyed his surroundings. The place was neat, sparsely decorated and appeared to be recently constructed. The rooms were bright, with white painted moldings and varnished wainscot in the parlor and dining room. The smell of roasting turkey and apple pie curled through the home. He also studied the young woman's curves as she walked.

"Have a seat, please. Right there on the davenport, Nicholas. I'm Eloisa, your brother's wife and this is your niece, Shirley. I'll go and wake up Leopold. It's about time for him to get up anyhow! Goodness! Wait until he sees you!"

"No, don't ..."

She interrupted, "Never mind! He got home at six this morning, and he's usually up by now anyway. Wait right here, Nicholas, and I'll go and wake him, and I'll put on a pot of coffee, and be right back. My Leopold is going to be so surprised ... this is so exciting!

"Come on, Honeybunch, let's go wake up Daddy!"

Nick watched her scoop up the youngster and leave the room with quickened step. He had no more than a minute to wonder whatever happened with his brother's marriage to Phryné. Blonde Eloisa and little Shirley were back in the room before his imagination could speed down that runway and fully take flight.

"He's up! I told him we had company, but I refused to say who was here, so boy, oh boy, he will be surprised! This I got to see, so the coffee can wait!"

They walked to the sofa, and she sat at the other end with her daughter between them. Eloisa and Nick sat waiting for Leopold. Sweet little Shirley was studying Nick.

Twelve years divided by two brothers equals six hours ...

After Leopold's expression of surprise, back pats and a hearty handshake, Nicholas and Leopold began their afternoon together knowing fully well that there would still be unfilled holes in the dike when the tide rolled out again.

Eloisa brought coffee and disappeared back into the kitchen with Shirley, leaving the brothers in the living room with the pot, two cups and some lady fingers.

The first thing Nick mentioned was that he had to be back at the Air Corps base in Palo Alto by midnight. He said it without forethought, stretching the truth to fit his fancy. Perhaps his subconscious drove him to be cautious, not wanting to press his luck, or squash his fear that old memories could return and cause an old fire to burn newer, deeper scars. Whatever the case, Nick believed that he needed to tread softly on any freshly plowed ground he and his brother could be turning over.

Next, he found it necessary to ask, "What about Phryné? What happened there? I expected to see her at your door because even the FBI told me that you two were married. Isn't Eloisa the gal that hung on Cafferty's arm all those years ago back in Buffalo?"

Leopold shifted in his seat, and started, "Phryné and I were married in Chicago, and we split for good right after we arrived in Los Angeles. We both made mistakes after that mess in Buffalo. I made some big ones, but she was almost my biggest. Getting married to her, I mean. Even if I gave it a second thought, it would still have been too little, too late."

Leopold sat straight in an overstuffed armchair, rubbed his open palms down his thighs to his knees and began to ramble, "But wrinkles can work themselves out, it seems. Phryné ended up marrying a movie producer and started working as a song and dance girl for Paramount Pictures. I was walking through a personal Hell after I got out here and began to suffer from nightmares, almost threw my life into the bay and was on a path to wrack and ruin. The Salvation Army helped me pick up the pieces of my busted life, then I went to sea for almost two years and joined the police force, found Eloisa years later completely by chance, married her and here I am in a new house ... a patrol officer with a beautiful wife and daughter, and another little one due sometime in May ... but how about you? You married yet, Nick? Any kids?"

Nick knew it was coming. It was his turn, and about halfway through the story about his hasty marriage of necessity with Nora, they took a break. Leopold grabbed the coffee pot, walked to the kitchen, and brought out a tin of Planter's salted peanuts*, and an unopened fifth of Four Roses bourbon. Leopold broke the tax seal with his fingernail and filled their coffee cups with the potent aged nectar. One cup was followed by another. An hour passed and a short pack* of Camel cigarettes went up in smoke.

Nick began his history, "I made Nora a victim. I took advantage of her innocence. We were young and I was dumb. The fire that killed Ma and our sisters turned my life inside out and you and Phryné flew the coop and were long gone, and I was alone and lost. I found Nora, we made Alexander and that's the end of it. I admit it: I was weak. Her family, their Old-World traditions, and a crazy, zealous pursuit of Catholic purity sealed my fate. After she got pregnant, Nora gave me a lot of nothing. Absolutely nothing, so I found what I needed elsewhere. But I promised Nora that I wouldn't back away from my obligations, and I haven't. She and our son Alexander have a home, clothes on their backs, and food in their belly."

Leopold asked, "If your wife won't be your wife, you know what I mean ... if she keeps it locked up and won't give herself to you ... why do you stay married, Nick? I mean, why drag your heart over burning sand and trudge through the dunes of that desert?"

"You don't need to worry about me dying of thirst in no desert, Leopold. I can whet my whistle for nookie, and I get my fair share of warm, fresh muffin. And believe you me, I can get what I need, whenever I want it or need it, no matter where I am. No stale stuff, either." Nick lifted his cup, and offered a ribald toast, "Here's to the invention of the zipper*." He swallowed more whiskey.

Nick guffawed at his own twisted humor and continued, "The truth is, Leopold ... the truth is ... that I've never felt obliged to stay in one place very long. If I did, my wanderlust and the muss and fuss of everything else would only drive me nuts. I got my pilot paper in 1930, spent six years crop dusting from Ypsilanti to the Yucatan and last year I joined the Air Corps. And now I'm still flying all around and looking all around for what ... and why ... I don't know. Maybe when I find it, I'll know … some magical, wonderful paradise in the clouds, maybe ... a place where I can hang my hat on a moonbeam.

"For a long time, I blamed you, Leopold. I blamed you for everything. I even blamed you for the mess my life had become. I was wrong. It turns out that I've made plenty of mistakes all by myself. I admit to some; others I don't. I don't think regret is a good thing. I think if you regret what you did, you'll never do anything worthwhile again. You live and learn. And looking back, I can say that I wouldn't change anything ... nothing at all. So far it's been a helluva ride and that's what life is ... one helluva ride."

The brothers looked at one another, their eyes stuck in an unsteady gaze with the haze that comes with a half-bottle of Kentucky bourbon. Perhaps ten seconds ticked off Nicholas' dual-dial Benrus wristwatch.

Leopold poured another half cup for himself. He sipped at the whiskey, set it back down to the coffee table and wiped his mouth and mustache with the back of his hand. "You blamed me, and me, truthfully, I blamed myself, Nick. So, I guess the jury was unanimous ... talk about a jury ... a year or so ago I heard that dago bastard Torricelli finally got what was coming to him."

Nicholas feigned curiosity and asked, "No shit? What?"

"Geoffrey, he's Ellie's brother-in-law ... well, he's City Editor at the Sacramento Bee and still has an old buddy back at the Courier in Buffalo ... anyway, a couple years back he told me and the wife that dirty wop Lorenzo Torricelli was killed by his own mob. They found his body full of bullet holes dumped on the upper west side waterfront and the investigation died right along with the crooked Mafia bastard."

For Nicholas, his brother's words sounded like the pages of an eighth-grade mathematics textbook being slammed shut for summer vacation. For three years, Nick tried to pull up the covers and forget what had happened on Grote Street in 1936. It was finally over. School was out.

Nick held his empty cup across the table for a refill. Leopold spilled a few drops during the pour. Hundred proof Kentucky was beginning to hamstring the Throckmorton brothers.

Nick took a large swallow, leaned toward his brother, and spoke in a low voice, "Torricelli had it coming ... and finally ... I can feel good knowing that justice played out in the end. And I can tell you this: it feels good to know he's dead. Damn good. I sleep better knowing the bastard is dead."

Leopold nodded in agreement and added, "Wish I could have been there to see the look in Torricelli's eyes when he knew he was getting the kiss off. I bet he shit himself. They do that sometimes, you know."

Nick let out a snide chuckle. "Yeah, I heard that. If I could have it my way, first I would've given him a painful gut shot ... laughed at him and then finished him off with one right square between the eyes. Then I would've unloaded the last four slugs into his chest ... one for Ma and one for each of our sisters ... Johanna, Ottilie, and Hilde."

Although Nicholas' off-the-cuff description sounded eerily similar to what Leopold had heard from Ellie's brother-in-law years earlier, he pooh-poohed it as sheer coincidence.

Eloisa appeared in the doorway, "Dinner's on the table, fellas. It's time to put your man-talk on the back burner while we eat ... and Leopold, Sweetheart, please take the turkey out of the oven, onto the platter and bring it to the dining room for me. Thank youuuu."

Eloisa had managed to have dinner ready and on the table by five o'clock. Roasted turkey, bread stuffing, mashed potatoes, green beans, and cranberry Jell-O* salad with Pet* milk faux whipped cream were served from miss-matched pieces of china bowls onto faded blue onion dinner plates. It was Nick's first home-cooked meal in over a year and as it would play out, it would be his last for quite a while – years in fact.

The small talk over dinner covered bits and pieces of Eloisa and Leopold's lives since their accidental meeting in the summer of '34. She colored the timeline of their five years together with a wide brush and was able to cover the biggest questions Nicholas had.

After the meal, the flyer, the cop and Four Roses were back in the living room and were later joined by Ellie, who managed to get Shirley into bed and asleep by 7:30. The two-year-old's curly blonde locks matched Shirley Temple's, her namesake. Not more than a half hour later, the conversation had played itself out.

The past is interesting only to those who have lived it. For everyone else, it's just a curious storyline that can become tediously repetitious. And bourbon builds the boredom.

Eloisa tried to cement a future get-together and suggested, "We need to do this again, when you can get more than a few hours of liberty from the Army, Nick. It would give us all the chance to properly catch up and I think it's important to keep the family bonds tight. I know, because I missed that for so many years, and I know you can appreciate what I mean by that. You, too, Honey."

Nicholas nodded, "I would like that Ellie, but truth is, things are changing quickly in the world and my immediate future is somewhat up in the air, if I can use those words. And even Little Orphan Annie sees what's coming: *We got to beat them at their own game*, is what she says."

Nick continued, "*The whole of Europe is on fire and it's going to spread* ... that's what I say."

Although Eloisa just smiled and considered that Nick was only joking, Leopold sensed that his brother was serious.

"Really? You see trouble, Nick?"

"Things are happening all over the world. And sooner rather than later, we're going to get involved. No matter what you read in the paper or President Frank tells you on his radio chats ... all hell is going to break loose ... without a doubt. Curtiss and Lockheed ain't making airplanes for the hell of it. They're making them faster with bigger engines, with superchargers and bigger, better guns. Next time around it will be serious."

Eloisa leaned forward in her chair, "You're scaring me, Nicholas ... do you really think so?" She studied him.

Nick shifted his weight on the divan, looked into her blue eyes, lit a cigarette, and added, "Hell, yes, but you don't have to worry, Ellie ... it won't happen here. It will happen on the other side of the ocean. That's where the storm clouds are forming ... just like the last one ... and your husband, hell, he's a San Francisco cop. He ain't going nowhere. He'll protect you." For a moment, Nick's eyes selfishly held onto her soul.

A few seconds of sticky silence passed before he went on, trying to switch the topic, "But this was a good day. It was a pleasure to meet you, Eloisa. You made one helluva meal and you got the prettiest little girl in the world. I'm so glad I found you both. Now we can get back to living our lives and knowing what we know for sure ... me and Leopold are brothers and always will be. We're the only family we got. Someday we'll do this again, won't we? You bet we will."

Although honey-colored Kentucky fog was blurring his thoughts and slurring his words, Nicholas knew his shallow platitude for what it was: a wordy, evasive goodbye. His brother was alive and well and doing just fine for himself. Leopold was content with his life, had a beautiful wife, a lovely little girl, a new home, and a secure job within San Francisco's police department.

The Throckmorton brothers shook hands, forced farewell hugs, and promised to keep in touch. Eloisa was able to get Nick's service number and address at Moffett Airfield. He made a hollow promise that he would forward his permanent mailing address as soon as he knew what it was. Nick boldly held Eloisa close with his hands at her hipline and gave her an awkward, mislaid kiss that graced both her lips and cheek. Eloisa considered Nick's misplaced hands and muddled kiss to be a result of the bourbon. It bothered Leopold, but he fought the urge to mention it or admonish his brother. He also believed that the drink was certainly to blame.

Leopold telephoned for a Goldengate Cab, and ten minutes later the Army Air Corps Lieutenant left Balboa Park for the train ride back to his Palo Alto barracks, his olive brown wool blanket, two-inch straw mattress, and metal bunk.

Nick was glad he had decided to look up his brother. The meal, bourbon, and conversation were good. The news about Torricelli came as a relief. Leopold may have become a policeman, but Nick had direct knowledge that the legal system itself was flawed. It was obvious that the cops had no control over the mob. Moreover, he saw himself rather than his elder brother as an enforcer of righteousness and an equalizer for lopsided justice. Most importantly, he had reaffirmed that he was good at what he did, happy to have gotten away with it, and could be damn proud of it.

The brothers would never meet again. They had grown too far apart since they left Buffalo in 1927. There wasn't any bad blood, but like oil and water, morality and reality, honesty and politics, best-laid plans and misfortune, some things don't easily mix.

1941-42: The Dipsy Doodle …

A dream, then reality...

The *M/V Jaegersfontaine** was slowly crawling upriver and approaching Rangoon, Burma, cutting through the dense sub-tropical air, spewing thick, black smoke from her funnel, sounding brass air horns, and leading the way with her bow painter and chain against the lazy current of the Bago estuary. The new, Dutch-flagged diesel freighter was under exclusive contract with the United States War Department for troop and equipment transport.

Nicholas Throckmorton, his pal Robert McElvoy, and one-hundred-twenty other eager young Americans stood along the port and starboard deck rails, catching their first close-up look at the British Crown Colony of Burma. The men watched, wide-eyed in anticipation of all things fantastic. The massive gold dome of the Shwedagon Buddhist Pagoda glistened in the distance, reflecting flashes of mystic, bright yellow light back at the tropical sun.

They had left San Francisco eighteen days earlier, knowing that Rangoon was only their port of debarkation and that their destination was Mandalay, about 400 miles north. The name itself was mysterious enough to evoke images of almond-eyed, black-haired, sorrel-skinned beauties in clingy sarongs. Some fantasized that the elusive Fennario*, or perhaps the mythical land of Shangri La*, could be found somewhere in hot and steamy British Burma.

As the Dutch freighter crept closer to the docks, Nicholas knew the romance was over. The sights and sounds of a far-away port in a far-away land did not disappoint, but the stench that slapped Nick and everyone else in the face was a stark awakening. He suspected it to be much like the jolt of waking up next to a fetid, filthy whore to discover that the singular clean spot on her body is a two-inch circle on her left breast. The odor drove even staunch McElvoy to retch. The place reeked. The river and its banks were awash with garbage, raw sewage, rotting jackfruit and bananas, in addition to all the imaginable flotsam of human presence and maritime commerce.

Since 1937, the Chinese had requested military aid and lobbied hard in Washington for assistance with their ongoing war with the Empire of Japan. Nick, Mac and their shipmates were the first contingent of the AVG* (American Volunteer Group) that had been put together to help the Chinese Air Force protect the only overland life-line to Free China: the decrepit Burma Road. On paper, a total of three hundred men with an average age of nineteen and a half years were listed as carpenters, mechanics, and laborers. The bunch of carrots that had been dangled in front of their American noses was too much for any GI jackass or government mule to resist. The Americans were essentially triple volunteers. First, the men resigned from their Air Corps enlistment; second, they agreed to help the Chinese fight Japan; third, they accepted their assignment to Burma. The pilots were to be rewarded with what could only be called extravagant wages and extremely generous bonuses. The volunteers were to have no uniforms and no ranks, only job descriptions such as wingman, flight or squadron leader, line chief, armorer, mechanic, and the lowly grunt.

Once ashore, the men stood dockside and were met by retired Air Corps Colonel Claire Chennault, a handful of Chinese Air Force officers, and two Curtiss-Wright engineers from Buffalo. British troop busses and halftracks drove them north to the Royal Air Force Keydaw Taungoo aerodrome, where they were to spend the next four months becoming particularly familiar with Curtiss P-40* fighter aircraft and receiving classroom and flight instruction on Japanese air combat tactics from Chennault and the Chinese.

They arrived at Keydaw airfield in the middle of a thunderstorm. Raindrops the size of quarters smashed down upon the roof of the military transport like cannonballs and crashed around them, creating a raging river where the rutted, dirt road should have been. It was a resounding welcome to the tropics.

On December 7, 1941, the Japanese attacked Pearl Harbor. For Nicholas, his fellow pilots, mechanics and ground crew, the Second World War officially began on December 20th, over Yunnan Province in China.

Over the course of the next seven months, it became apparent that "you cannot have a war without somebody getting killed." Twenty-three P-40 pilots were lost in the China-Burma-India (CBI) Theater of operations.

The Flying Tigers' P-40 Warhawks had gun cameras that verified the number of Japanese aircraft destroyed, either in the air or on the ground. It was valuable film. At $620 per month, and the generous Chinese *kill bonus* of $500 per aircraft, after one year with the AVG in Burma and China, Nick had allotted several thousand dollars to the Bank of Detroit. Lieutenant Throckmorton graduated from flying low and slow to low and fast and had become proficient at destroying enemy aircraft and support vehicles on the ground. He provided photographic proof of his penchant for pandemonium and proclivity for punishment of the enemy. His flying skills drew the attention of his commanders. Nick was issued a camera and a sidearm he was somewhat familiar with: a Smith & Wesson 38 caliber revolver. His Army weapon, however, had a considerably longer barrel than the snub-nose he threw into the Niagara River in 1936.

Either from Keydaw, Burma or any of a half dozen or more slapdash Chinese airfields in Yunnan province, Nick carried a Kodak Vigilant 620 in the cockpit of his Warhawk and provided the Group brass with pictures of Japanese airfields and outposts deep into China.

After the Flying Tigers were deactivated in July 1942, Nick was one of the few to rejoin the Army Air Force. Some of the other Tiger pilots became transport fliers in China, whereas hardnosed fliers such as Nick and Mac re-enlisted to serve elsewhere. He was given a promotion to First Lieutenant and Mac was awarded a commission as Second Lieutenant. Seven months of incessant combat had hardened the young McElvoy and further toughened the grizzled Throckmorton. Many more AVG volunteers had decided to return to America and civilian employment.

1942: Playing hopscotch with wallaroos...

Lieutenants Throckmorton and McElvoy were subsequently assigned to the 35th Fighter Group, headquartered in Brisbane, Australia*, and were stationed at Woodstock Airfield, Townsville, Queensland state. With seven months of combat flying under their belts, Nick and Mac were seasoned veterans; part of three new squadrons consisting of dozens of freshly trained pilots from the States.

Days after he and Mac arrived, Nick was promoted to Captain and assigned as Flight Leader of Bravo Flight, 39th Squadron, 35th Fighter Group, and began two weeks of familiarization with the Bell P-39* Airacobra and intense training in the new Lockheed P-38* fighter. It was a rigorous schedule: usually fourteen hours a day of classroom instruction, in-flight training and dodging pesky red kangaroos and smaller marsupials on landing and takeoff.

When the bi-weekly supply, ration and Red Cross shipment from Sydney arrived, the latest news and rumors spread over the base. It seemed that anybody or anything could have wings of their own. Spirits were lifted on the updraft of incoming scuttlebutt.

... and the Army Post Office delivers...

Australia was a world apart from Burma and China. Oppressive jungle, rice paddies, torrential downpours, and 95° temperatures were switched out for the rocky hills, wet summers, and dry 60° winters of the southern hemisphere. Although the Japanese had sporadically bombed targets along the northern Australian coast, it was markedly less hectic and quieter in the land of didgeridoos and koala bears.

Sleep in Australia was also conspicuously different than that in Burma, Siam, or China. There was simply no comparison between the muddy dirt floor of a bamboo and grass shack, a canvas cot, and a wool blanket in a short, four-man tent. When Nick and Mac arrived at Townsend, the Quonset* huts seemed to them to be on par with a Ritz Carlton hotel.

An unexpected windfall occurred at afternoon mail call on August 20th. For the first time since they had left San Francisco a year ago July, Nick and Mac received letters from home. Their mail had finally caught up with them. The only touch of home they had experienced during the time they spent in Burma and China was the occasional carton of American cigarettes off the supply plane from Calcutta, India. The entire AVG joked that the volunteer unit had in fact, fallen off the edge of the Earth. Eight months of redirected, rerouted, redacted, censored, misdirected, torn, and tattered messages from the States finally arrived. It was like winning the Irish Sweepstakes. Mac had two hands full, and Nick had about a dozen letters from Nora, half as many from Alex, and one from Eloisa. He checked the postmarks and read them in order, pouring over every little tidbit of news and trying to picture everything as he remembered it to be back in Mount Clemens.

Nora's letters were only lightly sentimental, short and generally antiseptic. He expected nothing more and quietly hoped she was happy. His son's writings jumped from one thing to another and were loaded with questions and comments that Nick knew he could never answer. He imagined Alexander sitting next to him on the cot and excitedly asking where he flew that day. Nick was confident that someday in the not-too-distant future the war would be over, and his son could know all the answers.

He opened Eloisa's badly worn, creased and soiled letter last, holding it briefly to his nose at the outside chance she had scented it. His name and service number were among only a few characters still legible on the envelope. The beat-up letter appeared to have been all over the Pacific before it had found its way to Australia.

Eloisa Throckmorton
~20 Cayuga Ave.
SF 3, Calif

Lt. Nicholas Throckmorton
O-32487530
c/o postmaster A.P.O. San Diego
35 F.G. 2/15th AAF

SAVE THE
BUY U S

REDIRECTED BY A.A.B.P.O.

January 23, 1942

████████████ San Francisco 3, California

Dear Nicholas,

I have struggled for days trying to finish this letter and there is no easy way to say it. It's been so hard that I have started it and tore it up countless times. I am writing this with a broken heart that I fear will never mend.

Your brother Leopold was killed in the line of duty on January 18th by a very disturbed man. It is not my intention to get you upset but I think I must let you know what has happened. The killer was angry with the ██████ at the loss of his son on the ████████ at ██ ████████. His wife called the police because he was drunk and depressed and getting violent and had been drinking excessively since the ████ ██████ attack and threatened to kill ████████ himself.

When Leopold and his partner responded and identified themselves as police, the man shot through the door with a rifle. The bullet hit your brother in the chest. I was told that he died quickly and didn't suffer. Later, two other officers arrived, and the man was seriously wounded and died at ████████ hospital There ██████████████████ I have enclosed ██████████████ and the obituary from my brother-in-law at ██████████ ██. All of this has turned my life upside down, but the members of the ██ ████ department have helped me so much.

Your brother and I were so fortunate to find each other after so many years and I am glad about the years we had together, no matter how much it was cut short. I am so happy that we were able to start a new life together. Leopold often spoke fondly of his "little brother" and I know he loved you very much. He didn't often get sentimental, but he was a kind and gentle man deep inside. I am so happy that you and Leopold got together again.

The only regret I have is that he won't be able to see his daughter Shirley and son Albert grow up. He would be so proud of them. Telling Shirley that her Daddy went to Heaven was the hardest thing I have ever done. Thank goodness little Al is too young to realize what has happened. Sometimes I cry, because he looks just like his Dad.

Although I am sorry I had to tell you this news I hope it finds you safe and well. I wish you the best wherever you may be and please remember that I will keep you in my prayers.

God Bless,
Love Always,
Eloisa

Nicholas set the letter down on his cot and let his eyes wander down the barracks to the flag hanging up against the far wall. The Stars and Stripes remained on silent, stoic display, and offered him no solace. For a minute or two, he simply stared at the red, white and blue fabric; lost in nothingness.

Although she wrote that she had enclosed newspaper articles, Nick didn't find any inside. He was at first befuddled at the Army's censors and couldn't help but wonder what Eloisa could have written or inserted that was so bad. He had known this practice occurred, but this was the first time he had seen such a letter. He then attributed it to the fact that it was written so soon after the Pearl Harbor attack and it originated in California. About half of the mail that he received from Nora and Alex had been opened, but nothing had been blacked-out. It was amusing and only slightly disquieting that the letters from his wife and son were deemed so innocuous as to not merit censure.

He decided that someday he would take the time and write to Eloisa, thank her for her letter, and reassure her that things always smooth themselves out over time. He could make a shallow promise that he might pay a visit to her and the children after the war.

Nick stood and looked down at the jumble and confusion he had created with the opened envelopes and the pile of handwritten letters, thoughts and wishes laying on his bunk. He quickly sorted out the pages written by his wife and son, and stuck them under the blanket, thinking that he might read them again later. He scooped up Eloisa's letter together with all the envelopes, crumpled and tossed them into the trash bin in the center of the barracks on his way out. The fact that he had just thrown away Eloisa's address never crossed his mind. Mac and everyone else were still pouring over their mail like puppies at a bowl of cornbread and fatback.

He made his way slowly toward the Officer's Mess, lighting a Camel, and trying to think about his up-coming weekend pass.   He felt out-of-place, uncomfortable, distracted, and strangely perplexed. A chill and one of those ever-so-brief shoulder-shaking quivers went up his spine.

As he crossed the boardwalk to the chow hall, Eloisa's news of his brother's death brought him to a sobering realization: his only blood relative in all the world was his son Alexander. Criminal violence had all but ended his bloodline.

He shook the eerie feeling off and wondered what surprise the Mess Sergeant would serve up for dinner. As it turned out, his evening meal of a lonely, lukewarm hotdog, mashed potatoes, and canned peas did nothing for his mood.

That night, Nick wrote two long letters home: one to his son and the other to his wife. While finishing his letter to Alex, he teared up and sensed a hole opening in his heart. He immediately pushed his mind to another place, to Eloisa and San Francisco. Despite the news of his brother's death, he knew he could have never again been close to Leopold and probably would not have written to him, no matter the circumstance.

His conscience grudgingly forced his thoughts back to Buffalo, his childhood, and all the little memories he and his brother once shared. Growing up they had grown apart; at first slowly separated by subtle differences, later torn by value and lifestyle conflicts, and a final, violent blow of tragedy and escape.

August 28, 1942: There's Something In The Air …

The Brisbane boogie-woogie...

With a whoosh of protest from its air brakes, the big blue bus came to a stop curbside on Anne Street, downtown Brisbane. It was a gloriously cool, starlit August evening in the Australian winter. The open-roof Leyland Lion was full of Army Air Force flyers from Antil Plains Airfield, Townsville; some fresh and curious, others seasoned and eager. The sound of their boots on the sidewalk was met with the laughing, cackling protests of kookaburras* perched on the power lines and streetcar wires.

The bus had stopped at the right place: the Transient Billets and Quarters Office, or what had been known as the Hotel Queensland before the war. It was still a hotel, but without the concierge, bell hops and desk clerk. Instead, there were uniforms of another sort.

Almost like tourists, the six pilots of Bravo Flight checked in with the Duty Officer, had their passes stamped and were issued Code of Conduct cards and a pocket-sized Geneva Convention Protocol. The four junior officers were given double-occupancy room assignments on the second floor. Nick's rank and Mac's time-in-grade garnered them private rooms at the Gresham hotel, around the corner on Adelaide Street.

For Nick and Mac, it was the first time in more than a year that the soles of their flight boots touched ground upon an English-speaking city. Arguably, it was their first time back in civilization since they had left California. It was a hard-earned weekend away from the smell of aviation fuel, grease, rubber and sweat. For the four other pilots of Nick's wing, it was a party that needed to get started. He kept it to himself, but Nick had a gut feeling that the other boot was about to drop. He had sensed something was in the wind days before the squadron was allowed two-day off-post privileges. The higher-ups didn't decide to grant casual furloughs for the hell of it. His thoughts wandered: *There must be something cooking. Why else would headquarters hand out weekend passes like Christmas candy when the Japs are bombing Darwin, the whole Top End, and having their way with the Philippines, Siam and Malaysia?*

He attempted to dismiss his wayward thinking and latent worry as nothing more than pure speculation. It made absolutely no sense to give such speculation any serious consideration. For all that, there was nothing he could do about it anyway.

The men had Friday and Saturday night to explore everything Brisbane had to offer. They were free until midday muster at noon on Sunday. Nick and his men agreed to meet at the Cocoanut Club at seven o'clock to allow time to check into their rooms and the chance to wash off the road dust. Out the door and around the corner it was not more than five minutes later that Nick and Mac had their elbows on the bar and hands around tall glasses of Bulimba Gold Top lager at the Hotel Gresham.

The hotel bar ran the length of the lounge; ten yards of polished maroon Malaysian walnut. Three bartenders in white shirts, black silk vests, and pin-stripe slacks were very busy with the largely American crowd. There was also a spattering of Aussie servicemen in the Hotel.

Nick pulled his Zippo* from his waist pocket, lit a Camel, and looked his wingman in the eye, "Between you, me and the lamppost, Mac, I got a feeling this could be our last dance with life outside the Army for a while."

"That thought crossed my mind, too, Captain. You think so?"

Nick drew deep on the cigarette, paused a second and continued, "Yeah, I think so. We got new war birds and new blood, and you can bet your ass that the brass will have us all up in the air damn quick. Uncle Sam didn't buy those new P-38 Lightnings just for us to fly around Australia, train new recruits, and scare up packs of kangaroos."

Mac grinned, took two swallows of beer and nodded in agreement.

Nick went on, "But let's keep it between you and me for the next couple days, Mac ... there's no need to give the men anything more to think about. And besides ... hell, yes ... they're young, but not stupid ... they probably already have figured it out for themselves."

Nick and Mac knew what was beyond the horizon. The other four flyers of Bravo Flight had no idea of what kind of hellfire the Rising Sun could bring to bear. They had been trained as to what they could expect and how to react, but could only imagine.

Captain Throckmorton and Lieutenant McElvoy finished their glasses of Gold Top and one more before they left the Gresham to rendezvous with the other four members of their crew at the restaurant and dance hall.

In downtown Brisbane, the Cocoanut Grove Dance Club at the corner of Adelaide and Queen Streets had become a haven for American servicemen. Seven days a week, the night spot served a slice of American pie to the Southwest Pacific and the soldiers, sailors, marines, and fliers half a world away from home. Steak and potato dinners, beer, women, music and dancing were the draw. Australian women were known to proclaim that the Yanks were *over sexed, over paid, and over here.* The city was awash with Americans and their cash, cigarettes, chocolates, attitude, and swagger. Like honeybees to Sweet William, Australian females of every size, description, age, and social standing were drawn to Brisbane from the far reaches of Queensland. The Aussie men could not help but be a bit envious of GI bartering items such as the nylons, perfume, and makeup that were always available at the American Post Exchange, but the American presence was accepted as a necessity of war. For the women, the GIs were a fresh, foreign, and exotic diversion with pockets full of spendable cash.

Along with Nick and Mac were four fresh-faced flyers from the Army Air Force training center at Randolph Field, Texas: lieutenants Andy Hill *(Handy Andy)*, Martin Sandoval *(Marty the Sandman)*, Saul Goode *(Goodie)* and Sherwood Newsom *(New Man)*. The men were ready for two nights of what was officially termed *R&R, rest and recreation.* Unofficially, it could be called *anything you can get away with.*

After dinner, Nick paid for the extra cover-charge that secured an up-front and close table for him, Mac and the other members of Bravo Flight. The dance hall was packed with anxious male and female patrons, all with the anticipation that the night held the promise of one to be remembered. Hundreds of people, each with their own idea of fun and fulfillment swarmed like ants on a picnic blanket.

Within fifteen minutes of settling into their table and ordering their first pitchers of Gold Top and Castlemaine XXXX, four auspicious Australian women claimed the vacant seats at Nick's table, and two more boldly brought their own chairs from along the nearest wall. Nick's table of six flyers had been stretched to accommodate six young women with their heads in the clouds.

Showman and bandleader Frank Coughlan of Sydney had put together the *Trocadero All Girl Dance Band*: a fifteen-piece, all-female orchestra created exclusively for the Brisbane Cocoanut Grove. As the king of Australian swing, Frank Coughlan recognized the lucrative marketing opportunity created by the military presence and exploited the American and Australian soldier equally. The dance band would perform from eight o'clock to eleven but was accompanied by the sale of alcoholic beverages only until ten.

At eight o'clock sharp, the band took the stage, greeted with boisterous applause, hoots, hollers, and whistles. The women were young and gorgeous, with perfect makeup and impeccably styled waves of short, curly hair. To a stitch, the ladies of the band were dressed alike: shimmering, silky ivory-white rayon[*] gowns with plunging necklines and intricate lace along every hem.

An airman yelled above the crowd, "I want you to be my parachute, Baby Doll!" and another, "It's the Caterpillar[*] Club!" The show had begun.

The band's first number was a sultry, rousing rendition of *There's Something in the Air*. The tempestuous beat of Aussie-altered American swing reverberated down from the tin ceiling, swirled and stirred around by massive rattan-blade fans, before it finally bounced up from the polished bamboo parquet floor, and sideways off the plaster and wainscot walls.

The blonde drummer held a snare brush in her left hand and a stick firmly in her right, braced between her thumb, ring and forefinger. She would snap rim-shots on the shuffle-eighth notes and brush on the straight. Six lovely sets of lips graced the mouthpieces of four saxophones and two trombones. Two young ladies teased and tempted accordion keys and buttons with their ruby painted nails. And not to be forgotten, three violins and three guitars in the string section were stroked and plucked. One of the classical guitarists was also the main vocalist, standing behind a large circular chrome microphone, warbling like a bobolink.

Nick and the men danced, laughed and drank with the six audacious Australian snuggle bunnies who had invited themselves to the big round table. Most flyers were of the opinion that loose women were about as useful as an ashtray in an open cockpit: good only for decoration and short hauls and useless on the long run. The reasoning was: anything that goes in fast never stays in for long.

The fact that the flyers had two full nights in Brisbane did nothing to subdue the emphasis on immediate fulfillment of physical desire. When the sale of beer and liquor ended unexpectedly just after ten o'clock, a sense of urgency drove pilots Martin Sandoval and Sherwood Newsom to leave the Grove early with two twittering young women on their arm. They were in the company of Anna Prentice and Jenny Taylor; two Kiwis who had claimed to be secretaries at the Royal New Zealand Commission of Trade and shared a flat two blocks away, around the corner from the American Consular Office. The quartet seemed to have a pre-planned mission, flight plan, and success assessment in-hand. Before they left, Nick quietly reminded the men of the 2 AM curfew at the Transient Billets.

Lieutenants Andy Hill, Saul Goode and two nameless women withdrew to a dark corner of the ballroom shortly after The Sandman and New Man had left.

Mac and Nick nursed one last pitcher of Castlemaine XXXX and continued to dance with their female company until the All Girl band called it quits about eleven thirty. They made a vague promise to the women that they would meet up again the following evening, said good-night with innocuous kisses and were back in their rooms at the Gresham at quarter-past midnight.

Sailing On A Sunbeam ...

Midmorning Saturday the young flyers, Andy, Saul, Marty and Sherwood met up with Nick and Mac at the Gresham for what was billed as a full English breakfast. Half a world away from the European war, Australia avoided much of the harsh rationing endured by her allies. The bleak reality, however, was that many of the menu items were limited. There were three options: smoked herring kippers with saltines; a New Zealand pan-seared rosemary lamb chop with potato and toast; or one egg, one slice of bacon, beans in sauce, and a biscuit. As appetizers or dessert, bananas, pineapple, and Tasmanian heavy chocolate were available in abundance.

The good news was that the food didn't come out of a little Army-green tin can or small cardboard box and the coffee didn't taste like it was percolated through the mess sergeant's sock. And truth be told, the food was appreciated. For a soldier, anything other than Army chow was a gift from the gods.

Lieutenants Sandoval and Newsom shared curious looks across the table during the meal, and Sandoval especially appeared to be on edge, fidgeting in his seat.

After the plates were cleared, Nick ordered a large pot of coffee and six glasses of brandy. He spotted the Sandman adjusting his jacket and trousers. Nick then smirked and razzed him, "Something bothering you, Lieutenant? Did your Kiwi oyster give you something special to remember her by?"

Initial silence was followed by a few snickers before the flyer answered, "No, Sir. I didn't catch anything. But we did get something. Me and Newsom picked something up for you, Captain."

"Did you think I needed something, Lieutenant?"

"It's a gift, Sir. A gift from all of us, really." Sandoval glanced to Newsom for backup.

New Man picked it up, "That's right, Capt'n. All of us wanted to get some kind of small gift for you; something special, and I think we found it last night, Sir."

Sandoval then pulled a bundle from under his jacket and set it on the table with a clunk. Something heavy was wrapped in a pair of olive green, GI two-button boxer shorts.

Along with the thump, the waiter reappeared with the coffee and liquor balanced on a tray over his right shoulder. He noticed the skivvies, smirked, and emptied his tray. Silence settled as everyone awaited his exit. Eyes moved all about, looking for some sort of hint of what could be expected. It seemed that only the Sandman and New Man knew what was wrapped up inside the underwear.

Nick smiled. "Well, it seems like you left me one helluva load inside those shorts, Lieutenant."

Quiet laughter and whispers drifted all along the table. "Those skivvies are clean, Capt'n. It's just that I didn't go looking for wrapping paper, Sir. Everything was closed." Sandoval pushed the parcel down the table to Goodie who then slid it across to Nick.

Nick gingerly used his index fingers, and continued the joke by slowly, carefully, unwrapping the surprise gift inside underwear. It was gleaming chrome.

Mac recognized it for what it was, "It's a fancy radiator cap, Capt'n! ... a chrome radiator hood ornament!"

There was some more subdued laughter followed by restrained cheers.

Nick picked up the chunk of chromed steel and examined it for all at the table to see. He detailed the item, "This is one of them winged ladies ... a *Flying Goddess** they call it ... a radiator cap ... no doubt from a '30-something Cadillac* Phaeton. It's from one of those long twelve-or-sixteen-cylinder saloons with a hood that goes on forever ... for about twelve feet. Where in hell did you get this, Sandman?"

"It's from one of those big ass Cadillac sedans sure enough, Capt'n. Last night on the way back to the billets, me and Sherwood spotted it, near the trade office where them dames work, and it just reminded us how you always talk about Betty Grable's titties flying in the breeze, and we figured it might be something that you'd like to have, Capt'n. So, we lifted it."

"Tell me you didn't steal this, Lieutenant."

"No, Capt'n. We didn't just lift it. We didn't steal it. We left a five-dollar bill under the windshield wiper."

"You were in on this Lieutenant Newsom?"

"Yes, Sir."

"Do either of you have any idea who might own the car?"

The Sandman looked to Newsom and back to Nick. "Since it's a Cadillac, I would guess it belongs to one of us, a Yank, somebody with plenty of sway or some cushy government job maybe, and not an Aussie ... Capt'n, Sir."

Nick took a cigarette from the pack of king-size Pall Mall* lying on the table and lit it slowly ... very slowly, while studying the two young pilots. He snapped his Zippo shut and spoke, "This afternoon or tonight, on your way through the streets or back to the Transit Billets, I want you to look for that Cadillac, Lieutenant Newsom."

To a man, everyone believed Nick would order the chrome ornament returned. He reached inside his jacket, fumbled with his wallet and began, "Today or tonight, New Man, I want you and the Sandman to look for that Cadillac. And when you find it, leave this five-dollar bill too."

The men gave out a 'hurrah!' and Nick motioned with two open hands for them to quiet down. He stood, picked up the hunk of chromed steel and continued, "Thank you gentlemen. I'm going to stick this chrome lady right where she belongs: on the cowl of Lightning number 14. On Monday, I'll have Crew Chief Wiles screw her right behind the barrel of the cannon ... right where I'll be able to eyeball her backside and line up my target right between her tight little cheeks and those feathered, upright wings. Beautiful. Thank you, gentlemen, thank all of you."

He grinned and began examining the ornament; looking back to front, along her back toward her flowing hair, "I'll have the only goddamn flying Cadillac in the Pacific ... goddamn beautiful. Her hair flapping in the breeze, tits and nose into the wind, and her round, tight little ass in the back draft. Beautiful ... damned beautiful ... a P-38 Phaeton ... The Equalizer ... no ... a flying Phaeton ... that's it! That's it ... *The Flying Phaeton*: six fifty-caliber guns and a twenty-millimeter cannon under the hood with two screaming Allison V-12's on either side ... beautiful. Hellfire from the heavens for Tojo[*]. A genuine flying American flamethrower."

He lifted his glass of brandy, toasted Bravo Flight, drank it down and ordered another pot of coffee with another round of liquor.

Thirty-three-year-old Nicholas was the veteran of the group by at least twelve years on Earth and six in the Air. The men in his command knew their Captain wasn't hardnosed or by-the-book, but never had they seen him so raucous. It wasn't just the spit-shine, creased khakis, polished brass, and silk scarf that identified the Flight Leader. Privately, Captain Throckmorton had been pegged with the nickname *The Old Man* not only from his cynicism, experience and serious, straight-up decisions, but the grey sprouting at his temples. Mac was the only Bravo member who openly referred to Nick as 'Old Man', and that was only when they were alone.

The men had earned their time off. Nick and his wing needed this respite from duty. August 1942 had been hectic for the 39th Fighter Squadron. New aircraft from the Lockheed assembly lines in Burbank, California needed to be flight tested, fitted out with armament and made battle ready. Pilots and ground crew worked in twelve-on and eight-off shifts. As a carry-over from the Flying Tigers and to enhance *espirit de corps*, Shark-mouth nose art had been painted on the nose cowls of the Lightnings' twin booms.

The dining room was beginning to thin out, with two other tables still lingering as the clock neared eleven. After the waiter had brought the third round of brandy, the Sandman suggested, "We can all chip in for this Capt'n."

Nick ordered his Wing, "You can, but you won't. You all can sign a Short Snorter* for me and I'll cash it in some other time. But for now, breakfast's on me. I just want to treat my Flight to something other than C-rations and whatever that crap is that the Army calls coffee.

"You men have done your Group, your Squadron and your Flight Leader proud ... completed ninety hours of training in your new Lightnings ... without bending any metal or dispensary calls. And now, well ... you can fly with the best of them. You all have warranted your Lightning wings."

The Sandman pressed for more, "We've all had the training, Captain ... but is there anything more, something extra ... something out of the ordinary that you could tell us?"

"Just what I've learned from flying up against the Japs with the Tigers ... but I've told you all that already ... the zoom and boom ... climb, dive and shoot ... zoom and boom. The P-38 isn't just an airplane. It was engineered to be a flying machine gun ... a bomber ... a fighter ... a cannon in the clouds ... a real tits machine. You men and me fly the fastest fighters at the highest altitude with the biggest guns ... by far.

Each and every one of us is the ultimate weapon. As a team, we're damn near invincible."

Nick looked to Mac for a moment, then moved his glance back to Marty and added, "To put it simply, it's two things: you have to put your mind right and keep your head on a swivel. You need to have eyes everywhere. You need to know that up there you're in a swarm of bees, straight-up. You must know who your Friend is, and who is your Foe; who's going to save your ass and who wants to kill you.

"And trust the man on your wing. Together, you fly in the sky, or you fall to the ground. Let the adrenaline kick in and allow your soul to become one with the machine. Understand that you are the ultimate enforcer ... Justice on the wing ... the Realizer ... like I said before. Together ... inside your plane, inside that beautiful cocoon of American stainless steel and aluminum, you, your ability to figure right from wrong, your brain, the engines and the guns, come together and become a killing machine. And don't be a phony. Be honest with yourself and know who you are and why you are here. Give your enemy a measure of Hellfire straight from the heavens. Kill the bastards. Remember Pearl. Remember home. If you know that and live that, you will live to see tomorrow. And together, we'll kill a bunch of Japs. And maybe you end up an Ace."

The plundered Cadillac was never mentioned again.

Saturday evening: Put Your Arms Around Me, Honey

... no lovin' ... no nothin' ...

The men of Bravo Flight were to spend one more night at the Cocoanut Grove listening and dancing to the All-Girl Band. Handy Andy Hill and Goodie Goode predicted they would round home plate the second time around, and for them, it wouldn't end up being just another night of bullshit, beer, and broads.

At eight-thirty, it was Nick who left the party early; barely half an hour after the music started. On his arm was one of the women from the previous night, who had initially introduced herself in a somewhat awkward manner. She had presented him with the quandary of exactly how to proceed, if at all, with a gratuitous relationship like the one Gladys had given him.

When she had sat next to him the night before, their interaction started this way: "I'm here with my best mate, Lois. Pleased to meet you, Captain Throckmorton. I'm Perpetua ... Perpetua Tummel and I'm working as a Red Cross volunteer ... sort of doing my part for the war effort. Most people call me *Pet*, maybe because I always try to be friendly, I'm not sure, but I guess so. I spend fifteen hours a week as a hospitality hostess at the Military Outreach Center, talking to Allied soldiers and helping them to feel more at home during their stay here in Australia. This is the first time that I've ever been in a place like this. My friend Lois Lefévre, we're best mates like I said, she's French, and was lucky enough to get out of Saigon in 1940 and escape the Japs, but she's the one who convinced me to come here tonight. I was able to get my next-door neighbor Ally for night nanny duty, so here I am."

Nick had allowed her to ramble on. She was visibly nervous and spoke quickly with only slight pauses between disjointed sentences. She reached into her purse, brought out a small paper sack, reached her hand inside and asked, "Pardon my fingers ... but here ... I know they taste better warm, but may I offer you a cherry sticky tart?"

Nick's imagination took off with her seemingly innocuous offer that somehow, either by coincidence or naïveté, had ended up on the wrong runway. It was all he could do to avoid an impulsive laugh or crude retort. There was something about this woman; something like the Vernors ginger ale bubbles that tickle your nose: uneasily amusing and deliciously tempting.

Among the women at Bravo Flight's table, Perpetua appeared to be the most down-to-earth and strait-laced. That, in and of itself, posed a very curious conundrum and problematic predicament for Nicholas. Perpetua and her friend Lois seemed to be a bit on edge and not completely comfortable or confident with their situation. Lois had sat with McElvoy the night before and was at his side once again.

Either in her early or middle thirties, Pet was barely five feet tall, had hazel eyes, and reddish-brown hair in a tightly curled bob. Although her form was petite, her breasts fought to escape the buttoned confines of her light blue woolen cardigan. She had the appearance of a working-class housewife, with a bit of the persnickety, wearing carefully applied deep-red lipstick, nails to match, and a touch of mascara. Her complexion glowed. A below-the-knee pleated skirt, taupe nylon stockings with perfectly straight seams, and dainty feet inside a pair of green T-strap pumps defied the image of a dance-hall girl. Pet was painted and well-dressed but not painted up or dressed down. She was fidgety and seemed on edge.

She explained that her husband was an infantryman with the Second Australian Imperial Force[*] and had been in North Africa since April of 1941. She spoke matter-of-factly, stating his last letters indicated that he was currently somewhere in the Middle East. She had obviously given some thought to her situation before venturing out to the Cocoanut Grove because, as her story progressed, she looked around to be certain nobody was listening.

She spoke softly, "Before the war my husband and I had a smashing fine life together: he held a good job at Curlew Fertilizers, we had a nice home, a little money in the bank, and two wonderful children underfoot. We were in love and dreamed of a darling little bungalow in an idyllic place like Wagga-Wagga[*], overlooking the Murrumbidgee River. But now, just like you flyers, I share a common enemy: Zero[*]. Your Zeros are Jap airplanes; mine is simply *zero ... zed.* It's not easy getting no loving and no nothing." She had nearly whispered her last sentence. Thoughts of love-starved Gladys flashed through Nick's memory. In only a few sentences, Pet had spoken volumes.

It was Perpetua who had taken the book off the shelf and opened it to the table of contents. Nick seized the opportunity and turned to the pages to his life story. He explained that although his teenage union with Nora had ended up being a marriage in legal standing only, he held no animosity toward his wife, and continued, "Nora gave me two things: a son and me. She gave me Alexander and allowed me to be myself. For that, I should thank her. The trouble is: she's not here with me and I'm not there with her. And even if she was and I was, it wouldn't change anything. Like you just said, my Pet: *zero is zero.*"

Nick and Pet had kept each other innocuous company that first night at the Cocoanut. When they danced, he held her close. Seated at the table, she would allow her hand to tease his thigh. They danced to the music of the Trocadero Girls; he drank Castlemaine draught ale, and she sipped at four glasses of Pinot Gris.

When he had mentioned that he and Mac intended to be back at the club again the next evening, a smile crossed her lips and she promised, "Good. I'll see you again tomorrow night, then ... Saturday. I'll arrange for Ally to watch the children one more night."

Nick looked deep into her eyes. "Good. I'll be here waiting for you, Pet, my dear."

The second night was more direct and on-point. They left the night spot after one drink and one dance with a plan of attack. In his room three blocks away at the Gresham Hotel, Captain Throckmorton obliterated Perpetua's *zero* enemy.

Business as usual ... late 1942 ...
After Brisbane, the party was over. It was back to war.

Once back in Townsville, Nick had his gleaming, flying lady hood ornament mounted to the nacelle of his P-38 while other pilots christened their birds with the name of their wife or girlfriend. A few others patiently waited for hand painted nose art of an alluring pin-up girl or cartoon caricature. By October 1st, the unit was in Port Moresby, New Guinea*, and flying incessant combat missions against the dug-in, formidable Japanese positions hidden in the dense mangroves along the northern coast.

Early in 1943, Nick was attached to the 43rd Photo Reconnaissance Wing. His Lightning, #44-66148, was repainted dull grey and modified into a four-camera, high speed surveillance and attack aircraft with auxiliary drop fuel tanks for extended range. Nick neatly lettered *The Flying Phaeton* in white enamel on the left and right armament doors. Following the outbound missions, he would oftentimes transform the return trip into a high speed, low altitude shooting gallery and mercilessly strafe the enemy.

For the next three years, the 39th dogged and engaged the Imperial Forces of Japan in the skies, mountains, and jungles of New Guinea, New Britain, Morotai, Schouten, Negros, and the Philippines. The effort came with losses. Saul Goode had been wounded early in the New Guinea campaign and was rotated back to Hamilton Army Airfield in San Rafael, California as a flight instructor. Sherwood Newsom and his aircraft were lost in a night training accident over the Coral Sea and Andy Hill crashed into the jungle during a bomber escort mission over Finschafen, New Guinea. Ian Caddigan, an experienced replacement pilot from the 475th, was killed before his plane could take off during a Japanese bombing and strafing raid at Wama Airfield, Morotai.

In the last quarter of 1944, only three original pilots of the 39th Squadron's Bravo Flight remained. Nick, Mac, and the Sandman were living in a four-man tent; stationed at Mangaldan Airfield, Luzon, the Philippines.

One hard-fought victory and one Pacific island at a time, the Americans were pushing the Japanese back to Honshu. With the passage of each day, there was hope that the War's end would soon be in sight.

7: SOLO FLIGHT, 1944

If I Only Had A Heart ...

November, Sydney, Australia

By November 1944, Nick had become starkly aware of the savagery of war. At every staff briefing he heard enemy troop assessments, battle projections, casualty reports, and disturbing details of Allied prisoner mistreatment. When his name came up in rotation for a seven-day escape from the battle zones on Luzon, there wasn't a moment of hesitation before he wished Mac and the men smooth landings and accepted his leave papers with a smile.

After a cold, noisy, six-hour flight seated on a metal bench aboard a C-47 Skytrain*, he landed in Sydney, Australia. With a bit of help from the USO* welcome booth, he was soon on the Woolloomooloo* trolley and on his way downtown. It was Tuesday: a starlit, delightfully warm summer night in the southern hemisphere.

The Kings Cross district of Sydney glowed with night life seven nights a week, fueled by Allied troops far away from home, war-weary locals, relaxed alcohol restrictions, and dozens of bars, dance halls, dens of inequity, and houses of ill repute. The night clubs on Bayswater and Victoria Roads burst at their seams with crowds moving to the sound of Australian-styled swing, imported American jazz, and British big band.

Nick explored a back-street underground maze of fish-and-chip vendors, tobacconists, haberdasheries, gin joints, and clubs. Partially hidden beneath a block of red brick Victorian townhomes and terraces, it was a surreal grotto, parts of which hadn't seen sunshine since the day they were built. The widest possible cross-section of humanity, with its feet massaging the pavers and bodies flowing along the streets, gave Kings Cross a pulse of its own. The cobblestone streets and brick walkways led along a two-block hodgepodge of Old-World wooden storefronts with flickering gaslights attempting to glow in an incandescent world. Directly above were second story balconies wrapped with wrought iron railings painted in bright primary lacquers or Mardi Gras jewel tones of purple, green and gold.

Nick stopped outside what certainly was a taproom. A large, carved wooden sign, arched multi-light windows and a frantic fiddle beckoned him from within. Once inside *J.P. Jernigan's Llandover Pub*, it took a moment for his eyes to become accustomed to the subdued light. The white plaster ceiling was no more than seven feet above the worn brick floor and supported by a crisscross network of wooden beams hanging precariously low for anyone taller than six feet. Against the brick inner wall were arched supports, buttressing the floors above. Nooks and crannies with candle-lit tables were snuggled tight, and separated by wooden half-walls that painted a picture of horse stalls. In the far corner, a gaggle of musicians on dulcimer, fiddle, harp, flute and guitar, played Gaelic folk more earnestly than well.

The music was playing, the stage set, the cast ready, and the curtain about to rise. In an instant, the next act in Nick's drama would get underway.

Nick moved further into the room. On the wall behind the bar, beer mugs of all description filled the shelves and fluted wine glasses hung from racks overhead. He worked his way toward the dozen draught taps at the bar and got the attention of one of the two barmen: a round, bald, flush-faced fellow with tiny tufts of white hair just above his ears.

Nicholas was about to cross paths with someone who would steer his life in an unpredictable direction. She was behind him, perhaps a yard away, moving forward and studying the American flyer.

The bartender stood with one pudgy, pink hand on his hip and the other on the bar. "Pick your poison, Yank."

Nick pulled a dollar out of his pocket, set it on the bar, eyed the names and logos on the draught handles and announced his choice with confidence, "Tooheys. A pint." He could barely make out his own words over the incessant din.

A voice came over his left shoulder, straining over the music and crowd buzz, "Catching a bit of Aussie culture, are you?"

He turned to find a friendly face, with a delicate smile and sparkling eyes. She was young and seemed to be starkly out of place. She had shoulder length, subtle strawberry blonde hair in ribbon curls, and sparse, dusky freckles crossing over her cheeks and nose. She wore an unflattering uniform of sandy-colored khaki: a mid-calf skirt, white shirt, and a single-breasted, hip length jacket. A red silk jabot and gleaming enameled red crosses on her epaulets and brass buttons brandished her vocation. She held a beaker of what was likely stout, cider or bitters.

He knew he was being played and leaned closer to her, "Is it that obvious?"

She smiled once again and only nodded. Nick scooped up his Australian change, grabbed his frothy schooner of beer and with a nod of his head encouraged the young woman to follow him, "Let's find ourselves a spot."

He stood on the balls of his feet, eyeballing the place and checking for available seating. He spotted a vacancy and nodded his intended direction, "Come on."

She lightly held his elbow, following behind him as he pushed and nudged his way to a time-worn, ten-foot pine trestle table with benches, on a wall opposite the bar. After several bumps and nudges, hollow apologies, acknowledgements, and meaningless *thank-yous,* they found themselves seated – in rather cramped quarters, but nonetheless seated. It was no quieter, but much more conducive to conversation and easier on the feet. Nick gave the young woman a nod, raised his glass and made a silent, impromptu, introductory toast. She smiled and obliged.

"You're a pilot ... a Yank."

"Nicholas Throckmorton, ma'am. Nick. You must have been reading my mail ..." He tipped his brimmed service cap to her, removed it and set it on the table.

She playfully studied him. "Well, it wasn't hard with that uniform; after all, this isn't fancy dress!"

Her eyes surveyed him, "I'm Gwen, Guendolen Peate ..." and offered her hand.

Nick accepted, and gave the obligatory, introductory handshake, felt her warmth and released, leaving their hands alone on the table, inches apart with only his hat standing guard.

She continued, "And of course, you can tell that I'm a Nurse Sister by my gaudy government-issue duds, but I can add that I'm here in Sydney on holiday ... to be particular: the last bit of a two-week holiday. I arrived today from Perth after a smashing week with Mum, Dad, and sister Jan. I'm with the 14th General Army Hospital in Darwin on reassignment order."

"I'm happy to meet you, Nurse Gwen, and yes, you're correct ... I am a pilot."

"I know, and it's not just that scarf. What really proves it is those silver wings above your pocket and that shiny brass winged propeller on your lapel. I've seen them before in my line of work, lots of times ... too many times, really ... and those twin silver bars make you a captain ... and besides all that, in plain sight ... over there at the bar you flashed your American passport."

"Passport?"

"You paid with a dollar bill! That's your passport to happiness; that's what they say, isn't it? And anyway, what drew you in here? The Welsh? I'm bloody certain that you're the only Yank in this boozer."

"Welsh? It sounds Irish to me."

She leaned toward him, as if telling a secret. "Shhhh ... It might be only a rowboat ride from Holyhead to Dublin, but to us Welsh, Ireland might as well be on the Moon."

"You're Welsh?"

"Mum and Dad are ... from Cardiff. But me, I was born here in Australia, in Perth."

After one more drink, she suggested they leave the autoharp, fiddle, and penny whistle behind and see a re-release of *The Wizard Of Oz*[*] at the Roslyn Cinema on Darlinghurst Road.

With only feigned hesitation, he gingerly jumped at the invitation, not wanting to telegraph his eagerness. "I guess so ... sure, why not? I ain't seen it, but I'm sure it's better than our monthly ration of celluloid war stories we see on that bed sheet that they hang up in the mess tent ... when we watch guys like William Bendix, Anthony Quinn, Bogart and Ronald Reagan save the world from the Krauts and Japs ... sometimes even the Bugs Bunny himself ... just to have something to watch. But once in a blue moon we get to see my gal Betty Grable, or Jane Russell, Rita Hayworth or even John Wayne or Randolph Scott in a cowboy picture."

He studied her for a fleeting moment and wondered exactly how old she was. She had flawless skin, eyes that glistened with wonder, soft lips curled in a youthful pout, and a silver voice untarnished by time, cigarettes, or drink.

He slowly crushed his cigarette into an old saucer reborn as an ashtray. With an awkward wink and a nod, he added, "Maybe a movie about rainbows, witches, scarecrows, and midgets would be good for a change."

With that, Gwen let out a tittering little laugh and exclaimed, "Ducky! We're going to the cinema ... we're off to see the Wizard, by Jove!"

He didn't realize it then and she certainly didn't intend it, but he was hooked.

After the film, he escorted the young nurse back to the Transit Quarters for Women on Brougham Place. On the walk back from the Roslyn, they stepped to the tune of *Follow The Yellow Brick Road,* holding hands, bumping hips and acting like kids.

She was effervescent, cheerful and seemed too young to be a nurse, much less exposed to the damages of war.

They shared a tender kiss under the streetlight at Victoria and Brougham, and promised to meet on the same corner at noon the next day, Wednesday. Contrary to his pattern with women, he had started down a road toward an unhurried romantic relationship that did not turn or detour immediately into a sexual liaison. It was Nick's first of five evenings in the company of Nurse Sister Guendolen Peate.

By eleven o'clock he was asleep in his bed at the Hotel Fitzroy.

Racing With The Moon ...

... and escaping under the stars ...

Gwen had laid eyes on Nicholas first, from nearly a block away, sticking out as the proverbial 'sore thumb' in his pink-and-greens*: his olive drab jacket and cap over a tan khaki shirt and trousers. As promised, he was there waiting for her: sunlight bouncing off polished brass, one hand in his left pocket and the other busy with a cigarette.

A smile crossed her lips as she approached. He spotted her and watched her sway. The two-inch heels on her oxblood service shoes were enough to push a bounce and wiggle into her step. Her shoulders too, moved with rhythm. For the day's meeting, she had applied lipstick and powder.

He took her in his arms; they exchanged hellos and an affable kiss. She teased him, "Were you standing here just waiting to chat up any skirt that came along?"

He teased, "As a matter of fact, I was. But I as soon as I got here, you showed up."

And she teased back, "That's a bit of cheek; even for a Yank!"

Two blocks away they discovered the Roosevelt Club* and Restaurant on Orwell Street. Once inside the hefty revolving glass doors, the foyer opened up with potted palms, wood panels polished to a glowing shine, and Persian carpets. Seven-foot carved wooden figures stood on either side of the dining room doors. They were painted up as dark-skinned Indian servants in red jackets, black trousers, bright white turbans and stoic smiles; each holding a blooming pot of large-leaf tropical Hoyas. Budgerigars of every color chirped and bounced about in tall, shiny brass bird cages atop candlestick tables.

Once they were seated and settled, they shared afternoon tea from a menu starkly abbreviated by wartime rationing. It was at the Roosevelt that Nicholas was introduced to a simple dish that he straight-up enjoyed: bangers, gravy, mushy peas, and mash*.

When Gwen told him she found it amusing that he could enjoy such a reviled dish, he defended his culinary taste, "Anything's better than pound cake or beans and Spam* fixed six ways 'til Sunday."

Nick found Gwen to be welcoming, friendly and very easy to talk to. Together, laughter was effortless. She made feeling good simple.

Following their meals, they moved from the dining room to the club and found a dimly lit corner table topped with a deep red tablecloth, a single flickering votive candle, and a small vase with a sprig of carmine grevillea. The place was at nearly half capacity by mid-afternoon with Aussie servicemen and some local women sharing drinks just as Gwen and Nick were. There was barely a handful of servicewomen and only one other American: an Army Air Force transport pilot.

Initially, Nick and Gwen started to unveil bits and pieces of personal history with large gaps in the timeline that allowed their undisciplined stories to jump about. The

186

insignificant or embarrassing tends to be either omitted or intentionally overlooked.

He enjoyed her company, easily immersing himself in the deep pools of her grey eyes and drowning in her soft, fluid voice. Encouraged by glasses of Tooheys pilsner and Bulimba Pear Cider, it wasn't long before the tales and experiences grew.

Gwen's story began, "I started nursing school at Saint Andrew's Mission Hospital in Singapore when I was nearly eighteen, and as soon as I finished, I believed that I had the world in my hands. I was fresh out of school; my father was a shipping broker at Dole Pineapple, and Mum worked a few hours a week doing the accounts at the tennis club. We enjoyed a quiet, respectable life. At twenty, I was a naïve young graduate working at the Woodlands Clinic, treating cuts, bruises, and dysentery at my first nursing job. I was rubbing elbows with a dishy doctor or two, and orderlies that could do in a pinch, if they had to. I was living in a closed community of Brits, Dutch, French, Kiwis, and Aussies with absolutely no knowledge of what the real world was like. Blimey, before the movie came out, I thought *The Grapes of Wrath** was the hangover you get from cheap wine."

She paused, sipped at her cider and went on, "Things slowly changed here but danger signs were ignored like the drop of a copper tuppence ... an unimportant, meaningless, worthless thud. Then, a year later, in February of '42, the rumors came true, and the nightmare began. The Japs came by land, swarming down from the North, not from the sea like the high and mighty military masterminds believed they would. My family and I got out of the Crown Colony by the skin of our teeth, just two days before the British surrender. In the black of night Mum, Dad, baby sister Janet and I jammed ourselves into a thirty-foot outboard dinghy with the Van Peldt family. So, from a stinky tobacco and palm oil warehouse on the Pandan wharves we escaped what was coming. Maurice Van Peldt worked with my father and along with his wife Oda, and maybe a half dozen of his and our Indian amahs, we made it out into the harbor in the dark, with no lights, and onto a Dutch-flagged ship named the Zaandam*.

"We came aboard under starlight, climbing rope ladders and we slept on skinny mattresses lying on the deck under a canvas shelter, and we were rationed to a biscuit, two kippers, one cup of tea, and a glass of water a day. The ship lugged south along the coast of Sumatra for a week before we docked in Perth, ten days out ... we learned later that the Japs were advancing all the way down Sumatra ... right behind us and eventually they took Java too.

"After our escape from Singapore and all the mess in Java, Hong Kong, and all the killing, I was angry, really angry and bursting out of my skin and not only because I was knackered and didn't have a fresh pair of knickers or a bath in a week, but I was so bloody mad at the Japs that I signed on with the Army Nursing Service*."

Nick listened intently, aware of the peril this young woman had endured. "And you said yesterday that you are stationed in Darwin?"

"As of right now, today, and according to the duty registry, yes. It's not exactly ordered by Parliament you know, because I'm technically a civilian volunteer, and I'm not required to go, but I'm being reassigned Monday to an Ambulance Unit at Port Moresby, New Guinea."

He knew exactly what she meant. Assignments were subject to change and all members of the service, civilian or military, were expected to hurry up and wait for orders. It was the nature of the untamed beast. The Army Air Force used hundreds of non-conscripted women to ferry aircraft all over the globe. Nick thought he could ease her anticipation and added, "My unit was in Port Moresby for about a year, then we took the scenic tour of the rest of Papua, chasing the enemy from New Britain to the Philippines, where we are now. Moresby is OK duty, Gwen ... the weather's hot and wet but the Japs shouldn't bother you now. We're keeping them busy in other places."

He wanted to steer the conversation away from war. "Tell me more about your life in Singapore, Gwen ... before the Japs ... must have been nice."

She went on with some childhood anecdotes but repeated herself that it was essentially a fragile life within a China cabinet of European transplants and transients. Nick did some mental mathematics and figured that Gwen could be no more than twenty-three, perhaps nearing twenty-four, and at least eleven years his junior. He decided against bringing the subject up specifically and started to tell her about himself.

He confessed that he had been flying since he was twenty, had joined the Air Corps in 1938, and from the beginning of his crop-dusting days he had seen his share of the world. Nicholas said he had left behind a son, Alexander, but did not acknowledge that he was married. He told Gwen that he had lost his wife Nora at childbirth, and rationalized his devious lie as the analytical, if not factual truth; without a wife to share her husband's bed, it's not a marriage. Although he had never said it before, so many times in the past he had considered the lie to be a legitimate explanation.

Now he had dared to tempt fate, taken the extra step and successfully convinced his moral core that the falsehood was gospel. He had danced around the bold-faced lie, doing the soft-shoe shuffle like a vaudeville song-and-dance man. Although he did not literally say his wife was dead, and did not use those exact words, he had an uneasy, inexplicable feeling. He felt he had just whistled past the graveyard.

"How old is Alexander and who's looking after him, then?"

Nick answered without pause, "Alex is sixteen now, and he's with his grandparents, Nora's mother and father. We keep in touch with the mail, exchanging letters. He writes often." He took a swallow of beer, trying to drown those words. As the beer crossed his tongue, traversed the gullet, and came to rest in the gut, he realized that his secondary lie about Dominik and Gabi would be likely be true had his first lie been the truth. To Nick, the second lie sounded as good as the first.

Nicholas had set the stage for dalliance. He was comfortable with his deception. If taken at face value, his story meant that Gwen could not believe he either was tied to a woman back in the States, or was a scoundrel who could betray spousal trust. He was uncertain where his relationship with the young nurse stood, or how firm her trust in him was, but the foundation was poured. Only time could allow it to harden.

It wasn't his story, but the numbers that stunned Gwen, "Goodness! You have a son of sixteen?"

He looked into her eyes, "Yes. Yes, I do. And I love him and miss him. And even though it's been so many years, I still think of Nora. So, you found me out; you got me, girl. I'm an old man of thirty-five."

She rested her chin in the palm of her hand for a moment, smiling before she put her arms around his neck, kissed him and whispered, "You're not an old man. Experienced ... used ... maybe ... but not old. And I doubt that you're used up."

Those few words lit a fire inside Nicholas with flames tall enough to melt the snow off Mount McKinley*.

They spent the rest of the afternoon at the Roosevelt, talking, laughing and nursing glasses of beer and cider. They sat close on the bench, partly due to the crowd but mainly because they wanted to. Nick discovered she wasn't wearing a brassiere, had youthful breasts as firm as ripe mangos, and once in a while, nipples as hard as aggie marbles. During some hugs and deep kisses, he had managed to slide a hand up her skirt, but, so far, she stopped him at her stocking top.

They shared a single shepherd's pie for dinner, and for the second night in a row on Gwen's suggestion, once again left the music behind to see a movie. It was Wednesday and at the Minerva Theatre on Earl Street, the feature presentation was Orson Wells and Joan Fontaine in *Jane Eyre*.

Except for the film title, it was an encore of the previous night. However, the kiss they shared under the streetlight outside the Transit Quarters was soul deep. They lingered, he held her tight, she trembled and pressed into him, but ever-so-slowly, they begrudgingly parted.

At eleven o'clock he was once again alone in his bed at the Fitzroy. Before falling asleep, he wondered if Gwen had noticed that the film centered on the romance between a young woman and an older man with a disabled wife. He acknowledged that she certainly must have.

J'attendrai (I'll Wait) …

… or perhaps I can't …

Thursday, Gwen and Nick walked along the waterfront and passed the morning hours dodging swooping gulls and talking above the birds' squawks of protest. They shared fish and chips wrapped in newspaper from a street vendor and made a brave but failed attempt at curried mutton.

By evening, they were back in Kings Cross. The ballroom of the Roosevelt was surreal. A world spinning within a world: a double merry-go-round; each going in a different direction: fantasy to the left and reality to the right.

The band had just begun their first set. Nick and Gwen were on the parquet floor, holding each other, dancing to the band's sleepy version of *J'attendrai* when Nick spoke ever so softly into her curls, his lips kissing her hair, "Look around, Gwen. We're invisible, all of us. Nobody really sees anyone. Just about every swinging Richard and furry Kitty is in uniform. The real people, all the regular folks, the citizens are somewhere in hiding. This whole place is make-believe. Everybody in here is ignoring the war; absolutely oblivious to the world outside."

She looked up at him with dreamy eyes and whispered, "I think I like it that way. Make-believe: you, me and nobody else." She began to slow her step, press her body to him, then whispered, "Dance a little closer to me."

He held her tight. His sly smile was hidden in her very soft, pale strawberry locks. He knew something was happening.

She spoke into his chest, "I signed myself out of the Transit hall for the rest of my stay, and gave my contact address as the Fitzroy on Dowling Street. I hope that's agreeable."

Mildly, but pleasantly surprised, he moved slightly away and stated, "That's my hotel."

"I know that, you banana bender!" She gave her special little laugh again, took his hand, and coaxed him off the floor.

Back at their table, Nicholas moved his chair close, covered her hands and fell into her eyes. "You've made up your mind about this, Gwen? Please, please do not think I want to push you into this. I love being with you and believe we have a connection we could build on, but we do not need to jump into this feet-first. In just a few days, a few hours, we'll be separated for what? A week, a year, forever ... who knows how long?"

Her very first words wavered; she blinked rapidly for a moment, but settled into what she wanted to say, "Every woman knows that some man will be the first at some time. When and who is an important decision that no woman ever makes lightly, given the chance. I've made my decision. I picked tonight and I picked you."

He leaned in and kissed her.

She pressed her hands into his and argued, "I want this to happen, Nick. Who knows what tomorrow will mean to either of us? Like you said back there, we're dancing, living, breathing in a fairytale world. For now, it's beautiful, colorful, and full of flowers just like Munchkin Land. Let's enjoy this while we can, see where this Yellow Brick Road leads and who knows, maybe I could get used to the idea of moving to America someday."

Nick quickly decided not to question Gwen's suggestion or dismiss her logic. "Let's drink up, Dorothy."

Gwen lifted her glass of malt cider and toasted him, "Tomorrow we can pick up my luggage, but tonight I'm off to the Fitzroy and the wonderful land of Oz."

Her words caught him by surprise. He nearly gagged on his lager and forced himself to uncomfortably hold back a swallow to prevent beer coming out of his nose. After a painful gulp, a cough, catching his breath, and a second, muffled cough, he stood, and offered his hand as she stood up, ready to leave.

She stuck her pocketbook under her arm and whispered a suggestion into his ear, "We should stop at the all-night chemist around the block so you can select the proper protection."

Nicholas remembered he needed lighter fuel, and perhaps the drugstore would have some for his Zippo. He sensed that he had a bag of firecrackers on his arm, and he was anxiously awaiting the chance to light the fuse.

"No man has taken me on this tour before Nick ... and although I haven't been in the neighborhood, I have seen the postcards and read a few of the brochures. But drive the tour bus slowly, please. I want to see all the sights."

Dancing to 'Deep Pacific' ...

Gwen had trusted Nicholas with her heart and core like no other man. The intimacy they shared that night strongly cemented the relationship for Gwen. If only for the duration of her stay in Sydney, she believed he would respect her in the afterglow of their heated, burning passion.

For Nick, it had been many years since he had felt comfortable with anyone. Contact with the world outside the Army camps was rare and any emotion beyond fear, anger or self-preservation was effectually nonexistent. What he had with Gwen was sparkling clean, intense, and refreshingly new. For him, she was the proverbial 'breath of fresh air' in every way imaginable.

Friday morning, they took a taxi from the Fitzroy to Gwen's temporary quarters near the docks, fetched and returned with her two bags of clothing and personals. After toast and coffee in the Fitzroy's tearoom, he wheedled and teased her to step inside Horace Gladstone's Bauble and Jewel Emporium on Victoria Lane. The most extravagant purchase he was allowed to make was a small, gold, puffed heart on a dainty link necklace. Then it was lunch at Pug & Harvey's, a matinee showing of *Casablanca* at the Roslyn, and another evening at the Roosevelt.

Spending time together was euphoric. Every step, every cobblestone, brick, and lamppost were unique. Every minute was precious and every experience a memory.

Things seemed to slow that evening. Gwen and Nick's emotions also slowed, perhaps knowing that they would be parting all too soon. He held her close on the dance floor, regardless of the tempo. They talked longer between dances and shared much more personal history. Gwen attempted to tease and quiz him with all the prying skills of Holmes and Watson.

"Haven't you met any other nurses other than myself? Any at all? You Americans certainly have medical personnel at your air bases, don't you?"

"There are two nurses in Mangaldan with us now, one doctor, one field surgeon, and two medics. But to tell the honest truth, I couldn't describe them to you, but then again, we just got there a week ago. I think they're just part of a temporary field unit and may be stationed somewhere more permanent later. But back on Morotai, there were four, and I wouldn't cast them off, but I never got to know them. To me, it's too personal, too private, to get involved with people you work with. You may need them someday to be not so personal. Did I say that right? Do you know what I meant?" Nick lit a Camel. He seemed to relax.

"I understand," she said.

Nick went on, "Like I said, back on Morotai there were four and there was one outgoing Lieutenant from Oregon ... no, it was Idaho. Boise, Idaho was where she was from, and her name was Pugwash, Pauline Pugwash. I don't really know if that was her last name but that's what everybody called her. She had a reputation, and I think maybe there were only two flyers in camp that didn't get cozy and canoodle with Pauline. I'm not sure who the other one was, but my guess is that it's Mac ... or maybe the Sandman. I never asked either of them.

"Another one of the Morotai nurses was Millicent Banks, and she could be viciously cruel. I think she was from Philadelphia or New Jersey ... somewhere back East. She could sit at a table in the Officer's Mess and smile that bewitching smile of hers, play a record, and dance with some GI and tease him, laugh and lead him on for hours, allow him to buy her drinks, and light her cigarettes. She would put him through all that, then pin him down, and pull his wings right off like he was a bug ... not really ... figuratively. She would get up, say 'good night' and watch the poor bastard crash and burn without batting an eyelash. One of the flyers she tangled with was one of mine ... from my flight, who came up in rotation for a sortie the following day and didn't come back. That was it. I reported her, and Major Farnsworth had her transferred."

Nick sat back in his chair, his thoughts drifting backwards. Remembering the loss of a pilot disquieted him. He crushed out his cigarette and took two swallows of beer before finishing, "The other two nurses kept to themselves or kept it private. Can't say that I blame them. In camp, it's damn hard to keep secrets. Impossible, really. Anyone who crosses the line and tries to hide anything is a damn fool."

He stood, offered his hand and they were on the parquet again, dancing to *Deep Pacific*. The band shamelessly extended the tune well beyond the normal. After the song ended, the reason became clear: Graeme Bell announced that *Deep Pacific* was one of the promotional records the band was selling copies of.

Instantly, Nick led Gwen up to the bandstand, "I'll buy one right now, Buddy, but you got to sign it for my gal. Sign it, sign it right on the label, not the sleeve: *For Gwen, Love, Nick.*"

If not the record, the memory of Nick's action would remain with Gwen for the rest of her life. She felt she was soaring on his wing, high above the Roosevelt, Australia, and the Pacific itself.

Back at their table, they agreed to one more round of beer and cider before calling it an evening and returning to Room 36 at the Fitzroy. Gwen expressed concern, "I don't feel at all comfortable allowing only you to keep spending your money, Nick. I can contribute ..."

"Never mind. Right now, I'm spending English money ... it's mine, but English. Think of it as repayment for lend-lease* or something like that."

"You need to explain that, Mister."

"My wingman Mac and me, we made some cash on the side in China. Back in '42 we were chasing the Japs, and flying in and out of make-shift airfields inside China ... sometimes with stones from Siam ... jade ... under our T-shirts or chutes for some Royal Air Force brass ... Colonel Percy ... Percival, I can't remember his last name ... paid us on the sly for carrying them with us from Kunming to Binyang, to another Limey and his name I can remember, because I know that he loved saying it: Colonel Montague Cranston of the Third Royal Tactical Air Force. A real mouthful and a real pain in the ass, he was. Him and his pal Percy were sending them stones on to Hong Kong right under the Jap's noses."

"You two were smuggling, then."

"I guess you could call it that. But we were killing Japs and blowing things up, too. Maybe some people would have a hard time figuring out what's worse. I don't."

There wasn't any more Army talk that night, either American, British, or Australian.

We'll Meet Again …

Much of Saturday was spent in and around the Hotel Fitzroy. Gwen had reminded Nick that it wasn't necessarily their last day together. He allowed her to believe it. *'If we only had more time'*, he thought.

He pondered: *'Then what? What would more time mean?'* There was no answer to that question. His thoughts drifted and allowed him to wonder what life in Australia would be like.

Nick was the first to wake up on Sunday morning. A breath of air through the balcony window allowed a sliver of sunlight to slice its way through the bamboo blinds and dance across her face. He was experiencing an emotional connection he hadn't felt at any other time in his life.

Nora was the end result of combining family tragedy, lack of direction, emotional hunger, immaturity, and hormones.

Gladys was half of an honest friendship that became steeped in pent-up sexual fulfillment brought about by opportunity and convenience.

Bonita, Llewellyn, Iris, Perpetua, and perhaps a half dozen others in the Western Hemisphere were just part of the ride, mere bumps in the road.

But this nurse, this Aussie named Guendolen Peate was different. Lying next to her and watching her sleep, he experienced a revelation. He was in the middle of an awakening, an epiphany. For the first time in his life, he felt a deep, honest love for another human. Not familial love, but a fastening, bonding, knotting two souls together kind of love.

And he knew that she trusted him; loved him.

For the previous three days and nights they were inseparable. Today, the harsh actuality of war would drop an impenetrable curtain between them. It was a certainty they did not want to acknowledge and neither wanted to hear the noise that it would make.

She awoke to a kiss on the cheek and exhausted the next hour in her lover's arms tossing, turning, and twisting the act of making love into a horizontal ballet. Very few words were spoken that morning.

Breakfast became lunch downstairs in the tearoom of the hotel. They traded service and home addresses from pieces torn from the Fitzroy's menu. Gwen had a report time of two o'clock at the Kuttabul Royal Australian Naval Base and time was quickly disappearing.

"I know I will see you again, Nicholas. I am as confident of that as I am that the sun will shine tomorrow, but in the meantime, please keep that airplane of yours flying above the clouds and your wheels landing on friendly soil."

"Have no fear, Gwen. When it comes to clouds, I prefer to wear them as a hat rather than shoes. I've been doing it for years and I stay under the radar whenever I can. It seems that I know lots of ways to be wicked, but all my life, I sure as hell have had a hard time falling in love. But you got me, girl. You got me good. I will always love you."

"We will be together after all this is over, I know it. I feel it in my heart, Nick."

He shifted his chair closer, held her hands in his and fell into her eyes, "There's so much more I want to enjoy with you, Gwen. I want life with you. I want to share things that I miss, forgotten, or didn't appreciate the first time around. Like spending hours with Alexander; the cool side of the pillow; to read the Saturday comics and laugh until it hurts; to feel the warmth of a woman I actually love; to sleep without the fear of bad dreams; to make love and feel the Earth move; to feel the morning sun warm my face; to enjoy a glass of beer with a head like custard; and to wake up next to you every morning."

The moment was committed to eternal memory with their kiss.

What happened next was forever lost. Together, they silently went through the motions and got done what needed to be done, and went where they needed to go.

The cabbie stopped about ten yards from the gate of the Kuttabul naval station. The driver set the parking brake, opened the back door for Nick and Gwen, set her bags on the ground and quickly got back behind the wheel. Obviously accustomed to farewells, he seemed in a hurry to get out of the way.

"Don't forget your promise, Nick. No long goodbyes."

"I haven't forgotten, Gwen, but honestly this is harder than I could have imagined ..."

She stood on tiptoe and kissed him. He held her, his hands nearly circling her waist.

"You look damn snappy in that outfit, Nurse."

She straightened herself, gave him a salute, "See you later, Captain," turned, picked up her bags, wobbled with her first step, and started toward the gate. An unconcerned sailor stood at attention outside the guard shack.

After a week with Nurse Peate, Nick felt that he had found a friend for life, the love of his life, and strangely enough, the most intimate female liaison of his thirty-five years. As he watched her walk past the sentry shack and into the maze of buildings, equipment, personnel, and vehicles on the docks, he felt the hole she left in his heart.

Nick couldn't watch anymore.

He got in the cab, "Back to the Fitzroy, bud."

He began to play with the idea of meeting up with her again and mused, *'I probably should take this seriously. I think I need to look her up after this bullshit ends. We'll keep in touch, and figure something out.'*

At 1800 hours, Sunday, 26 November 1944, Australian Hospital Ship *Centaur**, Red Cross designation #47, sailed from Darling Harbor, Woolloomooloo, Sydney, Australia enroute to Port Moresby, New Guinea.

Nick went back to Llandover Pub that night; the drinkery where he and Gwen had met for the first time. A few times he caught himself looking around the place to see if he could find her hiding somewhere in the dark shadows between the brick archways and murky cubby holes. With a crutch of Tooheys and Bishop's brandy, he hobbled through the night without Gwen.

On Monday afternoon, he managed to get aboard another gigantic, blue-grey C-47 for his return flight back to the Philippines. He had a headache without mercy; as fierce as a Tasmanian Tiger*.

Two howling 1200 horsepower Pratt & Whitney engines powered the nine-ton metal behemoth along the concrete and asphalt; lifting four crew, twenty men, and three tons of cargo barely five feet in the air before it ran out of runway. Protesting with creaks and moans, the big aircraft became airborne, banking slowly to the left directly over Sydney harbor toward a course heading due north over the Coral Sea and on to Mangaldan, the Philippines.

November 30, 1944 ... 27°16.98′S + 153°59.22′ ...

Hot tropical air, thick cigarette smoke and the sweat of four dozen men filled the inside of the large tent like a wet bar rag. The clatter of talk, buzz of whispers, and muffled laughter disappeared as the Executive Officer hollered *Attention!* and stood aside as a brigadier general, two colonels and a major walked to the front and took their seats. Before the November 30th regular Monthly Staff Debrief and Status meeting began, Colonel Kimball announced the creation of a new squadron of attack fighters for *search, engage, and report* duty in conjunction with the Luzon Offensive. Nick and one young flyer from the 471ˢᵗ volunteered immediately for the transfer and were informed that their papers would be processed within two days.

Nick's spontaneous decision only slightly surprised his wingman and friend, Mac. A week or so earlier, Nick had mentioned that he was anxious to see new horizons. Things were changing within Bravo Wing. The unit itself was swamped with ninety-day wonders* and new flyers from the States. Additionally, the battle-weary P-38 Lightnings of the 39ᵗʰ Squadron had recently been swapped out for new equipment: gleaming stainless-steel P-51 Mustangs*. Nick's Flying Phaeton was headed for a tired iron bone yard on Guam. Nick felt it was time to move on.

The debrief meeting lurched, and lugged along, gradually getting underway. After an overview of the Squadron Aircraft and Personnel Readiness and Morning Report was read, the junior-grade officers were summarily dismissed.

When the dust settled, and the sound of boots on wooden planks got back to bearable levels, the monthly meeting resumed. Personnel Projections, Quartermaster, and Motor Pool Utilization Reports, Leave Rotation Roster, and the unpleasant Casualty Release were read in endless monotone by the Group Information Officer: some Second Lieutenant without a name. The Information Officer changed from one week to the next and nobody ever seemed to know where they disappeared to.

The last thing covered during these monthly meetings was the Enemy Action And Response Assessment: sort of a Southwest Pacific Theater report card. It gave an overview of what had occurred, the results, and what was planned if further action was deemed necessary. The same Information Officer read all this additional verbiage in the same tedious, vocal drone. Nonetheless, this report always got appreciably more attention than the others. It contained information that affected the job at hand: troop movements, equipment inventories, intelligence appraisals, personnel levels, airfield readiness, and ordnance logistics.

These briefings contained overflow information that was generally days-old, had been de-classified, and made available for press release. There was always an overabundance of low-level intelligence during these sessions, but Captain Nicholas Throckmorton only heard the details of one noteworthy incident:

"The AHS Centaur* of the Royal Australian Navy was attacked at approximately 0400 hours on November 27th by a Japanese submarine in the Coral Sea, 24 nautical miles east-northeast of Point Lookout, North Stradbroke Island, Queensland, Australia: roughly 27° South and 154° East. Although clearly identified as a Red Cross Hospital vessel, the Centaur was torpedoed. The explosion set the ship afire and within three minutes it rolled to port and sank bow-first. The Centaur was enroute from Sydney to Port Moresby, New Guinea on a scheduled personnel and supply mission. Of 332 aboard, 268 have perished, including all 12 nurses of the Australian Army Nursing Service, all 8 Australian Army doctors and 180 of 219 members of the 12th Australian Field Ambulance. 63 survivors have been rescued by the USS Mugford, a Bagley class destroyer of the United States Pacific Fleet. A strong protest has been made to the International Red Cross."

Nick didn't move a muscle. His eyes were fixated on the gigantic map hanging on the wall behind the blackboard, beyond the Information Officer standing at the podium, past the four Field Officers seated at the eight-foot table, and far past the card table with a full pitcher of water and a dozen empty glasses.

Although Nick's eyes were glued to the specific spot of the attack, he only saw Gwen struggling with her bags, walking away through the front gates of Royal Australian Naval Station, **Kuttabul**. No more than twelve hours after the Centaur was torpedoed and sunk, the gigantic C-47 Skytrain with Nick aboard had flown directly over the sunken vessel.

Again, he heard her words, "See you later, Captain."

Three years of war and arduous encounters with the enemy had calloused Nicholas and numbed his humanity. Kamikaze attacks and the mass suicides of Japanese civilian populations on Saipan* and Guam gave testimony to the enemy's desire to fight to the death. Over the years, stark accounts of the Bataan* Death March and the general mistreatment of prisoners were verified by liberated populations. Further, he had convinced himself that his brother Leopold's murder was a direct consequence of the Japanese attack on Pearl Harbor. Ultimately, the sinking of the AHS Centaur cemented Nick's contempt for all things Japanese: living, dead, or manufactured. By Thanksgiving, 1944, his animosity toward the enemy far exceeded what he had once held for Lorenzo Torricelli.

Nick was a dedicated soldier; a hard wrought flyer willing to punish the enemy by whatever means available. He wanted to do more and was given the chance.

On December 1st, 1944, Major General Dennis Blackburn, Commander of the 5th US Army Air Force, held a lengthy, far-reaching interview with Captain Throckmorton. Also present were Colonel David Mayer of the Army Counter-Intelligence Corps, and Major Rayford Johnson of the Office of Strategic Services*, the OSS*.

Nick's transfer was approved and signed that afternoon.

8: STRAIGHTEN UP AND FLY RIGHT …
1945-46

... back to business ...

Two weeks later, Nick's security clearance was finalized. On January 16, 1945, Nicholas was promoted to Major and assigned to the 15th Aerial Reconnaissance Detachment of the 58th Fighter Group.

The 15th Aerial Reconnaissance Detachment did not exist. The 58th Fighter Group did.

Nick had begun to taxi down a different runway.

Robert McElvoy was promoted to First Lieutenant and took Nick's old slot of Flight Commander, Bravo Wing. Since Nick's boyhood in Buffalo, Mac was the closest thing to a true friend that Nick had ever known. Discounting family and Guendolen Peate, nobody else had ever gotten close to him. Nick's transfer and promotion had separated him from Mac for the first time since they had enlisted.

Starting with his initial flights as an Army pilot in 1938, Nick's ability to control an airplane got him noticed by his superiors. His years as a duster had taught him the skills that only come from hands-on experience. He had a love for the sky, an instinctive knack for flying low, a sense of the ground beneath his wings, and an eye for trouble on the horizon, be it trees or the enemy. Nick's reputation preceded his arrival at the 58th on Luzon.

Nick had arrived in Porac, the Philippines, at an airfield and encampment that only two days earlier had been hacked out of the jungle on the north side of Manila Bay. The driver tapped the brakes and brought the jeep and its passenger to a sliding, slippery stop at the boardwalk's edge. Black skies, a torrential downpour and a scrawny corporal in a rain-soaked slicker welcomed Major Throckmorton directly outside the Operations tent. It was just past midday, but with the blur of twilight. There were twenty-two new Republic P-47

Thunderbolts* tucked up against the tree line. Sporadic small-arms fire echoed from the jungle. Intermittent artillery rounds from hold-out Japanese positions could be heard exploding on the distant hillsides.

The young corporal needed to raise his voice over the weather and weaponry, "Welcome to the 58th, Sir ... Colonel Drew's waiting for you inside, Sir." The one-man welcoming committee picked up Nick's duffle from the back of the jeep and took ten long strides inside the tent. The pelting rain stung the back of Nick's neck as he exited the vehicle.

Inside, two men sat behind a folding table, lit by three bare bulbs, precariously hanging from the metal skeleton of the tent and swinging to the rhythm of the rain. A chugging diesel generator powered the lights and a ten-inch electric floor fan that wobbled and chattered noisily at full speed. Rainwater was leaking through the stretched, strained seams of the canvas roof.

The colonel barked to the soldier from the front of the tent, "That's all, Corporal, thank you. You're dismissed." He needed to bark; otherwise, he wouldn't be heard over the tropical downpour.

Nick stuck his hat under his arm, snapped and held a salute.

Thaddeus Drew was a veteran full-bird colonel with bristly, short white hair and sun-blackened skin as rough as alligator hide. An unlit cigar stub was stuck in the left side of his mouth. Still seated, he returned Nick's salute and spoke in a cement-mixer voice, "Good afternoon, Major, and welcome. Have a seat. I'm Colonel Drew, your new Group Commander, and this is General Garcia-Ramos of the Mexican National Air Force*."

"Thank you, Sir. Good afternoon, Sir ... General Ramos, Sir."

Nick was incredulous. His mind raced; *This can't be a joke. A bird colonel wouldn't pull a bullshit Chinese fire drill joke. Who in hell ever heard of the Mexican Air Force? And what in hell are they doing in this godforsaken hole?*

Nick took a seat on the only other chair inside the tent, opposite the Colonel and General, about three feet away from the table. He knew something was coming; he could hear the train rumbling down the track. The whistle wasn't blowing, but it was definitely getting closer.

The colonel pushed and rolled his cigar from one side of his mouth to the other, "I need to know what you're comfortable with, Major Throckmorton. Looking at your record I know that you're a good soldier, and a goddamn good pilot. Your last Group Commander had high praise for your talent and drive, Major Throckmorton, and stuck a Letter of Commendation in your APF. And General Blackburn himself signed your assignment papers. But ... what I want to know is this: how do you feel about your job, Major? How do you feel about your job in the Army Air Force?"

"My job is The Mission, Sir. My job is to believe in The Mission, ensure my men understand The Mission and carry out The Mission as ordered, Sir."

"Do you think you can learn Mexican, Major?"

"Yes, Sir." Nick's reply came without forethought. He felt goose bumps at the nape of his neck but was happy with his answer.

What ensued was essentially a job interview that would evolve into an orientation the following day.

Nick quickly studied the Mexican general. He was big, round, and wore a brown leather bandolier over his left shoulder. His wide, thick mustache seemed big enough to hide a ham sandwich.

Colonel Drew laid it out, "About 300 of General Garcia-Ramos' countrymen, pilots and ground crew, are currently winding up their training in Texas and California. In about two months, we expect them to be in-country, attached with the 58th, combat-ready, and flying combat missions as a squadron. These men know English, but I need you, Major, to know Mexican ... Spanish. We have an official from the War Department and an Army Ranger scheduled to arrive tomorrow along with a Puerto Rican Sergeant from the Signal Corps. These men will put you through some intense, but thorough crash courses, so you and the Mexicans can better understand one another."

Colonel Drew gave General Ramos a quick glance and continued, "I'm sure your flight experience will be extremely helpful to the pilots in dealing with the enemy, and I think that anything you can pass on to our Mexican allies will be appreciated. During the next couple of days, you will discover that this is a mission that consists of several different levels of participation, and soon it will be explained in detail. Are you on board with this, Major?"

"Yes, Sir." Nick was still expecting a punch line.

General Ramos spoke, "Have you ever visited Mexico, Major Throckmorton?" He had enough colorful campaign ribbons and medals on his chest to replicate a fruit salad.

Nick answered, "Years ago, I would fly over Mexico, gas up. and spend a night in Veracruz on my way to Honduras. And I have dusted my share of corn fields in Tamaulipas and Neuvo León … I also spent three nights in Tamaulipas State, in Matamoros, that seemed to last a week."

From the corner of his eye, Nick watched for a reaction from Colonel Drew but didn't get one.

Garcia-Ramos smiled and exulted, "¡Muy bien! Very good! You know something what to expect! I think you will like the working with the *Aguilas Aztecas*, my Aztec Angels, Major Throckmorton!"

The General was exuberant. It was impossible not to notice. Again, Nicholas looked to his colonel for some kind of rebound, or backfire, and again, there was none.

Colonel Drew reached into a worn leather satchel at the side of his chair and pulled up a bottle of Teachers Blended Highland Cream and three dirty, mismatched coffee mugs. He poured two fingers of the golden-brown nectar into each, pushed one across the table toward Nick and the other to his left, over to General Garcia-Ramos.

"There's no such thing as American whiskey* here in this Paradise, Major. And I know Scotch ain't no substitute for tequila, General, but it's all I got." Drew stood and raised his cup, "Here's to the Mission, gentlemen."

Nick also stood, following the colonel's lead, then the general followed suit.

Nick acknowledged the toast, raised his stained mug, and announced, "To The Mission, Colonel, Sir, General, Sir!"

Although that afternoon, it was not perfectly clear what the Mission was.

Adios, Muchachos … creating a work of art

... pencil, pen, chalk, oil, or watercolor ...

The following day Nick was introduced to three people who would assist in painting a clear picture of the Mission.

Agent Angus Munson of the US Department of State, provided the canvas and cast clear, but indirect light on the subject:

Discontented populations and unstable governments created the climate that allowed world war to erupt in the late 1930s. It would be in the interest of the United States to ensure that those conditions did not develop in the Western Hemisphere.

There were new jobs appearing on the horizon; jobs that would be important to American interests after the war. Well-qualified pilots, for example, would be in demand by any government or opposition group that should desire to train, establish, or upgrade an air force. US Army Intelligence and the Office of Strategic Services would provide those governments or groups with the experienced men and any aircraft they needed. Angus Munson explained that additional training was needed before Nicholas could become an OSS agent qualified for the Mission.

Nick agreed with Agent Munson that clandestine operations were essential for the Mission's success.

First Lieutenant Howard Loudermilk of the US Army 4th Rangers, set up the easel, drew the outlines, and mixed the pigments:

The forward-thinkers in Washington anticipated a huge surplus of planes and equipment after the hostilities in Europe and the Pacific ended, thus creating a market for many items that certain governments in the Western Hemisphere would find desirable. A man with proper physical training, ample flight experience, and a working knowledge of airplane mechanics would be an invaluable asset to any government or group wishing to establish a flying air force with world-class capabilities. The US Army Rangers would provide the training and tools to ensure that Nicholas Throckmorton had the required qualifications for any clandestine work.

Nick agreed with Lieutenant Laudermilk's belief in the survival of the fittest.

Sergeant Simón Vasquello of the US Sixth Army, 35th Signal Corps Brigade, finished the background, added highlights, and fine brush strokes:

Spanish is the primary language of Caribbean, Central, and South American countries. The US Army Signal Corps would provide whatever tools Nicholas needed to master Latin American Spanish* in under a year.

Nick agreed with Sergeant Vasquello that human interaction and foreign language skills were important.

From January 20th until August 1st, 1945, Major Nicholas Throckmorton was a student of intelligence tactics, survival skills, and language arts.

Nick's assignment to the 58th Fighter Group was only on paper. Although he did not fly in combat with the Aztec Angels, he did advise the Mexican flyers on evasion strategies and combat maneuvers. They were particularly enthused over the 'zoom and boom' (¡zoom y tronar!) Flying Tiger tactics practiced by the AVG in Burma.

I'll Make A Happy Landing ...

The Empire of Japan accepted the terms for unconditional surrender on August 15, 1945. The Second World War was over.

In late February 1946, thirteen months after he began his OSS training, Nick was released from duty in the Philippines and reassigned to the 8th Army Air Force for demobilization* and Honorable Discharge.

... *a reunion* ... *March 1946*
Okinawa, Ryukyu Islands, Occupied Japan

Sixty-five degrees on a bombed-out island in the East China Sea is cold when all you've known for the past eighteen months has been ninety-five degrees on another bombed-out island in the South China Sea. For Nick, temperature was the only qualifying difference between Okinawa and the Philippines.

The Officer's Club at Kadena Airfield was a far cry from a resort, but for the homeward bound flyers and penguins, scratchy records playing on a Zenith phonograph, canned Rainier beer, and hotplate hamburgers were Heaven on Earth. The noise inside the Quonset hut was an indecipherable buzz of human chatter and mechanical clatter. A familiar voice cut through the thick layers of racket, "Captain!! Old Man!! Over here! It's me, Mac!"

Across a sea of khaki, Nick spotted a waving, upraised arm and began weaving his way through the crowd of officers. The reunited friends shook hands. "Damn it all, Sir! You got promoted, I didn't know. Congratulations, Major!"

"Forget the rank, Mac ... it doesn't matter anymore. How the hell have you been, pal? You're looking good."

"Oh, I'm doing great, Old Man; can't complain. This war's over and I'm going home. We're all going home. It's only a matter of days now and I heard we'll be shipping out on Monday ... they say some tub is on its way from Calcutta to pick us up! Imagine that! All the way from India."

Nick was glad to see his friend again; it meant he had made it through. "Come on, Mac. Let's grab a couple beers and find a spot ... and lock down the landing gear and park awhile. And catch up ... it's been a while."

Nick and Mac carried four cans of beer from the makeshift bar of pallets and scrap sheet metal. They ended up at one of the tables at the far end, furthest away from the cold beer and loud talk. The remnants of battle were hung throughout the 48 by 20-foot Quonset as macabre amenities: parachutes as curtains on the four small window slots, a tattered Rising Sun flag, propellers and the odd blade, auxiliary fuel drop tanks, bits of ailerons and rudders, instrument panels from a downed enemy Betty and Zero, a bloodied kamikaze headband, and just about any other item that could otherwise be termed as war scrap.

"I bet you're looking forward to seeing your Alexander and Nora again, Buddy. Are they doing all right?"

Nick opened a can of Rainier, and answered, "I hear from Alex every couple of weeks, and for a kid who just turned eighteen, I would say that's pretty damn good. I don't get the chance to write as often as I like, but then again ... besides death and destruction, there really ain't much to write about is there?"

Mac's curiosity pressed on, "How about you and your wife, Nora? Any hope to rekindle the fire after you're back stateside and maybe save your marriage?"

Since the day they first met in Monroe, Louisiana, Nick found it easy to talk to Robert McElvoy. Now, seven years later, the kid from Asheville had proven to be a trusted friend and confidant. Together, they collected years of miles under their belts and have watched one another's back in bars as well as battles. With a quick metallic click, Nick put the flame of his Zippo to a cigarette and confessed, "Hell, no, man. That war was over the day it started. I didn't stand a chance against Nora's righteousness. I wouldn't ... couldn't ... surrender, so the only way out was a truce. I quit that battle and laid down my arms years ago."

Sadly, Mac could only listen.

Nick had broken the dam and released a torrent of words, "I could never understand why the Church has to be so damn vindictive. I cannot speak for you, but I think when someone walks through the doors for Sunday service, or goes to see the Chaplain, they should feel good about it. After all, it's supposed to be the House of God, right? Hell, if I didn't want to walk out feeling good, why would I go in the first place? And after the preacher gets done with that monotone lecture, they all give ... that's what it is you know: a lecture. When he finishes that, then he starts in with all the fire and damnation and tells everyone that they'll go straight to Hell if they don't drop to their knees and ask for forgiveness ... and I'm telling you ... I've looked around them congregations, and the pews are full of people that have had their wits scared out of them. I mean, they're scared to death, almost. The preacher tells everybody that they're going to Hell, and a lot of them poor bastards believe it.

"It's just my personal observation, but the world is full of good people on Sundays, or so it seems. But every other day of the week, not so much. And them Catholics, well that's a horse of the same color, but colored in with thick, blood red, and black crayons, and white candle wax. I know that from experience, my friend. They stand up there and tell you in Latin that you're going flat-out to Hell. Nobody but priests and nuns understand that dead language, so maybe that's a good thing. And now that I'm talking about them Jesuits, I think any faith that denies the humanity of its flock and even its clergy, whether they're a man or a woman, is simply living in the Stone Age. People are people and people do what people do whether they're sitting right up front in the first row on Sunday or they're wearing a starched collar or not.

"And they cannot eat meat at all on Friday. You know that ... and it's a sin, part of the dogma. What happens if you can't read the calendar? You go to Hell? What I'm trying to say is: I don't need no righteous, pompous preacher, or priest, or any white collar, telling me I'm going to Hell. Put it this way, after what I've seen and done in this war, I don't have any great expectations for salvation, but when that roll is called up yonder ... like they say ... I want to be at the controls of a *Flying Phaeton*, holding the stick, flying low, cannon blasting, and guns blazing ... and clearing the path for the righteous."

Nick lit another Camel and asked, "But this ain't no willy-waving contest here, Mac ... and I don't mean to stand here pissing into the wind. Me and Nora are done. I mean, I love the woman, I do. She's a good person and a damn good, caring mother. It's just a shame that I couldn't find the doorway through that wall of centuries-old tenets that separates us. We simply cannot connect as man and woman.

"Do you know what I mean? If you take the Bible literally, word for word, the whole world is going to explode someday anyhow at Armageddon … sometimes I feel myself getting stupider … by just trying to explain myself."

Nick didn't wait for a response, "Any of the other men here with you, Mac? Anybody I know?"

It was a few seconds before Mac answered, "I left Sandman behind at Le Shima Airbase because he didn't have enough points for the Magic Carpet[*], so I think he's technically part of the occupation for now, but next month I think he should be able to get back home to Tennessee. They told him he will have enough points by then."

Nick dropped his Camel to the dirt floor and crushed it out with his boot, "Sooner or later somebody's bound to get it right. Sooner or later."

... Chicago: three and a half weeks later, April 1ˢᵗ ...

After three days at Kadena Airfield, Okinawa, Nick, Mac and 3,500 other US servicemen went aboard the troopship *USS General Bliss** and spent fifteen days crossing the Pacific Ocean to Seattle, Washington. When they disembarked at the Port of Seattle, there was somewhat of a welcoming committee: a fleet of Army busses, six-ton and deuce-and-a-half 'cattle' trucks ready to transport the men to Fort Lewis for debriefing, final physicals, civilian orientation, and mustering out.

With seven years and ten months of active duty under their belts, it was yet another four days before Nick and Mac were officially out of the Army Air Force and aboard an eastbound diesel-powered, streamlined, passenger train.

At ten minutes past noon on Monday, April 1, 1946, they arrived in Chicago, Illinois on the Milwaukee Road's *Olympian* from Tacoma, Washington. They were no longer directly under the wing of the Army Air Force. They were essentially tourists; reborn civilians in a strange land: they were back in the United States.

The victory, post-war, and welcome home parties had ended six months earlier. When Nick, Mac and scores of other former airmen, soldiers, and sailors arrived at Union Station there were no ticker-tape parades, beauty queens, roaring crowds, fanfare, or marching bands. Two hotdog vendors, four newsboys, a rag-tag shoeshine man, and a three-piece Salvation Army Band were their welcoming committee.

The train terminal overflowed with unfamiliar sounds, sights and smells. The flyers' senses reached an anomalous altitude elevated by odors their nostrils had not whiffed and sounds their ears had not heard for six-plus years. Additionally, they were surrounded by a peaceful population of civilians and structures that were unmarred by explosions or gunfire.

Nicholas Throckmorton stopped in his tracks, looked to his friend Robert McElvoy and observed assertively, "You know, Mac, this is damn near like Christmas ... back when we were kids, little kids, I mean. If you were lucky enough to have maybe more than one present under the tree, you had to figure out which one to open first. Do you know what I'm talking about? Did you ever have that feeling of not being sure which one to open first? It's because you're a little bit afraid of opening the best one first. Do you know what I mean? You might open the one with the two-bit jackknife first, then you just know that the next one is going to be a pair of socks. Know what I'm talking about?"

"Yeah, I think so."

Nick dropped his bags to the platform with a thud and lit a Camel.

"You know what we're going to do, Mac? We're going to go ahead and open the first present ... open the jackknife. To Hell with it. Let's go find ourselves a bar." With a lit cigarette dangling from the corner of his mouth, Nick slung the straps of the duffle over his shoulder, picked up his barracks bag, and started from trackside into the station. "Come on, Mac. I've been waiting for this."

Nick knew exactly what was on the other side of the huge glass and brass revolving doors of Union Station. Directly across the street sat the Hotel Palmer. Down the street, to the right and half a block down South Canal at the corner of Adams Street, he would find Twin Anchors Bar and Grill. Nick had memorized the location, description and directions from the OSS departure briefing he had received from Angus Munson in the Philippines. He knew the time, key word, and name of the agent whom he was to meet there. Additionally, he knew the menu.

"First, let's get us a couple of rooms, Mac. Then we'll say hello to a T-bone steak and a beer. What do you say, pal?"

"Wilco, Nick. I can hardly wait. And tomorrow I'm going home. And for me, it'll be *Hello Asheville!*"

Agua Caliente ...

3 PM ... steak and potatoes ...

From the sidewalk, there was no doubt that a gin mill lay behind the aged industrial brick exterior. From one window, a neon sign beamed in green: *Pilsen Pilsner.* From the opposite side, another glowed in warm red: *Best. Chicago's Best.*

Inside the Twin Anchors, a thirty-foot polished cherry bar ran along the right wall. Eight large, stained-glass ceiling lamps hung from the varnished wainscot ceilings and cast mottled light onto the oiled white pine floors. Behind the bar, against the mirrored wall and snuggled between the rows of liquor bottles, sat an RCA Master's Voice round-top parlor radio tuned to WGN, 720 AM and the *Chicago Theater of The Air* program. Two faded souls in tattered work clothes occupied the barstools closest the door and worked on a bowl of French burnt peanuts alongside two bottles of Best beer. A middle-aged couple sat about halfway down; possibly drinking a late lunch. Odors of hot grease, fresh-baked bread, beer and cigarettes drifted together and wafted through the room.

There was a dozen or so tables scattered throughout the tavern, each with red and white gingham tablecloths. A four-hand game of Canasta was going on at one and checkers at another.

As soon as Nick and Mac sat down, a short, squat, round-faced fellow dressed in a white shirt, black tie, and shiny Woolworth slacks waddled over to their table. Mac was full of anticipation. The guy had arms like logs.

"Welcome to the Anchors, men ... you still in or are you out?"

"Out." Mac answered within an eye blink. Nick didn't offer an answer. His eyes were going over the room one more time.

The barman made a perfunctory excuse, "I apologize, men, the kitchen doesn't normally open until about four o'clock, but for GI's I always make the exception. I'll go back in the kitchen and light a fire under Frankie's ass. He needs ..."

Nick interrupted, "There's no need to go out of the way ... I'm Nick, and this here is my pal, Mac ... we're not in a rush, and we can wait, but in the meantime, a beer would sure taste good ... I would like a Detroit beer ... a bottle of Stroh's."

Mac added, "Me, too. I'll try one of them Detroit brews."

The barman forced a celluloid smile and nodded, "Two bottles of Stroh's then and it's not a bother about the kitchen; I'll tell Frankie to fire up the stove. It's not a bother in the least little bit, you see. The menu's written right over there on the chalkboard, fellas, and it's really short and sweet. I got fry pan chili with fresh hard rolls, or broiled T-bone with fried potatoes. That's it. And beer and booze, of course. And me, I'm Paul. Just plain Paul. You men got here a little early but at a good time, though. Even though it's Monday, the place will fill up quick in the next couple hours, just you wait. The boys from the rail yards and the river rat teamsters will pour in."

Nick's anticipation for his first clandestine holes-corners-and-back-room meeting faded. *Paul* wasn't the name of his contact, and the muscle-bound bartender clearly didn't recognize the key word. It was understandable: Nick was in fact, about two hours early. He had no recourse but to place his order, "It's steak for me, Paul, medium well if you please."

Mac duplicated Nick's order; Paul thanked them and was off.

Mac lit a Lucky Strike, and leaned back in his chair, "That's what I like, Nick. Nice and easy, straight-up, simple, short and sweet, just like the guy said. It's a good way to run a business."

Mac didn't get a comment from Nick, and handed him yet another verbal nudge, "What's your plan, Nick? Do you have anything lined up back home in Detroit?"

Nick was wondering if Mac could be the fly in the ointment, and if his presence could possibly have thrown a monkey wrench into his expected encounter. "No rock-hard plans yet, Mac ... haven't really given it too much thought, to tell the truth. I have enough dough in the bank to do me for a while ... but I can tell you what I'm going to do first thing ... I'm going to get me some civvies. I'm a little tired of the pink and greens."

Paul brought the beer and announced, "Your dinner will be out before too long, men. Frankie's got it under control. If you do decide to stick around for a while, some dames generally filter in, but some of them expect a free drink or a meal, if you know what I mean, and we got more bar and waitress help coming in for the rush. You can maybe make some good friends. We even got what we call 'Old Reliable', an old '39 Rock-Ola* jukebox tucked away in the back corner with some jazz and swing records. So, you feel free to stick around, because there's no stink on GI's. Not here."

Nick gave him a strained smile, "All that's good to hear, Paul ... it is ... bring a couple more Stroh's with the meal, OK? We probably will stick around for a little while ... we got no particular place to go."

Paul's response was, "Sure enough."

It could have been that Paul was leaving a coded message. Nick had no way to be sure; he was new at this.

... dim lights, thick smoke, and loud, loud music ...

The Twin Anchors began to fill up just as Paul had said it would, beginning about half past four. Nick was anticipating the interaction that was laid out for him in Fort Lewis and slowly nursing his second bottle of Stroh's. As the clock approached five, Nick and Mac moved to the bar and laid claim to two stools on the right end. With beer-fueled nostalgia, the men exchanged home addresses written on the backs of pressed-paper bar coasters. After his fourth beer, Mac started to supplement his alcohol intake with shots of Johnny Walker and was bravely feeding the cotton cloud growing within his skull, "Just prop me up against the bar, Nick. That bartender Paul said that we're among friends here."

Mac's unusual, inebriate behavior bothered Nick to the point where he considered that his friend could embarrass or burden him. Nick blamed his friend's reckless drinking on his sudden freedom, homesickness, and the excitement of homecoming, and decided that it was his duty to work through any awkward situation that Mac could create.

A waitress in a blue and white seersucker uniform appeared from the kitchen, pinned her greying hair back, tied her apron, and adjusted a brassiere strap on her way to join another who was already taking a food and drink order at one of the tables. A second bartender, younger, solid, and with thick, black razor stubble, began pouring drinks and popping beers.. Separately, Paul was talking with a raven-haired, tawny-skinned young woman at the other end of the bar. She was tall, with a toned figure, marvelous Mediterranean features, and dressed in a calf-length black skirt, a ruffled white half apron, and a flowered, short, puffed sleeve blouse. As an alewife, she did not appear to fit in. She looked into the mirror behind the bar, fingered a wisp of hair back off her temple and gave Nick and Mac a passing glance before turning her attention back to Paul. Nick caught her glimpse. The beauty and the barman shared a quiet laugh just as she picked up a bar towel and moved toward the other bartender at the far end.

Someone loudly asked that the radio be turned off. Paul looked toward the voice, nodded acknowledgement and fulfilled the anonymous request with the turn and click of a knob. With strained impatience, somebody stuck some nickels in the jukebox. Within sixty seconds the machine came to life with the sound of the Isham Jones Orchestra and Marilyn Thorne performing some signature swing: *There's A Wah-Wah Gal In Agua Caliente.*

Mac was studying the new arrival behind the bar, "That's sure one sweet looking babe down there, Nick." She turned and started toward them as Mac's slurred words fell from his mouth. "Here she comes, wing leader, right at us, ten o'clock high*."

She stood squarely in front of them, smiled at Mac and then directed her question to Nick, "Hello, I'm Jovita ... but it's much easier to say Joe or Joey, so that's what I use. Can I get you flyers anything?" She had a Latin accent that flowed like warm, brown Cuban cane molasses.

Nick was surprised and inquisitive, "I'd like another beer, another Stroh's ... a Detroit beer, if you would … please."

What had just occurred took Nick by surprise. He did not consider that his contact could be a woman, or that the name *Joe* could refer to a woman, and certainly not a good-looking woman.

Mac didn't hesitate to ask for another, "Me, too, I'll have another beer and a Johnny Walker Black, as well." He forced back and swallowed a beer burp.

The barmaid ignored him, and spoke to Nick, "What's your name, Major?"

"Nick. Nicholas Throckmorton from Detroit, but I'm no longer a Major … I'm out of the Army now, so you can drop the *Major* part ... Joey."

"That's good to hear, and I'm glad that you're back safe ... and that you and your friend here ..."

"I'm Mac, sweetheart ... Mac ... I'm Nick's wingman from way back. We're pals, real pals from way back ... when we were dusting and buzzing ... way back to bi-planes and Louisiana." Mac had stitched his words together like a cheap circus tent. He was unquestionably under the influence and far beyond the point of redemption or recall.

Joey asked, "I bet you can't wait to get home, can you? Exactly where is home, Mac?"

"I'm going home ... tomorrow. I'm going home to Asheville, North Carolina and my gal Mary Alice Dean ... she's been waiting all this time for me ... ever since high school."

Joey nodded, and Nick confirmed, patting his partner on the back, and explained, "Mac, he's my pal ... John McElvoy from Asheville; we flew together in the Pacific, and by chance, we met up again back on Okinawa, and he's been sticking right with me all the way back here."

Joey smiled, "Well, Mac ... tell you what ... Nicholas and I are going to make sure that you make it safely all the way back home to Ashville, so there's no need for you to worry about it."

Mac wound up on the receiving end of a Mickey Finn. His presence had created a problem for Jovita's rendezvous with Nick.

Half an hour after sunset, Nick and Paul maneuvered John McElvoy down the street to the Hotel Palmer. The desk clerk gave them an understanding smile and nod as they struggled into the lobby.

Nick offered an abbreviated, simplified explanation, "Just a bit too much celebration for my friend here." He and Paul continued hobbling along with Mac to the elevator, up to the second floor and room 204 where they allowed him to sprawl across the bed.

Paul pulled off Mac's shoes, loosened his tie and reassured Nick, "Don't worry about your buddy, he'll survive. When he wakes up tomorrow morning, he won't remember a thing that happened after six o'clock. He'll wake up with a hangover a lot less evil than the one more scotch and beer would have given him. I can tell you that from years of experience, my friend."

Nick set a packet on the night table that Joey had procured for John McElvoy's trip back home: a one-way Illinois

Central ticket on the next day's *Panama Limited* to Memphis, and an open-ended Greyhound Bus ticket to Asheville.

Nick stopped in the doorway and looked back as he and Paul were leaving. He considered his stupefied friend passed out on the bed.

Paul urged him on, "Let's go. He'll be fine."

"Yeah, I know. It's just that he was one helluva good wing man." Over the previous nine years, Nick had gotten to know Robert McElvoy a thousandfold better than he knew his son Alexander.

"Well, come on, Major, we're not done yet. We're going to your room and grab your bags and things. You ain't staying here tonight."

"I'm not a Major any longer, Paul."

Paul sounded annoyed, "Whatever you say, sir."

Rum And Coca Cola ...

... and so it begins ...

Back at the Twin Anchors, Paul led Nick through the small, noisy kitchen and down a dimly lit hallway to a beaten, worn, green enamel door. He opened it and stood aside, "It's been a pleasure meeting you, Mister Throckmorton."

Nick stepped inside and would never again lay eyes on Paul the bartender, waiter, and muscleman.

Joey was seated behind a small, four-foot desk with room enough for a rack of manila folders, a felt desk pad, a milk glass gooseneck lamp, an ashtray and an old black, pedestal telephone. She stood, motioned for him to take a seat on a wooden chair at the right side of the desk, and slid the papers in front of her into the desk drawer. A three-foot Mercator projection map of the world was on the wall behind her, and portraits of Presidents Roosevelt and Truman hung to her left.

She asked, "Your friend is safe and sound, snuggled in bed?"

"Yes."

Nick reached inside his uniform jacket for his pack of Camel and slid one out. Before he had finished the task, Joey had picked up the chrome Ronson desk lighter and lit his cigarette as it touched his lips. His eyes examined her form over the top of the blue flame.

"I know you were told what you could expect and given an overview, but I remember when I started in service all the questions I had, so I know that you must have some of those same questions. It can be somewhat staggering at first, can't it? How are you adjusting so far, Nicholas? Is there anything I can explain or help you better understand?" She pushed her chair back and crossed her legs. Her stockings whispered under her skirt.

Nick inhaled, nodded, let the grey cloud slowly out of his lungs and said, "Don't take this wrong … I was told my contact in Chicago was named *Joe*. I don't intend to be crass, but I didn't expect my contact to be a woman, or someone as young, and ... may I say ... good-looking."

Jovita was young, but not inexperienced at expressing herself. She nodded, and with the slightest hint of a smile, responded, "In actuality, I am a seasoned veteran at age 26. You will discover that the organization recruits very young talent and even I, as youthful as I seem, can find that challenging on occasion. So, between you and me, at 37, you're the silver-back gorilla in the room, Major.

"You see, your guide back in the Philippines, Angus Munson, is an ancient, old-world, red-ass baboon, woman-hater with a twisted sense of humor and thinks it's funny to tell everyone that my name is Joe. I am Jovita Maria Vasquello. You perhaps recognize the name; it was my father who was your first Spanish instructor on Luzon, and unlike me, you left him with a good impression of yourself, Major."

Just like Joe Lewis, she had landed a body blow that knocked the wind out of Nick's sails.

"I apologize, Joey. It was not my intention to insult you."

"Oh, I'm not insulted. You have quite simply proven once again for me that Angus Munson is an idiot, but you, Major, need to learn that it's best to keep some things close to the vest, and disguise your personal suspicions better."

She paused, locked onto his eyes and continued, "But that should come with time, Major, and to get back to where we started; is there anything more that I can help you with?"

"You referred to my old rank again and called me *Major.*"

"That only further proves my point that Munson is not only a jerk but that he did not fully explain things to you. That's what you are, Nicholas: a Major ... for now and for the immediate future. On paper, you are a Major in the United States Army Air Force. In truth, you are working for Central Intelligence. There is a promotion to Lieutenant Colonel just around the corner for you, and all that needs to happen is the funding for the rest of this month to kick in; I'm sure you're familiar with the way the military and government can function once they are able to get every gear grinding in a different direction, then work together on the next SNAFU.

"The most impressive skills you possess are those of a pilot and linguist, and that's what will be used for the time being, first and foremost. Your other attributes are keen also but can be classified as secondary ... things like your tenacity, loyalty, work ethic, and commitment to your assignment."

"But, Jovita, I was discharged at Fort Lewis ... discharged and mustered out with back pay, war bonds and travel pay."

"Put it this way, Nicholas: technically the answer is 'yes'; actually, the answer is 'no'. Consider yourself in a situation like the one you were in with the Flying Tigers. You existed, but you didn't. Nobody else but the Tigers knew who you were and what you were doing. Now you are about to become part of a new world; a secret world within a world ... you will live a dim, underground existence; sort of a dream, and stepping in and out of shadows. People will only see what you allow them to see.

"I'm sure you're aware that the OSS has ceased to exist, and things are rapidly changing, but as of today, right at this moment, we are called the Central Intelligence Group. Names change, but the mission is the same: stop the bad guys from stopping us.

"The war has ended. Hitler bumped himself off after millions died, and we had to bring the Japs to their knees before they would finally surrender.

"You see, Nicholas, to put it simply: the sun sets, the winds calm, the stars come out, the moon rises, the tide recedes and once again, all is right with the world. We keep it that way. It's our job. It's our mission.

"You and I, this bar, and everybody and everything in it are all part of a much larger world. We all got parts to play."

She stood, took two steps to a cupboard and brought back a bottle and two glasses. She then sat, smiled, poured and explained, "You will learn to appreciate the taste of Puerto Rican rum, Nicholas. And you will discover that it is a viable alternative to drinking water in many parts of Latin America."

Again, she crossed her legs, slowly this time, and allowed her stockings to hiss once again. Joey lifted her glass, "Welcome to the organization, Nicholas."

"To the organization." He studied her chocolate eyes over the rim of his glass.

"Day after tomorrow, Wednesday at noon o'clock, you will be a passenger on a C-47 from Douglas Field*, Chicago to Selfridge Army Airfield, Detroit. I'm certain you know where Selfridge is, and you can either reunite with your wife and son or not; the decision is yours. We have approved ten days of leave that you may use in whatever manner you like. Enjoy your free time, but I am sure you will also use it to put things in order."

She handed a crisp new manila folder to Nick and continued, "Beginning on page one you will find what is a brief outline of your first mission, Major. The folder and its contents are classified for your eyes only and stay here. But, continuing with what Mister Angus Munson told you before you left the Philippines, if you care to follow along, you will find that you are to inform your family that you have decided to re-enlist and return to active duty in the Southwest Pacific. The Group is well aware of your personal situation and has arranged that on June 1st, your wife will receive a Missing Air Crew Report stating that your aircraft failed to return from a routine mission over South China. Your family will continue to receive your monthly pay and allotments. When and how you ultimately want that particular situation to be resolved, Nicholas, will be up to you. Experience dictates that the earlier your status is resolved, the better it will be for everyone: you, the Group, and especially, your family.

"You are ordered to report no later than 1200 hours, April 14th to ... and you see the particulars there ... Jacksonville Naval Air Station, Florida."

"One question, Joey ..."

"Yes?"

"I'm flying into Detroit and not taking a train?"

"Correct. You're flying. Also, your air transport from Selfridge to Jacksonville has been arranged for the week of April 8th. We got planes and we use them ... something else?"

"No." Nick felt a bit foolish.

Joey continued as if there had been no interruption, "As Munson explained to you in the Philippines, you will be assisting various Latin American entities to establish working air forces with or without the direct involvement of the government or armed forces of the United States. Your relationship with Central Intelligence, however, will remain confidential. Your personnel status, your status on paper, will be much the same as it was initially with the AVG in Burma and China. The United States Department of Defense will be facilitating the acquisition of the fighter aircraft that have been deemed war surplus, and the Group will procure the personnel to deliver them.

"This next part presents a completely new operations scenario for us in Jacksonville, Nicholas, because it has just been actualized: the Agency has set up at a bar and restaurant, something quite like this one, very near the south gate of Jacksonville Naval Air Station, on the north side of Jacksonville, Florida. It's a scenario that has worked well for us because our people can come and go completely unnoticed from places like this. It's almost like a magician's trick, hiding in plain sight. Off the Naval Base, the Group can use this Florida location with minimal exposure, much like we do here in Chicago with Midway and Douglas Army Airfields.

"Across the street and a half block from the bar, the Navy base is tight as a drum. During the war, Navy sub chasers used it for their U-boat patrols all over the Eastern Caribbean, and the Army held nearly two thousand German POWs there.

"Our office in Jacksonville, the bar, it's called the Havana Hideaway. It will be your home base ... your home. It's where you'll hang your hat when it's not in your cockpit or on a runway in Panama or Colombia. I think you'll soon become accustomed to the Hideaway and Naval Air Station Jacksonville, or *NAS Jacks*, like they call it. I'm positive of that."

She paused, leaned forward in her chair and allowed a discomforting quiet to blanket the small office. The sounds of the crowded bar, only yards away, could not be heard.

Her eyes pierced into his soul. She led with a pointed question, "So what really prompted your decision to accept what Central Intelligence has offered you, Nicholas? What tipped the scales in favor of the Group?"

Her hand went to the top drawer and brought out a fresh pack of Chesterfield. Nick watched her lacquered nails open the cellophane wrap, tear the tax stamp, and pull out one of the king-sized smokes. She held it in pursed crimson lips and allowed Nick's brass Zippo to set it alight. It was the first cigarette she had in his company.

"I decided to join Central Intelligence because of all the wrong, all the time, all around me. By the time my unit got to the Philippines, my cork was pulled. My fizz was gone. Everything was wrong, a lot of it still is, and some of it always will be. But I want to try to do something about it ... try and set wrong things right as best I can."

"Your wife and son are your only surviving family members, correct?"

"Yes. The others have passed."

"Did the sinking of AHS Centaur influence your decision?"

Nick was taken aback ... way, way back. "You know about that? You people know about Gwen?"

"It's what the Group does, Nicholas. Intelligence. It's our middle name. Of course, the Group knows about Nurse Peate. You must understand that. Your Army files have references going back to China ... back to the Hong Kong jade and Colonel Cranston of the Royal Air Force. Your qualities were bound to get you noticed, Nicholas, so don't be surprised. But tell me, did the sinking of the hospital ship Centaur influence your decision?"

Nick paused, lit a Camel and answered sincerely, "Yes. I got upset over the sinking of the Centaur. But 'upset' isn't quite descriptive enough. At first, I had the desire to send each, and every monkey-faced bastard into the afterlife on my first pass, and straight to Hell on my second. It was two days before I got over it enough to sleep again. Guendolen was a jewel. For a while it felt like life was good ... I wonder if somebody had enough forethought to write down that personal, private footnote somewhere in my official file."

Joey poured another two inches of rum into their glasses and pushed the cork back into the bottle with a force of finality. "The Group is thorough, it needs to be, and uses whatever information any agency has on record. And I understand your personal feelings, Nicholas. It's normal, it's human and quite frankly, it would scare me if you weren't capable of them."

She was studying him. They sipped at the rum. "It's important that we know you, Nicholas. The Group needs to know what makes you tick. And if we're working together, we need to know each other."

He smiled at her. "Everything is pretty when it's new, Joey."

She set down her glass, lit another Chesterfield and exhaled a river of smoke from the corner of her mouth. "I'll tell you a story, Nicholas; the story of how I nearly quit this job less than a year after I started. It was June of 1942, and I was in the middle of my initial training at Fort Polk when they exposed all kinds of atrocities to us. Photographs, personal interviews, movies; everything from the Nazi executions of Czech Jews to the Jap enslavement of English, French and Dutch as comfort women in their Pacific occupied colonies. We saw film of children being shot between the eyes and heard the testimony of pregnant women who were forced to flush fetuses down a plug hole. I lost all faith in humanity and could have crawled into a cave and died. It was straight from hell; vile, repulsive, and filthy. My insides twisted, tightened, and I vomited until bile came up. One of my classmates was a petite, reserved Pueblo Indian woman from Colorado, and she told me something that has stuck with me ever since. She said: 'When the coyote forsakes hunger, and takes the rabbit for power, the eagle must fly.'

"What she said didn't settle my stomach, but I understood the logic. By allowing evil, we lose. It's the reason the Communists deny the existence of God: to devalue life. Life without value can be controlled."

Nick interjected, "I've heard it called, *The sword of the Lord.*"

Joey purposely, abruptly changed the direction, "Can you say that in Spanish, Nicholas?"

"Si. La espada de Dios."

"¡Excelente! That's very good, Major, and spoken without hesitation. That means that your mind didn't need to translate before you said the words. They told me that you're very good at what you do and that you learn quickly."

He finished his rum, set the glass down and pressed, "Years ago, I think it was in Matamoras, someone told me that Spanish is the loving tongue."

She replied instantly, "I don't know about that, but it's spoken by a quarter of the world's population. And it's the language that I dream in."

She stood; he stood. The electric wall clock read nine on the dot.

She took one step toward him, bobbed her head once and extended her hand, palm down. Softly, like a feather, he held it in his and sensed her warmth.

"It has been a pleasure meeting you, Nicholas, and I firmly believe we will work well together and be successful with our assignments. If you need anything tomorrow, stop by and see Paul or me; one of us will be here. Otherwise, I will see you next month at the Hideaway in Jacksonville. It will open on Wednesday, the 10th."

He was looking into her eyes; looking for some kind of tell-tale sign, some sort of clue to her cryptic presence and searching for something, anything to add and keep the conversation going, "Paul and me brought my bags back from the Palmer ..."

He watched her walk toward the door, the seam at the back of her hose flowing with the rhythm of her soft steps. As her hand turned the porcelain doorknob, she stood aside and dismissed him with a smile, "You're staying at the Astor tonight and tomorrow ... right now, outside, there's a taxi waiting at the curb for you. Goodnight and good travels, Nicholas."

Nick stepped through the doorway and turned, "Thank you, and goodnight, Joey. I'd be comfortable if you refer to me as 'Nick'."

She nodded, smiled and said, "Good. Goodnight then, Major." The door closed with a decisive click.

From his first glimpse of Jovita, she had fascinated him. He sensed that somehow, someplace, somewhere or someway, he had known her for years. Perhaps in a previous life. Perhaps he had dreamed of her just one time and she has occupied the furthest folds of his mind since. There was no way to be certain.

Joey was an enigma for Nick: a powerful, assertive enigma. But it seemed that she certainly knew him.

Coming In On A Wing And A Prayer ...

Wednesday, April 3, 1946 ... Detroit, Michigan

When he checked in at the Operations Desk at Selfridge Field the previous day, the desk sergeant handed him a sealed envelope. Inside were fifty dollars in travel allowance and a three-line message written on cotton bond note paper:

Nick - You have a room at the Capital on Gratiot Avenue. There you will find civilian attire, fresh uniforms, and brass. You will no longer need your model 10. Buen viaje y sueño bien.

It wasn't signed. He noticed that whoever had written it addressed him as 'Nick', and although it was likely that Joey was the author, he found it to be mystifying. The script was exceptionally neat, leaned left, and the author had addressed him in diminutive form. His attractive Central Intelligence contact had not used his name in that way, and she certainly did not appear to be left-handed. Those were distinct verbal and dexterous attributes that he should have noticed. He also found the authoritative, yet obscure reference to his #10 Smith & Wesson service pistol puzzling. Further, the fourth sentence in Spanish was wrapped in enticing ambiguity and could be translated into English one of two ways: 'good journey and sleep well' or 'good travels and nice dreams'.

The longer he thought about it, he realized that he could be reading way too much into those five little words.

Detroit appeared dirtier, noisier, and markedly more crowded than it did eight years earlier. He had noticed it in Chicago, and now in Detroit, that the urban noise also seemed much louder than he remembered. The steady tintamarre, buzz, and pulse of the city did not compare to cannon bursts, artillery strikes, or aerial bombardment, but the incessant din seemed to burrow into his skull with the tenacity of an earwig.

Inside his hotel room, he found his well-traveled duffle and barracks bag on the floor next to the bed. Three complete sets of new dress uniforms and two civilian suits hung on a wheeled valet clothing rack. On the bottom shelf were two dark brown cowhide belts, one pair of size 12, oxblood Florsheim wingtips, two pair of black service oxfords, and a cream Panama hat with a wide black band. The second and third sentences of the cryptic note he had opened at Selfridge became clear; inside a wrapped paperboard box were three sets of Lieutenant Colonel, silver oak leaf brass, a new military ID card, dog tags, and a Colt M1911 with an armpit holster.

Nick awoke Wednesday morning in room 108 of the Capital Hotel from a night of restless sleep that had forced him to quiet the world around him with wads of toilet tissue in his ears. It wasn't just the noise that had tunneled into his mind; it was the anticipation of his new situation and the curious note.

He dressed out of uniform for the first time in nearly eight years, and managed to get over feeling like a duck out of water. After ham, eggs and coffee at the lunch counter off the hotel lobby, Nick walked to the pawn shop at Woodward and Grand River Avenue and paid fifty cents for a worn, leather, attorney's attaché. His new shoes bit into his ankles.

On his way back to the hotel, he was starkly aware that nearly nineteen years earlier he had repeatedly crossed the same pavement on the way to his job at Garwood Mechanical. He successfully fought the urge to dwell on those memories. They needed to be passed by and replaced by matters of current and future importance.

Standing bedside in his room at the Capital, he moved the rolled cash and Chinese Yuan from the deepest bottom creases of his duffle bag into the briefcase, packing it around his Smith & Wesson service revolver and canvas holster. He broke the strings around a little bundle of letters, dug out a few odd snapshots and two that Mac had taken in Burma; back before the war had officially started. He tucked those, his old dog tags, and two Stroh beer coasters from the Twin Anchors into the attaché, did a cursory study of the contents, and secured the flap. The bag was packed and ready to go.

Nick hopped off the Gratiot streetcar at Griswold Street and hit the sidewalk in stride. Eighteen paces from the trolley stop and up a set of seven steps later, he pushed open one of the four heavy glass and brass main doors of the Penobscot Building. Inside, he walked directly to the Bank of Detroit platform manager's desk. He filled out the application forms and paid for two year's rent on a safe deposit box.

... *playing solitaire without a deck* ...

The house key was where it always had been: inside the garage, on the right side of the door, atop the jamb. It was half past one o'clock, and Nora was undoubtedly at Saint Mary's and eighteen-year-old Alexander was likely still in class at Mount Clemens High School.

Once inside the home, he could see that not much had changed since he had signed on with the Air Corps. There was new wallpaper in the hall and new curtains in the living room, but everything else appeared the same. The lone standout was a deep green, wool and linen tweed, button-tufted davenport, and a framed print of Rubens' *Raising of Christ and the Cross* hanging on the opposing wall. Upstairs on the dresser in Alexander's room he noticed a photograph he had sent of himself standing next to the Flying Phaeton in New Guinea. Generally, nothing else had changed inside the house at 12 Second Street over the last eight years.

His cursory search for a vase ended without positive result, forcing him to find a substitute from the back of the pantry, reasoning that his wife could switch it out later. The dozen red roses and spray of baby's breath from Macomb Florists looked just fine on the coffee table despite the old mayonnaise jar. So not to completely spoil Nora's initial impression of his ten-dollar floral splurge, he put the six pack* of beer he bought at Sloan's Grill into in the Kelvinator: minus one for immediate consumption.

There was naught else to do but wait. He settled into the green sofa and opened the bottle of Stroh's Bohemian. He waited patiently for nearly two hours, nursed the bottle of beer, ignored the occasional pang in his heart, and watched years of memories flicker across his mind.

When Nick heard footsteps on the porch, he got up and met his son at the door.

Alexander was jubilant. "I had a feeling you'd be home today, Old Man! I told Mom this morning! I just had a feeling! And I was right!"

It seemed that Alex had just wiped away a tear of happiness and the bear hug ended when Nora came home from her classroom assistant duties at Saint Mary's. Stark emotion and physical strength weren't present, but the hug Nick received from Nora came across as genuine. The kiss, however, was merely familial.

They had spaghetti and meatball dinners at Giorgio's Italian Kitchen that night and caught up on all the news that didn't warrant the space or thought in the letters they had shared over the years. Nora hadn't changed much in Nick's perception, and still wore those high-collared blouses and dark blue, ankle-length skirts. The singular outstanding impression Nicholas was able to take away from his homecoming was how much his son Alexander had matured, but managed to retain his youthful sense of humor.

The good times didn't last long. The whipped cream quickly melted off the cake. After supper Nick stretched the truth and told his wife and son that he had re-enlisted and was headed back to the Orient.

For Alex it was disturbing and bewildering. For Nora it was baffling, yet very familiar.

Alex played hooky on Friday, and he and his father spent the day trying to cement together what was never whole to begin with. They ended the afternoon on Woodward Avenue at the Empire Burlesque watching the Queen of Quiver, Darlene Tremour, shake her stuff and slap-stick comedian Duffy Simms make a fool of himself. It was, as Nick knew it would be, an afternoon of laughter; something that his son could not have predicted. On the way home, Alex helped his father select a gold crucifix necklace for Nora at Steinberg's Jewelers.

Nick decided to leave for Jacksonville on Tuesday morning, April 9th. His wife and son accompanied him to Selfridge Airfield and discovered that the departure hall at the airbase was as bare boned as Nicholas' farewell wishes. He gave Nora two Bank of Detroit savings account passbooks and keys for two safe deposit boxes. As a high school graduation gift, he handed his Bulova triple-dial aviator watch to Alexander … who sensed that his father's dispassionate actions were well rehearsed.

Outside on the tarmac, the aluminum wings and body of a waiting DC-3 glistened in the sharp spring sunlight. The big engines were rumbling at idle.

After a gentle kiss on Nora's lips, a handshake, bearhug, and pat on the back for Alex, Nick walked out the door and along the gangway to the boarding ladder. He stopped at the top step, took a deep breath, swallowed hard, turned to his family, and waved goodbye for what he knew could be a long time. Yet again, Colonel Nicholas Throckmorton was winging away. This time, however, he wasn't the pilot at the controls, and his precise flight plan was still being written.

(Phade To Black)

The story continues with:

The Flying Phaeton, Port Moresby, New Guinea, October 1944

THE END NOTES

CHAPTER ONE:

Hungarian and Austrian immigrants streamed from Europe after the First World War with the devastating breakup of the Austro-Hungarian Empire. In 1925, over 15,000 Magyar lived in and around the Delray neighborhoods of Detroit.

The BOI The Bureau Of Investigation was created in 1908, prompted by the 1901 assassination of President William McKinley in Buffalo, New York, and the need for an autonomous investigative service. President Theodore Roosevelt ordered its creation by Attorney General Charles Bonaparte. In 1924, a young J. Edgar Hoover was named as director, and tasked to put the Bureau's house in order. The BOI of 1927 was a meager national force of about 200 Special Agents. At best, it was inefficient, ill-equipped, undertrained, plagued by political corruption, outwitted and outgunned by organized crime. In 1935 its name was changed to the Federal Bureau of Investigation, the FBI of today.

Pin sticking and *ball running* was manual labor in bowling alleys prior to automation. Young men were perched precariously above the alley, stuck the bowling pins back in place. and sent the ball back down the return chute.

Listerine cigarettes were advertised to relieve sore throats and were first marketed in 1927. The brand was mint-flavored and short-lived, giving way to menthol cigarettes, the first of which was trademarked: *Spuds*.

Garfield (Gar) Wood was an American entrepreneur and machinist. He built wood-hull speed boats in his Detroit engine and boat works, held the world speed record several times and was the first man to travel more than 100 mph on water. In 1925, he famously raced New York Central's premier train, The Twentieth Century Limited, from New

York City to Albany and beat the speeding steam locomotive by 22 minutes. All of his boats were teak and named *Miss America (I thru X)*. On every race, he carried two small stuffed bears along as mascots, named Teddy and Bruin. Garfield Wood designed the PT boats the US Navy used during World War II up to and after the Vietnam War.

The Purple Gang was Detroit's most notorious and murderous organized crime gang in the 1920s and the early 1930s. Headed by the Bernstein family, the Purple Gang consisted mostly of ethnic Polish and Russian Jewish immigrants from Detroit's lower east side. The mobsters specialized in murder, extortion, kidnapping, and bootlegging. Rather than fighting them, Chicago's Al Capone became an ally.

Oshkosh Motor Truck Manufacturing Company was founded by William Besserdich and Bernhard Mosling. It has been headquartered in Oshkosh, Wisconsin since 1918, and employs about 13,000 worldwide. The company makes heavy duty construction and specialty trucks as well as military vehicles. The rugged dependability of Oshkosh equipment has nurtured a loyal following among construction and snow removal customers.

The Lafayette Escadrille was a fighter unit of the French Air Service (*Aéronautique Militaire*) composed of American volunteer pilots. Active in WWI from 1916 to 1918, the unit was named in honor of the Marquis de Lafayette, hero of the French and American Revolutions. A likeness of an Indian chief in full headdress was the fighter wing's insignia. After the war, many of the veteran pilots and mechanics continued to work in American aviation.

Douaumont, France is in north-eastern France. The village was totally destroyed during World War I. It is home to the Douaumont Ossuary, a graveyard and final resting place for over 100,000 unknown German and French soldiers.

The United States Army Air Service was created in 1917 because of the necessitated use of aircraft in World War I. In 1926, it became officially known as the Army Air Corps and was under direct command of the Department of The Army. On March 9, 1942, it branched out and became the Army Air Force with a dedicated Commanding General for its mission of ground troop support. After World War II, in September 1947, it became the separate entity of today: the United States Air Force.

Birth control in the Catholic faith was the "rhythm method" until the mid-twentieth century. Condoms, diaphragms, and cervical caps were "artificial" and condemned: "so many conceptions prevented so many homicides". It wasn't until the birth control pill that the Church began to turn away from the controversy. Since the "pill" contained hormones that occurred in nature, it eventually became tolerated, but not condoned or endorsed.

CHAPTER TWO:

The War To End All Wars was a reference to World War I and a phrase coined by Englishman H.G. Wells, author of *The Time Machine, War Of The Worlds, The Invisible Man,* and *The Island Of Doctor Moreau.* The term is occasionally erroneously credited to President Woodrow Wilson, who used the phrase once while he insisted that World War I "would make the world safe for democracy."

Baby formula was a homemade, handcrafted product in the early 20th Century, consisting of canned evaporated milk and Karo brand simple corn syrup. By the 1950's half of all American babies were raised on the concoction.

The Harmsworth Trophy was won nine times by Garfield Wood as driver and owner, with his mechanic Orlin Johnson seated next to him. The Detroit River course was five nautical miles around, laid out and measured by the Superintendent of U. S. Lighthouses. The races were run in three heats of two laps, and the country taking two of the three won the Trophy. In 1930, the flamboyant, openly lesbian, and eccentric English millionaire heiress, owner and pilot Marion Barbara (Joe) Carstairs had two boats in the race, *Estelle IV* and *Estelle V*. Joe drove the new *Estelle V* and Bert Hawker piloted *Estelle IV*. Neither boat finished the contest. As expected, Garfield Wood's Packard-powered, hand-crafted teak beauty *Miss America IX* took the trophy.

Pilot License #1 was issued on April 6, 1927, to William P. MacCracken by the Aeronautics Branch of the Department of Commerce. On May 21, Charles Lindbergh held license #69 and made the first solo transatlantic flight from New York to Paris. On June 30, 1927, Phoebe Fairgrave Omlie received the first pilot license issued to a woman: #199.

Diaphragms for contraceptive use were extremely popular among women in Europe in the 1920's but unavailable in the United States due to the restrictive Comstock Laws that prohibited the import of contraceptives. US production began in 1929 making the product legal for American women. In 2014, Janssen Pharmaceuticals discontinued its manufacture of the birth control product.

Pilots in the early 1930s earned about $8,000 annually. They were extremely well-paid members of a new breed of workforce that was unknown a decade earlier. Their pay was on par with congressmen, twice as much as a doctor, thrice as much as a dentist, and six times a teacher's salary.

Delta Airlines was born of Huff-Daland Aero Corporation during a time of private innovation, ingenuity, and nearly limitless funding by American enterprise and the military. Huff-Daland Dusters was a crop-dusting firm that later morphed into Delta Dusters in Monroe, Louisiana. The current Atlanta-based Delta Airlines owes its name to Huff-Daland's roots in the Mississippi Delta.

The Dust Bowl occurred over three periods of drought: 1934, 1936, and 1939-40. Dry soil was whipped by winds and created horrific dust storms. The worst hit farmlands were the Panhandle areas of Oklahoma and Texas.

CHAPTER THREE:

Elliot Ness was a son of Norwegian immigrants and an agent of the Bureau of Prohibition. His career was popularized as the man who brought gangster Al Capone to justice. In fact, it was the Treasury Department (IRS: Internal Revenue Service) that convicted Capone on charges of tax evasion.

Betty Grable (1916-1973) was an American actress, dancer and singer. Her career began in 1929 and fully blossomed in the mid-30s. She is perhaps best remembered as the favorite pin-up girl of World War II. (5'4" ~ 36-24-35)

House calls were standard practice for physicians in the 1930s. Forty percent of all doctor-patient encounters occurred in the home.

Ford Motor Corporation advertised their 1936 models as  "A beautiful Ford car with new style, new driving ease, new safety, easier steering and new design steel wheels. The price of a V8, five-window, two-door coupe started at $510. Add another $20 for the rumble seat and $5 for a radio.

Tinkertoy wooden construction sets were first introduced in 1916 and became wildly popular in the 1920s.

Ambulance service was nearly non-existent and extremely sparse until after WW II. The Detroit Fire Department received their first emergency transport in June 1927. It was a gift from private citizen Paxton Mendelssohn.

Hospital visitation rules were strictly enforced in the early twentieth century. From the Detroit Commissioner Of Health, April 1930: *It is not possible to permit relatives and friends of the patient to visit the hospital, only in cases of critical illness can patients be seen and then only by the nearest relatives. This adds greatly to the misunderstanding of the operation of such a Hospital. Rules have been set up,* *designed to protect the nurses, doctors, and others so that they can attend the patients with perfect immunity.*

John R. Williams (1782-1854) was a soldier, merchant and politician who became the first mayor of Detroit and helped organize the city's street grid system. *John R Street* was named before he passed. He actually named it himself.

Antibiotics were virtually non-existent for surgical applications until after World War II; the mid-1940s. Sulphonamide antibiotics (sulpha powders) were first available in the late 1930s but not widely used. Although it was discovered in 1928, penicillin was not developed for use until 1945.

Sutures, stitches, and post-operative pain management during the 1930s was almost always achieved by morphine. Appendectomy incisions of twelve inches or more in length were not uncommon. As a rule of thumb, surgeons used five stitches per inch to close an abdominal wound.

Sonja Henie won her third Olympic figure skating title at the 1936 winter games in Garmisch, Germany. The Norwegian skater became a national heroine in Norway and went on to a Hollywood film career. The 1936 Summer Olympics were also held in Germany, marking the last time both winter and summer games were held in one country.

CHAPTER FOUR:
Lupe Vélez (the Mexican Spitfire) was a Mexican film star of the 1930s and 40s; one of the first to succeed in Hollywood. Also nicknamed *Whoopee Lupe*, she had no qualms about saying she enjoyed the company of men. She had countless affairs and was once briefly married to Johnny Weissmuller, who played Tarzan in many films. She committed suicide in 1944. Pregnant out of wedlock, her death was rumored to be related to the morality taboos of the Catholic faith.

Mexican wrestling was a localized sport until 1933, when it was popularized nationally by Salvador Lutteroth, and took the country by storm. Today's wrestlers wear masks that bear historical significance back to the Aztec civilization.

Revolvers were excluded when *The National Firearms Act* became law on June 26, 1934, as President Franklin D. Roosevelt continued tinkering with American mores and economics. All other gun sales were slapped with a $200 excise tax ($4,150 in 2022 dollars). Buyers were required to fill out a purchase application for Treasury Department approval. Predictably, gun sales went 'underground' and gangsters continued to shoot up the countryside. The law is still on the books.

Work Progress Administration (WPA) was the largest and most aggressive of nearly countless "alphabet soup" federal agencies set up by the Roosevelt administration in the 1930's to help abate the effects of the Great Depression. In 1939 it was renamed Works Projects Administration to help remove any perceived association to socialism or communism.

Pörkölt ragout is Hungarian beef stew, or traditional goulash, spiced with paprika.

Thomas "Fats" Waller (1904-1943) was one of the most influential jazz musicians and composers of all time. It was in 1926; he was 21 years old and performing at Chicago's Sherman Hotel when he was kidnapped by members of the Chicago Outfit. He was blindfolded and taken to an unknown nightclub to perform for Al (Scarface) Capone's birthday party. Fats played for three days. He left several thousand dollars richer, and had a newly acquired taste for champagne. Fats' credits include *Ain't Misbehavin'*, *Basin Street Blues*, and *Honeysuckle Rose*.

Creole is a term of French origin for mixed race peoples and is used worldwide. Generally, the term permeated through colonization and the interactions of colonists with various ethnicities of native people. Once a scientific classification, racial identification (Caucasian, Negroid, Mongoloid, Dravidian, etc) is now considered pejorative.

The founding documents of the European Union reject all theories which attempt to determine the existence of separate human races. While the words of Thomas Jefferson cover mankind with a large blanket (*all men are created equal*), social standing often kicks the covers off that bed.

Ellsworth M. Statler completed the Hotel Statler on Niagara Square in downtown Buffalo in 1923. Boasting that it was the largest building in the state outside of New York City, the hotel taunted *a room and a bath for a buck and a half* and became instantly profitable. It had many 'firsts' in the hotel industry, including a wall switch for electric lights, a lighted desk, a private bath, and radio in every room.

Crapper is a term used for the toilet, privy, can or loo. Contrary to modern legend, the flush toilet was not invented by Thomas Crapper (1836-1910). However, he did invent some important components such as the ball cock. He also owned a company that manufactured porcelain toilets and washbasins on Marlborough Road, London, England.

Buck Moon usually occurs in July, when the velvet antlers of male deer push through their heads to signal mating season.

Bullets fired from a Smith & Wesson 38 revolver pack quite a punch. When exiting from a four-inch barrel, the slug can have a velocity of over 800 miles per hour. That's nearly two and a half times the speed of sound.

Boilermaker is a working-class cocktail consisting of a glass of beer and a shot of whiskey. The beer is served as a chaser for the liquor. A variation called a *depth charge* is created when the whiskey is dropped into the beer, shot glass and all.

CHAPTER FIVE:
Canned beer came to fruition after Prohibition, in 1935. A can opener, affectionately called a *church key*, was needed to punch a small, triangular hole in the top of the can. A smaller hole was generally punched on the opposite side to

allow air inside the can and facilitate easier pouring or drinking.

Ivory Snow was packaged in a box as laundry soap and hailed as *99 and 44/100 % pure*. The product was Ivory brand bar soap that was shaved into thin flakes. *Ivory Flakes* was a powdered formula that came along later and differed from Ivory Snow.

Cracker Jacks are a popcorn, peanut and caramel snack developed in 1896 by German immigrants Rueckheim, Eckstein and Brinkmeyer in Chicago. The 1908 song *Take Me Out To The Ballgame* gave the company priceless promotion with the lyric "buy me some peanuts and Cracker Jack". On the box was 'Sailor Jack' a likeness of young Robert Rueckheim who died of pneumonia at age eight and his dog 'Bingo' who was an adopted stray. Starting in 1917, the company included small, trivial toy "prizes" in each box.

Stroh's brewing company was founded in 1850 in Detroit, Michigan by German immigrant Bernhard Stroh. To survive Prohibition, the company began making non-alcoholic *near beer*, soft drinks, malt products, and ice cream. Ice cream production continued in Detroit until 2005. In 1999, Pabst Breweries bought the Stroh beer brand.

President Franklin Delano Roosevelt responded to remarks made by William Bullitt (US Ambassador to France) during a news conference on September 4, 1938, and suggestions made by British Prime Minister Winston Churchill on August 31, 1938, about a 'stop Hitler' pact, and affirmed American neutrality stating that the United States would remain uncommitted should the Nazis simply annex Czechoslovakia. *(Ref: News Conferences of President Roosevelt, vol. 12, 1938; De Capo Press, NY 1972)*

Selfridge Air Field first opened in 1917 on the shores of Lake Saint Clair in Mount Clemens, Michigan, and is still in operation. Over the years, the air field's name changed to Selfridge Army Air Field, to Selfridge Air Force Base to its current status of Selfridge Air National Guard Base.

Army Air Corps training was reduced from a full year to a mere nine months in 1939. Before a pilot was considered combat-ready, he had about 250 hours of flight training under his belt.

Fuller Brush Company was founded in 1907. Its door-to-door traveling sales model for household items became an integral part of American culture and was later recognized as a trail blazer with the hiring of a female sales force for beauty products. The company is still in business, generating the majority of its revenue through catalog sales and outlet stores.

CHAPTER SIX:

Stars and Stripes is an independent newspaper founded in 1861 and has been in publication since. It revolves around news generated about and for members of the armed forces of the United States. It has had a loyal readership and informative editorial policy since World War I.

City directories have been around since the 1800s. They predated and evolved into the massive telephone directories that have all but disappeared from today's world. Originally, the directories listed spouse, widow(er), occupation and address. Today, archived city directories are a useful resource for genealogists.

Aviator sunglasses were developed by Bausch & Lomb in 1936 and marketed as *pilot's glasses* by Ray-Ban in 1937. Flyers praised the unobstructed wide field of vision and light-weight frames, and the glasses became instantly fashionable with glitterati worldwide.

Thanksgiving had been celebrated on the last Thursday of November since Abraham Lincoln declared it a national holiday in 1863. In 1939, it was to fall on November 30th, leaving only 17½ shopping days until Christmas (at the time, stores were not open Sundays and only half-days on Wednesday and Saturday). At the urging of retailers, President Roosevelt changed the holiday to fall on the third Thursday of November. The move created havoc. All the calendars were wrong, the Thanksgiving football schedule was in question and schools, colleges and manufacturers across the country had holiday days disrupted. Much of the American public was irate and the holiday was renamed *Franksgiving* by newspapers throughout the nation.

Planters peanut company was founded in 1908 by Italian immigrants, Amedeo Obici and Mario Peruzzi. The men re-invested their earnings from selling roasted peanuts on the streets of Wilkes-Barre, Pennsylvania, to create the commercial food giant of today.

Short packs of ten or fourteen cigarettes were widely popular during the 1930s.

Zippers were developed by Gideon Sundbäck, a Swedish-American engineer as the *Separable Fastener.* They became known as "zippers" when BF Goodrich began putting them on rubber galoshes in the early 1920s. They were not commonly used on clothing until the late 1930s.

Jell-O gelatin was created in Leroy, New York by Genesee Pure Food Company in 1904. In the 1930s, *Jell-O salads*, containing everything from pretzel bits to lettuce were very much in vogue. In 1936, the company launched a very successful pudding product in chocolate, vanilla, tapioca, coconut, pistachio and butterscotch flavors.

Pet Evaporated Milk originated from the Helvetia Milk Condensing Company in 1923. It was economical, reduced product volume by 60% and eventually had a shelf-life of a year or more. American soldiers referred to canned milk as the *tin cow* during both World Wars. Briskly whipped with sugar, it could gain the consistency of whipped cream.

Fennario is a non-existent location that has become a musical and literary quandary quickening to Shangri-La or the Land of Oz. It's a romantic, mysterious place heralded by soldiers and sailors for centuries. With origins in an 18th century Irish folk ballad ("Pretty Peggy-O"), Fennario has been hailed in song for hundreds of years and covered in recent history by Peter Paul & Mary, Simon & Garfunkel, the

Grateful Dead and Hoyt Axton. As referenced in the embellished lyrics of Bob Dylan: *I've been around this whole country, but I never yet found Fennario.*

Shangri-La was depicted as the elusive paradise in the popular 1937 Frank Capra film, *Lost Horizon,* starring Ronald Coleman and Jayne Wyatt.

American Volunteer Group (AVG) began as a clandestine pre-war American operation initiated in the winter of 1940-41 by William Pawley (Curtiss-Wright), Claire Chennault (retired Air Corps colonel and mercenary), Chiang Kai-shek (Nationalist Chinese), and Lauchlin Currie (advisor to Roosevelt). See the next section, *The Odd Stuff* for more.

M/V Jaegersfontaine was a Dutch freighter built in 1934 that was under contract to the United States' War Department. By a single flip of fate, the ship entered Pearl Harbor on the morning of December 7, 1941, mere minutes before the Japanese attack. It fired upon the dive-bombing Zeros with its deck guns and was therefore the first "allied" counterattack on the Japanese during WW II. On June 26, 1942, she was torpedoed and sunk by German submarine U-107, 300 miles east of Bermuda. All 211 persons onboard were rescued from lifeboats by a Swiss ship. There were 86 US Army officers aboard, all enroute to England.

Australia is home to five species of Kangaroo: Eastern Grey, Western Grey, Red, Whiptail Wallabies and the prolific Wallaroo. About the size of the United States, Australia's 1943 population was 7 million compared to Great Britain at 47 million and the USA at 140 million at the time.

Kookaburras are heavy-billed, native Australian members of the kingfisher family about 12- 17 inches long. Their call is loud, somewhat obnoxious and very recognizable.

Quonset huts are half-round buildings made of sheet steel. Originally an English design, thousands were made during the World Wars. Their benefit was portability: quick erection and removal. The design is time-tested and still in wide use all over the globe.

Rayon is a man-made fiber of cellulose derived from wood pulp. It became popular during the mid-30s and by 1940 it was known as "mother-in-law silk" due to its silky feel.

Cadillac produced top of the line luxury model V-12 and V-16 powerhouses from 1930-40, making 4076 units during the eleven years of production. The 1934 Phaeton was the largest at 20 feet long. British automobile designer W.O. Bentley said in 1930, "The V-16 Phaeton is not only world class, it has outclassed the world."

Zippo manufacturing company of Bradford, Pennsylvania began making their famous lighters in 1933 and received the US Patent for it in 1939. Although the company officially ceased commercial production during WW II to conserve metal for the war effort, Zippo lighters were always widely popular and always available to GIs. To date, the company has produced over five-hundred million lighters and stands by their product with a free life-time fix-it-or-replace-it guarantee.

Caterpillar Club is a "brotherhood" of aviators who have successfully parachuted out of an aircraft under an emergency situation, such as enemy fire or equipment failure. The club was started in 1922 at McCook Army Air Field in Ohio and has grown into a worldwide organization. The name pays homage to the silkworm, the source of the silk used in early aviation parachutes.

The Flying Goddess adorned the hoods of Cadillac *Phaeton* and other large models as radiator caps/hood ornaments during the 1930's. The gleaming *flying lady* was about nine inches of polished chromed steel and weighed in at two pounds.

Pall Mall brand cigarettes were the first "king size" smoke at 85mm compared to the earlier standard 70mm length, which made them a bit more than half an inch longer.

Tojo: Hideki Tojo was the Minister of the Army and Prime Minister of the Empire of Japan from October 17, 1941, up until he resigned on July 22, 1944. His resignation came after American Army and Marine forces captured the island of Saipan. The name "Tojo" was a generalized term used by Americans to refer to the enemy. Prior to his arrest by US Military Police on September 11, 1945, he shot himself in the chest in a suicide attempt and was given emergency care at a US Army hospital. He was later tried for war crimes including inhumane treatment of prisoners and was hanged on December 23, 1948.

Short Snorter was a one-dollar bill *(Silver Certificate)* signed by flyers and others who met over a period of time. The aviation tradition started in the 1920's and *short snorters* signed by famous flyers have become highly collectable. Once a bill was signed, the person carrying it was required to produce it upon request and if not, a dollar or a drink was expected in return. Eleanor Roosevelt, President Roosevelt, Marine Corps flying ace Joe Foss and General Patton are among famous signatories.

Second Australian Imperial Force was formed to comply with an Australian law that prohibited foreign deployment of its military. In was created in September 1939 to support Britain with World War II in Europe.

New Guinea is the world's second largest island, behind Greenland. The island was discovered about 1540 by the Spanish and has a colonial history with Spain, Germany, Holland, England and Australia. The country of Papua New Guinea covers the eastern half of the island and is home to over 800 spoken languages. Much of the island is still undiscovered and cloaked in mystery. Cannibalism is known to have been practiced by pygmy and other isolated tribes on the island as late as 1970. In 1901, over 10,000 skulls were discovered on Gaoribari Island by missionary Harry Dauncey.

CHAPTER SEVEN:

Wagga-Wagga and **Woolloomooloo** are actual locales in New South Wales, Australia where you can listen to a didgeridoo while watching a wombat drop square poo. (true!)

The USO (United Service Organizations) was founded in 1941 and continues through today. The slogan "until everyone comes home" says it all. In conjunction with the War Department (now Department of Defense) they still provide aid, assistance and entertainment to service members worldwide.

The Wizard Of Oz was released in 1939 in the USA, 1940 in Australia, and became one of the planet's best-known films. It was an example of cinematography in its earliest art form, without any animation or computer-generated special optics or effects. The term *OZ* as a reference to Australia did not appear in pop culture until the 1980s.

The Roosevelt nightclub opened in Kings Cross, Sydney in 1939. Canadian entrepreneur Samuel Levi (Sam Lee) brought the North American bar scene "down under". It was sold to suspected Australian crime lord Abe Saffron in 1947 and provided years of corruption-fed entertainment, booze, gambling and sex. After many reincarnations, it is still in business today as an upscale club and restaurant.

Bangers, mushy peas and mash is high cuisine that has been savored throughout the British Commonwealth: sausages, mashed peas and mashed potatoes served with gravy. Stemming from the strict rationing of WWI, it is presumed that butcher shop sausages were called "bangers" because of the cheaper grades of meat and high volume of air in the product, which could cause the links to explode in the boiling pot.

Spam is a canned delicacy first introduced by Hormel Meats of Austin, Minnesota in 1937, and marketed during the

Great Depression as a valuable way to stretch the food dollar. During WW II and the lend-lease program with European countries, it was exported by the ton, feeding millions. The American soldier grew to love the stuff. Military humor dubbed it "Special Army Meat." An anonymous bit of GI poetry reads:

"Now Jackson had his acorns, and Grant his precious rye.
Teddy had his poisoned beef - worse you couldn't buy.
The doughboy had his hardtack, without the navy's jam,
But armies on their stomachs move – this one moves with
Spam."

The Grapes Of Wrath is a 169,500-word novel by John Steinbeck, published in 1939. The Great Depression epic became widely popular and was released as a feature film in 1940 starring Peter Fonda.

M/S Zaandam (2) was a single-funnel freighter/passenger of the Holland-American Line under contract to the US War Shipping Administration and saw extensive service in the seas around Malaysia. On November 2, 1942, it was torpedoed and sank 300 miles off the coast of Brazil by German submarine *U-174*. 134 of 299 aboard were lost, mostly American.

Australian Nursing Service was a civilian volunteer arm of the various Australian armed forces. The women did not receive the same status or pay as their male counterparts but driven by a sense of duty and desire to "do our part", the nurse sisters volunteered in large numbers to serve domestically and overseas. At the end of World War II, the nursing service became part of the Australian Army, Air Force and Navy.

Mount McKinley is part of the Alaska Range and the tallest peak in North America. Its summit (20,310 feet) was first verifiably reached on June 7, 1913. It is named after the 25th US President, William McKinley who was assassinated by an anarchist at the 1901 Pan-American Exposition in Buffalo, New York.

Lend-lease (actually "Act to Promote the Defense of The United States") was a massive foreign aid program enacted on March 11, 1941, prior to the United States' entry into WW II. Nearly 700 billion (US 1941) dollars in military aid was shipped to the United Kingdom, China, Free France, the USSR and other allies.

AHS Centaur was an Australian Hospital Ship.

☞Literary license was used to alter the chronology in Chapter Seven pertaining to this ship. The correct timeline is outlined here. ☜

The passenger/refrigerated cargo ship *Centaur* was refitted as a hospital ship in January 1943, repainted white, and clearly marked with large, red International Red Cross indicia and ship's designation number "47". It initially ferried wounded personnel from Townsville to Brisbane and from Port Moresby to Brisbane, to Sydney. On her second voyage from Sydney, she sailed with an Australian Army Field Ambulance Unit bound for New Guinea and was torpedoed by Japanese submarine *I-177* on May 14, 1943. The attack was at night, about 04:00 hours, catching most of the crew asleep. A torpedo struck the fuel tanks, setting the Centaur ablaze, sinking the ship stern first within three minutes. Of the 332 medical and civilian crew aboard, 268 perished including 11 of 12 nurses and all 8 doctors. Thirty-six hours later, 64 survivors were found adrift at sea and rescued clinging onto bits of wreckage by the American destroyer *USS Mugford* on May 16th. Navy riflemen on the ship's deck kept swarming sharks at bay. The ship lies at the bottom of the Coral Sea in 200 feet of water about 74 kilometers east of Brisbane, Australia. Map coordinates for the shipwreck are: 27°16.98'S + 153°59.22'

Tasmanian Tigers have been considered extinct since 1940, although there are still many unconfirmed sightings in the wild. Once common throughout Australia, its last known habitat in the wild was on the island of Tasmania, hence its common name. Closely resembling a cross of a hyena and wolf, it was the world's largest carnivorous marsupial, measuring about 40 inches long (plus a 20-inch tail), 24 inches tall and 40 to 60 pounds.

Ninety-Day wonder was a term given to new Army recruits who had completed a crash, three-month leadership course and were awarded a Second Lieutenant commission.

Saipan is an island in the Mariana Islands archipelago. The Battle of Saipan lasted from June 15th until July 9th, 1944. At the end of June, Emperor Hirohito sent out an imperial order in a radio message that encouraged the civilians of Saipan to commit suicide to avoid capture by the American forces. No accurate number is available, but it is estimated that between ten to twenty thousand Japanese civilians committed mass suicide off *Suicide* and *Banzai Cliffs* into the Pacific Ocean.

The Bataan Death March was a forced sixty-mile movement of about 60,000 Philippine and American POWs in April 1942. Oppressive heat and exhaustion took a toll on the prisoners along the way. The stragglers, wounded and fallen were bayoneted, shot, beheaded from horseback or run over by supply vehicles. Details of the atrocity were not made public until January 1944. The death toll has been estimated between 10,000 and 20,000.

OSS (*Office of Strategic Services*) was an intelligence service of the Unites States formed during WW II. It had agents attached to all branches of the military. It was disbanded in September 1945 and splinter groups were broken off into the Department of State and War Department. By 1947 it had developed into the Central Intelligence Agency (CIA). About 24,000 individuals worked for the OSS from 1942-45, among them Julia Child, Ralph Bunche, Moe Berg, John Schlesinger and John Ford.

CHAPTER EIGHT:

Mexican Air Force: (Fuerza Aérea Mexicana) had a contingent of approximately 300 (30 pilots and ground crew) men stationed in the Philippines. The *Aztec Angels* flew 96 missions in P-47 Thunderbolts with both USAAF and Mexican Air Force insignia. They were based on Luzon between June 4 and August 26, 1945, as the 201st Mexican Squadron, attached to the 58th Fighter Squadron, US Army Fifth Air Force. They officially returned home to a glorious parade in Mexico City on November 18, 1945.

Whiskey production was curtailed during WW II to assist in the war effort. American and Canadian distilleries did their part by making straight alcohol for the military. However, Scotch was readily available for two reasons: the British needed American dollars more than alcohol and some of the distilleries in the UK didn't have the ability to produce military grade or pure alcohol.

Filipinos (citizens of the Philippines) {male=Filipino female=Filipina} consist of several indigenous racial groups and speak 19 different languages. The most common is Filipino (Visayan and Tagalog). English and Filipino are the official languages of the Republic of the Philippines. Very few Filipinos speak Spanish.

Spanish is spoken by 400 million people on Earth. There are hundreds of dialects, but the main separation is between European (Peninsular) and Latin-American Spanish. However, the differences do not block cross-understanding.

Demobilization of the Army's land and Air Forces after World War II began in May 1945 and was given the name **Operation Magic Carpet**. Beginning with a total of more than 8 million (8,000,000) men, the final number of active-duty personnel was just over 9 hundred thousand (900,000) in 1947. The Army used an ever-changing "point system" for discharge priority based on duty type, performance reports, time overseas, and number of children.

USS General T.H. Bliss was a 523-foot troop ship built in 1942, mothballed in 1946, sold to Bethlehem Steel in 1964 and scrapped in 1979. With a crew of 350, the Bliss carried

3500 troops at a time on about 20 round trips from the US, Europe and the Far East.

Rock-Ola jukeboxes were first manufactured in 1935, when the company sold nearly a half million of them. David Cullen Rockola founded the company in 1927 and originally made weight scales, slot machines and pinball machines. During World War II, juke boxes were considered non-essential, and production was ceased. The company began manufacturing the M-1 carbine rifle for the US military and produced about 225,000 at a cost of $58 (1942 $) apiece. Rock-Ola jukeboxes and shuffle-board tables are still considered the 'Cadillac' of bar-room machines.

Ten o'clock (high) refers to a direction used in aviation from the horizontal as related to a clock face; it may be supplemented with the word **high** or **low** to describe the vertical direction. 6 o'clock low means down and below the horizon (under you), while 12 o'clock high means up and above the horizon (above you).

Chicago Midway and **Douglas Army Airfield** were used by the Army Air Force during WW II and are now two of the world's busiest airports: Chicago O'Hare and Midway International.

CIA, the Central Intelligence Agency, was born of several intelligence units following WW II. The agency originated from the OSS, which was officially dismantled in September 1945 by President Truman. In January 1947 Truman established the National Intelligence Authority and the Central Intelligence Group (CIG) became its operative arm. It is believed that the name was changed to the Central Intelligence Agency (CIA) because the acronym CIG carried the connotation of cigarettes.

Beer sales were restricted to bars in 1940's Michigan. Beer in six packs (an idea introduced by Coca-Cola in 1923) was marketed as an easy way for women to shop for beer. Canned beer disappeared from 1942-47 due to the war effort.

THE ODD STUFF

Aviation cocktail (or Blue Aviator) was a very popular drink in the late 20s and into the 30s: 2 oz gin; 1 oz lemon juice; dash maraschino liqueur; 2 dashes Crème de Violette or Crème Yvette for a sky-blue color. (You could skip the last ingredient[s] and simply add a half-drop of blue food coloring). Aviator sunglasses are optional but can be exceptional fun in the dark or flickering candlelight.

Pegu cocktail (or Pegu) was first concocted in the 1930s at the Pegu Club in Rangoon, Burma and has once again become popular: 1½ oz gin; ¾ oz blue curaçao; 1 tsp lime juice; dash of bitters.

The American Volunteer Group (The Flying Tigers) was formed in the winter of 1940-1941. The man behind its creation was retired Army Air Corps captain Claire L. Chennault, who lobbied for the Chinese in Washington. President Roosevelt signed an unpublished executive order on April 15, 1941, that enabled officer and enlisted personnel to resign from the Army Air Corps, Naval or Marine air services for the purpose of joining the American Volunteer Group. It was the first and only collection of American pilots and planes ever formed to serve in foreign conflict. The initial group consisted of 100 pilots and planes and 180 mechanics and ground crew. Generally, only 60% of the aircraft were in service at any given time.

On paper, the volunteers were employees of the Central Aircraft Manufacturing Company, a 'division' of Curtiss Wright in Buffalo, New York, so technically the United States could deny military involvement in the China-Japan conflict. The pay and benefits were more than extravagant for the times with pilot pay as much as $750 monthly plus a $500 bonus for each Japanese plane destroyed in the air or on the ground. The CAMCO volunteers were granted the right to return to their military positions upon completion of service.

The AVG was decommissioned on July 4, 1942, and currently, the 23rd Fighter Group based at Moody Air Force Base near Valdosta, Georgia is the only unit authorized to use the menacing 'shark mouth' nose art that was painted on the P-40s in Burma.

China paid eight million dollars for the Flying Tigers; three million of which went for payroll and bonuses, and five million for planes and munitions. Chinese diplomat Soong Tse-ven (T.V. Soong) boasted "the AVG was the soundest investment China ever made".

THE AIRCRAFT

Curtiss Jenny JN4 was first produced in 1917 by the Curtiss Aeroplane Company of Hammondsport, New York. After World War I, it became the building block for American aviation as private owners and small companies endeavored into civil aviation. From barnstorming to daredevil wing-walkers, the Jenny has had a long history. Tough and time-proven, nearly 7,000 were built at a cost of about $5,500 (1920 $).

Stearman C3 was first introduced in 1928 as a light commercial biplane. It proved its worth in rugged airmail service in the west and modifications for the application of agricultural pesticides and fertilizer. Stearman Aircraft of Wichita, Kansas produced about 125. A few are still flying.

Curtiss A-12 Shrike was the Army Air Corp's main fighter aircraft of the 1930's. Made in Buffalo, only about 35 were built. When World War II began, the airplane was already obsolete. Although nine planes were stationed at Pearl Harbor when it was attacked, none were ever flown against the Japanese.

Curtiss P-36 Mohawk was one of the first generation of fighter aircraft going into World War II. About 1,000 units were made in Buffalo, NY from 1935. The fighter was flown by 13 different countries from 1935 until 1954. With a powerful 14 cylinder, 1040 horsepower Pratt & Whitney radial engine, it was the forerunner of the successful P-40. At a cost of $23,000 (1943 $) the P-36 was the least expensive of the Army's WW II fighter fleet. Argentina's air force retired them in 1954.

Bell P-39 Airacobra was the main fighter in service when the United States entered WW II. The engine was located mid-fuselage, behind the pilot creating plenty of room in the nose for two 50 caliber machine guns and a 37 mm cannon. Two more 50 caliber machine guns were in the wings. About 9,500 units were built just north of Buffalo in Wheatfield, New York for $51,000 (1943 $) apiece.

Curtiss P-40 Warhawk was a single engine fighter plane manufactured entirely in Buffalo, New York from 1939 until 1944. The Curtiss - Wright Company sat adjacent to the Buffalo Municipal Airport on Genesee Street. A total of 13,738 airplanes were made at a cost of $44,892 (1942 $) each. Variants were used by many countries of the British Commonwealth.

Lockheed P-38 Lightning was a twin-engine World War II fighter plane developed for the Army Air Corps in 1938. It was nicknamed *two planes - one pilot* by the Japanese and the *fork-tailed devil* by the German Luftwaffe. After initial 'growing pains', the P-38 proved to be a versatile aircraft, and

was used in numerous roles including dive bombing, ground support, night fighting, long-range mission escort, and photographic surveillance. 10,000 were built in Burbank, California from 1941-45 at a cost of $87,163 (1942 $) apiece. It was the first fighter to fly at 400 mph and the only one to be manufactured throughout the war. The cockpit windows did not open, which forced pilots in the tropics to oftentimes fly in tennis shoes, shorts and parachute. Scores of used aircraft were exported to Central and South America.

Republic P-47 Thunderbolt was a highly functional single engine, oval cowl fighter manufactured in Farmingdale, Long  Island, NY and Evansville, Indiana from 1941 until 1945. More than 15,500 units were made at a cost of about $85,000

(1944 $) apiece. Pilots referred to this sturdy, heavy aircraft as the *flying bathtub*. Post-war, many of the planes were put into active service in the air forces of numerous countries throughout Latin America.

Mitsubishi Zero was a long-range fighter aircraft manufactured by Mitsubishi Manufacturing from 1940-45. Its official designation was the *Navy Type 0* fighter and was the main aerial weapon of the Imperial Japanese Navy. Nearly 11,000 units were produced. American flyers quickly discovered its weakness: no armor protection for its pilot or fuel tanks.

Douglas C-47 Skytrain is a military version of the proven, solid DC-3. It was first flown in 1941 and was initially put into service by the USAAF in the Southwest Pacific and CBI (China-Burma-India) theater of operations. It also saw extensive service in Europe and Africa. Many of the 10,000 built are still flying today.

North American P-51 Mustang was a long-range, high-speed fighter used extensively in WW II and the Korean War. Originally designed with an Allison engine, the powerful Packard V-1650-7 with twin superchargers became standard equipment. At more than 1700 horsepower, the Mustang had a maximum speed of 430 mph, and cruised at 360. The Mustang's speed, armament and dependability were the reasons that hundreds were still in military use well into the 1980s. More than 15,000 were built at a cost of $51,000 apiece (1945 $) at Inglewood, California and Dallas, Texas. The plane was used extensively by air forces throughout the world. The Dominican Air Force was the last to retire them in 1984.

GLOSSARY

Abyssinia	"I'll be seeing ya"
amah	(Far East) female house-maid or servant
APF	(military) Army Personnel File
Banda	Mexican music with guitars & trumpets
banana bender	(Au) silly goose, oddball
besotted	(British) intoxicated
blimey	(British) goodness, golly
blinkers	eye lashes, eyes
booby (boobies)	female breast (1930s)
boozer	(British) bar
breezer	a car without a roof or windows
budgerigar	parakeet native to Australia
bump gums	to talk, gossip, carry on conversation
cake eater	ladies' man
canuck	a Canadian
chemist	(British) drugstore, druggist
chrome dome	bald head, often shiny with oils
civvies	(military) civilian clothing
dago	Italian or Spanish (derogatory)
dame	vibrant woman
darb	something great or someone special
dishy	(British) attractive
dispensary	(military) first aid or medical unit
doll	attractive young woman
fancy dress	(British) costume ball
fella	man, gentleman (fellow)
G (G's)	a grand; a thousand dollars
gangbusters	(adverb) speed, vigor, strength
glitterati	fashionable persons, usually wealthy
gobble pipe	saxophone
gobbledygook	double-talk, nonsense
goon	gangster
greenbacks	dollars
gringo	(Latin American) American (derogatory)
gumshoe	(usually) private detective
güero	(Mexico) white person (derogatory)

Harlem stride	New York jazz piano style
hot squat	the Electric Chair
in cahoots	acting together
Jap	Japanese (derogatory)
joystick	(aviation) control stick
kamikaze	Japanese suicide pilot
kibosh	stop, squelch
kipper	dried, salted herring
kiss off	kill, get rid of
Kiwi	New Zealander
knackered	(British) exhausted
Kraut	German (derogatory)
latrine roomer	(military) toilet rumor
Limey	Briton (derogatory)
megillah	details, real story
Mess	(military) mess hall, cafeteria
mick	Irish (derogatory)
Mickey Finn	knock-out drops; chloral hydrate
modoc	flashy flyer (aviator)
moolah	money
morphadike	Lesbian (early 20th Century derogatory)
motor freckles	bugs on the windshield
muffin	woman of low morality
nookie	coitus, sex (from Dutch: *neuken*)
oyster	woman of low morality
penguin	(aviation) not a flyer
ring-a-ding-ding	good time
Rising Sun	Imperial Empire of Japan or its flag
scat	stylized improvisation jazz singing
share crop	promiscuous woman, usually a bar fly
shave 'em dry	jazz lingo: aggressive behavior or sex
short snorter	(aviation) a flyer's I.O.U.
slant	Japanese (derogatory)
SNAFU	Situation Normal All Fouled Up
snake charmer	woman used as decoy
sot, sotted	(British) drunkard, drunken
stompers	shoes
sunburn	a "suntan" in the early 1930s
sweet patootie	attractive woman (reference to buttocks)

tea	(British) lunch or dinner
ticker tape	strips of paper from telegraph machines; used as confetti
tits machine	(aviation) outstanding aircraft
Top End	Northern Territory, northern Australia
tuppence	(British) two pence
twit	fool
two bits	a quarter, 25¢
whockerjawed	wrecked, kaput
wilco	(military) yes; short for 'will comply'
wingman	(military) pilot to the right and just behind the lead plane in attack formation
wop	Italian (derogatory orig: WithOutPapers)
Yanqui	Latin American variant of "Yankee"
Yat	American (New Orleans) where you at?
zed	(British) the letter "z"

CHAPTER MUSIC TO CONSIDER

~ Songs contemporary to the story ~

'Deed I Do	Linnzi Zaokski
Midnight Special	Lead Belly
I Know That You Know	Nat Shilkret & The Victor Orchestra
Baby Face	The Buffalodians
Dead Man's Blues	Savannah Serenaders
No, No Nora	Spike Jones
The Car Song	Woody Gunthrie
Gimme A Little Kiss	Deanna Durbin
I'm Wild About That Thing	Bessie Smith
Blue Skies	Tim Zeitbumbe
Breezin' Along With The Breeze	Johnny Marvin
I'm In The Mood For Love	Vera Lynn
Footprints In The Snow	Cliff Carlisle
Just One More Chance	Sam Browne
Easy Come, Easy Go	Ruth Etting
Drop In Next Time You're Passing	Elisabeth Welch
Cielito Lindo	Lucha Moreno
Pistol Packin' Papa	Jimmie Rodgers
Downhearted Blues	Claire Austin

WPA	Louis Armstrong, Mills Bros.
I Know Why (And So Do You)	Paula Kelly and The Glenn Miller Orchestra
Hold Tight	Fats Waller
Shave 'em Dry	Asylum Street Spankers
Looking Around Corners For You	Chick Henderson
Inka Dinka Do	Jimmy Durante
Goodbye To Summer	Beryl Davis
Take Me Out To The Ballgame	The Gay Timers with their Hammond organ
The Masquerade Is Over	Bebe Daniels
Something To Remember You By	Anne Shelton
What's New?	Helen Forrest with The Artie Shaw Orchestra
Dipsy Doodle	Bea Wain & Larry Clinton's Orchestra
There's Something In The Air	Ruth Etting
Put Your Arms Around Me, Honey	Betty Grable
Solo Flight	Benny Goodman Orchestra
If I Only Had A Heart	Jack Haley
Racing With The Moon	Vaughn Monroe & Orchestra
J'attendrai	Rina Ketty
Deep Pacific	Graeme Bell & Royal Bells
We'll Meet Again	Sam Browne

Straighten Up And Fly Right	The Andrews Sisters
Adios Muchachos	Lydia Mendoza
I'll Make A Happy Landing	Sydney Kyte and The Piccadilly Band
There's A Wah-Wah Girl In Agua Caliente	Marilyn Thorne & The Isham Jones Orchestra
Rum And Coca Cola	The Andrews Sisters
Coming In On A Wing And A Prayer	Anne Shelton & The Ambrose Orchestra

IMAGE CREDITS

Aircraft silhouettes: United States War Department Manual #30-30 (1934-1945)

*

Cadillac *Flying Goddess* hood ornament: United States Patent Office, patent #92,358 Ternstedt Manufacturing, 1933

*

Lafayette Escadrille: United States Army Air Corps; New England Air Museum; Smithsonian National Air and Space Museum

*

United States Army Air Force unit patches:

39th Fighter Squadron (*Flying Cobras*), 35th Fighter Group, Fifth Army Air Force

*

Lockheed P-38 Lightning:

The Flying Phaeton: Family source.

POSTSCRIPT

The title spring:
(From Chapter Six, "Sailing On A Sunbeam") - "Beautiful ... damned beautiful ... a P-38 Phaeton ... The Equalizer ... no ... a flying Phaeton ... that's it! That's it ... *The Flying Phaeton* ... beautiful."

*

"Skillful pilots gain their reputation from storms and tempests."
Epicurus (Greek philosopher, 341-270 BC)

"War is Hell."
~ **William Tecumseh Sherman (June 19, 1879)** ~

"I would give anything to see that flyer flyin' tonight."
~ **Nancy Griffith, (lyrics):** *The Flyer (song),* **1994** ~

"If one took no chances, one would not fly at all."
~ **Charles A. Lindbergh (August 26, 1938)** ~

"I've a right to think!" said Alice sharply.
"Just about as much right," said the Duchess, "as pigs have to fly!"
~ **Lewis Carroll:** *Alice's Adventures in Wonderland* **(1865)** ~

"Thank you."

This novel was created with 100% recycled thought.

It Is Written in Stone

7 x 11 inch
Carved Fieldstone
Created in Pigeon Forge, Tennessee, USA
at
The Sandman's Workshop

Killroy was here.

As a self-published author, my readers are my best advocates.
Please consider a simple rating or brief review
on Amazon or Goodreads.
It is appreciated.

Made in the USA
Monee, IL
09 June 2025

8141bcf2-7efe-4e8c-a65f-7fae7fde5800R01